Book #3

The **Horn~Horn** Series

STARS ABOVE

# Horn~Horn

I0588844

# TOMMY LELLAN

PRAISE FOR The **Horn-Horn** Series

"Let me just say, this is my all time favourite fantasy series. The plot kept building upon itself drastically with every page."
- *Ceara, Goodreads*

"The f***ing bee's knees."
- *Tamara Presley, Goodreads*

"One of the most mind-bending fantasy stories I've ever read!"
- *Marina Levy, Goodreads*

"Got to be the most original series out there. The twists are insane. I found myself laughing because I was loving where it was going."
-*James McDonald, Goodreads*

"I see huge things for this series, and I can't wait for the next one."
- *Jesse Elliot, Amazon.com*

"I completely connected with the main character. Perfect for young adult fans who love humour and horror."
-*Rory, Goodreads*

"This was the strangest book. I just couldn't put it down!"
- *Merry Chapman, Amazon.com*

"A stand-up comedy. And then there are the amazing odd twists!"
- *Gloria, Amazon.com*

"This book was magic! It keeps you hooked until the very end."
- *Alex Murakami, Alextheshadowgirl Blog*

"Try reading this on a train and looking like a normal human being."
- *Charlotte Geller, Goodreads*

*For Cassie,*
*who passed away during the writing of this book*

"It is the stars,

The stars above us, govern our conditions.

Else one self mate and mate could not beget

Such different issues."

- WILLIAM SHAKESPEARE, *KING LEAR*

# PROLOGUE
## SLOWLY AND SURELY

The universe was vast. Ursula could never quite grasp the immense size of it, not in all her years of studies and tours across the constellations. There were always stories to tell, horrors to witness, worlds to claim.

As their deluxe travel bubble soared over the ocean at the speed of sound, the Queen of Danube looked out the nearest window at the rushing water, her mind lost to the vastness of it all. Around her sat Danube's most elite. Rich aristocrats, celebrities, elders, and the Heads of the Universe, all three of them. Their little airship, nicknamed Tic-Tac for its shape, may have appeared small from the outside, but inside it felt enormous to the passengers. There was a bar, a seating area, sleeping pods, and most glorious of all — three-hundred-and-sixty degree views outside.

"Duke Wilson, it's stunning," said Lady Moropa Angle, an elderly socialite with frizzy, pink hair. She was sitting next to Danube's second-in-command, legs crossed as she looked out at the horizon. "For the coldest time of year, I am impressed."

"Why, thank you," said Duke Wilson of Elmer. He was dressed in a tight black suit, his cape wrapped around his front. "I take it you'll be agreeing to the papers when they are delivered? We have the ruling in a few weeks. It'll be a loud parliament, but I highly recommend you attend."

"Oh yes, I don't see why not," said Lady Angle. "But first I may ask you for some details on the space we will be occupying in the coming months."

"Ah, we are nearly there, so I shall show you out the window. How does that sound?"

Within a few minutes, the ocean disappeared and an empty beach filled up the windows as they zipped into the small seaside town, invisible to anybody watching nearby.

"Horn-Horn," said the Duke, catching Ursula's eye briefly as she went to get another drink from the bar. "Currently holding one Child of Crux, previously King Frederick's. You recall the exchange to Queen Ursula on her birthday?"

"Could one forget?" declared the Lady under her breath.

"The Crux is named Zagreus Wendig the Third, previously the Three-Hundredth while rogue. He is now third in line for the... Well, you know..."

"And tell me about his newest owner?"

"A young human named Cassandra Gellar the First. Saved Queen Ursula's life, brought us up to speed with Rudnick van Pan. As grateful as we are to her, we must destroy her in order to retrieve Zagreus."

"Understandable. And is it Guiltursaar who will be taking her life? There are rumours spreading throughout Danube about it — although many of these started in Summers City, therefore I do not feel particularly assured of their validity."

"For once, Summers City is correct. The comet will hit this town in five months time and kill everybody within it. After that, we will look at other viable places."

"And how long will that take?" asked Lady Angle.

"Months, perhaps even years. Horn-Horn's destruction will be the perfect chance to test the waters, see if integration is possible. These humans, they... I am aware that it is frowned upon to suggest they are our descendants, but..."

"Oh, Duke Wilson," said Lady Angle at once, patting his knee. "You mustn't fear my scorn. I too am of the controversial belief that

2

they are indeed our children, and I know exactly what you are about to suggest. If they are only five hundred years behind us in technology, there will come a time soon where they will catch up enough to discover the magic infused with their DNA, and soon after each one born will start to acquire their own unique abilities. It concerns those on my board just as much as it surely must concern those in your Palace with even a hint of intelligence. After all, it is undeniable. Just last year, there were those reports of a child born off the coast of Barbados who could crawl through walls. And let's not forget the Roswell debacle. To think, they thought it was aliens. Ha!"

"Yes, all of those concern us greatly. The Heads of the Universe are watching this planet very closely. And you know of the swapped version, don't you?"

"Yes, I've heard. Hello, Queen Ursula, dear," said Lady Angle, just as Ursula came and joined them with a glass of brandy. "We were discussing the humans on this planet. Interesting creatures, don't you think?"

Ursula sipped her drink, but did not answer.

"I am aware, Duke Wilson, of the swapped planet, but can you bring me up to speed with *this* one? They say it only has four continents instead of seven. Quite intriguing! How do they manage to fit everything in?"

"A mixture of the same history, although parts are different. They don't have any form of homophobia here, quite the opposite in fact; and racism is now on the low-end, virtually disregarded... at least, it's not as insidious when compared. Many of the countries are also mixed together. Horn-Horn is on a super continent; I've forgotten the name off the top of my head. It's mostly like the Americas over there, along with Australia, Britain, France, all rolled into one culture... although France is off the coast of Florida here... One of the most interesting differences, at least in my opinion, is where Cassandra Gellar the First comes from."

"Oh, and where is that?"

"Salem, Massachusetts. She travelled with her family all the way across the country to get to Horn-Horn on the East Coast."

"But..." Lady Angle patted down her unruly, pink hair as she thought hard. "Salem is on the East Coast as well; how can they possibly..?"

"Ah, but it is not," said Duke Wilson. "A most incredible find on this planet, to be sure. Salem is on the West Coast here. Not only that, but it is a near mirror image of the same town on the other Earth."

"Well, that sounds rather remarkable, doesn't it?" said Lady Angle, smiling across at Ursula. "What a wonder! Does it have the same history, with the witch trials and so forth?"

"To a fault. In fact, it's rather unnerving if I do say so myself. Ursula, would you like to speak to everybody before we visit the Gellar property? We'll be peeping in the upstairs in hopes of seeing their Child of Crux through the window. You might want to remind everybody that we're invisible, in case they're worried we'll be spotted."

Ursula stood up, agreeing, and started to head for the front when suddenly one of the guests pointed out a window.

"Look! What is that?" they declared.

The guest was pointing towards a giant tree. As they passed slowly through the streets of downtown Horn-Horn, past the Mayor's office and towards the beach, they saw it in all its glory. A fifteen-foot tall pine tree, covered in golden lights and decorations of red and green. Even though it wasn't quite dusk yet, the lights were almost blinding to the shoppers on the chilled street below.

"A Christmas Tree!" said Duke Wilson, standing up and joining the others as they crowded around the nearest window. "I almost forgot. It's Christmas here. Another thing," he added to Lady Angle, "they have in common with the other Earth."

"What does it do?" she asked him, eyes locked on the giant golden star perched atop.

"Nothing at all. It is a symbol of peace. Of family. Hope. Alright, everybody, it's not like we haven't seen stars above shining the exact same way. Let us head towards Philips Street. Ursula, we'll sit down so you can speak now."

Queen Ursula pried her eyes away from the tree and looked out at the beach behind them. A light caught her eye, flickering briefly. It was the lighthouse up on the nearby cliffs. Her mind cast back to her time in Horn-Horn, and the people here. Knowing perfectly well that the crowd of entitled Danubians were watching and waiting for her to speak, she moved away from the window and went to the front of the Tic-Tac, where she placed her drink down on the ground and began to tell them everything she knew about the Gellar family, and how they were planning to systematically annihilate them before taking control of the planet.

# SUNDAY THE 9TH

# 1

# POWERS IN THE ATTIC

Christmas was, without a doubt, my favourite time of the year. Occasionally, when in the mood for nostalgia, I'd hark back to childhood days where I would sit underneath our decorated tree at night, gazing wide-eyed into the branches above, lit up by the colourful fairy lights. I'd imagine I was a little bird, or a chipmunk, safe and protected by the bushy pine needles. That was what Christmas meant to me. Not the presents, or the celebrity of the jolly fat man (I already had one of those in my life). It made me think of gingerbread. Pine needles. Cinnamon, and a wonderfully strange scent from my mother's wardrobe I have yet to figure out.

There was something else to it, though. Something I couldn't quite put my finger on. It wasn't just the olfactory senses kicking in, or the visual delights of reds and greens pitter-pattered throughout the month of December. There was a unique atmosphere to the world. Almost as if every living soul was unanimously at ease, at the same time. It was palpable. Christmas Eve in particular, I was *sure* of it. There was something in front of me, a comforting spirit of some kind, and if I reached out my hand I felt I could break through to the other side and touch it.

"I have no idea what you're talking about," said Hayley in the backseat of our car, once I'd explained these feelings. "Sounds to me like you're having mini-strokes every December. Are you allergic to anything Christmas related?"

"Of course not," I told her grumpily.

We'd been driving back from the mall. Hayley had recently acquired a Christmas job at the local bakery, which she'd managed to grab because JT had worked there temporarily last summer. I'd had no idea he held down a steady part-timer, as he seemed so aimless in his life, but the more I thought about it the more sense it made. After all, he was vague in his aimlessness. He could have been the Zodiac killer, if he'd been born decades earlier. Greg had a job at the mall, so of course JT had gotten a job at the same mall. It made perfect sense.

"These Christmas hours are going to murder me," my blonde friend told me as we pulled into our driveway. "They want me there at ten o'clock on the night school wraps up. I'll finish at six in the morning. That'll be a whole day of being awake! Isn't that crazy? Why can't they just bake their bread during the daytime, and not be weirdos about it?"

"Bakers have been doing it since the stone age," said Dad from the driver's seat. "That way, the bread is fresh when they open in the morning."

"So people who get up at midday aren't allowed to have fresh bread? Don't you think that's a little bit unfair, Mr. Gellar?"

"Hayley, I'm not Jesus. Don't come to me with your problems. Oh, by the way, Lesley went shopping today and got you that coffee brand you wanted. Pantomime..?"

"*Pandora*," said Hayley. "It's from Greece. It can keep me going for twelve hours straight. Steve got me onto it when I was ten. He thinks it's laced with..."

We waited in silence for her to continue.

"...peppermint..." she muttered, looking down.

I nudged her jokingly. "You forgot where you were."

Hopping out into the freezing night air, we were quick to rush inside our house. Within moments of entering the warm foyer, our dog Pigsworth came running to greet us with one of his pink and lime coloured pull-toys. Hayley kicked off her black sneakers, which landed in a heap underneath the coat rack. We didn't say a word, not one of us, and right here is where I should explain something to you.

Hayley was staying with us over the Christmas period. A terrible thing had happened, you see, a few days earlier. Her mother, Bonita, was out shopping when she was hit by a row of runaway trolleys. They knocked her into oncoming traffic and now she was stuck in hospital. And, as bad luck would have it, her step-father Steve had booked a stripper gig in Ibiza over the holiday period and couldn't afford to fly back. With nobody else to help out, Hayley had two viable options: Stay with us, or Ms. Weiss. And Hayley Gauche was not living with Jacqueline Weiss.

I for one was very excited. I felt like a kid having a sleepover, only this one would consist of many sleepovers, lasting until the first week of January (when Steve would return). Annie was the first to remind me of the little bundle of joy stowed away in my wardrobe, not that it bothered me. As Brendan pointed out, a simple wish could fix that. And it did. When Hayley arrived at our doorstep two days earlier, Zag was promptly banished to the attic. Not bothered by the idea, except for the fact that he apparently had a great fear of heights, I was delighted when he packed up without a word. He was of the same opinion: it was a sleepover, only he would be up there on his own with his clay head sitting on top of a box filled with unused menorahs. We'd barely heard a peep out of him since, although his big schtick would be to come into my room disguised as Brendan when he wanted to ask me something. Not realising it was him at first became quite tiresome, so I asked him not to do it anymore. If he wanted me, he'd have to magically make my ears twitch from afar. I would then pull on one of them if I'd heard him, twice if I was busy. Thrice if I'd pulled accidentally. It soon became very confusing and annoying, plus it set off my OCD, so we scrapped it altogether. I would instead make multiple trips each day up into the dark attic, rousing suspicion from my parents (who probably assumed I was hiding presents up there).

That night, as we gathered together eating dinner in front of the television, Brendan could barely contain his excitement. Tomorrow, he told me, was a very special day. His bully-turned-friend Aron Hasmutt was getting a tattoo, and apparently this was especially cool. He wouldn't let on what it was, waiting for the next day to reveal all, but Brendan was practically bouncing off the walls in anticipation.

"I wonder if it's of a polyp," he said.

Annie groaned next to him, not in the mood for his eccentric thoughts. "*Why* would he get a tattoo of *that?*"

"He likes them."

"Well, that seems pretty disgusting."

"Hey, maybe he'll get a tattoo of your face, then!"

The bickering died down as the ad-break ended. We waited in anticipation for the final scenes of my favourite show, *The Prefect Family*, before it ended for the Christmas break. We were dying to see what happened. Even my parents, who didn't usually follow the show, wanted to see for themselves.

Suddenly, an ad came on that changed everything.

*BANG!*

The sound of a gunshot.

"*AAAARGH!*"

A shrill scream. Red screen faded to black.

Then it cut to a slick exhaust pipe of a motorcycle, and a woman in a crowd screaming happily, panning back to reveal a motorcycle race being cheered on by many bystanders on a racing track-.An announcer started yelling:

"*Get your motorcycles primed! Horn-Horn's Twenty-Third Annual Motorcycle Race for Charity takes place 7pm, Friday the 21st of December! $30 entry! All proceeds going to local hospitals! Sponsored by the San Antonio Bundles-for-Babies Charity Fund! Be there or be square!*"

We humphed as it ended.

"I should enter that," said Dad.

"You haven't ridden your motorcycle in years."

"Well, Lesley, I've been meaning to get back into it. I've lost a lot of weight since moving here, and it's just sitting in the garage under a tarp, wasting away. To be honest, I can't remember why I stopped riding it."

"Family, commitment…"

"Speeding fines," added Annie.

"Reckless driving…"

"I thought it was because you were too fat!" said Brendan.

"No, Ichabod, I don't want you riding it again…" muttered Mom, talking over the show as it returned. This was breaking the cardinal rule. We instantly shushed her, for the conversation would have to take place during the next ad break. Still, the idea of it had wormed its way into our minds, and now all I could do was picture Dad's pride and joy, bright yellow, with a bumper sticker on the back that read: *'Too Fat To Carpool'*, hidden in the garage where it had been since we moved in.

———— . . . ————

Later that night as I got ready for bed, despite our agreement to the contrary, I felt a great tug at my ears. I gave up searching for my earphones and headed up to the attic. It was a giant space above us, reachable only by a flight of wooden stairs that folded down from the ceiling to the second storey landing outside Annie's bedroom. As I entered, I was struck by the warmth. It was refreshing, given how arctic it was outside. Even our own bedrooms had a slight chill which you couldn't get rid of with the central heating. Up in the attic it was cosy, as if an invisible fireplace sat in the corner.

"Hello?" I said, gazing cautiously into the darkness before me. It was a very large attic, stretching across almost the entire width of the house. A gothic sight, it gave me the spooks. With only one, round window near the front, the daytime would offer very little in the way of light.

"Over here!" called the voice of Zag.

I pulled myself up to stand on the nearest wooden beams. Brushing myself off, I balanced my way over to him, sitting near a stack of boxes. He was only there because of his size. Normally I knew he'd stay in the clay head, which was sitting right by the entryway. Today, however, he clearly wanted to talk.

"It's warm up here," I told him quietly, not wanting anybody downstairs to hear me.

"Heat rises, silly."

"Yeah, yeah. What's up?"

"Well… As you know, it's Christmas in a few weeks."

"I am aware."

"Can you tell me more about it?"

I thought for a moment. "About Christmastime? I don't know, Zag… Why don't you conjure the internet and read up on it?"

"I've already done that," he muttered. In his blue pyjamas and hat, he let out a wide yawn and climbed onto one of the dusty, unpacked boxes. He gazed momentarily at his clay head across from him. "There's too much to learn before it happens."

"Before what happens?" I allowed myself to lean on the nearest pillar, suspecting I may be here for a while.

"Before *Christmas!*"

"Oh. It comes around every year. It's not that special."

"That's not the way the ads interpret it!"

"What, the TV ads?"

"Yes, and who is Santa? I read up on Nicholas of Myra but he died a long time ago. Yet he's still wandering around? I thought you said magic wasn't used by humans. You contradict me."

"There's no such thing as Santa. It's used for kids."

"How so?"

"We tell them that Santa brings them presents. You know, to shut them up."

"So they wake up disappointed every year?"

"No, *we* give them the presents. The parents do."

"Parents buy them presents and say they're from Santa?"

I nodded.

"What's the point?"

He was right, and on behalf of all humans I felt very stupid. If you focussed on it too much, nothing about the situation made sense. We were telling them about a magical creature that didn't exist. It was a life lesson in disappointment.

"It's Jesus's birthday on Christmas, which confuses me."

"That's what it's about originally," I told him.

"How does Santa come into the equation?"

"I don't *know*. It's mainly to celebrate the birth of Jesus. Santa came into it a little later."

"It says Jesus is from the Christian faith... but aren't you Jewish?"

"Half. I don't believe in Jesus, but my mother does. So does her family. My dad's family are Jewish and believe in that, but he doesn't and so we don't."

"Aren't you celebrating a Christian holiday anyway? Why don't you celebrate *Hanukkah?*" He phlegmed as he said this.

My eyes drifted to the boxes with Jewish names on them, and could only shrug. We just didn't. There was no thought for or against the argument. But then the reason for it became the answer, so I told him: "We're not a religious family, Zag. We celebrate Christmas because... Christmas is less about Jesus, and more about family. To some people, Jesus *is* family, but... Not here. Christmas is an important time that we spend together as a family. That's just how we choose to look at it. There's nothing in it that's religious for us." I liked how smart I sounded on the fly, so I smirked at him in the darkness. "You're right, though. There *is* a magic to Christmas. Maybe not the magic you and I think about, but something else. Something... special. A feeling."

It was clear that Zag was not on the same page as me. He shrugged and shifted his eyes about, trying not to antagonise the crazy person in front of him any further. I suddenly felt horrible, realising that I was inanely flaunting my perfect family so casually about him, while his relationship to our home came down to the fact that he was an orphan without any family at all. I was his only connection to the outside world, and here he was spending the holiday season hiding in the attic like Anne Frank. As much as we liked to make him feel welcome, he simply wasn't real family. Mom and Dad had gotten their memories wiped due to the stresses of knowing about Danube, so Zag was a secret guest in our house once more.

"Don't you have... *any* family?" I asked. "Aunts or Uncles? Cousins? Evil step-sisters?"

Zag shook his head and decided to swing about a beam next to him, making his way like a monkey in the trees above until he wrapped his arms around the pillar next to me. "I am but a curse on the universe. We don't have such luxuries. Don't feel bad, though. I don't really care. I'm here and I like it..." He saw the look in my eyes. "I only wanted to know about Christmas because this will be the first time I experience it here. I like the idea of Christmas trees. I *love* the decorations. I just want to learn all about it."

"Alright, I'll search in the library and borrow as many books on Christmas as I can," I promised, and I kicked the attic stairs back down. As I started to lower myself, I could feel how drastically different the temperature was below. "God, we really need to up the heating down here. You're living in a tropical resort and it's wonderful."

"Up, down, here, there. Makes no difference. Don't have it on too high. You'll have a restless sleep," he said, and he turned into a puff of smoke that was enveloped by the orange clay head nearby.

I shut the attic door, now feeling lousy, and went for the thermostat at the end of the hall. I turned it up extra high despite his warning.

# 2
# FORGOTTEN

We weren't in our usual grumpy moods as we rose the next day. I was peppy, and could sense it off the others, too. Despite being a Monday, it was the last Monday of school for the year, so exciting things were happening during the week. Today was the day we got to put up the class Christmas tree, creating our own decorations out of school supplies. It was all very sixth grade material, and our overly worked teenage minds were excited for the reprieve of tenth grade responsibilities.

It was incredibly difficult to eat cereal at the kitchen bench in such a gigantic winter jacket, but that was exactly what Annie was attempting. She looked like the Michelin Man.

"Why don't you put it on when you've finished?"

"I'll forget to," she told me.

"You'll remember as soon as you take a step outside."

*"Nein!"* she declared coldly, stretching her neck to reach the spoon in her left hand.

Brendan was sitting next to us with his chocolate breakfast, fiddling with a toy in his hands. It was a figurine from one of his favourite programs: '*Tiro the Barber-Librarian*'. This hilarious cartoon was about a German spy who worked undercover as a Barber and a Librarian during World War II. Still, I felt like my brother was too old to still be playing with toys. Nonetheless, he wanted it more than anything and had given us many hints throughout the months of what he was expecting for Christmas.

"*HEY!*" shouted Mom as she came into the room.

We all jumped at her angry voice, and turned, curious as to who was in trouble. Brendan was in her line of vision.

"*What do you think you're doing!?*" she raced over and snatched the Tiro doll away from him. "This was wrapped! Why did you open it?"

"It had my name on it," he replied innocently.

Mom smacked him across the back of the head.

"You're too old for this, Brendan. If I find out you're sneaking around looking for presents again, next year I won't buy you anything. Have you got that?"

Brendan glanced at Annie and I for moral support, then gave up with a forceful kick to the table, his morning apparently ruined. His eyes filled with red-hot tears, and he muttered: "Fine," before sulking quietly into his cereal.

I felt bad for him, but Mom was right. We'd been through this. Year after year. He became a super-spy at Christmas. It was a tired act, snooping around and finding his presents each year. As a young boy it was sort of cute, a thing to tell people at parties to accentuate his cherubic fables. But then once he hit the age of ten we suddenly saw it in another light. He was ruining Christmas not just for us, but for himself. He'd never failed at finding them, and rubbing it in our faces. It reminded me of those weirdo professional runners, who would compete in small-town family-friendly charity runs just so they could win another medal. So unnecessary, and ugly to boast. Eventually as a family we'd decided to better Brendan each year by teaming together, but... He was far more wily. One year, Mom thought to hide his presents in the garden... or rather, *under* the garden. Still, he found them. She even went to desperate measures and tried to get Pigsworth to eat some of his smaller presents, intending to check his poop in the days leading up to Christmas. Dad, thankfully, talked her out of her craziness, but this served as the perfect example of just how maddening he was. Every year we would collectively keep our lips sealed on the subject until he found them. Therefore, understandably, having him sit so blatantly at the kitchen bench that morning with one of his presents in his hands was simply too much for our mother to take. Even though I hated to see my brother cry, I sided with her.

"Come on, Brendan," Annie and I said together, and we left him alone at the table to sob into his bowl.

———— . . . ————

If having a hearty breakfast that morning wasn't enough to wake us all up, exiting the house would've taken care of it. Annie and I cried and moaned in discomfort as we walked down the street for the bus pole. Despite our layers and layers of clothing, it was windy and dark and positively freezing.

"I think I need to invest in some duck down."

"With what money?" asked Annie.

"Mom and Dad's, obviously. It's freezing."

"Just think, January is going to be colder," she replied.

As usual, the bus hit the pole and we picked it up and put it back into place. Eleanore Parker raced to catch up to us as we hopped on board. She was bundled up as well, not looking especially great in her puffy jacket, but at least it was fluorescent pink, in case somebody in the crowded rows forgot to immediately notice her.

"Good morning, Cassie!" she said to me, her cheeks flushed a bright pink in the chill. She put her hands on my shoulders as we walked down the aisle, and departed quickly as she joined her two compadres.

I left to sit away from my sister, who knew I liked my alone time. I rested my beanied head against the glass, and closed my eyes. It was a great time to meditate over thoughts and feelings. And I had a lot of them. However, the scars of the past were finally healing and I was glad that things were settling down now. Just in time for Christmas. I felt relaxed, looking forward to school and the holidays, and relished in the bus's peacefulness.

Until somebody kicked my seat from behind. I ignored it the first time, but then it happened again. I sat up straight, alert, waiting. I tried to see the person in the window's reflection, out of the corner of my eye, but couldn't. When it happened again, I turned around to give them a good old staring. It was a small boy I'd never met before, surely in the seventh grade, red-haired and wearing a hoodie and a grey beanie just like mine. But as I looked at him, he gazed off as if nothing had happened. I turned back around, perplexed, until it happened again.

"What are you doing?" I asked him, facing fully around.

He shrugged. "I dunno."

"Please stop it."

He reached out and poked me with something sharp.

"Now you've got AIDS," he said ominously.

Creeped out, I faced the front again. I knew more was coming; when it did I decided foolishly to do nothing about it. Figuring he'd eventually get bored and stop, I waited as he poked and kneed and moved his foot about, trying to get a reaction from me. It wasn't until I was almost leaning fully forward from his indent that I grabbed my bag and moved. I gave him a quick angry glare before plopping down in the empty seat next to my sister.

"Some people on this bus need to be lobotomised…"

"Maybe he likes you," said Annie, checking him out.

"I'd rather projectile vomit out my ass."

Not long after, we drove through the front gates of Horn-Horn High-High. Yack-Spit-Hack dropped us off right by reception today, instead of round back in the bus zone, probably because of how chilly the weather was. As soon as the doors swung open, we fled for our lives to the warmth of our designated hallways. I caught up with Hayley as we ventured down the long Berry Hallway.

"Hey," she said. "Did your mother stink up a fuss?"

"About what?"

"You… didn't notice I wasn't home when you got up?"

"Oh yeah. Look, we keep forgetting you're staying with us. Maybe we'll remember tomorrow."

"Maybe…" she said hopefully.

"Where'd you go, anyway?"

"I snuck into JT's house."

"How did that go?"

"Well, at first I was stuck outside freezing. But then, you know, we did a reverse *Romeo & Juliet*. I serenaded him with abusive name-calling below, until he relinquished his rights and let me in."

"How romantic," I said with a sly smirk.

Despite having plenty of spare bedrooms for Hayley to lodge in, we both wanted to sleep in the same room. Her single bed was lined up against the wall, under my window. It was hard to get into my wardrobe with it in the way, but we were making do for the short space of time she was with us. Besides, I'd never had a proper friend like this before. It was all new to me, and I cast my mind back to the previous night, growing more and more certain that she'd fallen asleep before me…

"No, I was pretending," she confessed, as we neared the end of the exhausting hallway. "When I was sure that you were fast asleep, I snuck out the window and down the drainpipe and ran to JT's."

"All that way?" I said, curiously.

Although, I didn't even know where JT's house was. I'd yet to receive an invite. He must have lived in a street only a little further down the hill, possibly near Ms. Weiss on Flavour Street, otherwise Hayley would have gotten frostbite in her travels.

We burst through the doors at the end of the hallway and into the Fido Auditorium, which was filled like Grand Central Station. Students and teachers, parents, you name it, crossing here and there on their way to classes and appointments. A group of girls were practicing some sort of dance moves, and I even spotted Greg playing a game of basketball with some guys I didn't know.

Hayley and I walked over to the red entrance to our classroom, and went in to find almost the entire class already in there, despite it being early. Ms. Weiss was in the corner, fiddling with the thermostat. Eleanore and her pals must have bolted around the block to get here before us, as they'd been loitering in the front seats of the bus talking to the newly recovered Yack-Spit-Hack.

"Oh, great. The coat-rack is full," said Hayley, eager to shed her jacket somewhere.

Suddenly, JT and Greg walked in and stopped by our sides.

"Perfect timing as always, Jonathan!"

She gladly put her jacket over his head, and wiped her hands free after a good job. JT took it off and wrapped it over his right arm and chased after her to the back row. I smiled at Greg, and was surprised when he held out his hands for my own coat. Not one to squander a perfect moment, I swiftly handed it to him and thanked him quietly. We joined our friends in the back row.

A little while later, the bell rang.

Ms. Weiss, oddly silent this morning, pointed at the board above her desk. I squinted to read the small writing:

### 'INTRODUCTION TO ECONOMICS'
- What is economics?
- Write three pages on the matter until recess.

We all groaned. A whole period of writing. How exciting.

*When are we going to put up the tree?* I wondered, fidgeting.

Hayley put her hand up. "Can we talk amongst ourselves?"

Ms. Weiss went to her desk and sat down to sort out some coloured binders in front of her. She simply shook her head. No we may not, it told us.

And what a boring class it was because of this. None of the excitement I'd felt about the lead-up to Christmas was in the windowless room that morning, and I racked my brain trying to think of how to put my opinions on economics into words. I thought back to my conversation the night before with Zag, and how wonderfully I'd managed to communicate my ideas of Christmas to him. Today I felt more like Nell.

By recess, I'd only managed a page and a half, and when I handed it in our teacher gave me a predictable scrunch of one shoulder which seemed to tiredly say: *What can you do, Cassie? You're ordinary.* Her silent treatment wasn't just irritating me, either. Hayley was downright paranoid. As we sat shuddering atop the inside bleachers of the Fido Auditorium, she vented her frustrations.

"What if I decided I wasn't going to talk one day, just like that? With no explanation or anything."

"You'd get in trouble," said Greg.

"Exactly! Maybe as a class we should all give her detention. On the grounds of being a jerk. There are no rules stating that teachers can't be punished for their inferiority. We should protest in traffic, like those political weenies on the news."

"I think maybe you should just let it go," said JT, tiredly. "Hey, what day are we doing Kris Kringle?"

"Thursday," I reminded him.

"Excellent! I love Kris Kringle," said Hayley.

"Why, who have you got?"

She scoffed. "I'm not supposed to tell you."

"Oh, so it's me?"

"N... Maybe."

"It's not me," I informed Greg coolly.

"Shut up."

The possibility of Eleanore lurking nearby was always on my mind, so I was not surprised when she snuck up behind us with Wednesday and Friday in tow.

"*I* know who *my* Kris Kringle is," she said loudly, "*and* I have to say, I'm *very* happy with it."

Hayley snorted.

"You've probably got Ms. Weiss, you suck-up mental case."

"*No,* I do *not!*" she declared melodramatically, which was enough to give it away.

Ms. Weiss was definitely her Kris Kringle.

"Wow, Eleanore," muttered JT. "Your poker face sucks."

———— . . . ————

After recess, the entire class was back in their seats before any adult authority had even arrived. We were on our best behaviour, for an undeniable smell had greeted us upon filling the classroom. *Pine.* The Christmas tree was here, somewhere, which meant it was time to decorate it. Strangely enough, my mouth salivated in anticipation.

Ms. Weiss walked in with her handbag, face as downcast as earlier. "Schitt down, clash," she said in a strange way. When she looked up, she was surprised at how obediently we were already sitting. "Oh. Never mind. Anyway, sheeing ash it'sh the lasht week of shkool, I feel like shelebrating. I wash going to wait until lasht period, but I thought, why don't we decorate the Chrishtmash tree *now* inshtead?"

We gazed at her in wonder.

"What'sh the matter?" she asked with an animated wince. In this moment, her mouth widened, revealing a single metallic line across her front teeth.

"My *God!*" cried Eleanore in her usual dramatic flare.

"Oh, Mish. Parker, for goodnesh shake. It'sh jusht a moush plate. My teesh were shliding. Over the weekend I went to the dentisht, that'sh all. It'sh noshing worsh menshioning."

"So that's why you've been quiet all morning."

"I don't know what you're talking about, Mish. Gausche."

"But your teeth are fine," I said, offering some support.

"That'sh very nishe of you to shay, Cashie. Shank you. I'm shupposhed to wear them at all timesh, but troosh be told I'm having a few difficultiesh. Like forgetting it'sh in when I go to drink shomething..."

The few dental platers amongst us muttered in understanding.

"Never mind all that. You've dishtracted me. The strongesht men of the clash, pleashe help to bring the tree in from the computer room behind ush. We can put it in the left corner. Everybody elsh, don't be shilly, schitt back down again. Come on, schitt, all of you. I said *schitt!*"

While Hayley and Greg laughed enthusiastically into their shirts, five burly men raided the computer room in an attempt to show off their brawn. I noticed neither Greg or JT getting up, simply choosing to let the boneheads do all the dirty work.

We were handed scissors and white paper, cold popcorn in packets which caked our fingers in greasy butter, and diagrams of cut-out men with instructions. Excited, Hayley and I skidded our desks around a little bit so we closed ourselves off as a group of four. Giggling, we started on our tasks as the five macho men struggled to pull the tree into our room without completely stripping it of its pine needles. To our delight, Ms. Weiss put a speaker on the end of her desk and played Christmas music at a low level. She went and tszuj'ed the tree up, an air of professionalism in her eye, and Wednesday suggested straightening the slightly leaning tree a little bit. Oh but no, with it fully upright it would tip anyway. So back to leaning against the corner of the blackboard.

By the end of class, the tree had been accosted by very unflattering, handmade decorations. Hayley laughed at how stupid it looked, but Mary and Ama insisted it was not without its charms, even though it looked to me like a blinged-up footballer's wife. Our teacher was positively beaming, though. Proud of her achievements with the help of child slavery, she admired the tree from her desk.

"It'sh shimply shtunning…" she said.

Friday stuck up her nose. "You wha — ?"

Our teacher grunted in annoyance. With a giant slurp and a puddle of drool, she took the mouth-guard out and threw it in her drawer. "To hell with it."

# 3

# RABIES AND HOBOES

A cross the hall and far away, Mom sat in the Popolopodopollus Block of the school, at the reception desk that was usually occupied by Chloe Croxley. Sweating, she searched the messy work station for the remote to turn down the heating, only coming across dust bunnies and used tissues.

When Candice Croxley, Chloe's younger sister, finally wrapped up with a client in her office, she waited until the crying teenage girl left and then sighed, shrugged, and giggled.

"Ah, to be young," she said. "Hello, Lesley!"

"Hello, Candice. Oh, can I ask you a question?"

"Of course!"

"What are your living arrangements at the moment?"

Candice leant against the high reception bench, curious. "Apartment with a view of the beach. Why?"

"Is it very small?"

"Reasonably. You're exciting me, Lesley! What have you got planned? I don't think it's big enough to hold a baby shower..."

"No, I was just going to ask you for a favour, that's all. Brendan keeps finding his Christmas presents. This morning I went downstairs and saw him playing with a doll that he wasn't meant to have opened yet."

"Oh, dear!"

"I swear, I saw nothing but red. I'm... I guess I'm a little upset at how I reacted, but honestly Candice, he really does send me round the bend. He finds them every single year! It's like he gets off on showing us how much smarter he is. Maybe we should get him tested..."

"For rabies?"

"No... his IQ..."

"Ah. And my apartment falls into this, how..?"

"Well... I was wondering... if you would let me hide his presents at yours? It would only be until Christmas, and they're not especially large gifts. Would hardly take up any space in the closet."

"Of course, Lesley! I quite like this idea! Or... we could one-up it and set all the presents around my apartment as if I owned them. That way, if he breaks in, he won't find a big bag with his name on it."

"Candice, he's not going to break in. He's not a criminal."

"No, but he's smart! And I don't mean to side-track the conversation, but it's quite exciting to imagine all of the possibilities, isn't it? Let's say he's got the Suicide Squad as back-up. How would we hide his presents from *vigilantes*, Lesley?"

Mom knew she couldn't ration with madness. She instead took the cue of a schoolboy coming in for her next appointment to move on, content that the issue had been dealt with. She would take the presents to school the next day and then hand them over to Candice.

———  • • •  ———

Even though the promise of a much earned Christmas break was a mere four days away, Annie and I understood how exhausted we both were on the bus ride home. We didn't pester each other in the least. Unfortunately, Hayley was bubbly as ever. Ms. Weiss's inadvertent swearing was almost as exciting as Christmas, according to gospel. And she chatted about it non-stop while we walked up the short incline to our property. We passed the letter-box, my eyes skimming the front yard and spotting Ella-May Parker in the next garden over. She was tending to the overgrown vines on our shared fence. They were bare in the winter, so quite grotesquely orange and spindly.

"Hi, Mrs. Parker," said Annie and I together.

Ella-May smiled half-heartedly, in a snooty kind of way.

Inside, we were hit by the firestorm coming from the central heating. The three of us took to undressing immediately, and Annie slid across the tiles to get to the nearest thermostat.

"I feel like I'm in Ibiza with Steve," said Hayley.

Annie came back and nudged me, whispering gently: "Maybe check on Zag?"

"Why?" I whispered back.

"Heat rises."

"Oh yeah, I keep forgetting."

I took a quick gander upstairs. Zag was fine. The clay head was where I'd left it, and nothing was out of the ordinary. Back downstairs in the sweltering heat, I found most of my clan in the kitchroom: Dad, dressed colourfully, was making hot chocolates for us, while Hayley relaxed on the couch, and Annie sorted out her homework to spread across the demented coffee table.

"What's with the Hawaiian shirt?" I asked my father. I'd never seen him in one before, and hoped I never would again.

"I've lost too much weight to wear my regular shirts."

I ruminated on this for a while before saying: "No, Dad, it works the other way round."

"They're too baggy; they make me look like a hobo."

"I didn't realise hoboes were so fashionable these days... Hey, now there's an idea... Would you like some new shirts for Christmas?"

He grunted in response, mainly because he knew what I was up to. I didn't have a clue what to get my parents this year. I'd usually buy my mother perfume and my father a bunch of socks (he *loved* getting socks, and antacids), but they had become comfortable with these expectations, and it saddened me a little. I wanted to give them delightful surprises this year, so I was flat-out refusing to go down the tired perfume/sock route again. And they knew it. I wanted to buy them something big.

"You couldn't afford to buy me clothes even if you wanted to," Dad told me. "Besides, you'd have to go into one of those extra large places and we know how embarrassed you get in public. Take this mug in for Hayley, it's got Pandora in it."

Only slightly wounded by his dig, I took the finished drinks into the lounge and joined Hayley on the couch.

"Help a girl out, Dad. Annie's already bought your presents."

"Yeah," said Annie. "Socks. Just the way he likes it. His big toes point upwards; the nails constantly wear through the fabric."

"You should see Lesley's calves..." muttered Dad, and he joined us and created a warp in the couch as he sank into it. He took a sip of his hot chocolate and put his feet up onto the coffee table, purposely disturbing Annie's workspace. "Honey," he said to me, "don't take this the wrong way, but anything you buy me is only going to be bought with money coming out of my own pocket. I appreciate the sentiment, but if you're really stuck for ideas, just do what Brendan did five years ago and make me something in class."

I reddened, embarrassed. "You mean like *handprints?*"

"Alright, if you don't want to buy socks, I could always do with some new underwear."

"Ew, Dad, I'm not buying you underwear."

Hayley had somehow found a packet of popcorn and was chomping away quietly.

"Sounds to me like you need a job," she offered.

Dad saddled higher in his seat, his face lighting up like the Christmas tree in the corner. "*Yes!* Excellent idea, Hayley. That's what you need. You need a job."

"I'm not getting a job," I said with a smug laugh.

"It's good to try new things," said Hayley, smirking. Sometimes, she really reminded me of Brendan.

"Alright, if I get a job, you have to try eating cereal."

Her face dropped immediately. Game over.

"You *know...*" she said slowly, "that cereal doesn't agree with the dangly thing in the back of my throat. Do you *want* me to retch all over your shag carpet? Is that what you want, Cassie? Because I'll do it. Wheat should not be consumed when wet!"

"Don't change the subject."

"*You* are the one who changed the subject! Get a job!"

"Eat some cereal!"

"*Get a job!*"

"No!"

Both sides piped up furiously.

"*Why not?*" they asked me.

It was almost like I had stereo headphones on, pestering in perfect symmetry. I didn't even know what to say. Annie was watching eagerly, her eyes wide but tiny behind her frames. I looked at Hayley, then at Dad.

"I'm not getting a job!" I snapped.

Dad and Hayley leant back, both making a snarky 'mmm-hmm' noise, and it was all I could do not to smack their bozo heads together. I stormed off upstairs, furious at the attack.

*Who do they think they are, the Righteous police? Oh, because they have jobs, they h... Dad doesn't even have a job any more! He quit because we're so rich! What's the point in getting a job if I don't need one? There are plenty of things I could do in the world other than spend seven hours a day slaving over something I don't even care about...*

*Heck,* I thought as I searched my chest of drawers for the pyjamas I wanted, *why bother going to school, come to think of it? The same reasoning applies.*

Despite this grievance, it fizzled out the more time went by. Nighttime came, and I forgave Hayley. We chatted and laughed about school until we eventually fell asleep, which took me a little longer than usual. She liked to fall asleep with the TV on, while I couldn't really do that. I did not have an affinity for flickering light-sources in my room. I'd been spooked ever since I saw *Poltergeist* as a kid. So, I waited until she was dead to the world (for real this time) and snuck over to turn the television off.

# TUESDAY THE 11th

# 4

# IRKSOME ORIFICES

The next morning, I woke up to find Hayley lying half in her bed, half out the window. Her legs and waist were close to falling out. Quickly, I hustled over and pulled her limp upper-half back in. Still fast asleep, she'd been moments from falling two storeys into the chilly garden bed below. That certainly woke me up, so I decided to do Mom a favour and deal with 'Morning Brendan'.

"Hey, you. It's time for school."

My little brother shuffled under his covers, hidden entirely. "I can't go to school today," he murmured. "I'm not well."

"Having a rash from homework is not a thing. Unless you're allergic to cedar, which isn't actually that impossible. Still, hoist yer britches up..."

He clutched at his blanket when I tried to pull it off.

"No. Where's Mom?"

"I don't know."

"I need Mom."

"Oh, really?" I said doubtfully, hands on hips.

"Yes. Seriously. Please."

I sighed and left his room to fetch her. She was in her en suit putting on a pair of Christmas earrings, the word '*Ho*' on each one.

"You know I can't let you wear those, right?" I said.

Mom noticed the error in the mirror and heaved in disappointment, taking them off and chucking them in her drawer. "You'd think the clerk at the store would've said something... What's up?"

"Brendan says he's sick. Not going to school."

She took it in, muttered something under her breath, and strode out of the room to deal with him. A moment later I heard him cry out, and then she too let out a yell of surprise. I ran immediately to check on them, but everything seemed to be fine. Mom sat down on the edge of Brendan's bed and fussed around his eyes, which is when I noticed...

"What *is* that!?" I cried, covering my mouth.

Brendan panicked at my voice, and Mom hushed us both. "Relax, I'm sure it's nothing... *Ichabod! Ichabod, come here now!*"

Aghast, I turned away as my father thundered in. Annie and Hayley quickly followed. To my surprise, Dad pushed the three of us out into the hallway and shut the door behind him.

"What's going on, do you know?" Annie asked me. Her hair was up in rollers and she had white dots on her face from pimple cream. Hayley was rubbing her arms, teeth chattering.

"His... *eyes*... are glued shut," I told them in disbelief.

Through the door, Dad ordered us to get ready for school, telling us they'd be out soon. By the time we were sitting in the kitchroom eating breakfast, Mom came down fully dressed and ready. She didn't look happy, though. More distracted than anything. It was like we weren't even there; therefore she served no explanation as to what was going on upstairs.

"Mom, spill!" Annie demanded eventually.

"Brendan's eyes have glued shut, so your father's going to drive him to the Emergency Room in Alexandria. It's nothing serious."

"Are you telling us he put adhesives on his eyes?"

"No, he..." Mom seemed momentarily flustered as she packed up her work briefcase, and for some reason she lowered her voice. "I've heard of this happening before, but it's rather excessive for... I mean, there's the infection part, sure, but it only gets like that if you

32

cry yourself to sleep. But you really have to *cry*. Why would he...?"

"Maybe because you smacked him yesterday," said Annie.

There was silence as we thought back on the situation. That was yesterday morning. He would've gotten over it by last night, surely.

Hayley put her head down and focused entirely on consuming her breakfast.

"Not here. Don't care," she said.

"Mom, aren't you going to stay home with him? He's not going to school, right?"

"Of course not. And no. I've got students! He's fine, your father will be home all day. You girls catch the bus and I'll let you know at recess how he is."

"I'm happy to stay home. We're not doing any work in class this week. We're only watching old video tapes."

"No, Annie, go to school."

"Oh, Mom, please. It's an awful waste of time! Yesterday in Home Ec we watched Martha Stewart bake ornamental cookies with Miss. Piggy."

"Unless you're leaking fluids from your orifices just like your brother, the answer is no."

"Well," muttered Annie, "it *is* that time of the month, so..."

Hayley dropped her spoon and let the milk dribble back into the bowl. "Do you mind? Some of us are trying to eat cereal for the first time here!"

I turned to face my mother as the other two argued.

"Can I catch a ride with you this morning?"

She obliged, and seemed grateful that I'd offered to stay a little longer in case she needed more help with Brendan. And it was strange... For the briefest of moments I wondered if Zag had anything to do with this, but it was just not quite strange enough. Besides, Mom and Dad knew not of our previous magical escapades. If it seemed within the realms of possibility to them, then it likely was.

Soon enough it was time for the others to catch the bus. Despite her protests, Annie was particularly keen to be rid of her family's troubles for the day. As they rushed for the door, she stumbled in her efforts. Her copy of *World Politics* was missing and she wanted to read it during art class.

"I'm sure it's here somewhere," said Hayley, leaving quickly. "I'll stall the bus for you, friend."

But she didn't. Five minutes later she was on JT's lap while the bus drove away. She pulled the copy of *World Politics* out of her bag and snickered as Annie helplessly chased after them.

"That'll teach her to make me gag on her leaking orifices."

JT waited approximately five seconds.

"I am *not* asking."

Eleanore moved away from the safety of the front row and dangled above the pair of unused seats in front of them. She was dressed in a bright red top and green skirt, with the same green-coloured stockings underneath. She pointed to Wednesday and Friday, who were in matching clothing.

"Aren't we just darling?" she said tweely.

"Yes, *so* darling!" said Hayley effervescently. "So darling I could just rip off your heads and feast on the spider sacs inside!"

This was apparently too much for the Saviour, who sprang back and gulped. She collected herself, and turned her attention to the boy sitting underneath Hayley. "JT, I thought I'd let you know that my father and mother happily accept your request."

"*Their* request," insisted JT. He scratched under his beanie, for Hayley's mention of spiders made him suddenly very itchy.

"I'm assuming it's just the usual crowd?"

"Yes."

"Very well. And I too accept the invitation. Thank you."

"You're welcome."

Hayley rolled her eyes and mocked JT's polite response. "God, I hate this time of year. Everyone's so festive and nice."

"Heaven forbid!" said JT in a girly voice.

"I don't need you two becoming lovers," snapped Hayley. "That would tip me over the edge, and I'm nearly there already."

"Calm down. There's nothing wrong with Christmas."

"It hates me."

"How?"

"Well, for one it always reminds me of how cursed I am."

"You think *you're* cursed?" said Eleanore. "I'm the one who has to see your ugly faces every day."

"You're not cursed, Hayles," said JT.

"Yes, I am! Bad things always happen to me at Christmas."

JT grinned in amusement. "When has anything bad ever happened to you at Christmas?"

Hayley's eyes widened. "Hello? My mother! Steve! Homeless! Kindness of strangers!"

"I don't recall *you* being knocked over by a row of trolleys."

"Yeah," said Eleanore in agreement.

Hayley spun around and crossed her arms.

"This strange alliance you two have at this time of year is getting on my nerves. Shut it down."

With that, Eleanore lured herself away like a scheming little gibbon. However, her cruel intentions had left their mark. Although Hayley was sitting on JT's lap, the two couldn't have been further apart if they tried.

· · ·

I eventually made it to school, running late as Mom forgot two separate things and we had to turn the car around each time. She would be terrible at work today, I realised, for her job was mostly to listen to students, and she was barely paying attention to the traffic let alone me as I told her about my desire to spice up my Christmas present list. Her mind, most undoubtedly, was stuck on Brendan.

I scooted into class moments before Ms. Weiss angrily locked the door, and was sweating throughout the entire first period. By the time the bell rang for recess, Miss. Terr had already popped in briefly to tell us to get ready for an exciting single period playing basketball. I wasn't particularly happy with this, especially since I'd refused to shower earlier due to what I'd perceived as a relaxed day ahead. Agitated, I grew certain that my armpits were suddenly producing more sweat than usual.

"Oh, Cassie," said JT, catching me as we went out into the Fido Auditorium. "My parents wanted to know if your family would like to join us for a special Christmas dinner on the twenty-first."

Surprised, I wondered in the moment if this was the longest sentence he'd ever said to me. However, I was more distracted by how genuine he was in his invitation.

"I'll have to check with my parents, but count me in," I said, giving Hayley a perplexed look as she caught up to us.

JT smiled gladly at my answer, and Hayley cottoned on and told me how excited she was that I was going, as she would be there too. I was excited more than either of them, because I'd never met JT's family or even been to his house before.

Meanwhile across the auditorium, Principal Parker was showing some people around, almost falling backwards as some guys rushed around him with a basketball. Clearly angry at being embarrassed in front of his new company, he took the ball from the nearest student and hugged it, essentially confiscating it. He then pointed towards us and beyond as he continued talking to his guests about the new school.

A beautiful, slender woman with very tanned skin huddled into her giant jacket, looking quite unhappy to be in such a cold environment. The other person standing with them was an extremely tall man, freakishly so, wearing a full suit, top hat, with a heavy black moustache and an eye-patch over one eye. I laughed and subtly pointed so my friends would look.

"Check out the attention seeker," said Hayley.

We continued on, planning to head to the Vineyard and see if it was warm enough in there to stay during our break. But before we'd even left the auditorium, there was a ruckus behind us. I heard somebody say in a harsh whisper nearby:

"Her. *Her. Her!*"

Before I had time to turn, something hit me.

After that, darkness.

# 5

## HEL'
## ON
## WHEELS

I woke up shortly after, my head pounding. Lying down, I opened my eyes to see a blurry world in front of me; then the nurse's office came into focus. I'd only been in here once before, during orientation day... the second one, that is, when Principal ...Parker?... introduced us to the new nurse. It was a tiny cramped place, with only enough room for the single gurney bed I was on, and a few cabinets for medicines. Nothing high-tech or life saving if such trouble arose. And I assumed, then, that I was out of harm's way. But what had happened?

I moved my eyes from side-to-side and stretched my arms behind my back as far as they would go, and it was as I tapped on my skull gently that I found the source of the problem. I stood up, not dizzy in the slightest, and checked myself out in a mirror on the back of the door. I had a giant, purple bruise around one eye. Gaping for a moment, I touched at it gently. It didn't hurt. Yet above my fringe was where the sensitivity lay. Something had hit me, and I quickly remembered the moment before I was knocked out. I leaned in for an even closer look.

The door before me opened in, the corner smacking me in my good eye, and I fell backwards. The nurse cried out and grabbed me, and laid me back down on the gurney bed. Nurse Fletcher had short red hair tied back, and in the shock of it all her face was whiter than her uniform.

"Now-now," she said in her intriguing Belfast accent. "We'll have no more of this or else you'll have a black nose next." She rubbed my most recently accosted eye-socket vigorously. "This is to stop it from bruising as much. *Here…*" She went over to the wrapped steak she'd dropped upon opening the door. "You take turns now, keeping it on one eye and then the other."

"What happened?" I asked.

"Don't worry, dear. Someone will be here to pick you up soon. I'll be in my office next door. Scream if you need me." Nurse Fletcher seemed eager to leave, perhaps feeling guilty.

Alone again, I did as I was told and alternated between eyes with the steak. Somebody had thrown a ball at me, I surmised. Given I'd been talking on the basketball court, perhaps we'd… But no, Principal Parker had the ball, and he definitely wouldn't have thrown it. Either way, whoever did it must have put their back into it. It was enough to make a girl hallucinate…

Which is exactly what I thought I was doing when, moments later, a familiar face walked into the tiny room with as much energetic fervour as a Tesla coil. She couldn't possibly be here in front of me. It wasn't even down to magic, either. It was something so impossible that I stared in grim disbelief, my mouth hung open like a common loafer.

"Well!" cried my grandmother, grabbing my wrists and checking both sides. "Not what I thought it would be."

I pulled back, frightened and confused. My mouth was dry and a sudden inner quiver began in my chest, as if I had onset diabetes. "Grandma Helen?"

My mother's mother was definitely long in the tooth compared to the last time I'd seen her. Lengthy, straight grey hair tied up in a sensible bun, wrinkles galore on every visible part of her ivory skin. Her strangely watery, small eyes were still the frighteningly bright blue Mom and Annie had inherited from her. She didn't smile, but she looked glad to be of service to my shocked senses. And of course, hiding behind her navy blue pantsuit, her cane. The only thing really keeping her upright.

"I'm glad your memory is still intact. The nurse said somebody threw a ball at your head. Who did you offend?" She checked my scalp, feeling her fingers along my hairline, and when I winced, she backed off like she'd set off a firecracker. "Tell me who did this to you."

I took a moment to respond, and bit my cold bottom lip. "Where's Mom and Dad? Nurse Fletcher said…"

"*They* are occupied. Your father's at the hospital with Brendan and your mother is here somewhere… I just happened to be at your house when the school rang, so I drove right down."

"But… We… How many cars do we have?" I closed my eyes. Thinking this hard was giving me a headache.

"I had no choice. You will thank me when we're finally home. Besides, the cold will do you some good. Come, come. The nurse says you are fine to leave."

Grandma Helen was underneath my elbows, lifting me to my feet. She had purposely avoided answering my question, and as we exited the nurse's station into the empty main hallway, I managed through squinted eyes to see the car-park ahead. It was empty. We walked through the reception area and past Ms. Chin-Tucker, who smiled sympathetically and said: "Feel better, Cassie."

I barely smiled and said thank-you, as the lights around me were ghosting in a rather unusual way. Why was everything so bright, but… darker? It hurt my eyes.

We took one step outside and I closed in on myself, the winds harsh and relentless. Grandma Helen told me to hurry onwards, she would catch up. And then I realised. It was long after school had ended for the day; it seemed dark because it was nearly twilight, and the only vehicle in the front lot sat glaring before me.

Dad's yellow motorcycle.

I turned back to watch my grandmother as she hobbled slowly towards me. "There's a sidecar," she pointed out, feeling this would change my opinion altogether. "Your jacket is in there and it's a five minute drive. The fresh air will wake you up more."

I wasn't in the mood to stink up a fuss. My head was positively aching and I couldn't place myself in time. I put the jacket on and hopped into the bright yellow sidecar, buckling myself in. It had been years since I'd sat in there. Dad used to take us as kids for rides around

Salem, until he nearly crashed it one day when a cat ran out in front of us. Suddenly he was an irresponsible father and Mom barred any of us, including him, from ever using it again. Unless for emergencies, we gathered. And strangely, I suppose this was an emergency.

My German grandmother looked wildly out-of-place as she started the engine. I knew her hatred of motorcycles was deep, not just because of her disdain for my father, but also because of the run of absurdly bad luck she'd suffered throughout her life, which always seemed to come back to them. Her story was like urban legend in our household; I could recite it off by heart if necessary:

When she was a little girl, her father rode a motorcycle in Germany and she would often accompany him in the rear, clutching at his leather jacket for dear life as they soared down the cobbled streets of Bad Wimpfen in summertime. A few years after that, as Hitler's regime threw the country head-first into yet another fruitless war, she was walking home from the library one afternoon when she was struck by an officer atop an R75. Hip shattered at thirteen, she declared to anybody who would listen that motorcycles would cease to exist by the time she was through with them, promising to get better and study hard and then socialise until she garnered enough followers to ban the production of any motorcycles in Germany. Of course, nobody paid her any attention, as another nut with followers was causing greater concern. Still, Helen vowed to never hop on a motorcycle ever again. Which was all well and good to say, but to practice such restraints proved impossible from the moment she started dating Pierse a few years after the war. While her sore hip served as a reminder, giving her grief in the cold, she did as Pierse told her, saddling up behind him on his bike and accompanying him wherever he went like a good doting girlfriend. But then on a trip to Paris together for a rally, she was struck by another motorcyclist, this time a drink driver, while crossing the road. Finding it hard to believe, her hip was shattered again.

Many years went by and she refused to even look at a motorcycle. She met our Grandfather Victor, the two got married and moved to Canada and started a family. Between 1950 and 1995, she was struck by ten more motorcycles. *Ten.* It became a running joke in our family, and something that we really had to insist was true to people who refused to believe our story. Not that we ever blamed them. It all sounded horrendously made up, however Mom and Dad verified everything tiresomely, plus Annie and I witnessed her getting hit in 1992 while we visited in Canada. It was like the universe was out to get her, and she lay on the side of the road in agony, clutching at her hip, cursing at my fussing mother: "Nein! Nein!"

"Ma, let me check it, let me..."

"No, Lesley, I'm saying nine! Nine times! *Nine!*"

Now, Grandma Helen was a very vocal member of motorcycle *un*-enthusiasts, going so far as to join hater clubs, committees, and attending rallies that would bombard all sorts of motorcycle shows across the country with intense negativity. Signs, yelling crowds, blocking streets in their protests. She lived for it.

And yet here she was, faced with a dilemma. Fetch the wounded granddaughter at school on the devil's contraption, or wait until one of the parents came home to use their car. Well, as I sat like a melting snowman in clothing, frozen from head-to-toe as we made our way up the streets of Horn-Horn, I felt grateful that I wasn't still at school. I would be home safe and sound and in bed within ten minutes, and perhaps she'd known this and made a little sacrifice for me.

I looked up at her, riding steadfast, with the dark and gloomy clouds of early winter high above her, and felt a rush of gratitude.

———— . . . ————

I was still frozen when we entered the front door.

"What a chill!" said my grandmother, taking my jacket off for me. "Straight from Canada. I must have brought it with me. Into the living room with you, go on."

She pushed me forward and I went into the kitchroom, where Annie sat with Dad and Brendan. They were all in their pyjamas watching the television, except for Brendan who was wearing a blindfold. Upon seeing my hideous face, Dad jumped up, wearing a pair of mismatched socks I'd bought him last Christmas.

"Helen!" he said in disbelief. "What are you doing here?"

Grandma Helen remained in the hallway but her face was lit by the raging fire in the other room.

"I was saving your daughter. What's wrong with the boy?"

I snuck a look. In the ever-changing light flashes from the TV, I noticed the very blind Brendan sitting on the couch, stroking Tigger on his lap, tilting his head this way and that to understand the situation.

"Brendan, that's his anus," Annie guided his hand away.

Dad humphed as he watched his mother-in-law with unease.

"It's discharge from an infection. Helen... what... I mean, how are you? How did you get here? Lesley said she was..."

*Speak of the devil*, I thought as Mom swung open the front door. Her beige trench-coat billowing around her in the wind, she shut the door behind her and stared in at the situation. Fury was written all over her face and in her scarily bright blue eyes.

"Just *what* is going on?" she yelled.

She rushed past Grandma and came straight to me, but I had enough sense now that the attention was aggravating me, and I went and sat down next to Annie in the living-room. Unfortunately, the adults followed.

"Cassie, why did you leave the nurse's office? I told you I'd come and get you after my last patient."

"You did?"

"Yes..."

"I don't remember that. What happened?"

"When?"

I burst out in laughter. *"When everything!"*

Dad came over and managed to squish his giant torso between my sister and I. "Honey, you were hit in the head by a basketball. It knocked you out."

"I saw it!" said Annie. "Let's just put it this way: *Yowza*."

Mom's neck was arched in a peculiar way. She was stressed, I could tell. "We spoke in the nurse's office. A few hours ago? A full conversation. I can't believe it. Don't you remember any of it? You seemed fine."

I pouted as I tried to cast my mind back. It was a little bit freaky, to be honest. "Sorry," I said, giving an innocent shrug.

"Well, of course, that's okay. I'm just glad you're fine. The nurse and the doctor both said you were good to go. And I checked for you. You don't have to stay awake all night. I was worried about concussion, you see... Now, *you*," she said, looming over us to reach Brendan, and kissing his forehead. "I'm glad you're not as worried as you were this morning. I told you what it was. Now that you've heard a doctor in a hospital explain it, can you please relax? They said give it a few days and wash it with salt-water."

"I can't relax! It's Christmastime and I'm *blind*! How would you like it?"

"At this point, I'm begging for it. And..." Mom pointed at the window behind the television. I followed her gaze. The curtain was drawn, but it was billowing in and out slowly. "What's that about?" she asked the crowd.

Grandma Helen was fast on her approach for the kitchen. She took some vitamin powder out of a drawer, as if she'd been here before, and mixed some into a glass of water. She gave her daughter a dead-pan stare. "My cane slipped."

"We can't sleep in a house with a broken window."

"Why on earth not?"

It was always odd to hear my mother talk to her own mother, if only for one particularly suspicious fact: Whilst Grandma Helen was German, she'd been here so long that she had a regular accent just like me. But when she became angry or her emotions were heightened, a strange hybrid accent would emerge. It was almost as if she were secretly from somewhere in Eastern Europe, with V's replacing W's dotted across a poor man's German.

"What are you doing here?" asked Mom starkly. It could have been the sudden wind gust getting through the curtain, but the temperature certainly dropped after she said it.

No longer able to fend off the questions, Grandma Helen swigged back the drink and wiped her top lip, then took a refreshed breath and headed for the stairs. "I need to use the bathroom; don't pester me while I'm in there."

As a family, we grouped together on the couch in her absence, grateful for the brief time it would take for her to do her business before she came back down again.

"I bet she couldn't get in because nobody was home."

"So she broke the window," said Annie.

"To get in?" asked Brendan.

"No, doofus, to meld prescription eyewear with."

"Then she took Dad's motorbike to pick me up," I said.

All four of them turned to me, even Brendan with his eyes blindfolded. Mom and Dad immediately raced out the front door for a better look. Thanks to the window being broken, I heard Mom cussing loudly. Moments later they were back and we were in our huddled form again to discuss viable options.

"If she's going to ruin Christmas, I want to visit Aunt Rachael in Brooklyn," said Annie.

"You guys have to keep her busy during the day while she's here. I don't want her lurking around the hallways when I can't see what she's doing," muttered Brendan. "You know how weird grandmothers can be. She'll probably stand over me while I'm doing a poo because she knows I can't see her."

"You're insane, you know that?" snapped Annie.

Mom's thought process, however, was on a different level. She gazed off into space, spellbound by the absurdity of it. "I can't believe she broke into our house, and then stole the motorcycle," she said slowly. "That's not like her. Ichabod, I'll bet you anything she ripped off that *'Too Fat To Carpool'* bumper sticker the O'Flahertys gave you for your thirtieth."

"That's okay, they gave me a whole draw-full of them."

We sat together in silence, until we heard the pipes in the walls that signified Grandma Helen had finished doing her business. The old woman was quick to call out to us from the second-last stair, and as we turned to see her, I noticed she had changed clothes and was now in her bed-wear: a light blue silk nightgown that went right to her ankles. Her hair was down and flowed over one shoulder, past her bosom.

She smiled at us all calmly, and then said:

"I left your father, Lesley. That's vhy I'm here. I want to spend time with my family. I don't see why you make it out to be so unusual when it's not. I'm here for Christmas and I'll be staying in the guest-room. You must all be far more tired than I am," she said with a laugh, "and I am quite tired. I usually am, after interrogations."

With a glance above, she held her breath, as if listening for something. "This house is so draughty."

*That's because you broke the window...* I thought.

"There's also someone else up here."

My mind seized in horror as I thought of Zag.

"That's Hayley," Dad said. "She's staying with us."

"I think I frightened her."

"She'll be fine."

"Goodnight, everyone."

"Goodnight," we called back.

When she finally disappeared upstairs, we turned to each other for support, as the reality of the situation hit us hard.

This couldn't be...

Grandma Helen was staying for Christmas.

# WEDNESDAY
## THE
# 12<sup>TH</sup>

# 6

# HOGAN'S HARDWARE HUT

Something funny happened the next morning. I woke up in my bedroom, all alone, and for the briefest of moments I thought Hayley had sleep-fallen to her death out the window. As I darted upright, and saw that her bed was no longer there, I let out a sigh and collapsed back into my covers. But I was awake for the day. It was a vague memory, having Hayley and Annie push the spare bed out of the room. She would be staying with Annie for a few days, because Mom insisted I have my bedroom to myself. Despite the size of our house, none of the other free bedrooms were upstairs, save for the one Grandma Helen was now using. We had two perfectly lovely guest rooms downstairs, but they were so far away and cut-off from the rest of the house that they gave Hayley the creeps, and she flat-out refused to stay in either of them. Grandma wouldn't budge either, but that was because she was old and knew perfectly well how things worked. "That's why your bedrooms are upstairs, because you'll get the heat from the day while you sleep," she would tell us as kids.

All well and good when it wasn't summer, I guess.

The thing I didn't like about this arrangement was that Grandma Helen's guest bedroom was directly opposite mine, across the landing. If we both had our doors open, we could see into each other's rooms. Of course, teenager that I was, I kept mine closed at all times. But she was notorious for keeping her door wide open, even when undressing. Mom grew up with this behaviour, while Dad married into it and without fail would freak out whenever he spotted her in just her stockings (which apparently happened often).

"I'm very glad you upgraded," was the first thing she said to Mom the next morning, greeting us as she came down late for breakfast. She was ready for the day, having dressed in a rather dated navy blouse and skirt. Her metallic cane wobbled slightly as she struggled to sit down on a stool next to me.

"Upgraded what?" asked Mom, buttering her toast.

"This," she pointed up and around.

"Oh."

"All those little wooden treehouses you called homes. Very concerning, I'm sure you knew that, it drove me mad… Oh, you have Pandora. Don't mind if I do."

Annie, Hayley and I ate our breakfasts in solemn silence.

"Ma, when are we going to have a… chat about… things?"

"After breakfast, when the kids have gone to school," Helen answered happily. She stole a piece of toast off Hayley's plate and began buttering it generously.

"I work at the high school, so I won't have time then," said Mom, putting on a great big fake smile that showed nearly all of her teeth.

"Then tonight shall do nicely! So. *'Hayley'*. Why are you here?"

Hayley could barely contain her rage after having been robbed of her toast. She turned on the stool to face Grandma Helen fully, and I noticed her face was beetroot red again. She didn't have time to say anything before Mom snapped her fingers in front of their faces to catch their attention.

"She's a guest, and it's time she went to school. You too, Annie."

"Can't I stay home? I did *nothing* yesterday, and I've lost my *World Politics* book!" pleaded Annie.

"Oh," said Hayley quickly, reaching into her backpack. "Here you go, friend."

Annie grabbed her book gleefully, not questioning where it had been, then grew melancholy as Mom urged her to follow Hayley to the front door to catch the bus. Suddenly I found myself alone in the kitchen with my mother and my grandmother.

"Can't *I* go to school?" I asked, equally desperate. "I don't want to sit at home all day on my own. It's boring."

Mom eyed me and shook her head gently. I gobbled down my toast and, feeling strangely unwanted, made myself scarce upstairs. For a few moments the mother and daughter ate their toast in silence, looking anywhere but at each other. Mom threw her dish in the sink and then finished her coffee, and was about to leave when she stopped. She focused her eyes on the dishwasher and its solid red dot, trying not to let anger take over. She wanted to walk away, to save it for another time, but she had to say *something*.

"At no point during your trip across the border, in what I'm assuming was a bus, did you stop to think that maybe you should've called ahead? You know, as a courtesy. You didn't once think that maybe you should check in advance?"

Grandma Helen listened politely, then dabbed at the sides of her mouth with a napkin. She stood up and struggled to make her way across the living room.

"I didn't plan this trip."

"You plan everything, mother."

"Except to call ahead. Am I not welcome?"

"What?"

"It's your house, Lesley. If I am not welcome, then…"

Mom scoffed and went to grab her bag from one of the stools.

"Don't put words into my mouth. I spoke to Pa last night on the phone and he's as bewildered as I am. You didn't even tell him you were going. You think it's acceptable to leave your husband a week before Christmas? I offered for him to come and stay as well, but he doesn't want to, and now I feel bad that he's going to be alone for the holidays."

"He's not alone. He has Bertha."

Mom eyed her quizzically, then said: "Who's Bertha?"

"She's the reason why I left him."

It seemed nothing else needed to be said between the two. Mom shook her head, taking in the information slowly, and headed towards the door.

"I can't right now. I'll see you tonight. Leave the kids alone."

She grabbed her keys and stormed out.

Sitting up uncomfortably in my bed, I heard cabinets and doors opening and closing rather annoyingly downstairs. I still had a headache and felt really weird, and the more I thought about it the stranger the case became. How close had the person been, the one who'd hit me with the ball? I mean, was it... like... on purpose? I could vaguely remember somebody shouting... or was it whispering... *Her... Her...* Or was it: *Hit her... Hit her...?* My mind became distracted a few minutes later when the closing of doors ceased, and was replaced by rather quick footsteps above me. In the attic. I quickly pulled at my ear in aggravation, and a split second later Zag appeared near the wardrobe. He was wearing an elf costume again, which looked exactly like his usual pyjamas, only in red and green.

"I thought we ditched that?" he said immediately.

"Why are you being so loud up there?" I snapped, sounding like an uptight schoolmarm. "You are going to draw attention."

"Sorry," he said, his cheeks pink. "I have a visitor."

"Oh, really? Who?"

"Nobody. We'll be quiet, I swear."

He disappeared in a puff of smoke and glitter. It was just in time, too, as somebody immediately knocked on my door. My thoughts in tatters, I greeted Dad with a smile as he poked his head in. He said quietly: "How's your head?"

I shrugged in response. He looked as tired as I felt.

"I need to pop down to the hardware store. Guess what? I'm going to put the Christmas lights up on the roof tonight."

"Oh, yay!" I said enthusiastically. "I don't think the usual amount of lights will cut it this year."

"No, I know. That's why I want to go down to the shop, to buy more. What do you reckon, about three times as many?"

"*Four*," I insisted with a grin, even though we both knew this would be far more than necessary.

*Good*, I thought. *Make our house visible from Danube!*

"Thing is, I'll need a hand. You know, picking them out."

I nodded, listening. I knew what he was doing. I could tell he felt bad for me, cooped up even though I felt fine. Mom was a worry-wart. He was handing me an olive branch.

"Want some help?" I asked.

He grinned. "Meet you at the front door in five minutes."

"Wait!" I called immediately, and his head reappeared like a ghost in the door. "We can't leave Brendan alone."

Dad pondered for a moment. "You're right. And your grandmother's sussing out every nook and cranny downstairs. I'm sure she'll want to snoop in his room eventually."

I shuddered at the thought. She'd done worse. I went to say such a thing, when Dad appeared to slip on the door handle and tumbled forward. With a yelp, he checked behind him. Catching his footing, he put a hand to his heart in fright, and I too jumped and let out a little squeal at the sight. Grandma Helen had been standing behind him for goodness knows how long, listening to our conversation, and behind her was Brendan, eyes grotesquely welded shut. The sight of them both had scared us silly.

"I don't sneak," Grandma said to him, taking offence. "As you could hear downstairs, I'm a noisy prowler. Now, if you two are quite done talking about people behind their backs, I'll make a suggestion. Since you're going downtown, I'd like it if you could take us as well. I can escort Brendan around the mall for a while. You've treated him very badly this week and I want to buy him a present."

"How about that Tiro doll you weren't supposed to open, buddy...?" said Dad, ruffling the blind boy's hair.

"Ichabod, let me make a deal with you," said Grandma Helen, very clearly judging his handyman flannel shirt and paint-covered overalls in one fell swoop of a glance. "Take us downtown with you. You can drop Brendan and I off, then you and Cassie can go to the hardware store. When you've finished, you can call my number and pick us up."

As awkward as Dad was around his mother-in-law, he wasn't an idiot, and he let her know with one equally repugnant glance: "Uh, Helen, not sure if you've noticed but Brendan's got a really bad eye infection. He's not going anywhere."

"Fine, then I will tell Lesley tonight. As I recall, both Brendan and Cassie are home sick for a reason."

Dad scoffed at first, but quickly his face dropped in realisation. This was all she'd need to say to Mom to get us into trouble.

• • •

We were out the door ten minutes later. Dad, in the driver's seat, wasn't having any nonsense. He was quiet, the radio was on his favourite station, and he was driving as slow as he wanted. He gripped the wheel and stared straight ahead as I sat next to a blind-folded Brendan in the back, holding him to make sure he stayed upright. Grandma Helen sat in the front with Dad, but he didn't seem to even notice her.

"Dad," I chanced it as we drove down the road. "You fit into the driver's seat so well now. You really are losing weight."

For a moment I thought he was going to give me the cold shoulder, and I felt bad because I wasn't the one blackmailing him. But eventually he replied with a quiet: "Thank you, honey," before continuing on with his silent and serious driving.

———— · · · ————

The Horn-Horn Mall II's parking lot was absolutely jam-packed. There were lorries and vans, trucks and trolleys, people running to-and-fro, carrying heavy things back-and-forth in the Christmas rush. However, one thing was missing entirely.

"No motorcycles," said Grandma Helen with a smile.

I opened the back door nearest to me, and by the time I'd jumped down the two front-seaters were already cutting in front of me to help Brendan out. Then Dad unpacked the folded wheelchair from the back and helped Brendan sit down in it.

"Where did you find this thing again?" asked Dad.

"It was in the guest bedroom," said Grandma, "tucked away in the wardrobe. I really can't imagine why you'd have a wheelchair. It's not like anybody in your family needs it. Unless you did, before you lost...?" She gazed at him curiously, wondering.

Dad, offended, frowned. "No. Cassie, any idea?"

On a five second delay, I cast my mind back but couldn't remember any immediate family needing a wheelchair. Perhaps it was left over from the previous owners.

"I'll call you as soon as we're done, okay?"

It took Brendan a moment to realise that Dad was talking to him, and he nodded and gave the thumbs up at me.

"Don't run anyone over," I said to him.

"See you soon, racoon," he replied.

As Dad and I hopped back into the car, I bit my lips in curiosity. Had someone told him about my two black eyes, and was he being his usual sneaky self, or was it just a coincidence that he called me a racoon? Each bruise was so vastly different from the other. While the first one was a hideous black colour (almost green), the second eye-bruise from Nurse Fletcher was only blue and purple, but it had been a direct impact so it made my top eyelid swell out more. I'd caked on so much foundation and powder to cover them up, I was sure strangers would think I was doing whiteface. Luckily, I'd added a little of Mom's rouge and fuchsia lipstick to hopefully distract from the obvious. I looked like I had a mild form of elephantiasis.

*But you know what?* I reasoned with myself as we pulled into the hardware store parking lot. *You won't know anyone while you're out today, because everybody is at school!* This did make me feel a lot better. I was officially not trying today. I could be a meth-face at my own friggin' leisure.

The jingle of a bell didn't help as we walked through the front door. The hardware store was an old schoolhouse stripped many decades ago, with about twelve different rows of shelves leading all the way to the back, and then in another room were paints and holi-day aisles.

"Ugh," I said, wishing I'd worn a hoodie.

"Nobody cares who you are, sweetheart," said Dad reassuringly. "I don't even see anyone I know, and I wouldn't make a fuss any-how... Oh, Morgan! Over here! Hey! Hello!"

A good-looking young Asian man came over to us, wearing a purple flannel shirt buttoned all the way to the top, which was half-covered by a green *'Hogan's Horn-Horn Hardware Hut'* apron. I guess as embarrassed as I was looking like a beehive victim, he must have felt equally embarrassed at his own appearance. At least he got paid to look like that.

"Hey, Mr. Gellar."

"Mr. Gellar, pffft. Please. Call me Icky."

"... I don't think I can do that, sir."

"Yeah, Dad, ew..."

"Are you in for more paint?" asked the man named Morgan.

"No, not today. Morgan, this is my daughter, Annie."

"Cassie," I corrected him in horror, but Morgan cut in.

"Oh, the smart one? I've heard a lot about you. You know, I was a Science Labber through the eleventh grade and..."

"No, that's Annie. I'm Cassie."

"Annie," said Dad, and then he corrected himself again, but sounded like Stuttering Stanley in his attempt.

Morgan smiled awkwardly. "Sorry, you're..?"

"CASSIE," I said firmly. "I'm Cassie. I'm not the smart one."

Internally peeling off the insides of my skull, I smiled as Dad and Morgan got over the hurdle that was my life, and started talking business. LED's were becoming big nowadays. Incandescent was the only word I knew of besides from watts, and expensive. And lumbago for some reason. But my mind was too accosted to focus on what we came here for, so I saddled into my usual hermit hunch and decided to wade it out. Every once in a while Dad would catch my attention by saying: "See this, Cassie?" And I would add a 'hmm' noise as a signal that, yes, I was seeing what he was seeing, because I wasn't the blind one in the family. I think Dad picked up on the fact that I was feeling prickly, so he just collected a whole bunch of random boxes of wired and solars. Without the attention of his second born, this outing wasn't fun.

"Oh, look, Cassie," he said, almost as if trying to cause me more pain. "Over there, look at that."

He was pointing to a sign directly behind Morgan's shoulder. Through my slightly distorted vision, I grew even more aggravated by its nonsensical wording.

"*Stuff wanted?* What do they mean, *stuff wanted?* Like, spare parts? Bean bag beans? They should really be more specific, don't you think?" I said loudly.

Dad turned to check the sign again.

"No, honey, it says *staff* wanted."

"... Oh..."

I was definitely not the smart one.

Morgan didn't seem too disturbed by my serial killer attitude. In fact, he turned eagerly to look at the sign, then back at me.

"Are you looking for work?" he asked.

"Just a few hours over the holidays to start with," said Dad, answering for me. "We were just talking about it the other night, weren't we? She can't even afford to buy underwear!"

My mouth was open in rage, although it was in the shape of a smile. My teeth were fully on display... but my wide eyes, edged with crusted powder, told another story.

Finally, Dad caught the hint.

"We'll take a form to fill out at home."

Morgan grabbed one from a nearby counter and handed it to Dad, not me. I couldn't look him in the eye anymore. He'd already seen too much of me. I'd have to dump his body somewhere.

"Dad, I have never been so humiliated in all my life!"

I vented freely as we walked to the car. I pushed the trolley holding the boxes we'd bought because it was heavy, and I used it like a stress ball, pressing against it to release the frustrations inside of me.

"Why, honey?"

I laughed angrily at his obliviousness.

"Who must he think I am? Some nut job, surely. I've never even met him before! But I know he's... Oh, God. I'm going back, y'know, in my mind, replaying and... Ughhh!"

"Who, Morgan? He seemed to like you."

I squinted in disbelief.

"Were... you... even... *there?*" I declared dramatically, trying to wrap my head around my father's way of thinking. "I must've looked like I had Bell's palsy or something. What do you think, Dad, should I hand in my résumé on a couple of used tissues next time I ride my two-legged donkey into town?"

I put the trolley on an angle so it wouldn't roll away, and left it for Dad to empty into the back. I hopped in the front passenger seat and shut the door angrily behind me, crouching down in my seat and putting my feet up against the windscreen.

"Stuff wanted..." I muttered to myself. *"Honestly."*

Maybe the others were having a better time...

———— • • • ————

What Brendan and Grandma Helen didn't realise was that, as they made their way around the mall, many people who knew Brendan from around town were gazing in fascination at his oblivious, blindfolded form — sitting in a wheelchair, pushed by a woman they simply didn't know. It wasn't so alarming that anyone thought to call the police, but many questions were up in the air, and one particular individual was too curious not to venture forward and inquire.

"Hi, hello," said Cindy Tanner.

She worked at Horn-Horn's one and only 'Siberian Musky', a Russian conglomerate which sold candles and Wiccan stuff, mostly. Cindy was new to the scene, having shaved her head after dealing with the trauma of her rock-climbing accident, and finding her inner sanctum. Seven-thousand dollars in debt later she'd found her outer sanctum was a sucker, and had to work full-time to make up for it. Despite this, she remained open-minded the best she could, and bent down to touch Brendan gently on the shoulders.

"Hi Brendan, it's your neighbour Cindy Tanner. Remember me? Are you…?"

She almost retched as he took off his blindfold to reveal his goopy eyes. She quickly looked up in panic at Grandma Helen.

"Is he alright?" she mouthed as quietly as she could.

"Hearing's fine," said Brendan.

Grandma Helen didn't crack a smile.

"An unfortunate week, poor boy. But that's why we are out now. I'm taking him for a day-trip around town. I'm off to treat him to lunch!"

Cindy stood up, pleased with this response, and she leaned into Helen to speak more confidentially.

"I used to be a candy-striper when I was in high school, and I loved helping the younger kids, especially the ones with mystery illnesses, you know? Because, like… we all knew… deep down… that they were just making it up for the attention. But still, it's… Oh, not that *you're* faking, Brendan."

She stared at him for a spell in concern.

"What child would fake this?"

"I'm not his carer. I'm his grandmother."

Cindy gaped, wanting to shut up but knowing she couldn't.

"I'd have guessed his mother!"

With that she walked away, instantly burning in the cheeks at her total stupidity.

*I've gotta get back on the bandwagon,* she thought.

Brendan was pushed around, and in the darkness he could see slivers of light changing here and there. As it so happened, he could see the teensiest bit through all the gunk and eyelashes, but not enough to even count his fingers by. Still, the sounds and sensations around him really did heighten, just like everybody said. He could hear rogue birds trapped in the mall at his three o'clock… then at his seven o'clock… a baby was crying and a slushy machine was churning as they passed by. He could hear his grandmother's light breathing, and her jewellery as she turned her neck here and there to look at different things.

When at last it was time for lunch, they went into the food court. Grandma Helen helped Brendan up and sat him down at a spare table, and went to get something to eat. He could hear her cane clacking off into the distance. When she returned, she handed him a bowl of...

"What is this?" he asked.

"Try it!"

"You've given me boogers."

"How'd you guess?"

"Really, tell me what it is."

"Alright. It's German boogers... You don't trust me?"

Brendan sniffed the food before him gently, trying to figure it out. "No," he said matter-of-factly.

"That, I find shocking. After all, we are family. If you can't trust family, who can you trust?"

"Tell that to Oedipus."

"Right then, this ends now. I'm going to gain your trust. Do you want to know how?"

Brendan shrugged. "By breaking into song..?"

"I know about a big secret. I haven't told anybody yet. Then you'll know you have my trust."

"That sounds more like bargaining than trust."

Grandma Helen let out a hum and a sigh as she leaned back in her chair, exhausted by the boy sitting opposite her. She took to gazing about at the busy shoppers, thinking of what to say next. Not far away was Santa's Workshop, and an empty throne amongst candycanes and white picket fences.

"Christmastime," she said with another sigh. "A wonderful time of year. It's a hectic month. So hectic, one might be forgiven for forgetting something important."

Brendan had stopped fidgeting and faced forward, still unimpressed, but listening. Even though he couldn't see her, Grandma Helen looked him right in the eye.

"So, they forgot your birthday, kid."

Her words had gotten through to him, she knew it immediately. She could tell he was surprised despite his eyes being closed, as he'd frozen like a statue. He still looked remarkably unimpressed, although she suspected now it was only for show.

"I tried to book my bus to get in the day before, but it was really a last minute trip and I had no luck. You know, being this time of year. Lo-and-behold not a peep from the others about your twelfth birthday. I figured it out soon enough. You woke up on the day and saw a present with your name on it under the tree, so you opened it.

A simple mistake. When your mother hit you over the head for it, you figured it out pretty quickly. They'd really forgotten it this time. All of them. That night, you were so upset, you cried yourself to sleep. And look at what it has done to your eyes..."

Brendan sniffed his meal. "What is this?"

"Rouladen. My eyes almost burst from their sockets when I read it on the menu over there. In a food court, of all places, wonders never cease. I don't know how to feel. But it has reminded me, I will cook for the family on Christmas Eve. Fleischsalat, Kartoffelpuffer, to compliment your mother's most favourite food, schnitzel."

"She does love the schnitzel," he agreed.

Tentatively, he stabbed at some with a plastic fork. Little by little, he managed more and more. When at last he finished and scraped the bowl empty of onions, he lifted his head to face in her direction.

"Why are you here?"

"Well," she said, "for starters... Your family is in shambles. Your sister has two black eyes. Your other sister probably sleeps standing up. There's tension... tension, all around. I don't know where it's coming from, and I don't like it. Every time I enter the front door, I can feel it."

"What's the real reason you're here?"

Grandma Helen squinted one eye and waited for him to figure it out. It didn't take him long.

"*Horn-Horn's Annual Motorcycle Race*," he said, grinning stupidly. "I should've known."

"We have a very good plan of attack, mostly comprised of rotten eggs," said Helen proudly. "I found these people... locals... on a website. Protestors. They said they used to be quakers, but then it stopped being cool. Or... 'rumbling' is the word they used, I don't know. I struggle enough as it is understanding talk on the internet. I'm too old. But those people, they seemed very... eager. You'll see; we'll bring that motorcycle race crashing down. Preferably without any actual crashes."

"You know it's for charity, right?" said Brendan. "Grandma, you should leave them alone."

"It's not about the charity, it's about the principles. Motorcycles are death traps. I've been hit twelve times, and yet I am one of the lucky ones. They are a menace to everyone and everything, whipping left and right between cars, speeding, two in a lane, cutting through alley-ways, riding over pavements... They're incredibly dangerous, and it's ridiculous they haven't been outlawed by now. People might as well ride Penny-farthings on the highways."

Brendan couldn't help but snigger.

"You're pretty overdramatic for an old woman, you know."

Grandma Helen's phone started vibrating noisily in front of them, startling them both. She answered promptly.

"Yes. Alright. Give us two minutes."

She hung up.

"Home time. We'll grab that ice-cream on the way out, and I'll show you what I've bought for you at home. Now, you keep my secret, and I'll keep yours..."

She helped him stand, and then sit again in his wheelchair.

"Agreed?"

"Agreed," said Brendan, putting his blindfold back on.

All at once he felt a great sense of relief, but he couldn't exactly understand why.

————— · · · —————

Despite my bruises and swellings, I was expected back at school by my parents the next day. They had an awful fight that night, brought on by Grandma Helen, of course. She blasted them from left, right and centre about their parenting techniques, and in turn Mom blasted back, mentioning some woman named Bertha back in Canada. I felt most sorry for Hayley, who awkwardly sat on my bed during the repeat of *The Prefect Family* mid-season finale. The yells from downstairs seeped in from under the door.

"Have you ever noticed how unrealistic this show is?" I asked my blonde friend, hoping to distract.

"Duh, it's a soap opera."

"But, look. Thomas Noel is taking his shirt off. *Again.* For no reason. Oh, come on, they're in a blizzard!"

"I'll not have you criticise Thomas Noel in my presence."

"Did you know that they shoot this in New York, too? My aunt works in a gallery that they use sometimes for night scenes."

Hayley nodded, eyes glued to the television.

"I know everything about this show," she said, as if in a trance. "Production numbers, guest stars, filming locations, executive producers, casting budgets, you name it. A passion I share with 'The Vapid One', believe it or not."

"Wait… Eleanore likes *The Prefect Family?*"

"Of course. She's our age, isn't she? She even entered our class in some competition to meet the cast, but it's happening sometime around Christmas so I guess we didn't win."

I bent over to pick Tigger up, as he crawled out from under Hayley's bed.

"You like Uma Harlow the best, don't you, Tigger?" I asked him in a cutesy voice. "She's so pwetty!"

"They're all pretty, that's why they're on TV. And that Thomas Noel, I swear…"

Hayley ogled as his abs flexed on-screen.

"If I wasn't with Jonathan, I'd drop out of school and stalk his ass in real life. Be one of those homeless people who camps outside his apartment waiting for him, eating from his trash, lingering on nearby rooftops. I'd even cut off my hair as a non-violent protest against his girlfriends…"

"Those are some very specific life choices."

"Well, it would be a very specific situation… Gotta pee."

She flung her legs over the side of the bed. As she got up to leave, Annie pushed the door open, already in her nighty.

My sister let Hayley pass before saying in a hushed voice:

"There are rats in the attic."

"What makes you say that?" I asked.

Annie checked around her to make sure the coast was clear, then muttered: "Unless Zag is running around making a fuss. He seems more like the subtle type. Tell him to stay in his clay head."

I looked up at the ceiling, thinking about his mysterious visitor earlier that day. No way he would still be at it, right? I'd have to have a word with him, just in case.

Oh, I'd do it tomorrow.

Everything could wait until tomorrow.

Besides… maybe it really was rats.

# 7

# KRIS KRINGLE

The entire house was startled awake in the middle of the night by the screeching of a rat in the attic. At least I hoped it was a rat.

Hayley, still sleeping with Annie, yelled very loudly at it to shut up, which seemed to do the trick. However, come daylight, the residents of 12 Philips Street were still quite jittery from the shock of it. After all, it had been quite fierce, sounding like a demonic monster of some kind. Dad offered to set some traps in the attic, but Annie and I insisted on doing it for him so he wouldn't stumble across Zag. While we were up there, our red-headed friend promised us he'd only had one visitor since moving to the attic, and that the possibility of rats would explain why he'd found his plate of dinner to be half-eaten the night before. Despite our groggy early-morning brains, Annie and I made some 'emergency wishes': a fresh plate of dinner and a giant fruitcake for desert appeared in front of Zag. He scoffed them sheepishly, then returned to his clay head.

The rat concert had really spoiled the festive mood, too. As the grandfather clock ticked closer to nine, we found ourselves rushing around downstairs. There was a symphony of banging, ramming, cussing under our breaths, unnecessary fussin' and moanin'…

And let me tell you, I was the worst of the lot. I'd woken up not just on the wrong side of the bed, but on the wrong side of the *North Pole*. My bruised and puffy eyes were the least of my concerns, for today I had Kris Kringle to contend with. An event which ordinarily should have brought positivity and light to all involved was instead sending jagged shocks of anxiety into my stomach. For some reason, I was obsessing over what would happen the moment I revealed myself to Greg. Upon opening my present, he might spit in my face. Or laugh and call me a moron. Perhaps he'd shoot me dead on the spot. Knowing how unlikely these scenarios were didn't stop me from imagining them. Still, I made sure the wrapped present was under my arm as we finally left the house for the bus stop.

"The garage door is open," said Annie curiously, as we crisscrossed through the bare oak trees in our front yard. "Has it been like that all night?"

"Maybe Hayley opened it in her sleep," I suggested.

Hayley turned angrily. "Say what?"

The three of us walked down the street towards the bus pole, huddled in our jackets against the cold wind. We spotted JT making his way up the hill to join us. He was in his usual black ensemble, but today he was also sporting a Santa hat instead of a beanie. He took it off upon meeting us, and bowed like a gentleman.

"Good morning, ladies," he said, trying not to stare at my grotesquely swollen face.

Hayley wrapped her arms around him. "Why are you taking the bus this morning? I thought your father was dropping you off."

"Change of plans," he said to her, and then looked at me: "Did you find out if your parents can make it to our dinner next Friday?"

I put a hand to my mouth. "I'm sorry, I completely forgot!"

"Forgive her, boy, for her brain's been battered by basketballs bouncing by!" declared Annie randomly.

I could tell JT hadn't made his mind up about my sister yet. He gave an affirmative gulp to address her, then turned back to me.

"If you could find out by tonight?" he said, wincing as he

pressed about it. "We need numbers, for the catering."

"I'll ask Mom about it when I see her at school. Wow, catering? How fancy is this thing?"

"You have no idea..." Hayley snorted.

She gently pushed me out of the way as the bus slammed into the pole next to me, knocking it over. We picked it back up, then hopped on the bus, followed behind by a very rushed Eleanore, Wednesday and Friday. All of them were dressed to the nines in girly Santa outfits. Plastic holly strands wrapped around their braided hair, make-up flawlessly distributed in reds and greens. Without jackets, though, they shivered in the cold, their bare legs popping with fresh goosebumps.

*A modern tragedy,* I thought. *To be numb for the sake of fashion.*

---

At school we rushed like starved coyotes for the classroom, clambering inside and warming ourselves by the heaters on the walls. The Christmas tree had wilted overnight, causing some of its higher and heavier decorations to fall to the ground.

"What's happened to it?" Tanya asked as we gazed at the pile of fallen pine-leaves around its base.

"Anyone water it yesterday?" I asked, for I'd been absent.

That was the solution, it seemed. Hayley quickly ran for the nearest bathroom and filled a small bowl found in our teacher's desk. By the time the tree was watered, Ms. Weiss had arrived for the day. She too was dressed for Christmas, wearing a Santa hat as well as a cute red and green knitted jumper with an image of a Christmas pudding on it.

"Everybody," she called in her usual way, clicking her fingers. "Everybody! Do as I say. Stay standing, please."

Half of the class sat down, while others tumbled slightly at her surprise order. Swiftly, our teacher ordered us to move the desks, pushing them as much as we could against the walls so that the centre of the room would be free.

It only took us about five minutes, arranging and rearranging, stacking, making sure not to put any against the door in case of a fire drill. Once the task was completed, we were ordered to sit down in a circle with our Kris Kringle presents.

I could barely contain my excitement, more so for seeing other people receiving gifts than my own receiving of one. I hated getting gifts from people. It made me feel very uncomfortable, as if saying thank-you wasn't enough. I always felt like I really ought to go out and organise a kick-line in order to prove how grateful I was. However, the dishing out of gifts was my specialty.

Ms. Weiss magically flopped down to the ground in one ultra-flexible move, crossing her legs with wrapped gift in hands. She was about to start, when somebody else beat her to the punch.

"I'll go!" declared Friday aggressively.

Since she'd been the first to sit down in the circle, it seemed only fair. Not bothering to wait for those with aches and pains to settle, the Saviour declared: "My present goes to... Tanya Tanner!"

Everybody clapped after influence from our teacher. Friday crawled to the centre of the circle, where she met Tanya, and handed the wrapped gift to her.

"Merry Christmas!" she smiled.

Perhaps sensing a trap, Tanya thanked her unsurely. When she went back to her sitting place, she unwrapped it, revealing a Dr. Seuss book. She smiled politely, holding it up for show.

"Ooh!... *Fox in Socks!*"

"Have you read it?" asked Friday, smiling from ear-to-ear.

Tanya examined the cover more than was necessary, blushing slightly. "Can't say that I have..."

"Oh, you'll like it," Friday insisted, smile dropping. "It's about a freak who learns to fit in..."

She caught Ms. Weiss's arched eyebrow, and retreated.

"To socks, that is."

Before any more nonsense could start, Eleanore put her hand up and declared furiously that it was her turn. Santa hat tucked in her desk somewhere, she crawled to the centre of the circle and flicked some loose hair behind her ears.

"My present goes to... Ms. Weiss!"

She smiled cutely as the perturbed Ms. Weiss came to join her in the middle. ("Called it," muttered Hayley.) Eleanore handed her something large, in green wrapping paper covered with candy-canes.

"Why thank you, Eleanore!"

Our teacher seemed earnest in her appreciation, and she ripped the wrapping away to see what was inside. A blue box hid beneath; in the light of day we caught the words *'Little Miss. Perfect'* printed on the front, in neon pink.

"Ohhh... What's this?"

"It's a fashion kit!" declared Eleanore, delirious with delight. "Now you can dress up really pretty and look fashionable just like us! See the little girl on the front? How glam does she look in this funky *Hello Kitty* ballerina dress?"

"Eleanore..." said Tanya quietly. "That's for little kids..."

"So is *Fox in Socks*. What does that say about you?"

Ms. Weiss frowned. "What does that say about *me?*"

"That you're beautiful and young!" insisted Eleanore.

Ms. Weiss opened the box eagerly.

"You've got a point. My goodness, how lovely!"

She pulled out a long, sequinned dress fit for a banquet. It was a quarter of her size, but she didn't seem to notice. Her eyes were too dazzled by the glitter.

"I'll get changed into this as soon as recess is upon us. Thank you, Miss. Parker."

"You're so very welcome, Ms. Weiss!" declared Eleanore.

JT pretended to gag on his index finger.

Wednesday was next, her present for William. It was a book on how to get by if you were a victim of frostbite. The sides of the book even had indents in it. Given William had lost four fingers the previous winter to a kitchen chopping-board, it was a rather useless present, but he seemed pretty happy with it.

Ms. Weiss followed. To everybody's surprise, she called Hayley to the centre of the circle. Hayley rolled her eyes, expecting the worst, and sure enough was handed a small paper bag with a pair of plastic handcuffs and a key inside. I suppose it was our teacher's way of getting the message across that she didn't think Hayley would be out of them very long. But it surprised me on a deeper level. Jacqueline Weiss could be a stone cold bitch when she wanted to be.

"Oh, it's just a little joke," she insisted, chortling after a mild backlash. "They're not real. They're made for Halloween, see?"

Hayley scooted back to her place next to me, and leaned in to say quietly: "Joke's on her. I love them."

Tanya had a present for JT, which was a black beanie with his initials sewn on the front. This was a glorious gift, and JT promptly ditched his Santa hat to wear it proudly.

Hayley had a present for Jared. The two weren't exactly on good terms, ever since he'd accused her a year prior of anti-semitism... although he'd actually meant 'anti-autism' given he had Asperger's syndrome. Presently, she handed his gift over in a half-ripped plastic bag. It was a light-blue jacket, just like her favourite one. She'd also stuffed a bottle of blue eye-liner in there, since he often wore some.

"Thanks," said Jared, surprised. I think he liked it.

Once everybody but Greg, Ama and I had handed out their presents, Ms. Weiss started gathering bets from some students as to how the remaining trade-offs would go.

Ama gave Ray one of those fake fish you hang on a wall, which would start to sing when the button on the side was pressed. Poor Ray was pretty underwhelmed, but Hayley got a good kick out of it.

While this was happening, I retreated into my own world for comfort, panic slowly rising just like it had earlier that morning. For, as soon as Ama and Ray had revealed themselves to one another, I knew what this meant. Who the two remaining Kris Kringles were.

"What are the odds?" I heard Eleanore whisper to Friday, looking sneakily across at me.

I tried not to turn my head, choosing instead to wait nervously until Ms. Weiss pointed at us. Greg caught my eye, but I didn't move until he did. Hayley must have set it up, I realised as I crawled on my hands and knees to join him in the centre.

I was glad my face was caked in foundation today, because I was sure I was blushing like William Shatner. I'd of course known all along that *I'd* picked Greg's name out of the hat the previous week. But I'd had no idea until this very minute that *he'd* picked *my* name.

We met in the middle of the circle. He brushed some of his dark hair away from his green eyes and greeted me with a smile. I smiled back, sure that my face was actually expanding in the moment, ballooning like a pufferfish.

The entire class let out a playful "*oooooh!*" noise; I ignored them and shakily held out my wrapped gift for him.

"M... Merry Christmas," I said quietly, gulping far too loudly.

Suddenly, yet another possibility rushed over me. What if he didn't like *The Prefect Family?* What if my gift of the first season on DVD wasn't something he really wanted? Perhaps he was the only teenager in the mother-effing country who didn't like the bloody show. It would be my luck, too. I'd just assumed he enjoyed it, because Hayley did, and JT did, but had I ever actually heard him specifically say he watched and enjoyed it and loved repeats as much as I did, and why oh why didn't I already have a copy, I could have just *leant* it to him to see if he liked it first, *well great Cassie congratulations on being the world's biggest moron, you might as well etch the word 'dunce' into your forehead and move to Yemen —*

"Here's yours," he said, cutting through my madness. I think he was going through the same thing as I was, for his eyes were ablaze in an obvious panic, his pupils dilated. He thrust his wrapped gift into my trembling hands.

"I have an idea," said Ms. Weiss suddenly, clicking her fingers. "Since you two are the last ones, why don't you open your presents at the same time? I'll count to three…"

She insisted on everybody else joining in.

"One," they called. "Two… Three!"

Greg and I tore away at our wrapping. I focused on mine, ignoring the outside world, and was met with a white box beneath. It took me a moment with my nervous fingers, but I managed to pry it open and was met with my own present…

The first season of *The Prefect Family* on DVD.

For a split second, I thought we'd accidentally double-swapped. A momentary lapse of hand-eye coordination resulting in the returning of gifts. My heart couldn't beat any faster than it was already going; I turned the box over in my hands, and then looked up to meet Greg's eye-line. He was figuring things out just as slowly I was.

Eleanore was the first to spot the anomaly.

"Oh. As. Actually. *If…*"

The lead Saviour sat up on her knees and stretched her neck to get a proper look at the event.

*"They got each other the same present!"*

An immediate uproar began; every classmate crawled as fast as they could to crowd around us. There were nudges and laughs, heckles and even a few screams. It became so loud that Ms. Weiss eventually called for order; still, it took about a full minute for the chatter to die down. Greg and I stayed where we were, frozen, embarrassed.

"Stars above, what an amazing coincidence," our teacher said, fanning herself with her hands for a moment and smirking. "Alright, alright, everybody. I guess this calls for an early recess. We've only got movies to watch today, so you can make it an hour long. Consider it my personal Christmas present to all of you. Miss. Gauche, you must be feeling rather grateful, getting two presents in one day."

Hayley clearly wasn't impressed. She sarcastically smiled as widely as possible, giving the thumbs up with both hands.

# 8

# POPPING P'S

The hallways were deserted, since the real recess wasn't for another half-an-hour. I left my friends in a desperate attempt to have a moment to myself. I couldn't be around Greg for a while. Just a little while. I needed to calm down, and that old headache from yesterday was settling in behind one of my eyes.

I took a chance to see if Mom was free to talk, and as I walked into the Psychiatric Department I saw Chloe Croxley sitting at her desk on the phone.

"Yes, Audrey. Three. I don't know why I have to pronounciate so properly to you on here. Well, I don't hear any interference. You sound properly pleasant to me, and I have perfect pitch... No, I will not stop using the letter P! I'm sorry if it gives you a popping headache! Yes, maybe I am doing it on purpose now! I..."

She looked over at me, and then put the phone down.

"She hung up."

"Maybe she was *peeved*," I joked, popping my P.

"Perhaps," said Chloe in a daze.

"Who was that?"

"My... It doesn't matter. How are you, Cassie?"

She squinted, perhaps wincing as she looked at me in pity.

"How are the eyes? I see the eyes. Now I know what your mother meant when she said the eyes."

I really didn't want to talk about how ugly I was today. I told her they were fine, and asked as sternly as I could for my mother. As I did, a man jumped out from behind the counter, frightening me senseless. He'd been there the entire time.

"What, ho!" he cried upon seeing me.

I still wasn't sure if I was safe, and it wasn't until Chloe introduced us that I calmed down.

"Cassie, this is my... friend, Pepper. He's here fixing the speaker system. Pepper, this is Cassie. Lesley's daughter."

"*Enchanté*," he said rather wankishly, holding out his hand for me to kiss. Wasn't it usually the other way around?

"Hi," I said, choosing instead to shake it.

This man was something else. It was like he was dressed in a disguise. His frizzy black hair sat up as if he'd been electrocuted. He had a gigantic nose, and sported an overly theatrical moustache. His most alarming feature, of course, was the fact that he had an eye-patch over his left eye, which helped me recall the fact that I'd seen him with Principal Parker the day before yesterday, right before I was struck by the basketball. Although he was wearing a top hat then.

"You," he said quickly, pointing. "Yes, that's right. You were the one the other day who..." He didn't finish what he was saying, for Chloe scolded him in a husky snarl.

I tried not to focus on his bizarre eye-patch. Having been raised well, I didn't dare ask what the issue was, but the judgemental socialite in me assumed he was either troubled, or severely eccentric. On top of this, he was wearing a full dinner suit with a black tie, and I noticed a gold pocket-watch in his vest pocket.

"Are you an electrician?" I asked, noticing a bunch of silver and orange wires tangled together in front of him.

"That I am," he said, and then he smiled in such a way that I felt rather uncomfortable. "Are you a student?"

"Pepper, don't patronise her," said Chloe in annoyance.

The man before me collected his equipment from underneath

the bench, and made his way around to my side. He held in his right hand a giant silver tool kit, and written in block writing on the side was: 'PEPPER O. SALT'.

*Of course his name is pretentious,* I thought.

"The speakers should be connected again," he said to Chloe. He checked his pocket-watch and leaned against the closed door. "Shall we dine at, say, midday?"

"Twelve-thirty," said Chloe in a monotone.

"I shall remain heartsick until we meet again," he said, bowing.

As he did this, his pocket-watch slipped out of his pocket. He bent further to pick it up, and in doing so his tool kit fell open. He collected everything, clumsily recovering, sweating slightly, and waved once more at us before leaving.

"Are you dating him?" I asked.

Chloe neither confirmed nor denied, but instead shrugged as if it were a desperate situation not amongst her proudest of accomplishments.

"I was dining on my own last Thursday," she said. "I do it a lot these days. I'm hoping to catch my future husband's eye as he's passing by the restaurant, but so far the only interest I've gotten is from those Gomer Pyle types... You know, always on the look-out for a desperate woman's weak spot. Then, before I knew it, *he* was sitting at a table across from me... I was dazzled by his good eye. It's so *blue*..." She stared off into space for a moment.

"It *is* blue," I confirmed for her.

"Anyway, I quickly realised we were in the same boat."

"Eating alone?"

"Yes. And he's cute enough, a little mysterious with that patch. He came over and asked if I'd care for some company, and I thought... Why not?"

She gazed off into space yet again, this time thinking about something evidently grim.

"He's not very bright, but I suppose the charm of the dinner suit got to me. He *always* wears it."

"Why?"

Chloe shrugged.

"I haven't asked. I'm probably afraid of the answer. It reminds me of what a magician wears, and I quite like magicians. The only reason he's here today is because we needed an electrician this morning for the speakers, so I called him and here he is. I guess you could say things are getting serious."

She chortled, but sank back into her seat.

"The saddest thing is, he reminds me of my sister."

As if her ears had been prematurely burning, Candice Croxley came out of the back-office like an excited Labrador.

*"Enchanté!"* she said elegantly.

One look at my face and she slapped her hands to her cheeks.

"Oh, no!" she uttered, darting around the bench to embrace me in a tight hug.

Her breasts were *huge*, that was all I could think about as the smell of cinnamon and wood-chips washed over me. She was in a green woollen sweater, much like Ms. Weiss's. When she moved away, I got a better look and realised it featured a knitted image of a small house in silhouette, with Santa's reindeer above, peeing as they flew over. A speech bubble coming from inside said: *"Smells like rain, dear."*

I laughed immediately, forgetting my troubles, and then stopped and met her eye-line. She was serious. Very serious. She dabbed at my hair and then stroked my cheeks.

"Are you alright, my lovely? Oh, I've been so worried since your mother told me about your concussion! You. Look. *Dreadful.*"

Candice bolted out into the back-office again. A few minutes later she came back, carrying a small black purse-like thing which turned out to be her make-up bag. She searched and searched inside.

"Now, let's see. We've got eyeliners, rouge, foundation, a door-stop I use to plump my lips with, moisturiser, Vicious Trollop... Aha! Sit down over there."

I did as I was told, sitting on the leather couch in the waiting area. I was grateful for any help, and she gave it to me by adding lipstick and eye-shadow. By the time she was done with my hair, even Chloe was arching her neck to see for herself. In a compact mirror she fished from inside her bag of magic, I saw my reflection and tried not to cry.

"Wow, that's so lovely."

Candice smiled, glad to have helped. She tapped me gently on the head and went over to her sister at the desk, stealing a candy-cane from a bowl and unwrapping it.

"I seem to be helping a lot of Gellars out this week. Your mother, dear Cassie, has asked me very kindly to hide all of Brendan's Christmas presents in my house."

She clapped merrily at the thrill of it all, and slightly choked on her treat.

"I've heard he's a bit of a buzz-kill this time of year."

"Massive understatement," I said, collecting myself. "He already found one of them the other day and... let's just say Mom wasn't too impressed."

Candice knew about the Tiro doll, of course, but went silent as a long-stretched strand of a brain cell reignited and she caught on to something.

"Oh. Is that why you're here, to see your mother?"

I nodded.

She gleefully ran out the back again and returned moments later with my mother. Upon seeing my face of make-up, Mom put on a very forced smile.

"Hi, honey. Looking..." she gulped, "good?"

"I wanted to ask you before I forgot," I told her. "JT's parents want us all to go to his house for a Christmas dinner next Friday. Can we go? Please?"

My mother and, surprisingly, Candice were both delighted beyond belief at the invite.

"Of course we'll go!" said Mom. "I've wanted an excuse to meet JT's parents since we got here. Oh, what'll I wear?"

She turned into a teenage girl before my eyes, twirling for Candice.

Was I missing something? She didn't make a fuss over meeting Hayley's mother before her accident. I don't think she even bothered to ask about Greg's parents.

"So I can tell JT that we'll be there?"

"Yes! Of course. Go tell him," she insisted. "I'll call your father and let him know. Oh, I hope your grandmother doesn't expect to come along..."

She rushed to the nearest phone in a frenzy, and I left her office feeling more confused than when I'd arrived.

At least it made me forget about Kris Kringle.

# 9

# BIG TROUBLE IN LITTLE PHILIPS STREET

A s the day wore on, the sense of it being Christmas really kicked into gear. Mostly everybody was dressed in either Santa hats or red and green sweaters, some of them sporting flashing earrings, and as lunchtime ended and we walked towards our giant red classroom door, we saw somebody familiar through the glass window.

"*Santa Claus!*" cried Hayley.

She pushed Greg aside, ran into the classroom and embraced the jolly fat-man fully, lifting her feet high and wrapping them around him. Watching from the doorway, we marvelled as the man in the Santa outfit let out a girly shriek, and crumbled to his knees. The two of them fell heavily to the floor. As we were the last to return from lunch, the entire room was full of witnesses. Hayley rolled off him, blushing at the mess she'd made, and the Santa man grabbed at the middle of his back.

"Hayley!" cried Ms. Weiss, standing up from her desk in shocked delay. "Mr. Arnold has just had back surgery! What were you thinking? Mr. Arnold, are you alright?"

"*Who does that!?*" the man named Mr. Arnold shrieked.

Soon, things calmed down. We went to our seats, and he recovered enough to put on a happy face. With that, Ms. Weiss told all of us to listen in. Mr. Arnold, moving cautiously, grabbed a large brown sack from underneath the only empty desk in the room.

"Ho-ho-ho!" he said merrily, pretending again to be the real Santa Claus and putting on a deeper voice. "Merry Christmas to 10W! I come bearing gifts from afar! As some of you are aware, a lovely young woman by the name of Eleanore Crapchel Parker entered a competition last month. Can anybody tell me what that competition was for?... Yes, you."

He pointed at Jared, who had his hand raised.

"For Farmer John to paint a pig mural on the backlot?"

Mr. Arnold paused.

"... Not quite, no," he replied.

Upon hearing her name from the row in front of us, Eleanore's butt was so far off her seat that she might as well have been standing. Mr. Arnold, or Santa, instantly picked her as she raised her hand highest of all.

"Yes?"

Eleanore was breathing funny, like in Lamaze class. Wednesday and Friday, on each side of her, took to fanning her down with their text books. Eventually, she managed to speak, sounding serious.

"My name is Eleanore Parker, and... I am the one who entered us in that competition."

"Can you tell us what that competition was for?"

"A charity ride with the cast of *THE PREFECT FAMILY!!!*"

Wednesday and Friday stood up and the three of them began to scream. Like, 'being murdered' screaming. My headache roared like a jet engine, and I covered my ears. I wasn't the only one, either.

Mr. Arnold pulled out some fancy envelopes from his sack.

"On behalf of the producers of *The Prefect Family*, we invite you, Eleanore Crapchel Parker, and one guest, to join the cast and crew of your favourite show on a Zeppelin ride around Horn-Horn, next Friday night, the twenty-first of December!"

Nearly the entire room of students stood up in a rush and

joined the Saviours in their excited yells. Suddenly I became aware of a microphone attached to the man's fluffy lapel. This was being recorded. This screech-fest was going out live to people. To the radio? Were there cameras? What was going on? I was so confused.

Hayley finally had enough nerve to speak up, so she bravely raised her hand and called out over the crowd.

"Does this mean Thomas Noel is coming to Horn-Horn?"

Mr. Arnold nodded warily, but it was too late for him.

Hayley flung her desk sideways, smashing it against the wall and frightening Greg half to death. She let out a gigantic scream of her own, which started low and then reached the same heights as the Saviours. With that, she barrelled down the aisle and embraced poor Mr. Arnold.

Once more, he crumbled under her weight.

———— · · · ————

Annie and I gossiped about it like crazy from the moment I ran into her on the way to the bus. Not that I needed to talk to anybody else about it, for even Ms. Weiss was excited about the impending visit from a dose of *our favourite celebrities*. Eleanore was suddenly the most popular girl in school, although she didn't have time to take it in yet for she'd fainted mid-scream in class. We hadn't noticed at first, because Mr. Arnold was buckled over in pain garnering all of the attention.

But he was fine. Annie and I walked past him as we exited the main Reception area. He was lecturing Principal Parker on appropriate behaviour.

"These students need to learn there are *boundaries!*"

The bus was like a can of soda left in the freezer for too long — fit to burst, and very cold as well. Everybody was yell-talking as we drove along the road, rambling on, excited, gleeful, almost manic.

As Annie and I hopped off down the street, we were still chatting breathlessly about it until we strolled up our driveway.

Immediately, we stopped talking *and* walking. There was a police car pulled in by the open garage.

Mom was coming out of the front door. I was surprised, expecting her to have been at school like she usually was this time of day. Dad followed her out, then a tall police officer with shades on.

"We've been robbed," said Mom, spotting us.

I gasped, putting a hand to my mouth.

"What did they steal?"

I thought about all the wonderful things I owned, the tech stuff, my keyboard, TV, Legs of Luxury, the wardrobe...

"Your father's motorcycle," she said sombrely.

Annie and I kept silent. The only sound to be heard was the cop's smart black shoes grinding down the gravel drive as he slowly inspected the place one more time.

"Insurance," he said to my parents.

"For the fifth time, we *do* have insurance."

"*'Too Fat To Carpool'*?" I gasped. "How did this happen?"

"They think it might've been overnight," said Mom quietly. "While everybody was asleep. The front window is broken from your grandmother's cane, so they would've snuck in there."

"They *only* stole the motorcycle?" my sister asked.

Dad nodded and wiped a tear from his cheek. He was staring off at the oaks in the front lawn.

"I can't believe it. And at Christmastime. I was going to enter into that motorcycle charity ride next week, too."

"Oh, honey," said Mom sympathetically, rubbing his right shoulder to comfort him. "No, you weren't."

"Where's Grandma?" I asked, my mind full of suspicion.

Mom pointed inside. Annie pressed her forehead against my shoulder as we walked towards the front door, leaving the policeman to chat to our parents alone.

"I feel dizzy. Do you feel dizzy?"

Agreeing with her, I suggested we sit inside, make Belgium hot chocolates, and calmly debrief about that afternoon's many ridiculous events.

———  • • •  ———

Mom didn't care about the competition Eleanore had won, and how it affected us. She was far too concerned with the motorcycle, and the window being fixed, and at the idea of burglars lurking around downstairs while we slept. Desperate for another pair of ears, we even attempted to explain it to Grandma Helen, but she sneered and clicked her tongue midway through, reminding us that sex on TV was ruining the world, which really had nothing to do with anything.

"You're such a buzzkill, Grandma," said Annie.

"Maybe. But when your fifth baby sucks the Methamphetamine right out of your crystallised bosom, don't come crying to me."

Not even understanding her this time, I snuck upstairs to get ready for bed. Hayley was giving me the silent treatment tonight, because after class we'd accidentally ditched her. In the rush and craziness of everything that was going on, I'd forgotten she was living with us. I knew it wasn't a long-term grudge, though, and was confident that by the next day we would be right as rain.

Taking a moment on the landing, I pulled down the attic steps and stuck my head up into the musty space above our house. All around me was darkness, spoiled here and there by a few cracks in the roof-tiles, and tiny reflections from the light I was letting in from below. I saw the dozen or so boxes from the move, the rat-traps, Dad's old Santa costume thrown into one of the corners in a heap, and the clay head sitting where it always sat. Just as still and unremarkable as yesterday, and would be tomorrow.

As a stream of shimmering smoke danced around the clay head and turned into the form of Zag, I wondered if he would be bashful around me after I accused him of all that noise the previous night. However, he was not. His face was alight and his cheeks were puffy from smiling.

"Cassie!" he said, glee plain on his face. "Santa is *real!*"

"Oh!" I said, taken back. "Well, of courses! Didn't you know?"

"No, I knew, I knew," he said coolly. "But after doing some research, I found out his name is Nicholas! And, and, he really *does* bring presents to children on Christmas Eve. He said he's been doing it for years! See, Cassie, I *knew* you humans had to have *some* kind of magic."

Tired, I smiled and let him gush. For in that moment I realised that despite where he came from, and what curse he carried, before me sat the very definition of a child. Instead of telling him the truth about Santa again, I held my tongue and said simply:

"That's great, Zag!"

"I still don't feel it, though," he said. "That *feeling* you told me about. Maybe it's a human thing."

I shrugged, simply glad that he was glad. Everybody deserved a childhood where they could believe in Santa. If Zag wanted to experience a real, human Christmas, who was I to stand in his way?

# 10

# A HONK FROM
A HEARSE

I woke the next morning to somebody crying out in another room. I went to my door, opened it a crack, and listened
intently. Grandma Helen's shape was under her covers
across from me in her own room, rising gently up and down as she
slept. So she hadn't heard it. Maybe I'd dreamt it.

No, but there it was again. This time it was two moans, and
through Annie's bedroom door. I immediately burst in, only to find
the two temporary roommates in quite a state. Hayley was sitting on
the edge of Annie's bed, her hair everywhere. Annie was standing by
the open window, her nighty dishevelled. They looked at me, exhausted and angry.

"Someone wanna tell me what's going on?"

Annie closed the window and stormed past me, heading for
the staircase. Hayley patted down her frazzled hair, trying to ignore
me, but I cottoned on quickly.

"You were sleep-walking out the window again."

Hayley snapped.

"Oh, like you're so perfect. I have a long day ahead of me. I need some caffeine. Your stupid sister better not take the last of my Pandora. Move."

She stormed past me, running after Annie. A few moments later I heard their yells of distress again, this time as they battled it out over the coffee-machine.

———— · · · ————

*"LESLEY!"*

While we were eating breakfast, our father's high-pitched voice bellowed down the staircase. Pigsworth and Tigger, both originally lounging like lovers by the open fireplace, leapt up and bounded away, almost knocking Annie off her feet as she crossed to the kitch-room with her breakfast.

Like tired kids after an overdose of sugar, none of us youngens in the house were keen enough to snoop, or ask what was up. Mom and Dad had an almost audible heated conversation in their bed-room. Brendan, next to me, was just starting to peel the last layer of flax-coloured gunk off his eyelids. When he could finally see through one eye, he squinted up the staircase in wonder.

"Maybe Grandma's dead."

We groaned at his morbid thought, and Hayley threw her banana peel at him. Thankfully that wasn't it. Eventually they came downstairs, looking ever so pissed, and Mom decided she would tell us what was going on.

"Your father received a…"

Dad slammed the front door as he left.

"He received a text from your Aunt Rachael… That's Ichabod's younger sister," she added for Hayley. "Looks like she'll be staying with us for Christmas."

Annie, Brendan and I gaped in astonishment. Hayley looked at us, then at Mom, hesitantly.

"Good news or bad news?"

"Great news!" I cried, but I could tell my mother wasn't so hot on the idea.

"Actually, she's not staying *here*," said Mom suddenly. "Your father told her that Grandma Helen is with us. The two don't get along very well."

"That's an understatement," muttered Annie, still bitter about her eleventh birthday party and the insults thrown.

"So… where *is* she staying?" asked Hayley cautiously.

With a friend who lived in town, that's what Mom said. She wouldn't mention who that friend was, and instead prompted us to hop up and leave for the bus, which was conveniently timed. As we walked out the front door with our stuff, we spotted Dad coming out of the garage. He was trying to unravel some of the remaining Christmas lights. With life's array of events flying at us like naked dodgeballs, he'd not managed to get started on decorating the exterior of the house. People driving past at night were beginning to boo us for being humbugs.

"Seeya!" I called to him with a quick wave.

Instead of responding in his usual manner, he continued delving into his decorations box.

I knew why he was acting this way. His relationship with Rachael was off-kilter. They didn't share the same bond that Annie, Brendan and I had. Partly because Rachael was really into Judaism. Like, *really*. Everybody on Dad's side was just as connected to their faith as she was, too. Papa Asher and Nana Esther weren't exactly zealots on the subject, but they expected things from Dad that were unreasonable. As our father would so lovingly tell us from time to time, the original names picked out for us were Peninah, Tzipporah and Elyakim Gellar. I mean… can you imagine? Tzipporah. My name would have been *Tzipporah*. That's a silent T at the start, by the way. When I think of the torment I would have faced at school! I think Mom considered these names for maybe… ten minutes, before she put her foot down each time. Annie was eventually named after Anne, Mom's great aunt. Cassandra came from my father's favourite book, *I Capture the Castle*. Brendan, on the other hand, was the name of a tissue brand Mom had noticed in the shops when she was nearly due, and took a liking to it. Often, whenever she finished a sad movie for example, she would say: "Oh, somebody bring me a Brendan to blow my nose on!" and we would drag Brendan over to her kicking and screaming.

Because the names they chose for us weren't especially meaningful, Nana and Papa took great offence to it. And boy did they let us know. Mount Vesuvius wasn't as dramatic as these two elderly Jews. But at the end of the day, as Mom said to them over and over again, her children were not going to grow up with names that would take them six extra years at school to learn how to spell and pronounce. Not the kind of people to admit defeat, Papa and Nana often used Rachael as a spy, dropping her into Dad's life from time to time to gather information and report back to them. I'm sure they were sending her in yet again, this time most likely to suss out the new, multi-million dollar house we lived in.

Regardless of her espionage intentions against my father, I couldn't wait to see her.

———— · · · ————

Hayley disappeared as soon as we got to school, muttering that she was simply going to the Teacher's Lounge before class. Not bothered, eager to hear any more news about *The Prefect Family*, I ran to the Fido Auditorium on my own. Just as I got there, Greg ran straight into me. Things flew, elbows jabbed. It was like a meet cute, except with a few hearty swear words thrown into the chaos.

"Hey, sorry," he said. "Have you seen Hayley or JT?"

I was still a little shy around him since the Kris Kringle deba-cle, plus this violent collision made me blush.

"Hayley was on the bus, but JT wasn't. Do you think he'll skip, being the last day and all?"

"I hope not," he said, looking around.

A Greg without JT was like a piece of toast without pâté. Some would argue, useless. As predicted, our beanie'd friend didn't show up. But Hayley arrived soon after class started, sporting a mug of coffee. It was the second of many that day, for she was starting her first night-shift at 6pm. She was snappy, but well and truly on form.

"No, Hayley," muttered Greg, halfway through class. "I don't *care* if Santa's nipples are pink or brown."

"That's covert racial discrimination, Gregory."

Sadly, that was the most interesting aspect of the entire day. The rest was a bit of a dud. Ms. Weiss bid us a teary farewell at the beginning of the first class, even though we only had three weeks off.

"I imagine I'll see you before then, Miss. Parker," she said with a massive grin on her face.

She was, of course, gleeful as ever that her very own student had won the Zeppelin prize. Any qualms she had with the Saviour were long gone now, which didn't bode well for us regular folk.

Eleanore wouldn't reveal who her plus one would be, though, and it was the second most interesting part of the day. People poked and prodded her for information, but she insisted she was sworn to secrecy. Everybody figured it would be either Wednesday or Friday, although Hayley pointed out that neither of them looked particularly happy. This suggested equal naiveté on their parts. Anyway, it didn't bother me all that much. I had to keep reminding myself that it in no way affected me. I wouldn't be riding in that Zeppelin with her, because she *loathed* me. I wouldn't even be watching it either, since we would be dining with JT and his family. Unless his parents let us sneak into the other room and watch it.

"Do you think," I asked, turning to my only male friend, "that Mr. and Mrs. Walker might let us watch the Zeppelin ride on their TV next Friday?"

Greg, who had been listening to Ms. Weiss, ducked his head even lower, thinking.

"Uhhh… They don't own a TV."

*Bozhe moi!*

I tried to comprehend this. JT didn't have a television? Like, at all? How did he *live?* I had no idea his parents were so strict. I'd pictured them innocently enough in my head, two middle-aged black people with permanent frowns on their faces, the way I imagined all middle-aged parents to be.

With this new piece of information, a white band appeared around their collars in my mind.

———  • • •  ———

There was a strange sense of sadness as the day came to an end, early at two o'clock. Ms. Weiss said another teary goodbye, hugging each of us as we exited the room. I thought about what Christmastime would be like for her, alone. I relished in the thought that the next time I'd see her, she'd have her garden gnomes back (Pothosia had promised in her letter to return them on Christmas morning).

"Thanks for being such a great teacher," I decided to say.

Ms. Weiss gave me an earnest smile, but it was ruined as a few of the rougher guys in the class chortled and called me a suck-up on their way past.

*Snap out of it,* I wanted to say to myself. *You'll be back before you know it. Wax your balls, Gellar.*

Bundled in jackets and beanies galore, the student body moved as one like a school of fish for the exits. I was swept up in the expected bus crowd, and Annie and I linked arms upon meeting. We were just about to hop on when a ferocious honking came from the parking lot beyond. We stopped to stare at the culprit: a brown Cadillac hearse.

"Who died?" muttered Annie.

As our curiosity petered out, we turned toward the bus again, but the driver of the hearse wound down their window and yelled.

*"Hey, Gellar!"*

A black-haired lady was looking at us, waiting for recognition. Annie caught on before I did.

"Rachael?" she said sceptically.

She turned to look at me.

"It's Aunt Rachael."

*"Aunt Rachael!"* I cried, and I bounded away from the bus.

As I got to her window, I noticed a few things. One, her hair was longer. Two, she wasn't wearing her big Sally Jessy Raphael glasses anymore. She still had all of her beads and necklaces, though.

"What is going on with your eye region?" she asked me in her husky smoker's voice, waving a hand around her face. "You gotta wear sunglasses more, and stop squinting."

I was quickly losing steam, but Annie ran around me to sit in the front with her. Aunt Rachael gave her an enthusiastic embrace as she hopped in, and finished it off by looking out at me.

"Cassie, get in the back."

"Are you here to pick us up?" I asked.

"No, I'm here to perve on the children. Get in."

I obliged, my mind flinging from one thought to the next.

"Mom told us you were in town, but she didn't say you were picking us up after school," said Annie.

"That's because I didn't tell her. We'll let her figure it out when you don't hop off the bus."

With that, she chortled and then coughed up a lung.

"Strictly speaking, I'm working from home. I've been doing some of my best artwork for that Pauline Goddard studio, you know the one in New York, with all the Ziegfeld Girls? I've got a really steady gig there, they seem to like me, even that horrible Lenora I told you about. Anyway, because of the wonders of technology, she's letting me go mobile. So I thought I'd take the opportunity and visit my family for the holidays! Isn't that wild? I mean, I was going to visit you in the next year anyway, but the timing worked out perfectly."

"I can't believe you're going to be here for Christmas."

"Me too," said Annie.

We couldn't stop grinning.

"Nobody's more excited than I am, trust me. To get away from the Peeping Tom that is my landlord is a blessing in and of itself. And so far I'm digging this town, although I've only driven past the beach, and... down a road called Periodontitis Parade..? I'm sure I read that wrong."

"No, that's right. It's just off Toothpaste Boulevard."

"Well, that explains why Icky chose to live here. It's one of *those* towns. You feel that? Secrets. They make things vibrate. Where are all the dead bodies?"

We burst into laughter again, even though what she said wasn't that funny. But she was Aunt Rachael. She could read the ingredients off a carton of milk and it would sound hilarious.

"Okay," she said slowly, side-eyeing us suspiciously. "Nobody's ever that happy to see me. What's going on?"

Annie was the first to tell her about the Zeppelin ride and Eleanore and the cast of our favourite show, but I added dot points and afterthoughts, whilst she was still talking. I could tell that Aunt Rachael was having a hard time keeping up, but we didn't care. We were on a sugar rush, and I think she knew we'd calm down eventually. But how could we! Oh, the most amazing thing, we told her. Thomas Noel and Uma Harlow were going to be in *our* town, at *our* school next week. It was beyond exciting, it was ludicrous, it was amazing, it was...

*"The best thing that's ever happened in the history of mankind!"*

I finished in a giddy cry. I breathed in and out for a while, and looked to Annie, who was also finally winding down.

"You're not on the bandwagon, are you?" asked Rachael.

"Huh?"

"Never mind. You're both in a tailspin. I really had no idea my company was worth so much to you. I'm flattered, really... Hey, help a girl out here!"

She pointed with her free hand to the road. Somehow we'd driven up the street and were now waiting at a green light, while an old lady in front took her time prepping to go.

Our aunt checked in between the two front seats as we waited.

"Cigarettes, cigarettes… Do you remember Audrey Mercy? Squat girl my age who always used to run into things back home? This might be before your time…"

Annie and I shook our heads, lost for whom she meant.

"Since that heinous Nazi is staying with you, I'm bunking with Audrey and her husband, Luke. She's very pregnant, or as he likes to say: *They're* very pregnant."

Annie and I pleaded desperately for her to reconsider. After all, she was our amazing Aunt Rachael, youthful at thirty-nine in ways we could only hope for in our impending sag. She was fit, she was stunning, she had the Jewish accent and the wit and the style, and she wasn't afraid to tell it like it was; but she was also wonderfully thoughtful and bright and merry all the time. Dad loved her as much as any brother loved a sister, but I knew he wasn't fond of her the way we were. She was our role model, our favourite, and to have her here was simply topping off the best week of our lives. But now, just like that, it was being taken away from us.

All because of Grandma Helen.

As if by a mystical, menacing force she knew we were coming, the old lady in question stood by the front door, watching the hearse spiralling down the driveway. Aunt Rachael let out an annoyed mumble and cursed, but didn't stop. She drove the hearse right into the open garage, crawling deep until she nearly hit the back wall, in the space where Dad's yellow motorcycle had once been. As we all hopped out, we heard a gentle cackling of evil laughter.

"Who died?" asked Grandma Helen, arms crossed.

Rachael mocked her, crossing her arms and cackling forcefully.

"Hello, Helen. Haven't seen you since…"

"Annie's eleventh birthday."

"Has it been that long? Hmm… Time flies when you're having fun. Excuse me."

She pushed past somewhat violently, and Grandma Helen gaped in surprise at the roughness of it.

Annie and I didn't say a word, but as we walked into the foyer we felt the intense heat radiating from the vents above us. The window had been fixed earlier that day by some handymen, which meant our household was safe at last from any further robberies.

"Wow," said Rachael, stopping by the flight of stairs.

She had never been here; it sounded like she was not so much impressed with her brother's new dig, but… merely surprised.

"Icky really did it. He upgraded."

Possibly hearing his nickname, Dad walked in from the back hallway. He was sporting a navy v-neck and jeans, and held the blue rake from the shed. Upon seeing his darkly clad sister in front of him, he hesitated for a moment. Was he planning on walking backwards, hoping it would reverse time? If he wasn't thinking that, it sure looked like he was.

"Home-time already?" he asked us.

"Last day," I said, unsurely. "We got let out early."

"Where's Hayley?"

Annie rushed a hand to her mouth, genuinely shocked.

"We forgot about her again!"

"She'll be fine."

"Damn right I'll be fine," came her voice from behind us.

Hayley walked in the open door, taking off her jacket.

"I'd be pissed off, but the joke is on you because Eleanore handed out mince pies on the bus, and I took two for you but ate them outside. So ha. Mr. Gellar, do we have enough milk in the fridge to make a coffee?"

Dad nodded and she ran off, not bothering to stay and say hello. Well, it was fair, I guess. She was starting night shift soon.

"Love the new place," said Rachael, after awkwardly hugging Dad. "I'm guessing there's enough room here for me?"

"I thought you were staying with Audrey Mercy."

Rachael shrugged and took a few steps up the flight of stairs, arching her neck to look around.

"Yeah, but I figured, she's heavily pregnant, Luke's got insomnia. Plus it's Christmas. Anyway, these two Chatty Cathy's convinced me in the car. I can sleep on the couch if you want. You know my affinity for couches."

"How long are you staying for?"

"Undecided."

Dad's breath was held, and he put a hand to his forehead.

"Alright," he muttered.

Annie and I screamed in excitement and rushed to link arms with Rachael, then guided her through the nearest hallway to show her the second guest room.

Left alone, Dad avoided his mother-in-law's eagle eye.

"I hope you know what you've done, Ichabod," said Grandma Helen finally, in a low voice. "You've opened Pandora's box."

Hayley walked by, mug of coffee hugged close to her body.

"No, no," she said, catching the tail-end of the conversation, "it's already open. Help yourself."

SATURDAY
THE **15** TH

# 11

# SCHOOL,
# SPORADICALLY

J ust as I woke up the next morning, Hayley came in to go
to bed, having moved back in the day before. She looked
drained of all life and had her hair up in a bun. As she
crawled under her covers by the locked window, I reminded her that not only did she still have her bakery uniform on, she
was also wearing her apron. And backwards, at that.

"It twists around when I'm working…"

"*All* the way around?"

While she slept, I snuck downstairs and hung out with Annie,
Brendan and Rachael. Our aunt had been pretty quiet the previous
night. Sneaking out around midnight to fetch her things from Audrey Mercy's house downtown (which was fine because Luke Mercy
was a night owl), she'd tripped in the foyer on her way back up the
stairs, disturbing Helen in the process. But it wasn't the end of the
world as one would've expected. The two weren't on the same taran-

tula venom that had poisoned their tongues during Annie's eleventh birthday party. They'd obviously called a truce, for whatever reason. Now, as Rachael sat next to me on the couch, she didn't seem too bothered as our grandmother came downstairs and made her usual ruckus. Ignoring her in my peripherals, I also noticed how refreshed my sister looked. Brendan did too, even though his newly freed eyes were still puffy and red from the infection. I wasn't sure what it was about the day after school break-up, but it always happened — it was as if our minds subconsciously knew what to compartmentalise to allow our entire bodies to relax. We must've slept deeply, I realised.

To my surprise, half an hour later, Mom and Dad came downstairs fully dressed. Mom in her dark green businesswoman's suit and alternative Christmas earrings, and Dad in his ugly Santa sweater that was slowly becoming baggy on him.

"I've got a meeting at the school," said Mom, as they rushed to grab themselves some coffees. "Your father's coming with me. Does anyone need anything from the shops? I'll pop in on the way home."

"No," we all called, but then Brendan dared ask: "What's the meeting about?"

"Your precious darlings," she responded, but to me.

Completely clueless, I humphed in disapproval.

She finally elaborated: "The producers from *The Prefect Family* have requested a luncheon with all of the staff, so we won't be home until this afternoon."

Annie and I jumped up. "Oh! Can we come?"

"No," said Dad firmly. "Rachael, how was the couch?"

Rachael stretched in her pyjamas. "We're *involved*."

"Dad, please can we go?" I begged him. "If it's a luncheon, maybe they won't even mind all that much! I mean, it's not like it's a proper meeting or anything. It's the weekend. Maybe you have to look after your kids, they don't know."

"But we don't. You're both nearly adults."

Brendan climbed up on his armchair to get a better vantage point of his parents behind it.

"If you take Cassie and Annie," he said to them, "I promise I won't keep looking for my Christmas presents."

Now *this* was conflict. There was a strained silence, broken only by the flailing snoring sounds of Hayley upstairs in my bedroom. Finally, the two of them sighed.

Mom said: "Be ready in ten minutes."

Annie darted for the stairs, but I stretched and got up slowly, as I was already dressed and had brushed my teeth. All I needed to do was comb my hair and cover my bruised face with more make-up.

"Wow, Brendan, thanks," I said. "We owe you one."

"Trust me, I know."

"If you two are going, so am I," our Aunt insisted merrily.

"Rachael, no…"

"Hush your fat face, brother. I am the guest of this house, at least one of them, and given the alternative is to stay at home with… her…"

She nudged her head towards Grandma Helen, who was yelling at the microwave.

"… I think I'd rather take my chances. Besides. I watch that show, too, you know. I'm hip. I'm in on the now."

Mom breathed in heavily as she stared at Dad, thinking hard.

"Fine. We'll make a day of it."

———— · · · ————

There were no words for how excited and gleeful we were as we drove downtown twenty minutes later. Annie, Rachael and I sat in the back seats gas-bagging, while Mom drove and Dad stared out the window forlorn.

What was up with him?

Mom was particularly tight-lipped about the details of the meeting, but also very scary and strict when she told us what to do once we got there. We parked in her designated spot, and as we hopped out there came a chill bounding across the baron landscape. It was so weird being back here only a day after we'd wrapped-up. The school looked eerie without its students.

"Lesley!"

Eric Parker raced out of the nearest building to greet us. He didn't seem phased that Mom had brought along extras; in fact, he was beaming with delight.

"Thank goodness," he said. "Most of the staff have politely declined so there's only a handful in the Teacher's Lounge. Hello Ichabod, Annie, Cassie… and…?"

"This is my sister-in-law, Rachael Gellar," said Mom.

Rachael was in her usual black. A heavy trench-coat almost covered it all. She smiled nicely.

Eric pointed at her. "Audrey Mercy's friend?"

"Yeah," said Rachael, taken aback.

"She works here when she's not heaving with pregnancy."

"She does?" Mom and Rachael said together.

"Cooking for the cafeteria. We hired her for today, too; some light catering. Just small things, you know. She mentioned you were staying with her."

"Was, but now I'm staying with my brother."

Rachael wrapped an arm around Dad's, and he tried to wriggle out of it, but she wouldn't allow it at all. She almost got violent in her determination.

"We haven't seen each other for nearly a year. Not since the last heart-attack, right, brother?"

We were led into one of the outer offices, through a side door. Up a few steps until we could hear some voices coming from nearby. The heating was on in here, for the closer to the Teacher's Lounge we got, the warmer. This was good, as none of us had ventured out of the house with too many items of clothing, except for Rachael. I was in a red plaid shirt and jeans, while Annie was in almost the exact same wear.

Principal Parker was right. There weren't many people attending, and to my disappointment there weren't any stars of the show, either. Ms. Weiss was there, sitting down talking to Eleanore, who was in a stunning ruby dress. Miss. Terr, my gym teacher, was talking to a few people in suits. A brunette woman was there, too, with shaggy brown hair, wearing an oversized aqua woollen jumper. She was associating with a *heavily* pregnant woman, situated by a long table full of scones, sandwiches, a punch bowl and an array of fruits and tossed salads.

"Audrey, this looks phenomenal," said Rachael, walking over to the pregnant woman and breaking up the conversation.

"Thanks! I... Oh no, I'm not talking to you," the woman named Audrey replied, and she gorged on a ham sandwich.

"I'm *sorry.*"

"It's too late for that. Luke and I were expecting you for Christmas, so now we're going to have to project that love onto this stupid little cretin instead..."

She rubbed her huge belly.

This was the first time I'd ever met Audrey, and I knew that I liked her already. She was the same age as Rachael, and very tanned for this time of year. Despite her size, which would be chubby any-way, her face was incredibly round and dumpy looking. Her long, dirty blonde hair was straight and flat on her head, and sort of wispy. Perhaps the baby was draining her of her essential oils and nutrients, because she looked tired. But she smiled kindly and her glowing hazel eyes landed upon Rachael's company.

"Annie and Cassie…" she said, and she fake bemoaned. "Why have I never seen you two in school before? I only stopped working here a few weeks ago."

I shrugged. "Our mother makes our lunches."

"To be young like that. I bet you still carry around lunchboxes."

Rachael fished in her pockets and brought something out, dangling it in front of her friend.

"Here, you can have your key back."

"Keep it," said Audrey.

Rachael hugged it to her body, touched by the gesture.

"No, I mean, throw it away. We have to get a new lock because of the damage you made trying to sneak in last night."

"I thought I was using the right key!"

"It was a cork-screw."

Rachael inspected the many items on her keychain, angry at herself for not realising at the time. She looked up at Audrey, who frowned in disappointment, but then her good-naturedness came through and she grinned happily.

"Just because I'm smiling doesn't mean I'm not mad," said Audrey. "Anyway, this is Netti Zawistowski, one of the show's producers."

The petit woman in the aqua sweater, who had been standing there listening awkwardly to the conversation, acted as if somebody had suddenly wound her up like a toy mouse. Her face became animated and she said hello to us as we were all introduced. I marvelled at her giant blue eyes, but also at how drastically gaunt she was. She looked ill, and unhappy.

"I am big fan of small town," she said, with a thick accent. "Never heard of until this week, but is now in top five of all places I be to. Top five."

Audrey nodded as she listened.

"Netti is also one of the star's sisters. Did you know Uma Harlow is Polish?"

"You're Uma Harlow's *sister?*" I said in surprise and awe.

The more I looked, the more it became apparent.

"We are twins."

Annie and I laughed, because of course this wasn't true. The two of them may have shared the same gigantic eyes and pinched nose, and sure their hair colour was exactly…

"Oh wow, you are too."

Eleanore barged her way between us, and went to gobbling down some pieces of sliced banana. Midway through picking a few grapes from a bunch, she said her hello's and went to leave. But suddenly she addressed my sister.

"Annie, tell me. Have you done something different with your skin lately? Like, cleaned it?"

Annie stared wild-eyed, preparing to duck-and-roll.

"No."

"Well, you're looking radiant."

"Th-thank you."

With that, Eleanore left to return to the couch with Ms. Weiss.

"Why's that girl dressed like Jessica Rabbit?" asked Rachael.

I was still caught up with the remarkable similarities between Netti and her famous sister. They really *were* twins, but she was so dressed down and without a lick of make-up, and those cheekbones were ridiculous.

"Is Uma… I mean, is your sister going to be here today?"

"Nie. Only producers and staff. We are wanting to go over plans for ride next week. Are you one of, uh, girls going… to, how you say… on flight?"

"No, that would be her," I said, pointing to Eleanore in her stunning gown. Of course she would dress like that around TV producers. "Her and a friend. We only came today because our mother works here, and we…"

"… were hoping to see Thomas Noel," said Netti, grinning.

Annie and I looked down, feeling embarrassed.

"I would love to sit with you both over lunch, if that is possible?" Netti said to us. "Record you, so you tell me what you like about show? Am always interested in hearing from public, yes? About good, bad, improve quality of programming."

"Yes, absolutely! We'll definitely sit down with you!"

"Will both of you be here next Friday to watch Zeppelin take off? It will be on football field of school, down there."

Suddenly I remembered. JT's party. Saddened by the thought, my heart sinking, we told her no.

Netti frowned.

"That is shame. A lot of stars will be shaking hands. You never know what might happen."

Annie smiled at me sadly. Bitter regrets and resentment over next Friday's dinner were slowly settling on my heart.

"I don't like crowds," said Rachael suddenly, "so count me as one of the millions watching from the couch."

"If you pop your head out the window at right time, you might see Zeppelin fly over!" said Netti. "I know Uma will be glad so many fans of show. Nice to be on bandwagon, yes?"

Rachael's eyebrows raised. She looked at her pregnant friend.

"Speaking of bandwagon, Audrey, this is for you. I forgot to return it last night. I'm sorry."

She whipped out a small paper bag and handed it to her.

"Thank you," Audrey said.

"What is it?" asked Annie curiously.

"Just some of her spooky healing crystals. Jasper, Amethyst, Lapis, Tiger's eye…"

Our aunt turned to point at Mom and Dad, who were standing next to the newly arrived Chloe and Candice Croxley.

"Hey, Icky! Save me some of that pie you've got there."

To our surprise, something heavy hit the window nearest to us. We looked over in time to see something black collapse on the ground. Audrey was first to the door leading outside, surprising in her state. Annie and I peered around her to see what it was she was crouching over.

A blackbird.

"That poor little thing," said Chloe, leaning over my shoulder.

Behind her, I noticed her electrician friend, Pepper O. Salt, who twirled his oversized moustache in curiosity.

"It's an omen," he said gravely, his only visible eye squinting.

The blackbird twitched on its back for a moment. Then before we could do anything else it collected its senses, flipped around, dodged past us and loudly flapped its wings as it went on its way.

"With one bullet," said Netti, and she pinched the back of my right hand for some unknown reason.

⸻ • • • ⸻

The luncheon lasted another two hours, but it was extremely informal. A few more of the staff arrived, some of them also bringing their eagle-eyed children, and a producer named Cora Corali spoke intensely for twenty minutes about how the following week's event was going to unfold. In a nutshell: the stars and producers would arrive at the school, which would be in total security lockdown for the whole day, and have the entire place to themselves. The special guests, being Eleanore and her friend, and their families, would get the Teacher's Lounge as their *'ensuite'*, where make-up crews and producers would stay with them all afternoon. At 6pm, the front gates would open to the public and the press, and they would all be guided down to the football field at the back of the school grounds. Allocated seating, billboards and an entire side of the bleachers for the cameras, it would be full of entertainment. Musical acts, comedy routines, much like how it looked when we had the fair last month. All of this would be leading up to the big moment. The Zeppelin, coming across the bay from an undisclosed island, would initially only have the two pilots and a camera crew aboard. As it would come over Horn-Horn, the cameras would capture the town at night and all of the pretty Christmas lights. Then, as it moved closer to the bay, there would be fireworks above the football field, finishing at 7:30pm. Fifteen minutes later, the Zeppelin would land on the football field, the cast, crew and special guests would board it, and up it would go again. It would spend an entire hour in the air essentially doing laps of the town, and in that time every passenger would dine. Interviews would be given, special guests would be treated to prizes galore, and a 'great reveal' would happen. Shortly after that, another burst of fireworks from below, and then the Zeppelin would descend and land safely on the football field once more. Everybody would leave, and that would be that.

Eleanore could barely contain herself every time she was asked a question, and I couldn't help notice Eric Parker glancing across at me every few minutes. I also noticed he kept nudging his daughter and jerking his neck towards me from time to time. I tried not to read too much into it, but a tiny part of me was thrilled. Maybe she was getting ready to ask me to accompany her on the ride. I knew that fish flying in the skies of Pakistan was a more likely scenario; yet there he was cricking his neck, and there she was eyeing him angrily with an *'Alright, alright!'* look that could kill.

As Mom and Dad did their round of goodbyes, Annie and Rachael helped Audrey pack up all the leftover food she'd prepared. Surely enough, Eleanore sauntered over to me. She tripped on her ruby dress at the last minute, but recovered gracefully.

"Congratulations," I said to her honestly.

"Thank you," she muttered, looking distracted, watching the food tables as they were being disassembled. "So Cassie, look. Here's the thing. I have been elected as conveyer of a message. But it goes against everything I stand for in life. So instead of telling you, I thought it would be best if I instead give you a heads up. Does that sound alright to you? I know you're sensie."

If this was her way of inviting me onto the Zeppelin ride with her, she had a funny way of wording things.

"Why me, though?" I asked.

Eleanore kept her voice down.

"You have to understand, it's a tradition."

"It's a what now?"

She sighed, and started to move away.

"Just be ready by nine tomorrow morning, okay?"

"For what?"

Eleanore couldn't stand being asked the obvious, apparently, and she slipped out of the room faster than you could say 'red leather, yellow leather'. I'd been invited to do something tomorrow, but it was top secret, and she didn't want to invite me but was being forced to...

It had to be about the Zeppelin ride, right?

# 12

# HOT CHOCOLATE HORRORS

Chloe, Candice and Pepper O. Salt struggled into Candice's apartment downtown, carrying with them giant vats of left-over food from the luncheon. Chloe put her stuff down and raced off to the bathroom, while the other two placed the food they'd carried onto the kitchen counter.

Pepper hadn't been in Candice's apartment before, and he was surprised at how cramped it was for such an expensive block. Nearby sat a child's firetruck toy by a sliding door which led to the outside balcony. Near the front door were other gifts — a complete box set of the original Power Rangers series, a small electric keyboard, a doll in a box... Then, underneath the Christmas tree in the lounge-room sat seventeen individually wrapped presents, one of them very clearly a child's bike.

"Do you have a... little brother?" asked Pepper, trying to brush down the puffy box of black hair around his forehead.

"No, I'm hiding a friend's presents here. Her son likes to snoop around for them at their house."

"How c-cre-erk-clever!" he said in parts, for his moustache, which was clearly fake, tickled his nose.

Candice smiled politely as he eventually sneezed, despite feeling strangely uneasy around him.

"Have you got any kids?" she asked him.

"No, not at all. I myself am still a child, as I collect... Oh, hang on, is that..." Pepper noticed the toy in the box by the door, reading the name on the front. "That's a *Fräulein 'Frown-Lines' Schneider* doll from the *'Tiro the Barber-Librarian'* line of collectables! Have you seen the show it's based on? Banned here, you know. Set in Berlin during the Second World War. It follows a spy who works during the day as a barber for Nazi commandants, and at night is part of a secret espionage ring that masquerades as librarians. Every episode they come *this* close to getting caught by the Gestapo. Genius program. It's from the creators of *The Prefect Family*, you know."

"Isn't it a cartoon, though?"

"Yes, but it's deep. I only caught it recently for the first time. I think you'd really like it. Oh, it's the original seven incher! I am impressed. He must already have the *Tiro* doll. Who's the lucky kid?"

"Brendan Gellar," Candice couldn't bring herself to say any more. All she knew was that the young scallywag would not be finding his presents early this year.

"So nice of Audrey to give us these chocolate brownie blocks," said Chloe, emerging from the bathroom still doing up her belt. She held a paper bag under her right arm. "Did she say *why* she wanted us to have them?"

Her question was directed towards Pepper, who shrugged.

"She was busy packing up when she gave them to me. All she said was to pass them on to you. Something about a bandwagon."

"I have no idea what that means. But wouldn't you think, being so pregnant, she'd want to keep them all for herself? I know I would."

"Yes, but think about *after* the baby is born!" said Candice. "Besides, she's a generous lady by nature. I think I heard someone say she cooks things for free at Christmas time, and gives baked cakes to charities and so forth! How bloomin' marvellous! It's obviously a labour of love. And I'm not complaining. That's a lot of brownie! We'll be set until New Years!"

"What's this *we* business? I'm spending Christmas alone with my cat Dleifrag. We've sort of got a tradition going."

Candice snatched the paper bag off her as she lumbered close, and watched in dismay as Pepper wrapped his giant arms around Chloe. Then she sniffed the contents.

"They smell funny," she remarked.

"Audrey loves using Asian ingredients, that's probably why. Here, let's try some. Pepper?"

"No thank you, I am on a low-calorie diet for the stretch of December. Need to lose some weight around the middle."

"But you're a Scarecrow."

"Flattery will get you nowhere. Perchance, ladies, could I interest either of you in some of my delicious homemade pumpkin soup? The secret ingredient is leek. I could bring it around later tonight, along with a few Christmas movies I own."

Chloe pulled a DVD from her handbag. "Way ahead."

"Plus, we want brownies. We want brownies!" The sisters began to chant together. "We-want-brownies! We-want-brownies!"

Pepper swirled his black man-cape around himself, and his left hand landed with almost impossible precision on the front door knob. "In that case, I bid you farewell. Goodbye, Candice, kindly host. And goodbye Chloe, my beloved—"

"Okay, bye, then."

He left as quick as lightning. Perplexed by his increasingly bizarre behaviour, the sisters went into the kitchen to make drinks, and helped themselves to some of the brownie mix. Despite the odd smell, they tasted delicious. Candice almost moaned in delight.

———— • • • ————

As daytime came to an end, a brief snowstorm whooshed through town without a single sound. Annie and I watched from the front door as it covered everything, and quite heavily, but it ended after only a few minutes. I breathed in the chill air and allowed my mind to wander.

"Can one of you please give me a lift to work in an hour?"

Hayley was trudging down the stairs, her hair a great big mess of knots. She was still in her pyjamas and nearly collided with Grandma Helen as she raced for a bathroom break.

"I'll do it," I offered, knowing Annie was still a little wooden around her after the window incident. Which, as I thought about it, felt like a very long time ago.

As I prepared myself upstairs, throwing on some jeans, heavy socks and a thick pink jumper, I checked to see if the coast was clear and went up into the attic. It was hot again, almost overbearing. Squinting into the darkness, I thought I saw a sudden movement. A rat? It had to be.

"Zag," I called.

He appeared like a ghost, waiting for me to speak first. I did indeed have a question to ask him. "Remember how I made a wish for there to be no more wishes during Christmas?"

"I do, party pooper."

"Can I change that?"

"Not unless it's an emergency," said Zag, and he tried to spy down the attic steps. "Is everything okay?"

"Oh yes, everything's fine. I just... next Friday, there's a... and I want to... Never mind." I let out a great big sigh of ennui.

"I've been doing more research," said Zag suddenly. "On Christmas. *Santa Claus*. It makes sense the more I read about it! There's *Old Saint Nick*, and then there's *Sinterklaas*. And you said before that it was all about family to you, and Nicholas has been talking non-stop about family... but if you let Santa into your house at Christmas, he..."

"Zag, you're getting too technical with this," I interjected. "There's just a feeling to it. You're not meant to analyse and deconstruct everything, or else it ruins it."

"I'm not like you in that sense; I can't just observe the impossible and chalk it up to magic."

"You literally grant me wishes! I'm not... this isn't... let's not argue," I insisted. "If you don't see things from my point of view, then I guess you'll never really know what Christmas is all about!"

His reaction to this was, strangely, quite adamant. He would continue with his research on the subject of Christmas. Distracted by his thoughts, he said a brief goodbye and plunged back into his clay head. Left alone in the darkness again, I remembered the shadowy rodent figure I'd seen earlier and disappeared back downstairs.

———— · · · ————

Candice let out a blood-curdling scream as her decorated Christmas Tree reached out its spindly branches to grab her.

*"Calm down!"* it yelled angrily.

"I'm not going to calm down! You're a bloody talking tree! Chloe! Help!"

Chloe was wonkily coming out of the bathroom, and froze in mid-place. Her sister was, without a doubt, being strangled by her Christmas Tree. Terrified, she rushed into the kitchen and opened the cupboards, desperate to find a set of matches. When she found some, she ran over to her struggling sister and lit a dozen in her hands. The tree reacted, letting go of Candice and making a huge jumping effort to return to its corner.

*"Back off, Yuletard!"* shouted Chloe.

Candice hugged her sister, shaking as she did.

"Oh, Chloe, it was horrible!" she sobbed loudly. "And now I smell like urine and pine needles!"

The horrific set of circumstances had materialised slowly throughout the night. About an hour earlier, a pigeon had smashed into the glass door leading to the balcony. When Chloe went to see if it was alive, she was astonished to discover a dory fish flapping around in its place.

*Do fish fly?* she found herself wondering in the moment, not sure of the correct answer.

Soon after that, as they settled in to watch another movie, the actors on the television would glance at the camera from time to time. It was as if they'd become aware of the sisters, trying to ignore them as they focused on their acting. Eventually, during a final intense scene, the main actor called for everybody to stop, and then asked Chloe and Candice to please stop watching them, as it was very distracting. Evidently spooked by the whole commotion, the sisters turned off the set and decided to give each other a Christmas present early. When they went to look underneath the tree, they found that all of their presents had been replaced with beachballs. Perturbed, Chloe went to the bathroom to collect her thoughts. While in there, she heard Candice scream and quickly rushed out to see the Christmas Tree attacking her.

"Are we going mad?" asked Candice.

Before either could come to any proper form of conclusion, the tree and all of its beachball crones decided to lunge together. Candice let out another scream, Chloe grabbed some car keys from the hallway table, and the sisters fled for their lives.

Downstairs, underneath the apartment block and into the private parking lot, the two of them ran as if the entire world was having one giant earthquake. They banged into each other and tripped over their own feet; finally Chloe saw up ahead that wonderful light olive Gremlin car of Candice's sitting in its usual spot. As they reached it, Chloe tried to open the passenger side door with the keys, but her hands were shaking terribly. She threw them to her sister, who managed to unlock her door. She hopped in, opened the other door, and let her sister in.

Suddenly, a smack on the window. Chloe turned to see the Christmas Tree looking in, frowns appearing within its branches. The dozen or so beachballs arrived, jumping upon the bonnet and roof aggressively.

"Jesus Christ!" yelled Chloe.

"I've wet myself again!" cried Candice.

"Drive!"

Candice started the engine, reversed the car, and the two girls drove away in a hurry. The tree and the beachballs initially gave chase, but were eventually lost to the darkness. The sisters drove along in a hush for a long while, allowing the silence of the night to calm their shell-shocked nerves. Neither could bring themselves to say anything. Where were they going to drive to, anyway? Who knew? The streetlights seemed darker tonight, the festive lights on houses failing to bring the needed source of vision to the darkened roads as they usually did. Finally, Chloe realised why…

"Headlights," she said, reaching across the steering-wheel, flicking them on for her sister.

———— . . . ————

I tensed in fright as a pair of headlights lit up the road, barreling straight towards us. I swerved out of the way, and the car which had appeared out of nowhere disappeared just as quickly into the darkness behind us.

"Ghost car!" I cried.

My nerves on edge, I lingered at stop signs and drove quite drastically under the speed limit for the rest of the trip to the Horn-Horn Mall II where Hayley worked. In the back seat with her earphones in, trying her hardest to mentally hibernate until the moment her shift started, she had no idea how close we'd come to death.

"Come in," she insisted ten minutes later, as I nudged her

awake. "I want to show you where I work."

The mall was a strange place to be at night, just as peculiar an environment as the school during the holidays. Not only was every shop closed, but lights were dimmed and I felt a little nervous. As with many instances in my life since seeing *Jurassic Park*, I envisioned two scary velociraptors emerging from around a corner and giving chase. I imagined in a brief panic what I would do, where I would go, and if I would survive.

The bakery was next to the dental surgery, which seemed very strange to me. As we slipped behind the counter, I immediately spotted two other people about my age. One of them was from our school, I knew that much. The other was Asian and reminded me of that Morgan guy from the hardware store.

"Oh!" I said, almost choking on nothing, and he turned around to see us. It *was* Morgan from the hardware store. Immediately embarrassed, I could do nothing but gape like a trout at him, while he set to cleaning some giant metal death-trap machine in front of us.

"Cassie, this is Morgan," Hayley introduced us. "Morgan, this is my best friend, Cassie."

"Sure you're not Annie?" he said, smiling in amusement.

Hayley inspected him curiously. "That's a weird thing to say. Her sister's name is Annie. Are you psychic?"

I wasn't quite there yet, and I knew my cheeks were badly flushed. I held out my hand for him, and thankfully he shook it without any qualms.

"We've met before," I said in a quiet voice. "At the hardware store. You work here, too?"

Morgan kept a tight grin. "'Tis the season to earn money."

Hayley wasn't in the mood. She ignored what Morgan was doing and sticky-beaked in the back to see if the big, scary boss man was there yet.

"I've got to go. Look around if you want. Thanks for the lift."

I told her she was welcome, and stood still for a moment once she was gone. I was unsure. Were Morgan and I knee-deep in a conversation, or a curt meet-and-greet? I couldn't tell.

"So," I said slowly. "Uh… Need help doughing?"

Morgan paused and then shook his head.

"You're not allowed, sorry. Health and safety. Are you planning on coming back to the hardware store with your résumé? We need help after Christmas."

"Oh, yeah, no, I will. I'll print it off tomorrow."

Going over my previous statement in my head, I had to face the fact that he was most definitely measuring up my intelligence in that very moment.

"About time," he replied.

All at once his smile was warm and not judgmental in the least. His eyes were shining in a way that made me think of freshly baked cookies on Christmas morning, and his teeth were that sort of impeccably healthy white a pair of veneers could never replicate. All I knew, as I backed away like a robot to head home, was that I liked him. For whatever reason. I would without a doubt be taking my résumé in to the hardware store.

Tomorrow. Maybe. I needed time to prepare.

"Cool," I said, thinking back to when I'd misread *'Staff Wanted'*.

Suddenly something in my mind snapped. It really tickled my funny-bone. *Stuff wanted,* I thought as Morgan waited for me to explain why I was smiling so goofily. It wasn't helping my case with him. *Stuff wanted, stuff wanted, stuff wanted...*

I waved and turned without another word, and cackled heartily as I exited through the automatic doors of the mall.

At least I could laugh about it.

# 13

## THE
## MARGUERITE TROUBRIDGE

I spent the previous night warding off Grandma Helen and Aunt Rachael as they tried to garner votes over what to watch in the living room. *A Muppets Christmas Carol*, or the classic 1951 version, *Scrooge*. In the end, Mom intervened and let Brendan choose what to watch (he chose *Die Hard*).

With total and complete intention of waking up early and making a résumé before Eleanore came knocking for this surprise something-or-other, I fell asleep without setting my alarm. A rookie mistake. I awoke the next morning to Annie, who was calmly hovering over me like a curious Golden Retriever. I jumped up, nearly karate-chopping her neck in the moment, then quickly dropped my head to rest again as I set to maintaining a normal heartbeat.

"Could you be any weirder?" I mumbled into my pillow.

Annie's gaze was something else. "They're here…"

I lifted my head slightly and squinted with one eye open. Why was she fully dressed? Hayley was snoring away in her bed by the window, body contorted in such a way that it made her look like she was fresh from falling off the top of a building. Still, Annie pulled my cover away, then went over to Hayley, and promptly poked her enough to wake her up.

"Be gone, demon!" she snarled, and she tried to bite Annie's fingers as they lifted her own cover away. "Just got to… and now you… oh, let me sleep…"

I noticed a movement by my open bedroom door. There was a group of people peering in curiously. Stunned, I sat up and pulled the covers to my shoulders. JT and Greg were there, joined by Eleanore, Wednesday, Friday and Tanya.

"Good morning, girls!" said Eleanore loudly.

Hayley sat up automatically and checked the clock. She smacked her forehead with a palm. It dawned on me that she'd been expecting them. With that she jumped up and grabbed some random clothes from her pile near the wardrobe, and left to get changed in the bathroom.

"What's… everyone doing in my house?" I asked shyly.

JT turned to Eleanore with a sly look on his face. "I asked you to do one thing. One."

Eleanore put her hands up angrily. "I *did* tell her! Yesterday. I told her to be ready by nine in the morning. It's *not* my fault. She's *your* friend. I think she's secretly handicapped."

None of the Saviours looked happy to see me, and the more they peered about my bedroom the more coiled their facial expressions grew. Hayley stormed out of the bathroom in a pair of brown dungarees and a white top. She grabbed her light-blue jacket and put on her galoshes. She looked pretty crap, to be honest. She came over and pulled me out of bed.

"None of you have permission to be in here," she told the crowd, and she slammed the door in their faces. "Ugh. I need Pandora for this."

"For what?" I asked, glad to be alone again. "Huh? Hayley… what is happening?"

"We're going to Jonathan's to decorate. For Christmas."

I begged for more details.

"We do it every year. It's no big deal. Sort of a tradition. You don't have to come if you don't want."

"No, no, I'll go…"

I insisted. I had an indelible fear these days of missing out on things, even if I had no idea what they were. Even if they crushed my hopes and dreams of being invited on the Zeppelin ride…

———— . . . ————

"So, this is weird," I said.

I was walking down the frosty street by Eleanore's side.

"Spare your flappers the usual comedienne routine of pointing out the obvious," the lead Saviour replied in her high-pitched voice. "We're hanging out for one measly day of the year. We always do it."

"But *why?*" I asked for the twentieth time.

"It's something we've always done," said Tanya. "JT's house always needs decorating, so we put our differences aside and help."

"It's still weird."

"Not really," said Tanya. She was dressed in a million layers, yet still hugged herself as we walked through the chilly morning haze down Philips Street. "I think it's very human and Christian of us. It would make Jesus of Kryptonite proud."

"Stop calling him that," insisted Wednesday.

As we got to the end of the street, which met with a slightly distorted T-section, I looked across the way to see the ocean between the last of the teenage oaks. It was a grey, dull day and nothing was going to change. Clouds were hanging low from all sides and seemed to stretch on forever.

"Will everybody from our class be there too?" I asked.

"No, just us," said Friday, acknowledging the crowd of those who had been in my bedroom. "It's a sort of… Well, we do it for the sake of JT's family. His parents think he only hangs around with rich people."

"Not all of us are rich," said Hayley with a resentful grunt. "They only let me come along because I'm his girlfriend."

I turned to JT in pity. "Oh, do your parents have a complex?"

There was a moment of intense pause, and I tried to read their faces. Most were looking at their shoes.

Promptly, we turned left instead of our usual right, heading uphill. I wondered when we would get to the shortcut I'd discovered recently, that would lead us directly into the lower streets of town. However, with just one street sitting behind our own, we ventured higher into Gentleman's Court. Three houses were on this street, all of them mansions. The closest was a vast property with hardly any trees on it, just a hilly arena of dull-coloured grass and a few rocks here and there. A large mansion sat atop the hill, towering above everything else. It was three storeys high, of a dark wood, and the entire place looked deeply unfriendly. It reminded me quite remarkably of the Addams Family house.

I succumbed to the chill of yet another winter blast, and watched in concern as Hayley strode right up to the giant iron front gates and forced them open. I wanted to say something, to protest, but then the rest of the clan followed. Fearful to be left alone again, I clutched at Annie's puffy jacket coat-tails and ducked as I followed into the property. I immediately pictured a dozen and one black Dobermans racing from around the corner to chase after us. I waited until Hayley and JT reached the front steps of the mansion before finally calling out for them to stop.

"What are you guys *doing!?*" I whispered, my voice high.

It seemed Friday was the only one who had an inkling of anything that was going on. She trotted the short way back down the hill and grabbed onto my shoulders.

"Cotton on, Cassie. JT isn't JT at Christmas. He's Jonathan Thomas Abraham Walker the Third. He's a well mannered, polite and sophisticated member of our superlative society. And his family is filthy, stinking rich."

Perhaps I was a little bit overwhelmed in the moment, as this information sunk right in without a fuss.

"Ah. I do see that now, and did not know that before."

"Didn't your parents ever mention JT's mother to you?" Eleanore muttered, turning on her heels as the group continued up the hill.

"Why would they?"

Eleanore refrained for a moment, then turned to my sister.

"Wow, you really are the smart one."

Disgruntled but at the mercy of my feeble mind, I continued to follow them as they made their way up to the mansion. On the veranda, which seemed to wrap around the entire house, I noticed a long range of black couches and swings, with many potted flowers and even a cat scratcher by a window. Through these windows, one could only see a scattering of gold from the light-bulbs, for the frames inside were draped in net curtains to block prying eyes like my own.

The front door was of large mahogany, with a giant window that looked in through distorted glass. JT sure enough grabbed the handle, opened the door, and invited us in.

"Mom! Dad!" my friend called out.

The foyer wasn't much to go by, as it was a narrow hallway with a dark brown staircase to the left. He told us all to stay there, and then ran off into an adjoining room.

I was still having trouble keeping up. If this week was planning on outdoing itself any more, I'd need a hospital room to recover in. The others took off their jackets, while noses and cheeks suddenly burst with colour from the change in temperature. Hayley was the only one who didn't look too impressed. The others, I noticed, had a crescent-moon look to their eyes, manic or excited.

"Did you know JT was rich?" I whispered to Annie.

"Of course. I'm not stupid."

I wanted to poke her in the kidneys with my knuckles, but before I could do that JT returned with two extra people in tow. A very tall, thin and glamorous woman reached with outstretched arms as if planning to give everybody a great big hug in one. She was dressed in a sublime maroon-coloured dress and carried on her neck a giant, dazzling emerald necklace. Behind her was a man about JT's height wearing a tweed jacket over a dull-green vest, sporting beige pants and shiny shoes. He was holding a half-finished glass of red wine loosely in his right hand. The two of them were smiling as if they'd recently won the lottery. For all I knew of JT, that's exactly what had happened.

"Ah, the *friends*," called the woman in a sort of pigeon voice, almost as if calling to her bird-family across the bay.

Unlike my turn with Netti Zawistowski, I recognised this woman right away. My jaw dropped.

"Yes," said JT, turning to us with little bother. "You know everybody here, mostly. Except for these two."

"Ah, hello," said the woman, and she reached out a hand to Annie. "You must be Cassandra."

I raised my hand, annoyed at how often this was happening.

"Mom, *this* is Cassie. That's her sister, Annie."

"Hello," she said to me, her eyes sparkling with intensity as she locked both her hands around my right one. "Jonathan has told me so much about you, Cassandra."

She was pronouncing my name the way I hated, and it wasn't the correct way, either. *'Rahhhr'* instead of a quick *'rah'*. It was for the pompous, the imperially diseased minds that thought the way a name was pronounced meant you were better than others.

"You're Marguerite Troubridge, aren't you?" I said quickly, popping my hand up again as if I were in class. "The French opera singer. Our mother loves you…"

I said this last part without thinking. Maybe Mom wouldn't want me telling her that.

Marguerite smiled bashfully and pointed to the others.

"Yes, well, that's all part of the rouse. It's my stage name, a business façade. Jonathan is my darling boy, and coming home to him makes those trips abroad worthwhile. I do apologise for never coming down to visit your family in Philips Drive, but I've been very busy since August."

I kept my free hand to my heart. "Sorry, I'm a bit… I wasn't expecting to meet somebody famous today."

The others around me, those I'd momentarily forgotten about, laughed in a sort of nervous way. Marguerite let go of my right hand, which was most likely sweaty, and shook Annie's. JT stayed on me, and introduced the man in the tweed jacket.

"Cassie, this is Jonathan Thomas Walker the *Second*."

"Your name is Jonathan as well?"

"Yes, but everybody calls me Tommy," said his father, Mr. Walker. He had an amused look on his face, most probably a defence mechanism. Or, as his wine suggested, he was so rich that he couldn't possibly find serious worth in meeting anybody new. It reminded me so of JT and the dazed and uninterested looks he would often give in class. Obviously it was hereditary.

"Dad used to be a lazy-eye expert. Top of his field."

"Yes, before I married a famed opera singer."

"Oh, and what do you do now?" I asked.

"Nothing. I'm the husband of a famed opera singer."

As the 'hello's and 'cheerio's and the 'isn't this weather abhorrent's and the 'you're a third?'s fizzled to a bored chatter, Marguerite eventually acknowledged Hayley.

"Hello," said my blonde friend, tired and grumpy.

"Hello," said Marguerite, and she sucked in her lips and turned her attention to Wednesday. She grabbed at her cheeks to make them rosy. "Oh, my dear Madam Shalom! I feel like your mother and I never catch up these days. Are you still on that old farm by the steel mill?"

Wednesday nodded, feeling the pain of the pinch, her eyes watering. "Yes, we're still there! All twelve of us!"

"Remind me, I must give you the number of my dermatologist. Your skin is getting out of hand."

"I'd *love* that, Mrs. Walker, but… my darkness is not a pigment issue. I'm black. Black and from Africa… originally."

Marguerite gave her a sceptic side-look, stepped back, then moved on to the last Saviour.

"Friday, Friday, Friday. You know, I don't think I've seen you since last Christmas."

"Your Christmas Dinner!" Friday soaked in the attention.

"How could I forget?" said Marguerite, and then she moved on to Tanya, who had to be at least an entire foot shorter than her.

She looked down, and for a moment I thought I saw a scowl, but it turned into another smile and she hugged the girl. She let go and grunted at Greg, who grunted back in an equally informal way which suggested they saw each other quite frequently, and then, at last, Marguerite made one more step back and examined us all in the foyer.

She breathed deeply, took in the moment, and said: "Now, are we on good terms with one another?"

"Yes," the others answered.

"Keeping chummy at school? Having each other's backs?"

"Yes," they called, Annie as well this time.

I watched with intrigue. They were all gathered around. JT even had his arms across Wednesday and Eleanore's shoulders. Mr. Walker stepped in suddenly with a Polaroid camera and snapped a photo of us. I wasn't prepared, and I knew that my infamous red eyes would show up like a deer's on a highway.

"I'm glad the elite of Horn-Horn are still such pals," he said, tucking the camera under his right arm and shaking the polaroid as it developed with his free hand. "It really does mean a lot to Marguerite and I."

All of a sudden, I couldn't hold it in.

It was like a rush of diarrhoea hitting me in public without a bathroom to escape to. Only this time, it wasn't poop about to come out of me. My emotions were at an all-time high and before I could run off to contain myself, I let out the biggest belch of laughter one could possibly imagine.

The entire group jumped in surprise and turned to stare at me as I doubled over, clutching at my thighs in desperation. My eyes watered and I knew the giant vein on my forehead was bulging outward.

It was everything. The Zeppelin ride, meeting Uma Harlow's twin, Aunt Rachael surprising us, Zag's stupendous glee at the idea of Santa Claus, the sudden realisation that JT was filthy stinking rich, and on top of that, his mother was the famous Marguerite Troubridge of whom we owned a dozen CD's and vinyls.

As if this wasn't enough, I suddenly remembered something else. I tried to speak, drooling through my episode:

"Nuhhh... Nuhgh..."

"Is she trying to say napkin?" asked Marguerite.

"Who cares? She's having a fit."

Finally, at long last, I managed to muster up enough strength to blurt it out: *"N... N... Need help doughing!?"*

With that I buckled over, crippled by the hilarity of it all.

Bloody Morgan. It was happening again.

# 14

## SPAT
## AND
## SPIT

"Y es, I promise," said JT.

"I mean it, though. No more of that," said Marguerite, arms crossed indignantly.

"Look, will you just let her back in?" snapped Hayley, pushing the two of them out of the way and opening the front door.

I was a changed woman. My hair was slightly damp from the sleet outside, and I felt like a mangey dog asking to be let back in after going for a quick dip in a muddy pool.

"I'm sorry," I said solemnly.

"My dear," declared a cross Marguerite, to my utmost embarrassment. "Are you on the bandwagon?"

I shook my head, gazing down. "...No..?" I guessed.

"Well, come in then. You're not of much use standing out there, and you look like you've recovered. Besides, I've had worse encounters. I once shook a fan's hand shortly before learning it was a part of his erogenous zone. Now, in the time you've been out there, I've shown the others the main rooms to be decorated. We have all of the modern audio technology, so if you ask the house to play music while you work, it will happily oblige. House, put Marguerite Troubridge on shuffle."

'*Tie Me Kangaroo Down, Sport*' started playing loudly.

"No!" she yelled over it. "Marguerite Troubridge! The *peaceful and SERENE COLLECTION!*"

The track changed immediately, through either witchcraft or the aforementioned technology. The gentle weeping of a solo violin seemed to emit from all around us, and I recognised it as the song she had indeed covered on one of her albums.

"We named the audio intelligence unit '*House*', so it feels like we're asking the house to play something," JT told me. "Except sometimes it plays house music instead, which is… not… pleasant."

"Careful, Jonathan," said Hayley slyly. "You don't want to set it off again."

"The house?"

"No, Cassie."

JT gave her a grim look, and turned back to his parents.

"Dad, where are the coloured lights?"

His dad tucked his hands, now free, into his armpits after finishing his wine.

"I've already brought them up from the basement. They're in the main parlour, with the rest of them. Now, your mother has a bit of a headache from the weather. She's going to lie down, while I do some present wrapping in my study, alright?"

"Alright!" I said effervescently, hoping to get back on their good side. "Have a nice nap, Mrs. Walker!"

Mr. Walker smiled nicely at me, and helped guide his wife up the stairs. As they got to the top of the first bend, Marguerite flung out her arms and joined herself in singing the chorus to '*O Holy Night*'. She continued until they disappeared further upstairs and through a door.

"What the hell is wrong with you?" Eleanore asked me immediately, and she grabbed my arm as she pulled me down the hallway.

Flushing again, I noticed Hayley and the others chasing our tails. We walked into a giant parlour room, decorated in the most beautiful teal, while a second storey row of bookshelves circled around the room above, with ladders and steps to reach the higher books. The rest of the group, including Annie, quickly set to work on opening the decoration boxes around us.

"I've never had such second-hand embarrassment in all my life! Honestly, Cassie, you're like a Jack-in-the-Box sometimes."

"I'm sorry. A lot has been going on this week."

"I'll say!" said Friday, laughing.

Ripping out of Eleanore's grip, I went to a nearby ottoman and sat down on it. Next to me was a giant opened packing box, with 'Parlour Four' scribbled on the side in shoddy permanent marker. I curiously peeked inside, admired what I saw, and pulled out a big long twist of silver and golden tinsel. As I set to untangling them, I looked up and noticed the curvature of a tree behind me. I turned fully around and marvelled at the astonishing size of their Christmas Tree. It had to be two storeys high, at least, and in fact was too tall for the parlour room we sat in. Half-decorated, it was bent horribly and the top-half stretched almost to the other side of the room.

"Dibs on not doing that," I said, pointing to the undecorated section near the ceiling far above.

"It's good luck to put the star on top of the tree," said Eleanore. "Therefore, I'll be doing it."

"You always do it," said Tanya.

"And we always let her," sighed JT.

"Is it really the top of tree if it's halfway across the ceiling on the other side?"

"Shush up!"

"Guys," I interjected, growing annoyed by their snappiness. "What's with this whole pretend friendship thing?"

Nobody spoke of it. When I brought it up again, Greg answered. He'd been in the corner and I'd forgotten he was there, having been so quiet for so long.

"Mr. and Mrs. Walker don't know about what happened. We do it to spare their feelings."

"About how you guys can't stand each other? Why did they think you were friends to begin with?"

Hayley's eyes shifted uncomfortably from JT's to Greg's.

"Because we used to be," said Greg blankly.

*Had I known about this?* I wondered.

No, I was sure this was more brand new information coming to me from the same radio source as the previous shockers.

"When we first started high school, we were all friends," said Eleanore, keeping her head down as she untangled some red tinsel. "Ms. Weiss lumped us all together with a couple of ninth graders, who were meant to show us around in our first week."

"But they picked on Wednesday and JT," said Tanya. "When the rest of us tried to stand up for them, they locked us in the unused gymnasium at the back of the school. And we got stuck there overnight."

"All night?" I muttered in incredulity.

"Felt like forever," said Greg, and he shot Tanya a look.

"It did," agreed Friday.

Wednesday cracked a smile. "At least it gave us time to bond, which was the whole point anyway."

Hayley immediately piped up. "Pssshhh! The only bonding I did that night was with my eyelids. Best night's sleep I ever had."

"Yeah, you sleep-walk," said Wednesday aggressively. "You kept trying to pick my braids for cotton. Jerk."

"Did the ninth graders get in trouble?" I asked.

All of them said yes in the same exact tone, which told me any further questions were not appreciated. I looked down at my tinsel and thought about it some more. When did they stop being friends? This Breakfast Club overnighter obviously did something, enough to eventuate into this gathering every year.

My mind was fried out. I took a deep breath and lifted my head, catching my sister's gaze. We were the odd ones out in this story... and I was sick of being the odd one out.

— • • • —

"I swear to God, if you drop me, I'll sue your jeans off!"

These words spilled out of Eleanore's mouth as she balanced precariously on my shoulders. We were already on the second storey, and she held the final decoration — the evening star — in her hands. As we ventured near the edge of the upper-landing, my tippie-toes stretching as far as they could, it felt like I was docking a gigantic structure in space. The more I aimed for the left, the harder Eleanore swayed, letting out a comical sounding 'whoa-err-urrgh' each time she did. I couldn't point her just a tad this way or that, because she would instead swing about wildly, caused by what she told me was her extreme vertigo.

"If you fall, you fall," I decided to say wickedly.

"Shut up, shut up, but aim, but shut up!"

Wednesday carelessly threw something heavy and loud into one of the boxes below. She was irritated.

"*Both of you* shut up! Conserve your energy for the harder tasks. Like when you have to use the rock-climbing equipment, to dangle the Santa legs from the chimney later."

"Oh, we can't do that any more," JT informed her. "Too many calls to the police."

Eleanore had nearly reached the tree top. For a moment she put the star in place, but then slipped out of its reach before she had time to clip it on.

"We're nearly there. I just need you to stand on your impiety tippie-toes. Stretch! Stretch longer, Cassie! Stretch your toes like Rose DeWitt Bukater!"

I gave in to her demands, and a moment later I heard the click of the little clip on the back of the star. It was done.

Unfortunately, my legs gave in at the same time. Eleanore roared like a whale as she tipped back-and-forth on my shoulders.

With one giant underwear-revealing tumble, she quite crudely barrelled over the banister, colliding with her two friends below.

———— · · · ————

Daylight came to an end quite abruptly that afternoon, the sun setting prematurely beyond the hills at four-thirty. Snow reappeared and then faded, and as Mom arrived home from a full day of Christmas shopping on her own she was greeted with the entire family sitting together in the lounge-room.

"Nobody look!" she cried as she heaved past us with many handfuls of presents in bags.

When she returned from hiding them upstairs, she came and sat between Brendan and I on the couch. Puffing from the exertion, she turned to stare at Grandma Helen, then to Aunt Rachael, Dad, and to Annie and Brendan before speaking to me.

"Cassie. Why is everybody getting along?"

"*While You Were Sleeping* is on next."

"Ooh!" she uttered, and changed her position to get comfy.

An ad for the motorcycle charity ride started. Grandma Helen boo'ed and threw her left slipper at the screen, missing entirely and hitting Tigger on the ground.

"How was everybody's day?" asked Mom.

"Well," I said. "Annie, Hayley and I visited JT's house to decorate, and Eleanore fell on Wednesday and Friday, and then they went to hospital."

"That's nice, dear. Ma, what about you?"

"Let's see," said Grandma, honestly thinking. "I got up. Sat down here. That's about it."

She paused for thought.

"Oh, I pet the dog for a while."

"That's not much of a day."

"Pigsworth would beg to differ. Anyway, try having arthritis in your toes and going up and down those stairs. I practically crossed the Desert of Paran."

"That reminds me for some reason," said Mom. "I hope you don't mind, but we all have plans Friday night, so you'll be keeping yourself company…"

Mom was thinking ahead, thank goodness, for the Walker party. I was glad to see that my parents were on the same page as me in purposely not inviting her to tag along.

"I'll be fine. I have the carollers to look forward to."

"The c… Oh, no, Ma, please don't spit on the carollers again. I thought we convinced you to aim your digressions toward more deserving folk."

"What? I love them," Grandma lied through her teeth, trying to shirk Mom's protests. "They'll be happy to be spit at. In Germany, spitting on someone is a sign that you love them. It's very true; Victor can vouch for it. The night you were conceived, Lesley, your father and I vere *drenched* in each other's saliva."

"I mean it, don't spit on any of those carollers. It's a small town. We're bound to know them. Besides, some of them will be children."

"Even better!" Grandma Helen cackled, tossing away her innocence as if it were a great act of deceit. "Ha! It would serve them right. *Noise pollution.* All they do is tour the town, knocking on people's doors, singing at the top of their lungs. Imagine if we did that in August. We'd be locked up."

"You are not spitting at the people who make up that congregation," Mom promised her. "Even if I have to put you in a straightjacket or tie you up with a blanket."

"Doesn't matter. I'd still spit."

"Hell, I'm with Rijkaard for once," Aunt Rachael piped in. "Let's hock at some holy hymners!"

Grandma Helen, per usual when it came to anything Rachael had to say, simply turned away from her coldly. It was just in time for another motorcycle ad. Angrily, she grabbed her second slipper and threw it at the TV, hitting it directly in the centre.

"They just showed this ad! Vhat is going on with the world? Ah, now this. This race is what I'll be doing next Friday, Lesley. Forget spitting at the carollers, I'll be going downtown and spitting on the bike racers as they drive past. One of them might be driving your stolen motorcycle, Ichabod. I hope so, and I'll smile and laugh and spit at it too."

A fierce chill swept through the room. Nobody spoke, and nobody moved. Even Pigsworth stopped licking and held his breath.

I think deep down, Grandma knew she'd finally crossed the line with Ichabod Gellar. His frozen-with-rage corpse, sitting next to Brendan, was somehow the scariest thing we'd ever witnessed.

"I'm going to bed. Goodnight."

The old lady had never left a room so quickly in her life.

# 15

## AND A SQUEEZE
## AND A SLIP

Hayley was so brief in her vertical appearance the next morning; her arrival home almost didn't wake me. She collapsed heavily on her bed and within minutes was snoring. I didn't bother to help her into the covers. Instead, I got dressed and went downstairs. Aunt Rachael was on the couch fast asleep, having stayed there all night again. I'd told her about everything before going to bed the previous night: how I'd thought Eleanore was going to invite me on the Zeppelin ride, but that it was simply a misunderstanding. Then I told her about how one of my best friends was rich and I'd never known. I even told her about Morgan. With a push and a prod, she'd insisted we go to the hardware store bright and early with my résumé.

Despite my enthusiasm, though, she refused to get up when I nudged her that morning. I was surprised by her demeanour — she was crabby and insufferable.

"Leave me alone…" she muttered into her pillow, and she rolled over to face the back of the couch.

Perplexed, I returned to bed and watched television on mute. A repeat of *The Prefect Family* was playing, and I turned on the teletext to follow along.

By ten-thirty, I could hear people moving about the house. Gleeful, I ventured into the hallway and greeted Mom and Dad as they were getting dressed in their bedroom.

"Do you kids fancy going to the mall?" asked Mom, rubbing moisturiser on her arms. She was in another red and green get-up, and sported giant hoop earrings with Christmas lights on them.

"Yes, but please take those off."

"Stop telling me what earrings to wear!" she scolded me lightly, and after a quick once-over in the mirror she decided on something more low-key. A pair of reindeer earrings suited instead.

Unfortunately, Dad was refusing to change out of his bulky knitted snowman sweater, with a giant stuffed carrot protruding a mile from the centre of its face.

———— • • • ————

"Christmas shopping! Christmas shopping!" squealed Brendan, sitting between Annie and I in the back-seat.

I groaned, annoyed.

"I can't wait until you're a teenager."

It was freezing outside, and in our giant jackets there was bare-ly any room to move about. I wasn't as eager as my little brother, but I was a world above Annie, who stared forlornly out of the window at the tiny piles of snow as we drove past. My sisterly wisdom told me why she was so depressed. She didn't have any friends to buy presents for. We were all she had.

"I hope you're planning on buying a present for Hayley," I said, waiting for her to turn so I could lock eyes with her. "She told me she bought something for you."

"Why?" Annie asked curiously. "We're not friends."

"Yes, you are. Sort of."

"Only through you."

"If you don't get her something, she'll feel pretty lousy."

Annie turned to think about it, but surprisingly the conversa-tion wasn't over for Brendan.

"What about me?" he asked.

"You're not getting dilly. Hayley thinks you're a freak."

"Fine. I'll poo in a box and give it to her."

"*Brendan!*" Mom and Dad yelled, disgusted.

. . .

As Aunt Rachael drifted in and out of sleep on the couch, small sounds came and went. Tigger trotted in and snacked from his bowl in the foyer. Birds chirped in a group as they flew overhead. A car drove past.

Then, a heavy thud upstairs.

Rachael remained still, eyes closed, for an entire minute before her conscience got the better of her. Struggling, she hopped off the couch and went to the staircase to gaze up.

"What was that?"

Nobody answered.

"Hello?" she called loudly.

Still nothing.

Rachael heaved herself up the stairs and onto the second landing, where she stood still for a moment to inspect everything around her. Most of the doors were left open, except for the one at the end of the hallway with a crack down the middle.

She sniffed the air. The old woman's scent was wafting about, which meant she'd walked by recently.

"Well, I tried..." she sighed to herself, turning around.

Then there was a scuttle above her and another thump, and she spotted the attic door in the ceiling, its cord swinging gently. She gasped and covered her mouth — a movement to her right startled her. She locked eyes with Helen, lying on the floor of her bedroom.

"Oh!" she exclaimed, rushing forward.

Helen grabbed onto her as she came over. With a little bit of heaving and pulling, she was lifted back onto the bed. When finally sitting upright, Helen turned to her saviour gingerly, loose strands of grey hair partly over her eyes.

"Are you alright?" Rachael panted, sitting by her side.

Helen pointed across the room. "My cane slipped. On what, I don't know. But my hip. My, my hip..." She motioned towards it, and Rachael deigned to press sensitively against her nylon skirt.

"That doesn't feel right."

"It's dislocated again. I need you to punch me there. Very hard. Don't worry, it'll pop back in."

"You're quite morbid, has anyone ever told you that?"

"Quickly, do it! Twelve collisions with twelve motorcycles makes me a professional on the matter. Right here! If you don't do it, you will have to drive me to the hospital."

"Don't tempt me, Bubbe."

"I *mean* it."

If Rachael Gellar knew one thing, it was how much she disliked Helen Kent. But she also knew that she didn't hate her enough to wish her ill, and punching anyone let alone an elderly woman was not something on her bucket list.

She sucked in her lips, then her belly, and stared deeply into the woman's bright blue eyes.

"If this doesn't work, you can't blame me."

"Hurry up!"

With one hard and determined thrust, Rachael punched her in the hip and sure enough something moved. It was the most disturbing feeling of her life. She reeled, relaxing her hand, and groaned in her own discomfort.

"I need to take a shower after that."

Helen grabbed onto her cane tightly, eyes closed as she dealt with the pain. A moment later she stood up and turned to the cringing girl, kicking one of her feet gently.

"Stop complaining. It was more painful for me."

"It *worked?*"

"Of course. I told you I've been through this before."

"Then just call me the miracle worker!"

"Thank goodness somebody was home. The others have gone out shopping for the day. Except for that girl in a coma."

"Well, I was also a girl in a coma. You're lucky I'm a light sleeper. Good thing you leave your door open all the time. You wise, wise bigot, you."

Helen huffed, and sat back down on the bed next to her.

"You are a *very* rude young woman."

"If slips and falls could break my balls…"

Rachael picked at the old woman's skirt again.

"What happened to your hip, anyway?"

"I have been hit by motorcycles twelve times in my life."

Rachael paused for thought. "Oh, I thought you were joking…

Well, I don't believe *that*."

"It's true. Twelve times. Part of me wants to get to thirteen. It's my lucky number."

"Of course thirteen is your lucky number. So… Any twins, or…?"

"I really don't understand your humour."

"Join the cults," sniggered Rachael. "You know, last time we had an argument in the family home, I believe we both stormed off. You better not forget who saved you a minute ago."

"Are you waiting for me to say thank you for saving me? Fine. I'll say it. *Thank you.* And are you referring to Annie's birthday? Why do you have to bring up that day, it was so long ago, I don't understand. I don't like to think about it."

"You think I do? You really hurt my feelings, you putz!"

"Well… maybe you did too… you *arschgeige!* The last time I checked, having an opinion wasn't a crime."

"You know what you said."

"And I stand by it!"

Helen crossed her arms and looked away to finalise the deal, but a moment later she turned back.

"However, I am not unkind. If my words hurt your feelings, I apologise. That was not my intention."

Rachael comically tossed her head to the side.

"It's the end of times…" she said slowly. "My God, I can feel it. The devil herself has fallen; it's the twelfth sign of the Apocalypse! A thank you *and* an apology in one sitting."

"You are wasting oxygen," said Grandma Helen. "Instead, why don't you tell me what it was exactly that upset you so much?"

"On what occasion? I have a filing cabinet at home…"

"Annie's birthday. Everybody seems to be labelling me this and that these days. I might as well know what I am doing wrong."

Aunt Rachael prepared herself, taking in a deep breath.

"Our cousin Ronny was chasing after the twins, because they were only two back then, and I made a remark about how it was a shame fallopian tubes come in two's. Then you said something along the lines of: 'Thank goodness neither of yours work'."

"*That* is what offended you? My girl, there are *wars* going on in the world, deaths and rapes and murders. You should thicken your skin! I still don't apologise. It was a small remark and I don't understand how it offended you so much. As I recall, you practically flipped the table we were sitting on to verbally insult my parents and ancestors. How can…?"

Rachael stood up.

"Nuts to this. I'm going. I want some take-away food. I might go to the shops. Don't slip over any more because I won't be here to help you up. And…" she cupped her hands around her mouth as she got to the doorway, and yelled: "You're *welcome!*"

With that, she quickly rushed down the staircase, just as Hayley yelled: "Shut *up!*" from her bed.

# 16

# THE FIGHT
## BEFORE CHRISTMAS

There was something about the air quality in malls that always made me feel… fatigued. Annie, Brendan and Dad had wandered off together, while I followed Mom as she ventured into a department store called: *'KAK! SPINALDI'*. I'd yet to spot any presents to buy for my friends, let alone family members, and as Mom admired a rather oddly shaped reading-lamp, I wondered out loud what I should get JT for Christmas.

"Why don't you buy him one of his mother's records?"

"Okay Mom, I love you, but that is literally the dumbest thing I've ever heard. Anyway, it can't be too expensive. I only have ten dollars to spend on him and Hayley."

"Did you send your résumé to that hardware store yet?"

"No, not yet, but I *will*," I promised. I needed to work myself up to going in there again.

"Until you get a job, you don't have many other options, do

you?" said Mom, and she called on someone to help explain to her what the object next to the reading-lamp was. It looked like a half-melted space-heater.

The man she called over was big and fat, with a thick accent and a heavy black moustache.

"That is Plat," he told her.

"Plat? What's that?"

"What's that? That's Plat."

"*Plat?*" said Mom, pronouncing clearly.

"That!" said the man, pointing at it.

"I'm sorry, I don't understand."

"Kak! Spinaldi."

"Ah, okay. Thank you," she said.

The man walked away, and she shook her head at me.

"I'm so glad my mother wasn't here for that. Oh look, this dress is half-price! And it's a *Cavraldi Empire*."

She gasped and ran her hands along the navy mermaid gown, which had a split down its side.

"I need something for the Walker dinner. What do you think?"

"Navy really brings out the German in you," I said.

She ignored my words and decided to get it anyway. I continued following her as she looked around the store, feeling light-headed the more we walked down the aisles.

"Since you're spending left, right and centre, can't you guys just *give* me some money? I mean, Brendan doesn't have to get a job for his allowance."

"He's eleven. You're old enough and this is something we've discussed before. I'm not getting into an argument with you over money. Especially when you have a girl staying in your bedroom breaking her back over the school holidays to earn some for herself. You don't hear her complaining."

"No, *you* don't hear her complaining. I most definitely do. Maybe I should start charging those tiny cellar spiders in the corners of my room. They get free board, you know."

"Don't be silly. Spiders can't pay rent."

"Well," I muttered jealously, "maybe they should…"

"This is exactly what your father and I said we didn't want for you three. You think because we have money coming out of our ears that we're going to let you run around with credit cards and buy everything and anything, and do whatever you want."

"Trust me, I am fully aware of your restrictions. I don't even have my own car because you're so obsessed with saving gas."

"Listen to yourself!" she snapped, almost causing a scene, and her cheeks went red. "When we get home, I want you to print your résumé, and then we're going to drive *straight* to the hardware store."

"Only if you can catch me!"

"Cassie, get back here!" she yelled.

I rushed out of the store and power-walked angrily through the busy plaza. The noises were loud, the music coming from every store meshing together unpleasantly. I finally sat down in an empty chair behind the nativity scene in Santa's Workshop.

Putting my sunglasses on, I began to cry.

Maybe I was being selfish. A lot of people in the world had it worse. I was privileged, I knew that, and was grateful for it. If I wanted a car, why couldn't I have one? Even thinking it, I knew how it would sound to anybody else. But in my mind it seemed such an incredibly innocent request. I was more upset, however, with the altercation we'd just had. Seeing as we were cut from the same cloth, I knew that Mom was probably crying as well.

"HO-HO-HO!" the mall Santa was upon me, mightily ringing his bell. "Merry Christmas! Have you been a good little girl?"

I crossed my legs, smiled politely, but turned away.

He rang his bell about an inch from my face.

"Have you been a *naughty* little girl?" he asked. "Perhaps you need a good *spanking!*"

Horrorstruck, I noticed the man behind the white beard was dark. I took off my sunglasses to check properly, then smacked JT's arm angrily. "You scared me half to death."

"I'm sorry, does a black Santa offend y..."

He paused in his joking, noticing my wet eyes.

"Hey, are you alright?"

"I had a fight with my mother over something," I told him.

He came to sit down next to me, and I gave him the twice over. "Why are you... What are you... Huh?"

"Holiday work," he told me.

I waited a moment before I responded, to him and to the universe. "Are you kidding me? *You* have a job? But you're rich as well..."

It sounded stupid when I said it out loud, and I couldn't tell if JT was annoyed by my words. He side-eyed me for a moment and then sniffed my clothes.

"You're starting to smell like a Saviour again."

*Are we just rich, bratty kids?* I wondered.

Which was worse: not having a job because you're rich, or getting one and working your butt off even though you don't need to? As I thought about it, I realised that not only was I rich, but I had a Child of Crux in the attic and any woes I felt were completely absurd. I was neither right nor wrong. And deep down, I knew that the only thing I wanted to do in life was to make my parents happy.

"I need to get a job," I told him.

JT pulled down his Santa beard and stared in earnest.

"My condolences. Really, it's not that bad. Sure, I get kids who pee on my lap sometimes, but it's *very* unlikely you'll get a job with that in the description. Unless you... No, there's really nowhere else that could happen. I guess *maybe* if you played Musical Chairs at a retirement village? Even that would be a stretch. Point is, nobody will go to the toilet on you, so be happy."

I wiped my nose on my sleeve.

"I'm going to apply to that hardware store a few blocks away."

JT smiled.

"You'll enjoy it. Trust me."

"Thanks."

A moment later, a very heavy woman came rushing up with a walkie-talkie in one of her hands.

"JT, there you are. Park your keister on Santa's Throne, *stat!* We don't pay you to sit around, you know."

Black Santa stood up and smoothed out his red top.

"Yes you do," he said merrily.

With that, he left.

As the Gellar-clan collected by the exiting doors an hour later, I ignored Mom and she ignored me. Annie, Brendan and Dad obviously caught on to our vibe, so on the way home they steered the conversation away from any potential sore spots. However, my conversation with Jonathan Thomas Abraham Walker III was oddly enlightening. I wasn't really that mad at my mother anymore. When we got home and parked in the open garage, I offered to help her bring in the shopping, and she accepted.

The fight was over.

# 17

# SUDENTRY LEADS THE WAY

The sun finally set, somewhere far away, although the snow was so heavy it was impossible to tell in which direction. Chloe was behind the wheel now, having swapped places with Candice six hours earlier. At last, just as she turned the full beams on, the car made a little beeping noise and an orange light appeared on the dashboard.

"I told you no miracle would befall us, you idiot!" snapped Chloe, lips parched. "This fuel gauge isn't the second cruse of oil!"

"Well, it doesn't help the situation to be so negative," said Candice, stretched out on the back seat.

"It does help, actually. I feel much better after cursing! *Now* what are we supposed to do?"

"Keep driving!"

"To where? This snow-storm has been going all day and we don't seem to be driving on any kind of roads anymore, or hitting *anything*. Do you think maybe we've driven into the desert..?"

"Remarkable!" said Candice pleasantly, thinking about it. "A blizzard in the desert! What are the odds?"

"Might as well pull over. Save fuel. Conserve energy."

"Hug one another."

Chloe sighed apprehensively.

"Yes, I suppose that too…"

She slowed down until the car was at a stand-still.

With the engine off, total silence filled the vehicle interior. When Chloe finally switched the headlights off as well, they were both surprised to discover that they weren't greeted by immediate darkness as expected. Instead, a very obvious yellow light was coming from somewhere to their right, off into the distance, through the heavy snow.

"See! Everything happens for a reason," insisted Candice. "If we hadn't stopped now, we'd never've noticed that light over there! We'd have kept driving on *that* way, instead."

She pointed out the windshield.

"What should we do?" asked Chloe.

"Go towards it, silly!" said Candice, collecting her things. "We can't just stay in the car and freeze to death. There's something over there. Grab your stuff and rug up, and we'll get going."

Chloe did as directed, too tired and stressed to argue. She put on her brown beanie, zipped up her jacket and put on her black gloves, and hopped out of the car. As her sister readied herself in the back, she took a moment to check in the trunk of the car for anything that could help them.

To her surprise, a yellow dog leapt out just as she opened it. She flew back in fright, and it stopped by her side, panting heavily.

"When… how… huh?"

She leant down. It was a Labrador, or a border-collie or something that looked like a dingo.

"Have you been locked in the trunk this entire time?"

She noticed it had a collar on, and a silver round tag reflected in the strange yellow light.

*"Sudentry,"* she read. "Hello, Sudentry. What a funny name. Can you smell your way to that place over there?"

She pointed ferociously towards the direction of the yellow light. The dog followed her gaze and, thinking she was throwing something, ran off into the blizzard.

"No, wait!"

Chloe knew, somehow, that he was never coming back.

Candice finally hopped out of the back. Chloe was not surprised to find her ballooning in size. She'd kept a mountain of clothes stashed in her back seat for occasions such as this. Now she was wearing all of them to keep warm.

"Who are you barking to?" she asked.

Chloe explained.

"A real dog?"

"Yes, Candice, a real dog."

"In our trunk?"

"Yes."

"Alive?"

"Of course it was alive."

"In there, the trunk?"

"Yes, Candice."

"A *living* dog?"

"Yes."

"In that trunk?"

"*Candice!*"

"I'm sure you were just imagining things. We've been driving for... must be a day now. We're tired, we've both urinated and defecated multiple times, slurped away at the snow when we were thirsty, and had the heating on full blast. If there'd been an actual living dog in there, it would have died hours ago."

"But it *was* alive, Candice, and it jumped out."

"A dog?"

"Yes!"

"In our trunk?"

Chloe sighed and scratched underneath her beanie.

"It ran off in the direction of that light. Let's follow it. Maybe we'll find someone who can tell us what the hell is going on."

"I'm not one to agree with phantom pooches, but alright!"

With that, the two lost sisters ventured on foot further and further into the mysterious, hellish blizzard of death.

# TUESDAY 18TH

# 18

## THE
## ASTOR

There was a sigh. There was a creak. There was a…
*Splat!*
"Ow, what the…?"

Hayley lifted her head from her pillow, after having face-planted onto something sturdy. It was a small plate with a slice of something chocolate trapped beneath a layer of cling wrap.

Across from her, I sat up in bed and wiped my eyes of sleep.

"Mom saved you some sticky-date pudding from last night. She's convinced you're not eating," I told her with a yawn.

"I'm eating too *much*," Hayley insisted, placing it gently on the floor. "Every time there's some dough left over, I gormandise. I'm going to look pregnant by the time Christmas is over. What date is it, anyway?"

"The eighteenth."

*"Is that all?"*

With that, she rolled over and fell straight to sleep.

For the rest of the morning, we all busied ourselves downstairs as the blonde guest snored away in my bedroom. Aunt Rachael was in a much better mood today, so she helped us as we went out into the front garden with Dad. He was determined to finish putting the Christmas lights up. A task usually completed by the end of the second week of December, I think he'd underestimated the size of the house compared to our old one in Salem. He'd never admit defeat, though. Rachael, Annie and I watched as he climbed the ladder we were holding and balanced his giant torso across the right-sided window that led into his ensuite.

"When I say so, throw me the first set," he told us.

With a giant heave of noise to assist me, I did as directed. He caught it, nearly losing his balance. Then he said: "Brendan!"

Quickly, a small hand shot out of the open window with a stapler gun. Dad grabbed it. Entirely focused, he spent the next ten minutes staring straight ahead as he felt around the edges of the newly-painted gutters. It was like he was walking a tight-rope, the determination in his eyes almost comical.

*Five grey elephants balancing,* my inner child sang.

Three hot chocolates and eight descents later, he placed his feet on the ground by the left side of the house and bowed.

"Thank you, thank you," he said proudly, and then wiped his red nose of snot. "Now, if one of them doesn't work, I'll use them to hang myself in that tree over there."

Rachael smacked him across the side of the head.

———— • • • ————

The silence was like nothing the Croxley sisters had experienced before. As they sat in the pink kitchen, linoleum floors worn out and grotty, Candice stirred her cup of tea. The clinking spoon sent jolts through Chloe's brain.

They were alone. For now. But around them in the hotel were a few other people, all of whom gave no explanation as to where they were. Candice was happy to take things as they came, but Chloe knew she was right to feel suspicious.

"There's not much else we can do until it stops snowing," said Candice, sensing her sister's unease. She took a sip of her tea. "It is strange, though…"

"Which part?" snapped Chloe, in a harsh mutter. "When we fell off a cliff, or when we landed on the roof of a hotel in the middle of nowhere?"

This was true, of course. During the previous night's walking escapades, the sisters spent nearly two hours on their feet, never reaching a destination. The snow was slow but steady. Not even the slightest wind accompanied it as it fell; the only noise to be heard was from their crunching feet and sniffling noses as they struggled on their way.

Then at some point, Chloe heard Candice cry out in front of her. As she went forward to see what the problem was, the ground left her feet and she found herself falling, until she very quickly smacked into something solid. She nearly broke her back in the process, jarring her elbows as she landed unexpectedly on the brown tiling. Still assisted by the very strange yellow light, the sisters helped each other as they climbed down. They fell into some snow-covered bushes and looked up at the triple-storey building.

A giant sign, half-covered by snow read: 'ASTOR'.

The yellow light was emitting from the neon sign saying 'Vacancies'. Chloe promptly thanked the Lord and rushed indoors, Candice following closely.

Inside, with the heaters blasting and the walls a grotesque fuchsia, their eyes landed upon the first human they'd seen in over a day, standing behind a wooden reception desk in front of them. A tall woman with pointy features, and mid-length blonde hair which sat underneath a white beret. She smiled at the sisters and beckoned them over.

"Hello there! Well, come in. You two must've gotten lost in the snowstorm. I'm Vonda, and this little fellow is Sudentry."

She pointed down to a little Shih Tzu with long brown fur, and two little pink bows on its head and rump, who came over to the sisters and sniffed at their wet boots.

"Did you say... *Sudentry?* We were just chasing after a dog named Sudentry, weren't we, Candice?"

"Yes! Is this the same one, Chloe?"

"No, it was a bigger dog. How... strange..."

Immediately suspicious of the circumstances, Chloe scowled. She glanced around the reception area, trying to figure things out.

"Unfortunately, the manager Mr. Pollux isn't with us any more," said Vonda, opening a giant log book in front of her. "So if you have any enquiries they'll have to go through me. And Sudentry."

Candice was equally joyous in her response, bursting forward.

"Hello, Vonda and Sudentry! I'm Candice Croxley, and this is my sister Chloe Croxley. Do you have a phone we can use?"

"Or a bathroom," muttered Chloe from behind.

Vonda cringed. "No phone service here."

"Where are we?"

"In our hotel," said Vonda.

"Which town?"

"We're just past February Seven."

Chloe stopped taking off her layers and focused her attention on the woman. "Do you mean the *date?*"

"No, that's the name of the district we're in. February Seven. It's about eighty miles from... where you're from."

"What a peculiar name for a district!" said Candice, rapt. "I once knew a drunk in Earls Court who was a paraplegic, and his name was February *Milligrams*. Of course, he legally changed it to that as an adult. I'm not sure why he bothered, because we all just called him *Milly Bad Legs* anyway."

Chloe pushed her aside. "If the phone lines are down, how are we meant to call for assistance?"

Vonda smiled nicely. Chloe noticed she had some very vibrant blue and pink bracelets on her left arm, which she jiggled as they got too close to her wrist. She came out from behind the counter, touching Chloe gently on the shoulder.

"We're at the mercy of the snow, I'm afraid. Some lovely men tend to drive past every once in a while in their snowmobile — with a little luck they might arrive soon and assist you ladies. It hasn't snowed this steady in a while."

"Yes, it's relentless. I've never seen anything like it!" said Candice, her positivity yet again irritating Chloe to no end.

Vonda quickly offered for them to join her in tea and biscuits in the parlour room. They gladly agreed, and followed her through the back office. The parlour room was small but manageable, and continued the hotel's tradition of fuchsia walls. Around a putrid lime-green linoleum table sat three other people: a tall man with a scraggly red beard, a squat woman with slicked back short hair, and a bald dwarf with big, hazel eyes, sporting a Cuban cigar in his mouth. The three of them were playing cards, and Chloe noticed that Vonda raced back to an empty seat with a row of five placed down in front of it.

"Oh, it's my turn!" she said in a tizz, and she flipped up her cards to play. "I'll just be a minute," she called to the sisters.

As the game continued in silence, Candice couldn't help but notice that the squat man was grinning at her. He placed his cigar down into a glass ash-tray and plopped his hands across his bulging stomach. He was probably in his early forties, but his nose was red and his cheeks puffy from obesity, so he looked younger.

"Karloff, do you have an ace of spades?"

"Go fish," the bearded man replied.

"Hold on a minute," said the woman with slicked-back hair. "I thought we were playing poker."

The three of them leant back, evidently tired of it. It was at this moment Vonda pointed to the sisters.

"Everybody welcome our new guests. Chloe and Candice are from… where?"

"Horn-Horn," said Candice quickly.

They let out an affirmative throat noise in understanding.

"That's just…. south of here?" said the dwarf. "West? North? I don't know where we are."

"Somewhere out in the abyss," said the bearded man. "I'm Karloff. This confused hybrid of a human is Gianna. And…"

Before Candice knew what was happening, the chubby man with dwarfism was by her side.

"I'm McGideon…" he said gently, and he grabbed her right hand to kiss it. "Are you Chloe or Candice?"

"Candice."

"Beautiful name, regardless."

Disturbed by his sleaziness, Candice hid behind her sister.

"Vonda," called Chloe. "Is there any chance we can bum a couple of rooms off you? I can't tell you how tired we are."

Vonda laughed as she collected the cards.

"There's not much else you can do in this storm. I'm just glad the electricity has lasted so long. We've got plenty of rooms. We're the only ones staying here tonight, except for Atsina in Room One. She's our permanent resident, very old, doesn't like to be disturbed. That's just off the landing. I've got a much better room for you two, anyway."

"I'd prefer my own," said Chloe with a nice big smile on her face. "I've got sleep apnea. I snore like my neck is being sliced into by a blunt chainsaw."

This was yet another well-prepared lie she gave out in times of a much-needed excuse to get away from her sister.

Vonda eventually led them upstairs. It was an old house, really, and must have had at least a dozen renovations in its time. Around the curling staircase they climbed until they reached the landing. Chloe was surprised at how decadent it was compared to the re-strained lower half. Lavish paintings, ethnic vases, a row of potted bonsai trees. A large, bejewelled chandelier shimmered above them. The sisters held in their surprise.

Finally, at the end of the hallway they reached a dead end. Vonda turned to them, with two keys in her hands, and pointed to a door on her left, and a door on her right.

"I thought I'd let you choose."

Chloe quickly grabbed the right key and entered room twenty-three. Candice took the other, just as Chloe's keys locking from the inside rattled the door.

"Goodnight," she called to her sister, who didn't respond. "Thank you, Vonda. You've been a god-send tonight!"

Vonda smiled, and headed back towards the staircase at the end of the long hallway.

"Your sister, she's… nervous."

"Chloe unfortunately lacks a sense of adventure!" said Candice with a reassuring smile. "I'm sure once she's had a long, hot shower and a decent night's sleep, she'll feel good as new."

"Alright, well, you come and see me in the morning when you're ready, and we'll see how far along they are."

"Far along?"

"I mean…" she laughed to herself, and then looked down, sud-denly noticing something missing. "Sudentry? Sudentry, Sudentry!"

She ran off to find her beloved pet.

Candice went into her bedroom, exhausted and in need of a long, hot shower of her own. The room was brightly lit, the walls painted beige. Her double bed was freshly made, and a TV sat un-plugged on a chest-of-drawers.

Suddenly, a thought struck her. Not sure how to comprehend it, she decided instead to curl up under the covers and let her mind wander freely.

———— · · · ————

The next morning, she sat with her sister downstairs in the garishly pink kitchen. Unable to believe how strong the storm was, they pestered a very perky Vonda about getting help. She was of no assistance. All she kept saying was: "We can't do anything until the storm eases up!"

"It's been going for *days!*" snapped Chloe, and she grabbed Candice's stirring hand to stop her from clinking against the sides of her cup of tea. "These nincompoops seem to be alright with it, but I'm not."

Candice checked over her shoulder. That strange man with dwarfism was reclining on a sofa in the other room, but he'd positioned himself in such a way that she fell directly into his line of sight.

"Oh, they're not all bad," she said to her sister. "You've got to look on the bright side of things."

"Oh! Alright!" said Chloe, and she stood up forcefully.

She rushed over to the closed curtains in front of them, and pulled them apart. The room was bathed in harsh daylight, which was almost blinding due to the snowfall.

"Bright enough for you, Candice?"

She came to sit back next to her sister, squinting as their eyes adjusted. She whipped out her phone again, checking for a signal. Not even one bar.

*At least you're safe,* a tiny, optimistic voice called from the back of her mind. And, Chloe had to admit, she was glad for 'The Astor'. Without it, they'd have perished overnight. Still, the people here were indeed unusual. Vonda definitely had something wrong with her. The bearded man was slightly cultish, and the girl Gianna was aggressive in nature. She cooked her bacon as if she had a vendetta against it. Who knew how long until the storm of the century would let up, or their phones would work again? On top of that, how long until…

A very strange realisation popped into Chloe's head. She went over to the window to check, and then sat back down in her seat to finish off her coffee. Her face must have drawn concern from her sister, who put her own mug down and stared, worriedly.

"What's the matter?" asked Candice.

Chloe frowned.

"If this storm has been raging for days, why hasn't the snow piled up past the window? This place should be buried by now."

Candice didn't need to ponder, having thought the same earlier.

"Something fishy's going on…" muttered Chloe.

# 19

# STUCK IN A HUT

Given we'd been in a terrible argument the day before about it, Mom decided not to accompany me to the hardware store. Aunt Rachael agreed to take me instead, which was good because she'd promised it anyway. In a much, much better place than yesterday, she was practically bouncing off the walls as we drove down Hypoallergenic Boulevard. I wasn't much better, although my state was due to nervousness.

"What's his name again? Rodney?"

"Morgan..."

"I'm going to call him Rodney," she said, pulling into the parking lot. She hopped out of the driver's seat and started walking towards the hardware store, which looked warm and inviting with the many Christmas lights glowing in the windows. When she turned to chat to me, she stopped and stared at the car. I hadn't moved yet. Slowly, she came back and made me wind down the window.

"I don't think they have drive-thru here," she remarked.

"I can't do this," I said to her quietly. I tried to control my hands from shaking any further.

"Of course you can! You're Cassie Gellar. You're a strong, independent teenager, and you don't need anybody telling you otherwise. But what you *do* need is a job, so up-and-at-them."

She grabbed my right sleeve and pulled me out.

A minute later we were through the door. The bell jingled merrily, too sharp for my liking. It drew attention to us again. Not that it mattered, as the place was almost completely empty.

"I don't see a stunningly beautiful man anywhere."

"Shush!"

All of a sudden, Morgan was upon us. He smiled brightly.

"Cassie! Hi, welcome back."

He put his hand against my left shoulder warmly. I was too in my head; I could practically feel the symbolic gears moving about as they insisted I interact in the moment.

"Hello, Rodney," said Rachael.

He hesitantly held out his hand for her to shake, and they introduced themselves. Suddenly they were talking to each other about me, and I felt like I had cotton wool shoved deep in my ear canals. Finally Aunt Rachael said: "Isn't that right, Cass?" and I backtracked in my mind, catching on to what they were talking about.

"Yes! Here!" I said, and I shoved the rolled up résumé into Morgan's crossed arms. Unprepared for the onslaught, the two pages fell to the floor. We both immediately bent over, knocking our heads together as we did. When he grabbed them to pick them up, I grabbed them to pick them up. In a horrible moment, I realised my force was so brute that it had ripped both of the pages in half.

"Oh…" we said together, unsure of how to continue.

Even Rachael looked embarrassed. "That was quite a sight to behold. Look, it's a hardware store. You've got some sticky-tape around here somewhere, right?"

Morgan pointed to the front counter, where a vibrant yellow dispenser sat by the hairy right arm of a colleague on the phone. Aunt Rachael went off to get it, momentarily leaving us alone. I was still in a state of shock. I didn't have enough senses about me to feel embarrassed yet. However, Morgan's cheeks were red enough for the both of us. Still, putting people at ease was a part of his job and I think he knew it, for he immediately changed the subject.

"I'm so glad you came. For a while there, I thought maybe I'd scared you off."

"Nope," I said.

Slowly but surely I was re-entering the world of the living. I could feel the heat of embarrassment rising in my neck, yet somehow forced it to stay there.

"I've been busy with stuff, and... Do I still have a chance here?"

"Oh, definitely," he said, guiding me towards the counter where Rachael was doing her best. "We've got a few on staff, but they're all useless. Except for trust Jose here, who's really good. You know, for a man of... limited English..."

The phone rang again. The hairy-armed man by Rachael's side answered, proceeding to converse without pronouncing any H's:

"Ah... Hola, Hogan's Horn-Horn Hardware Hut on Hypoallergenic, Jose speaking. Sí, hammers and hinges... No, you need hangers and hosepipes to handle a... Ah, that's haberdashery. This is *hardware*. Ah, a hot glue gun would be hazardous handiwork..."

He paused.

"Hello? Hello?"

With that, he hung up and shrugged at Rachael.

"Al mal tiempo, buena cara, am I right?"

"Good job, Princess," she replied.

With the résumé taped together, Morgan gladly took it and shoved it in the large pocket in front of his dark green apron. He shot me a soldier's solute and winked, and then excused himself as his name was called over the speakers. With that, Rachael helped guide me away, as if I were part-blind and needed assistance.

Well, maybe I did. That had gone terribly, I realised.

Mostly.

"Awww, Ricky was so lovely and kindly," said Rachael, as she struggled to start the engine of her car. "Just what every girl wants for Christmas."

"Rodney," I corrected her.

"Ha! *Morgan*. See, I remembered. He reminds me of Theodore Laurence. Maybe he'll go for your sister next. Do you feel good about everything, kiddo?"

I shrugged in the passenger seat. It really was too soon to tell. Or was she referring to the part about where I'd hopefully be working there soon? Either way, my mind was obsessed with that terrible interaction.

"Aunt Rachael, does it get any easier?"

"What's that?"

"Talking to guys."

"Sure it does! Once you desensitise yourself. Alcohol will help. You'll get the gist of it. And I know you don't like hearing this, but you're young. Things will change as you get older. Then one day you'll find you're my age and withering like a corpse in the desert."

I turned to face her. Such grim words tinted her positive message. I noticed, as she reversed out of our spot, that she had a hint of bitterness to her expression.

Perhaps that was her answer, then.

Maybe it *didn't* get easier.

· · ·

There wasn't much to do in the hotel during the day. Chloe and Candice found themselves more often than not partaking in a confused game of poker, or Go Fish, or Solitaire, with the other guests. It felt like hours flew by, and the smoke from McGideon's cigars filled the air and tinted it purple.

Karloff and Gianna were the only two on the ball. Eventually, Gianna snapped at Chloe for not realising it was her turn. Taken aback and feeling nauseous from the smoke, Chloe placed her cards down and went out into the front room. There, she pressed against the large square window of the front door, and squinted out at the ever-brightened snowy landscape beyond.

*Where are we?* she thought to herself hopelessly.

"I'm sorry if I offended you."

The voice behind her startled her once more. Chloe turned and saw Gianna by the empty front desk. Her hair was newly gelled back, and her giant brown eyes watched intently.

"Don't worry about it," said Chloe, and she continued to gaze out the brightened window.

"I need to control my temper. My life is very stressful, but I shouldn't take it out on you. Does your husband ever get mad?"

Chloe surmounted it to be a wafer-thin attempt at sussing out her marital status, so she lied. "No, but he would love it here."

Gianna hid her disappointment well, and laughed.

"When the cat's away, the mouse will play."

Chloe ignored her words. "Why are you so stressed?"

Gianna fiddled with the bell on the edge of the desk. She scrunched up her features and shrugged.

"Try living here indefinitely, and see how you feel. Sometimes I think we'll be stuck here forever…"

She came over to Chloe's side, and squinted the closer she got to the window.

"It's easier to wrap your head around when it gets dark."

"How long have you been here for?"

"A very long time."

Chloe felt a sense of unease, a slowly shifting force which settled heavily in her chest.

"This snow's never going to end, is it?"

Gianna met her eye, and shook her head. "No."

Disturbed, Chloe could do nothing more as a tight fear wrapped around her throat. A moment later, Candice ventured from the parlour room. Looking just as ill from the smoke, she covered her eyes from the outside glare.

"Sister, it's your turn."

Chloe suddenly snapped.

"*I'm not playing your stupid deformed card game, Candice! I'm getting a little bit fed up with these living arrangements! I don't know why we can't get a straight answer from anyone, I don't know what this snow deal is, or where that dog Sudentry disappeared to, or why your Christmas Tree went bananas! All I know is, if this blizzard doesn't let up by tomorrow morning, I'm walking!*"

"Don't be stupid, you'll die out there," said Candice and Gianna at the same time. "Jinx!" they said to each other, pointing, and then they said it again: "Jinx!"

"Dying out there is better than being locked in here forever. I don't like it, Candice. There's something not right about this place. And the people, who…" she noticed Gianna by her side… "bless their unusual hearts… are not helpful in the slightest. I'm just about ready to torch the place! At least then people from far away will see it burning and come to our rescue."

Candice rubbed her shoulders to calm her down, and as she did this she failed to notice Gianna backing slowly out of the room and into the parlour. Seeing her sneak in, the other guests at the table stopped their confused card game and waited until she turned around to face them. Perplexed, they watched as she shut the door, and then, putting an index finger to her mouth, she urged them to stay quiet. Gently, she put her hands on the table and addressed them all equally.

"I think Pollux brought us the wrong ones again," she said.

Karloff tossed his cards to the table angrily.

"We just washed the last one off the rugs."

"Is the basement locked?"

"Yes. They can't get in."

"We'd better tell someone, then," said McGideon, wheezing.

"But Pollux has gone. Nora says he'll be dead by now."

"No, someone else."

"Who, Vonda?"

"*No.* Atsina in Room One."

# 20
## ELEANORE'S PROPOSITION

I was jabbed in the arm while I slept. Which was really good timing, because I'd been dreaming about snowboarding on a giant version of Ernest Borgnine's face. Just as the gap in his teeth opened up to swallow me whole, I awoke to see Hayley standing over me. She looked as glum as she usually did this time of day.

"You forgot to pick me up."

Groggily, I wiped my eyes and tried to remember what year it was. "Huh?"

"You told me last night that you'd pick me up after work."

It all came back to me, and I sat up in surprise. "Oh gosh, Hayley! I'm so sorry. I totally spaced. How did you get home?"

"I hitchhiked."

"You... Really?"

"Hell, no! Are you crazy? This isn't the thirties. I called Jonathan. He says you owe him lunch."

"I'll give him a call and apologise," I said, flapping my right arm against the bedside table to feel for my phone.

"Not now, he's gone back to bed. Hey, have you seen my pink underwear? I swear I left it on the bed for when I came home."

"Maybe Brendan stole it," I joked, but she didn't laugh. Taking it as a sign of distress, I asked what I already knew: "How was work?"

"I want to die," she said, and she stripped to her bare essentials and hopped under the covers. "Remember when life was simpler? We'd get up at seven-thirty, go to school and be home by three-thirty. Those were the days. I guess it's true what they say. You don't know what you've got until it's gone."

"Yeah, but we go back in like two weeks."

"And I'll appreciate every minute."

"What are you gonna do with all the money you're saving?"

"A few bondage things for the bedroom. Nothing too kinky, though. Jonathan likes it vanilla. Besides, he has sensitive skin."

I had a funny feeling she was being sarcastic.

"You're not saving up for anything else, like a house?"

It seemed Hayley found this rather an absurd thing to enquire about, and she turned to face me, head resting on one arm.

"I mean, I know I'm the ripe old age of sixteen, but do I look like I'm going to own a house in the next ten years?"

"You could. See where things go."

Especially peeved for some reason, she scrunched her nose up and said: "I'm not making a million dollars an hour."

"Never mind, sorry I asked."

"No, I get it."

"Get what?"

Hayley stared me down, trying to understand me from a simple look. When it seemed she couldn't, she positioned herself more comfortably.

"You and I lead very different lives. I'm literally squatting with your family because I have nowhere else to go."

I kept silent, unsure of how to respond.

"You wake up every day in your mansion, with your family. You don't have to worry about that sort of stuff. You don't even need to get a job, not really, because life is set out for you so perfectly. And I'm not bitter about that, I'm really not, but you... You see things from a safe distance. Look at those people, so poor and gross, oh well, I'm in the mood for Belgian waffles."

"I know you're poor!" I stupidly tried to defend myself.

"Yeah, but you exist in this tiny little world. Free of any real qualms, and you don't even see three feet in front of you."

"That's not true. I've got qualms. You have no idea how many qualms I have…"

"Can't be that many. You don't see what other people around you are going through. You just do what's best for you."

"Why are you attacking me?" I sat up in bed.

"Because you're defending yourself," she sat up, too.

"Because *you* keep telling me I'm selfish."

*"You forgot to pick me up this morning!"* her voice rose higher than mine. "What was your excuse? You *forgot?* Oh, I probably don't have a clue what you're going through, it must have been pretty big! So many qualms! Qualm this, qualm that. To be rich and have so many qualms! In your super luxurious life there must be *so* many stressful things to distract you from your one responsibility this week."

"I'm not comfortable having you in my bedroom."

"Well, too damn bad. You made a *commitment* for the holidays. I'm not going anywhere. Add that to your list of qualms."

Hayley turned over in her covers and ignored me. But that was it. I was out of there. I wasn't going to step one foot in my bedroom for the rest of the day.

———— · · · ————

*Rattattattatt!*

The knock at the door was so terse and sharp, it almost went unheard. Brendan, still in his bed-wear, answered and let out a shrill cry of alarm. By the time Annie and I raced from the living room to see what was happening, Eleanore Parker was already in the middle of the foyer. Taking off her purple gloves, she gazed around in distaste. Sporting a giant neck-brace after her fall at the Walker mansion, she'd managed to wrap a gigantic pink scarf with fluffy baubles around it, masking it almost perfectly. Although now she looked like she had the neck of a giraffe.

"Your little brother should be muzzled," she said quietly.

"Can I help you?" I asked, bored of her face.

"No, you may not. I am not here to see you. But thank you for asking how I am, Cassie! That was very sweet of you. Especially since I know how concerned you are over my well-being, after you carelessly threw me over the edge of that bannister the other day."

"Well, thanks for putting my mind at ease!" I said brightly, equalling her pretend jest. "If you're not here to see me, then who are you here to see? *Annie?*"

"Yes, actually."

"What?" said Annie, hiding behind me.

"Come."

Brendan snorted, easily amused.

"I've come to see Annie!" she let out a tired sigh. "May we converse in your dining room?"

Annie and Brendan looked up at me, as I was clearly the leading member of the household. I promptly waved my arm to the right in an exaggerated gesture, asking them to lead the way. Down the hallway we went, into the dining room. Eleanore took the head of the table and, as I switched on the lights above us, I was surprised to see that close up she had her face caked in make-up. Perhaps her fall had caused some bruising. Much like my face the previous week. I pitied her in the moment and decided not to bring it up.

"So," she said, settling into her seat. "I come with a proposition…" She noticed that not only was Annie sitting down next to her, but I was as well. And Brendan sat on the other end. She rolled her eyes, choosing not to stink up more of a fuss, and went on. She pulled some papers from inside her puffer jacket and handed them to Annie. "I'm in a dilemma right now. If my fall had been any more serious, I'd still be in hospital and probably would be until after Christmas. Luckily, Wednesday and Friday took the brunt of the collision for me. As such good friends should. While my injury is mercifully just a strain, Friday broke her elbow, and Wednesday… Well, Wednesday won't tell me about her injuries. I'm not sure why. Even though they're not in hospital anymore, their doctors have insisted they take it easy over Christmas."

"Why are you telling us this?" asked Annie, curious.

"I'm getting to it. Since they're out for the jolly season, this leaves me up a certain creek without a certain propulsion tool. I have one spare ticket to the Zeppelin ride in two days time. I must not go alone, you understand. Socially, it would be suicide. Like hell I'd let myself stand alone in a cabin with the cast of *The Prefect Family*, looking like a friendless loser. It's just not going to happen. In any parallel universe. Ever."

"Naturally, it's just the worst!" I agreed sarcastically.

"So wait," said Annie, frowning. "I'm not sure I understand. Do… you… want me as your backup, in case somebody else can't go with you? I'm your last choice?"

"No," laughed Eleanore, and she slid a piece of paper across the table to me. "*Cassie* is my last choice. If all else fails, Cassie, I want you to agree to go with me."

Flabbergasted, I looked down at the paper she'd sent my way. Some sort of a legal agreement to sign. It was literally headlined: '*Backup Concierge*'.

"And me?" asked Annie.

Eleanore rolled her eyes, which must have been a nervous tick since she did it so often. Her lips puckered, and I could tell that this was extremely hard for her to say. "No, dearest Anne. I want you to go with me."

"As a backup?"

"*No.* I want you to go with me! *Please will you go with me!* I don't know any more English sentences that can explain this to you! There's nobody else to ask, and Daddy has been pressuring me for weeks."

"To take *me?*" Annie squinted. "Is anybody else at this table having trouble comprehending what's going on?"

"No, I understand perfectly," said Brendan. "We've slipped into *The Twilight Zone.*"

Eleanore feigned amusement, and then handed Annie one of those same legal agreements. "Here's the thing. Number one, you're new to the school. Relatively. Number two, you're head of the Science Lab, an extra-curricular activity. You're also one of the smartest students in the school. Look at this as a business opportunity. For the both of us. And Daddy. I get the benefits of being seen on television with an elite member of the student body. Daddy gets on the good side of the school board at last. Horn-Horn High-High appears on television as if it doesn't have the same social limitations most low-brow public schools are known for. You get to represent your town, yourself, your intelligence, all the while hanging out with rich socialites and television producers. It's like winning a Golden Ticket."

"I see," said Annie, looking down. "So it's not because you like me and want to be friends with me, it's because I'm… a dork?"

Eleanore stared on doubtfully, looking gravely upon this outlook with trepidation. "Does that offend you?"

"Not in the slightest, I take it as a great compliment! Yes, I will go with you on the Zeppelin ride, Eleanore. Thank you for asking me. Now, where do I sign?"

Five minutes later, Eleanore was rushing out the door. As if her posture wasn't grand enough in general, her neck-brace exacerbated the situation. It also made her look even taller. Papers signed, she battled the chilly winds and strode across our lawn and out of sight. As we closed the front door behind us, Aunt Rachael came in from another room and asked what was going on.

"Oh, nothing!" said Annie. "I've just been cordially invited to attend a school function based on merits, not on looks. Excuse me while I rub it in."

"You only said yes because Thomas Noel is going to be there," I snapped jealously.

"That too!"

Aunt Rachael smirked.

"You're not talking about the Zeppelin ride, are you? I thought they cancelled it because of the strong winds coming."

Annie and I gasped deeply, and rushed to the family computer in the parlour room. The only decoration of the twentieth century, it looked odd in the corner amongst the mahogany sideboard and the chiffonier with the detailed and spotted mirror. Checking the internet, there were indeed rumours that it was going to be cancelled. But, as somebody reported, there was a lot of money going into this fundraiser. If the motorcycle race downtown was still happening, so was the Zeppelin ride.

"Thank the good Lord Jesus," said Annie.

"Or *HaShem*," insisted Rachael.

# 21
## BLACK & WHITE

As we sat eating lunch together quietly, I found myself feeling increasingly unwell. I knew what it was. It was a sort of fatigue from being inside for too long. Given the state of the weather, I was in no place to venture outside. Grandma Helen, who'd made herself extremely scarce of late, insisted that in her day she would walk five miles to and from school regardless of the weather.

"Good for you, Grandma," said Brendan. "I'm sure when I'm your age I'll be cussing at my grandkids for teleporting everywhere. When *in my day, we had to drive a car.*" He put on a mocking voice at the end, and we all laughed.

To our surprise, Helen pointed at him and scowled.

"Don't make me use my danger finger," she said.

That was enough to silence us, for we'd heard many stories about her danger finger, and the terrifying powers it possessed.

As if the universe was seeking retribution for his disrespect, the phone rang while we were clearing our plates. Not thinking much of it, Grandma Helen answered. Grinning as she spoke, all I heard clearly was: 'Play-date' and 'two in the afternoon'. When she hung up, she came to join us on the couch.

Brendan had picked which movie to watch, something called *'This Boy's Life'*. Just as she settled into her place by my side, Helen turned to Brendan and said:

"My dear boy, I have some wonderful news. Your friend Aron Hasmutt just called, and invited you to go over and play this afternoon. I knew how delighted you'd be at the news, but saw how deeply involved you were in your TV program, so I didn't want to bother you. Therefore, I agreed for you."

Brendan scowled suspiciously.

"Alright… When is it?"

"Today at two," she said, stretching her legs. "I'll drive."

"No!"

"Oh, but I must. Given your parents have gone out for the day, I am your legal guardian and there is simply no other way. Plus, you mess with the bull, you get the horns."

She cackled to herself merrily, until she checked the description of the movie on the television.

"Goodness, no, we're not watching this."

———— • • • ————

Naturally, there was little talk as Helen drove Brendan downtown at two o'clock. The snow made it difficult to drive on the roads, so the trip took twice as long as usual.

"What's this boy like?" she asked, breaking the silence.

"Fat."

Grandma Helen tapped the steering wheel, almost as if she suffered from a nervous tick.

"Really?"

"Yes, really. He's fat."

"I'm sure he has other qualities."

"He got a tattoo of a fishhook because his father used to take him fishing when he was little."

"How old is this boy?"

"My age."

"And he has a tattoo? I don't think much of his parents. Alright, why are you two friends?"

"Because we both like *Mighty Morphin Power Rangers.*"

"Is that a thing?"

"Yes. Oh! And *Tiro the Barber-Librarian!*"

"Sounding much better than just 'he's fat'. You know, your father is fat. You mustn't make fun of people who are fat. Have you ever seen the movie *'Marty'?*"

"No."

"You should. Open your eyes a little. See people for what they're worth, not how they look. We're here."

Helen stopped the car outside a very large double storey house. Wooden, painted a state blue which would look more pleasant during the warmer months. A row of hedges lined the veranda. Hunched over on the front porch, attending to a broken step, was Mrs. Hasmutt. Recognising her right away, Brendan undid his seatbelt and opened the door to get out.

"Wait," said Grandma Helen.

She had her hand against his chest, urging him to stay still. Staring like a hawk at the woman, it wasn't until Brendan asked if he could go that she reached for the town map in between the seats.

"420 Rose Boulevard..." she checked the map, then the note she'd written after speaking to Aron on the phone. "This is it. Who's that?"

"That's his mother. Can I *go?*"

Without saying another word, she let him leave. He ran up the broken steps, speaking briefly to the black woman who was in her late-thirties, and then went inside.

Grandma Helen waited a moment before driving off.

———— • • • ————

As late afternoon came, I was feeling listless and more sickly than ever. Annie was visiting Eleanore's house to go over Friday night plans. Aunt Rachael was out grocery shopping for Audrey Mercy, who was too pregnant to do it herself. With Mom and Dad out for the day, that left me alone in the house for the first time in ages. Well, besides from Hayley, but I was choosing to ignore her existence as she slept upstairs.

Soon enough, when I'd exhausted Pigsworth's and Tigger's concentration, I stood by the banister leading up to the second landing and let out a gigantic sigh. Finally, desperate, I decided that I would just have to spend time with the one person in this house who probably needed it the most.

"Zag?" I called, popping my head into the attic.

He promptly materialised into view, a sight which I would never get used to, as it looked like a ghostly mist from another dimension seeping into view. He sat there on a beam opposite his clay head, dressed in a miniature Santa outfit.

Beaming his buck-toothed smile, he declared: "Merry Christmas!" and a parade of confetti shot out of thin air, covering me.

"It's only the nineteenth," I told him.

Zag seemed perturbed by this. He looked back at his clay head. "Alright, well then... See you later..."

He looked like he was about to dive back in, so I grabbed his tiny right wrist to stop him.

"Wait. Do you... I mean, should we hang out for a while? Nobody else is home so you could... come downstairs, if you want? Like old times."

He tiptoed as he did, treating it like sacred ground. Only a few weeks ago he was trotting around barefoot like he owned the place. Now he was a hidden force above. This was his free time to venture out of his cage, like a dog in a kennel while its family is away on holiday. Nothing had changed, of course, in terms of the layout of the house. However, he did marvel at the size of the Christmas tree in the corner by the piano. I turned on its lights, and he stared up at it in awe.

"Did you know these originated in sixteenth century Germany? I guess you could say, because of your mother's side of the family, you're more connected to this tradition than most others!"

"I did not know that, no," I said, and I thought of something. "How long since you ate?"

"Not long," he said without thought. He leaned in and sniffed some of the branches. "It's *plastic.*"

I grabbed a wrapped bagel from the kitchen bench, sliced it in half, and put the two pieces in the toaster.

"Brendan is allergic to pine needles, so we can't have a real one. Plus, Mom is a bit of a nature advocate, so she doesn't like to support cutting down real trees. She says it serves no lasting purpose and is unnecessary."

"Your mother is right," said Zag sternly, thinking about it. "She must be related to Martin Luther, another forward thinker, who some believe was the originator of putting lights in the tree. Of course, they were candles back then."

"Where are you learning this stuff from?" I asked.

I was curious as to why he was so profoundly knowledgeable all of a sudden. Was it down to the boredom of being left alone? Surely he had other things to spend his time learning about.

"Santa told me," he said.

The toaster popped just as I laughed. I buttered the bagel and then spread on some peanut butter and jam.

"Santa, hey?"

I handed him a slice and we ate together on the couch. He hoovered it up before I'd even taken two bites. Still, he managed to speak through stuffed cheeks.

"I've asked him a few things here and there. He's smart."

"Who is this?" I asked, confused.

"Santa, the guy you were telling me about. He comes to me when I want to know things."

"Not the... It's not the *real* Santa, is it?" I asked.

Maybe it was. My inner child dared to hope.

"Yes, the real Santa! Who else would it be? He knows a *lot* about Christmas. And motorcycles. He's a funny guy. I'll introduce you to him if you want."

I suddenly became afraid. Not for my life, of course. What I was afraid of was actually meeting the real Santa. I didn't doubt Zag any more, because he came from another world and dealt with magic on a daily basis. I didn't know half of what the universe had to offer, and I was fine with that. But the very idea of him conversing with the real Santa Claus made me nervous, as if he were a television star on a Zeppelin ride.

"No thanks, I'm good," I told him.

"Well, any time," he said.

Ten minutes later we were out in the back garden, hidden from potential snooping neighbours between the back oak trees and Mom's frozen garden bed. It had snowed overnight a little. There wasn't much, but we gathered some up and had a snowball fight. I managed to get Zag more than he hit me, and for a few moments I felt like I was playing with a real human child. His cheeks were rosy in the cold, and although he was only wearing light clothing, the rest of his skin looked pale and frozen. When he finally landed a snowball square in my face, I turned and remained for a moment. It'd hurt more than I'd expected it to, and I realised that my bruises from last week weren't quite healed. Pretending I was fine, I swung around and hurled another snowball square at his face. It hit him with brute force, and he fell backwards, cracking his skull against some rocks on the edge of the garden bed.

"Zag!" I cried, and I rushed over.

He wasn't moving, and as I lifted him up his head went limp. A moment later he regained consciousness and smiled up at me: "What's the matter?"

"You hit your head," I said, checking the back for blood. "Are you alright? I'm so sorry, it was my fault, I threw a snowball too hard, I shouldn't have…"

Zag wriggled out of my arms and stood up, brushing his backside of snow. "Don't worry about me. You can't hurt me."

I stood up as well, relieved but my pride wounded.

"That's reassuring. I didn't mean the snowball hurt you, Zag. You hit your head on those rocks."

"Oh," he said, and he rubbed the back of his skull. "That's okay. It still can't hurt me."

"You're not invincible," I muttered.

"Of course I am. You can't kill me. Nobody can."

With this new information, I shuffled on my feet and imagined cutting off his head with the pruning sheers from the shed.

"I don't believe it," I said.

"Okay," he laughed. "Didn't you read up on us? Everybody knows you can't kill a Child of Crux."

"I didn't know that… So, what happens if your body gets mutilated, or something?"

"Then I live forever as multiple body-parts. I'll try and piece them back together, but I won't be dead."

"You'll be like Frankenstein?"

"I don't know who that is. And if I get caught in a nuclear blast, the grains of my atoms will still exist and I won't die. I'll eventually latch onto something else and make that my body."

"Zag, this is horrible news. Will you ever die?"

"Oh yes, don't worry, Cassie. I'll die from old age. Whatever form I'll be in. *But you cannot kill a Child of Crux.*"

I was quite haunted by this idea, however it also made me feel a strange sense of relief. I didn't have to worry about him in the same way anymore. Mind at ease, I let out a short giggle and picked up another snowball. I hurled it at his face again.

"Ow! I can still feel pain, you know."

"Sorry."

In perfect timing, Pigsworth bounded out of the doggy-door and greeted us with a wag of his tail, and Zag set about chasing around with him and throwing a stick. I felt a pang of sadness as I watched them play. Running across the back garden to-and-fro, Zag squealing with laughter as he hid behind a tree and was then chased by our border-collie back to the side gate. In an hour he'd be back in his clay head, hibernating until Christmas was over.

"Zag, are you sure you don't have *any* family left?" I asked him again, double checking.

"Not that I know of."

I shrugged. "Okay. Just wondering."

I was disappointed by his answer. If he knew of some far off relatives, maybe he wouldn't be considered a cursed Child of Crux any more. Still, these were matters I'm sure the higher authorities had thought of long before I'd come up with them. The Heads of the Universe, or whatever they were called. My mind let it go, and I wondered instead if there was any way we could keep him downstairs for longer. Without wishes, I realised, this was absolutely impossible. Especially given the house was filled with guests.

— · · · —

Grandma Helen spent an hour driving around. She went to the mall, bought a few more presents for people, went to the hardware store, and even bumped into Mom & Dad as they sat together on a mini-date at a café for afternoon tea. Still, she was concerned about something. When two hours had passed, she drove back to the Hasmutt house on Rose Boulevard, and knocked on the front door. Shivering in her light layers, she was eventually greeted by the same black woman who'd been on the doorstep earlier. She was tall, with long straight hair, and was dressed in a blue top almost the same colour as the house.

"Are you Brendan's grandmother?" she asked.

Helen smiled, although put on. "Is he ready?"

A moment later Brendan came out of the front door, still in mid-conversation with an overly peppy boy about twice his height. Mrs. Hasmutt waved goodbye and dragged Aron back into the house, and Brendan, high on life, dumped his chattering onto his grandmother instead. Something about Tiro's amazing abilities. It wasn't until halfway home that he realised she wasn't talking at all, and finally he simmered down.

"Gee, Grandma, are you alright?"

"I'm fine."

"Then why aren't you talking?"

"Sometimes it's best not to talk."

The next few minutes dragged by. He wondered if he'd done something to offend her. As if knowing he felt this way, she finally hinted at what was on her mind.

"You didn't tell me Aron was..."

Thinking nothing of it, Brendan laughed for a moment.

"Grandma, are you saying what I think you're saying?"

Helen didn't answer him, but Brendan could see it in her now: a burden festering beneath her bright blue eyes. All those stories he'd overheard growing up, those misgivings and prejudices Helen had been accused of, that he'd never seen in her.

"He's my friend."

Grandma Helen looked like she was busting to say something, and as she scrunched up her mouth, she twisted her grip on the steering wheel.

Finally, she muttered: "It doesn't matter..."

# 22
## ROOM
## ONE

They'd had a terrible, lurking and sinister feeling all day. The snow was finally thinning in parts, and as the sun set somewhere out of sight in the hazy distance, Chloe and Candice sat by the bay windows in the dining hall and thought about the spot of bother they were in.

All day, the other occupants had dodged their questions, slinking out of conversations. Was it a good thing, or was it a bad thing? They'd isolated themselves, most likely after Chloe let loose earlier that day. Perhaps she'd offended them, or maybe they were afraid of her now, looking at her like a crazy person.

"No, that's not it," said Candice surely, frowning as she looked down at her fiftieth cup of tea for the day. "It's almost as if they're up to something."

Upon hearing these words, Chloe checked behind her in case one of them was slowly creeping up on them. Karloff was also on her radar after vanishing from the hotel for up to an hour around midday, and returning with a bloodied arm. As McGideon, the man with dwarfism, set to fixing it in the kitchen, Chloe and Candice overheard them talking about 'biting the hand that feeds you'. Disturbed at the notion, they'd not pried any further about it. But even Vonda, who had scarcely been seen since the previous night, seemed more on-edge than usual. When Candice caught her cleaning some of the rooms and decided to start a light conversation with her, Vonda responded with one word answers. Even her little dog Sudentry stayed away.

"I don't know how much longer I can stay here, Candice, I really don't," said Chloe, choosing to fixate on her own cup of tea before her. Her eyes were twitching like mad. "If things get stranger, let's just grab our stuff and make a run for it. I've never heard of a blizzard in this part of the world lasting for more than a few days, so the odds are we'll wind up somewhere else."

The sun finally disappeared at long last, and soon the lights flickered on automatically and the sisters were met with their slightly distorted reflections in the darkened window-panes.

Then, the lights went out. Somewhere nearby they heard a low-hum. A surge of some type. With the snow falling steadily again outside, the darkness surrounding them was pitch black. Chloe felt around and found Candice's hand, and the two remained frozen in their seats, ears strained. Behind them, the slightest of sounds. Soon they became aware of a presence next to them, one which had not been there before.

A harsh and succinct scraping noise followed by a bright light flicked into existence by Candice's left cheek, and the two of them flinched as the match lit the candle before them. Held in a china saucer, a face emerged through the darkness. Vonda was in front of them, and in the candlelight she looked from one sister to the other.

"Follow me," she said in a whisper.

This was it. This was the time to run. But with no light to aid them in their escape, they were at the mercy of such darkness. In what little light the candle offered, the sisters could see now that the other guests were already in the room, crowded near the door that led into the dining room. With heavy footsteps, groaning pine floorboards, the brushing of clothes against door-frames, Vonda led the crowd into the front reception area. When everybody had come through, she nudged to the staircase leading above.

*There's the door,* Chloe tried to catch Candice's eye and speak volumes with it. *The front door. We can make a break for it. Candice. Look at me. Look!*

Her sister was drawn to the candlelight like a moth, and she followed Vonda up the creaking stairs, the three guests shrouding her and blocking her from Chloe's view. She could do nothing but follow.

At the top of the landing, Vonda fumbled in her side-pocket for a set of heavy keys. She checked them with her free hand, and went to the nearest door. *Room One.* The door was black. Vonda unlocked it and pushed it open, letting out a hideously loud groan which was quite shrill in the silence. The darkness beyond was almost indistinguishable from the dark wood of the door.

Chloe watched in concern as Candice took the lead, hypnotised by curiosity. Vonda followed, then Karloff, McGideon, and last but not least, Gianna. She held out her hand for Chloe. Believing it to be a sign of kindness, Chloe trustingly took it, and followed them into the darkened room.

Now that she was in there, she realised that it was just like all the other rooms, only more dated. Furniture from a very long time ago was decorating every inch of space. With maroon curtains pulled over the windows, and a small single bed in the corner. As the candlelight flickered for a moment from a ghostly presence, Chloe's eyes noticed a black dressing-gown hanging on the back of the closet door. Who's room was this? Before she had a moment more to think, she realised in horror that the dressing-gown was in fact a person, and it moved away from the door. Chloe cried out. A pale white face appeared in the middle of the frame, and as Vonda moved closer, more details emerged. It was an old woman, wrinkled beyond her years, with a strange hooked nose. She had no teeth, for her lips were sucked in, and her eyes were pale blue and sunken greatly into her skull.

"Why are you here?" the woman said in a high, dry voice.

Vonda looked to the others, and then at Candice and Chloe. She cleared her throat to speak.

"We're so sorry for bothering you this late, Atsina. The thing is, we had another... you know... a little while ago, and... Well, these two aren't quite... You know."

The old woman looked at Chloe and her brow crinkled. Was she angry, or simply pensive?

"It's not Christmas Day yet."

"No, not for nearly a week," said Vonda. "Atsina, these two sisters wish to leave. Given it's Christmastime, I was hoping…"

"Wait downstairs for ten minutes, until you see the lights coming. Then go outside with your belongings. Gentry and Uriah will follow."

The others froze, unable to speak. A gentle crackling from the candle was all that could be heard, until Vonda quickly thanked the old woman, and ushered for them to leave the room. Gianna was the first, and Chloe followed, then the rest. As they gathered in the hallway, Chloe shaking, Vonda waited until she'd closed the door and locked it, then the lot of them snuck down the stairway for the reception area below. Vonda placed the china bowl with the candle atop the tall waiting desk, and rushed into another room. She returned a moment later with two giant fur coats, and handed one each to Chloe and Candice.

"Put these on and grab what you came with. Quickly, you've only got ten minutes."

She ordered them back upstairs. The sisters hurried in silence down the long hallway and into their rooms, where they fumbled around in the dark searching for whatever they could find. After a few minutes, the most they could bear out of fear, they scrambled back down the hallway and downstairs again. With their bundles of clothes in trembling hands, they noticed that Vonda was by the front door. It was wide open and beyond it they could see the falling snow.

A tiny creak sounded from behind them, and Candice was the first to spot the three guests. Karloff, Gianna and McGideon, pale and eyes wide, were cowering by the parlour door. Once spotted, they sank back into the darkness.

Chloe need only share a glance with her sister. Without another moment to lose, they barged through the open door and stood out on the decking. Vonda, using her spare hand to protect her candle-light from the winds, gazed off into the distance.

"Thank you for staying," she said.

With that, she turned and walked back inside, locking the door behind her.

The candle did something quite strange, then. The sisters watched it through the window, lighting only Vonda's emotionless face, and it gradually faded and faded until they realised it wasn't a light coming from inside anymore. It was a reflection of a light coming from behind them, through the snow.

They turned, and to their surprise the glowing orange ball of light came with a distant sound. Soon, the sound roared and the light broke through the snow, and amongst the dramatic furls of ice sheets and sleet they saw at last their means of transport. A giant orange snowmobile, with an enclosed cabin, and giant headlights atop. As it bounded towards the hotel, the sisters thought to wave at first. However, they were shaken and wary after the disturbing events that had transpired. And it was coming right for them.

# 23
## CHIGGER BITES

I woke naturally. Lifting my head, I spotted Hayley already in her bed, snoring gently. So we were still fighting then. Fine by me.

I was surprised to find Annie's bedroom door already opened for the day. Sometimes she was weird like that. It was almost like a statement, as if she wanted to say: Look at me, my door is wide and I have more of a life than you. Also, smell my scented moisturisers.

Downstairs, Mom informed me that my sister was, yet again, at Eleanore's discussing the next night's journey.

"Are you really okay with her riding in that Zeppelin?" I asked, watching as she made Brendan some breakfast. "I heard it's going to be really windy tomorrow night. A little dangerous, don't you think? Also… dare I mention the H word?"

"Horatio Spafford's family died on a steamship, not an airship," called my brother from the couch.

"I meant the Hindenburg."

"Hmmm, I think I know what's going on here," said Mom.

"What?"

A smirk was spreading across her face. "Do I detect a hint of sibling jealousy?"

I scoffed at the idea. "Don't be ridiculous! Even though it's statistically proven that celebrities do more drugs than any other people on the planet."

"What are you going to do with your day?" Mom asked me as she heaped the plate of baked beans on toast onto Brendan's lap.

"Wait to hear from the hardware store, I guess."

"Any homework?"

"We didn't get any for the holidays."

"So you really don't have anything else to do with your day?" she asked me sympathetically.

I shook my head sadly. Mom grabbed a bowl from the fridge.

"Good. In that case, you can take this over to the Tanner house. Shelby and I are taking a collection of Christmas-themed custards tomorrow night to the dinner party, but we're mixing them together in a sort of... Well... It's less mushy than it sounds. Thank you," she finished in a sing-song voice.

Disgruntled, I gave in. I was usually on the ball with my mother's clever rouses to get me to do things. As I aged, she evolved. So, twenty minutes later I left the warmth of the house and battled the raging winds and sleet through my front garden, paranoid of having one of the giant oaks fall on me. I jogged past the Parkers' closed front gate, and down the Tanner driveway until I reached the front door. I rang the doorbell, heard their quaint welcome, and a moment later the heavy door opened and two hands yanked me inside.

"Chigger bites!"

It was Shelby Tanner, Tanya's equally petite blonde mother of around fifty years of age. She shut the door behind me and locked it.

"Do you have chigger bites?" she asked me, taking the giant chilled bowl.

"I don't even know what sound you're making."

"Now, you mustn't confuse them with jiggers!" she said.

She unfurled me from my scarf and unzipped my jacket, hanging them on the coat-rack by the nearest window.

"You look healthy, though, so I guess you have neither. Wonderful to know. I've been itchy all morning. Robert says it's the lack of moisture in the air from winter, but I suspect chiggers!"

It was lovely and warm in here. Last time I'd stepped foot in this house, I'd showered the room with a hose after a fire broke out. Now it had new carpet, freshly painted walls, and a charming beige Tetris-shaped couch with matching pouf. Sitting by another window at a small table was Cindy Tanner, the eldest daughter. She was still bald, a fashion statement which didn't suit her now that the shock-factor had worn off. On her lap was a tiny little brown Brussels Griffon. As soon as I dared look, it let out a shrill bark that caused us all to jump.

"*Venus!*" scolded Shelby, walking into the kitchen. "Heaven forbid someone blinks. This is *not* the Third Reich, young man."

The dog named Venus jumped of Cindy's lap and trotted off down the hallway. I took a moment and sneaked a peek to see where he was going, but he flung his head back around and caught my spying eye. Stopped at the bottom of the staircase, he huffed, as if to say: '*How very dare you!?*' before trotting away.

"He's just angry," said Cindy. "If you were the colour of baby crap, wouldn't you be mad?"

Shelby paused at the fridge door, thinking.

"I suppose I would be. I never thought of it that way. How are you, Annie?"

"*Cassie,*" said Cindy angrily.

"I'm fine thanks, Mrs. Tanner. My mother wanted me…"

"Yes, I know, and here is mine," she said, dumping an almost identical bowl into my unprepared hands.

I nearly dropped it. She laughed at my apparent carelessness.

"Are you looking forward to tomorrow night? It's a big thing, this party, you know. You're very lucky to be friends with someone as elite as Jonathan Walker."

"Mother," said Cindy, now flipping tiredly through a magazine, "not everybody is as hell-bent on total devotion to social hierarchy as you are. Maybe she's hanging out with him because of his personality."

Shelby found this deeply amusing, and addressed me merrily.

"My eldest always makes me laugh the most! Tanya, dear, your friend Celeste is here!" She disappeared down the hallway.

Cindy watched me curiously as I decided to sit down on one of the wooden bar stools. Smirking, she scratched the back of her shaved head.

"Have you been here since the fire?"

"No," I told her.

"It's not the first we've ever had, but it was the straw that broke the camel's back. Notice how new and sterilised everything looks now?"

It wasn't to my taste, but I told her it was lovely.

"I hate it," she muttered, lighting a cigarette. "Practically sending me into a suicidal depression. It's either that, or my debt. Makes me feel like we're living in a goddamn spaceship. You know..." she pointed at me, "some people say that Kubrick was ahead of his time. The same ones who glorify T. E. Lawrence. All I see are bipolar egomaniacs desperately trying to avoid the inevitable gravitational singularity."

"What are you whinging about now?" said Tanya, who had snuck up on us. She was wearing a pink tracksuit, and her hair was up in a bun.

Cindy didn't answer, and instead got up to excuse herself, leaving through the back sliding door to smoke in peace. The patio beyond was protected by a sheltered entertainment area. Still, she huddled as she inhaled her cigarette.

"What's up?" said Tanya, unplugging her pink phone from a charger next to my arm.

"Oh..." I said slowly. "Nothing much. I just brought something over for your mother. From my mother."

"Right, for the dinner party. I can't believe how quickly that has come around. Crazy, huh? And to think, Eleanore won't be there for once. Talk about a Christmas present."

I was about to ask why Eleanore wouldn't be there, then remembered. "Oh! Did you hear? She asked my sister to go with her on the Zeppelin ride."

Tanya was about to exclaim her disbelief, when we both turned to the sudden shadow of a figure looming behind the Tetris-couch. Since nobody else was in the room, we paused. Then the head of a boy with glasses lifted up, noticed us looking, and ducked out of view again.

"Derek," said Tanya in a pleading, tired voice.

I didn't really know what was going on, but I wasn't frightened any more. By Tanya's tone, this person was meant to be in the house, although his lurking was definitely creepy. As Derek stood up, I noticed he had fluffy, short blond hair, and was wearing a navy-coloured tracksuit. It was almost identical to Tanya's.

"Go upstairs and take that off!" my blonde friend cried, pointing to the hallway. "And don't go into my closet ever, ever again."

Derek was covered in facial acne. It was almost as if he'd used a very aggressive face-wash, which had given him a bad reaction. They were practically poxed, and shiny, ready to burst forth with pus. Evidently going commando in one of Tanya's tracksuits, it seemed uncertain which circumstance brought him more shame, and he rushed away to get changed.

"Who was that?" I asked.

"My cousin. He's staying here for the holidays while my aunt and uncle get some work done. They live in Norfolk."

"How old is he?"

"Nearly twenty-one."

"Isn't he a little old to be…"

"Wearing my clothes and spying? Trust me, *I know*. He's actually pretty great, once he comes out of his shell. Despite his short… comings. Hey, what are you up to for the rest of the day?"

I thought for a moment. "Not much."

"Do you want to go down to the Pop Shop for some lunch? I haven't been there since the accident, and I'm dying to snoop!"

Venus had returned. Tanya picked him up to scratch him.

"Count me in," I said gladly, smiling down at her little pooch. He was scowling at me somehow.

"Great. I'll ask Dad if I can borrow his MG, and we'll go. Oh, I think someone's ready for a kiss!"

I smiled uncomfortably, but Tanya leant Venus in closer to my face. At the last moment, he lunged. However, I'd been prepared and avoided any lacerations. Tanya, mortified, practically threw him to the ground in disgust.

"Venus! Bad boy! Don't do that! Be nice! You're a very naughty boy! Go to your suite! Go, go on, go!"

I gazed at his dry anus as he trotted indignantly down the hallway again.

*Even I don't have a suite,* I thought jealously.

———— . . . ————

Unfortunately, once asking her father to borrow his flashy car, Mrs. Tanner insisted we take Derek. Sitting in the same automobile as him proved to be unpleasant, for he had a rather earthy scent to him.

*"Pour Un Homme de Caron,"* he said in the back, as Tanya slowly drove down Rasputin Lane.

Were we meant to know what that meant?

The Pop Shop was extremely busy, and it wasn't even noon yet. Tanya found the very last spot in the parking lot, which was a tight squeeze, and as we walked in the newly renovated doors we stopped dead in our tracks. Directly to our right was Eleanore in her neckcast. Wednesday and Friday, both looking unharmed and in matching pink puffer jackets, were sitting by her side in their booth. Hiding between Friday and Eleanore was none other than my sister, also wearing pink. She wasn't wearing her glasses either, so I knew that even though her eyes landed upon me, she didn't have a clue who she was looking at.

"Of course they're here," I muttered.

Derek grazed up behind me for a moment, and I leant forward as if preparing to walk to a table. But there weren't any spares. Suddenly, to our surprise, the Saviours put their hands up and called our names. They wanted us to join them.

"Do you think it's a trap?" asked Tanya.

Eleanore was smiling.

"Most definitely," I said.

Still, it was better than standing around near the exit. Every time somebody came in or left, the chill from outside hit us in a most unpleasant way. So we squeezed into the tiny Saviours booth, neither smiling or groaning. Manners had been drilled into us at a young age. Just because these cruddlings were ruder than a drunk Yankee didn't mean we had to be.

"Good morning to you all!" said Friday chirpily. She'd straightened her hair, and it looked a bit darker than her usual sharp red.

We said hello back, but I wondered what their deal was. My friendship with Tanya depended on the day at this point. But Annie was here. Yet the girls definitely had a malicious look in their eyes.

"Hello, Derek," said Eleanore grimly. Apparently she'd met him before. "How are…"

Tanya told her to stop wasting her breath, and pulled a pair of earbuds from her pocket. She handed them to Derek, and he put them in his ears and played music from his console. A moment later, his eyes wandered to the rafters, innocently lost in his own world. *Mercifully* lost in his own world.

"Uh-oh," said Wednesday, muttering under her breath just in

case. "Somebody call an ambulance. There's been a smash on Fifth and the victim's face is worse than a Picasso painting!" Friday laughed along with her after that, but the rest of us didn't find it very funny. Sure, Derek's face was bad, but was it really Rose Marie bad?

"So Cassie," said Eleanore, turning her whole body due to the neck-brace. "After our little debacle the other day at the Walker mansion, I didn't have time to tell you and your sister about how completely forbidden it is to mention that hang-out to anybody else. Or did I? I can't quite remember after falling so suddenly from the banister you pushed me from."

"I didn't push you."

"Either or. But let me make it clear. We only hang out on that one day, every year. If you attempt to befriend me during school hours, I will pretend you are the ghost that haunts the old abandoned train station, and scream. Okay?"

"I don't want anybody knowing we hung out either."

"Good. We're already having enough trouble coming up with an excuse as to why we're so damaged. At least Friday's and Wednesday's injuries aren't obvious. Nobody's going to ask *them*."

"I think they might," said Wednesday.

Eleanore rolled her eyes. Obviously this was an ongoing discussion. "Yeah, well, how can I make something up about your injury when you won't tell me where it is?"

"I told you. It's personal."

"*I* broke my elbow. See?" said Friday, and she tried to take off her giant jacket to show us. After a few moments, and not one to ask for help, she gave up. "Well, it's in a cast."

"What are you guys doing here, anyway?" I asked them. "I didn't realise Annie was a Saviour of Tomorrow."

"She is most definitely *not*," said Wednesday furiously. "However, as Eleanore has picked her to go on the Zeppelin ride, they have work to do."

"What kind of work?"

"Oh, plucking, waxing, manoeuvring sans eyewear... Mostly all stuff *she* has to do," laughed Eleanore, nudging my sister. "She's not going to be my guest at a banquet aired on live television for the program I love most unless she stops looking like manure on a Spin bike."

A rage boiled beneath the surface of my skin, and I'm sure my cheeks flushed. But it was already overly hot in there, with the customers surely passing the maximum amount allowed in such a small venue.

"Dearest Wednesday and Friday won't admit to it, but they're mad at me for not picking either of them for the ride tomorrow," said Eleanore, oblivious to my anger. "With two broken body parts, though, we just can't take the risk."

Friday scowled and finished off her milkshake.

"You planned to ask Annie *before* the fall!"

"Details," Eleanore scoffed, waving her off. "Anyway, we've got to go. With a little bit of luck, my optometrist will check Annie's eyes for contacts, and send them out for delivery before tomorrow!"

"That's ridiculous, and impossible," said Tanya.

Eleanore and the others stood up.

"You don't know Carl Zimmerman very well."

"Good luck with your broken eyes," I told my sister, who didn't meet my eye-line. I turned to Friday. "Good luck with your broken elbow. Eleanore, your neck. And Wednesday, your... uh... *whomst.*"

I said it as a throwaway, and laughed, expecting it to be way off. However, Wednesday didn't say a word, and her cheeks practically lit up with embarrassment.

"Is *that* what you broke!?" cried Eleanore in disbelief, as they shuffled out of the café. "You broke your *VAGINA!?*"

———— · · · ————

We stayed for forty minutes or so, all three of us tucking into pulled pork sandwiches. By the time we decided to leave, Derek had well and truly come out of his shell.

"Naturally, if I wasn't accepted into Harvard I'd be jumping across the pond quicker than a hypothetical tachyon, but Oxford's elite *are* superstitious in a nincompoop sort of way, thus the dilemma extends its stay!"

Tanya pulled into my driveway, and I almost exited before she stopped. I was tired from so many things; I couldn't bear another awkward goodbye.

Shutting the front door behind me, the chore of unraveling my many layers meant I didn't have time to escape before Hayley walked down the stairs in front of me. Her hair was tied back, a sight she'd rarely shared with me before, and although she was still in her blue pyjamas she looked more awake and lively than I surely did.

"Oh. Hello," she said.

"Hey," I said with a forced smile.

She took my distance as an insult, and immediately scowled. With that, she went on her way into the living room, and I haphazardly decided to follow. Brendan was in there with Aunt Rachael, and the two were playing some sort of game with their bare feet.

"What are you doing?" I asked.

"Thumb Wars," said Brendan.

"Uh…"

"It's more challenging when you do it with your toes!" declared Rachael, and after a moment she let out a furious sigh and collapsed back in her armchair. "It's like threading a needle. Hey, where did you go before?"

"Out with a friend. Where is everybody?"

"No idea," said Brendan. "Mom and Dad left twenty minutes ago, and Grandma is still asleep."

I checked my wristwatch. It was rather late for her to still be in bed, early bird that she was.

"Maybe she's dead," said Brendan.

"Stop saying that."

"Which friend were you out with?" asked Hayley.

I turned my head, not enough so that I was facing her, but enough that she knew I'd heard.

"Tanya."

"She's being nice again?"

I remained with my eyes locked on Rachael's feet.

"For now. Why are you up? Don't you have work in a few hours?"

Hayley seemed to relax, as if her grudge against me lifted in a single moment.

"It's my weekend. I have tonight and tomorrow night off. Then I'm working until Christmas Eve. Then I quit."

"You quit, or you finish?"

"Same thing. I haven't told them yet. I only wanted this job until Christmas anyway. Bonita has a lot of money stashed away in a savings account so I'll just live off that until she's better."

Flummoxed by this revelation, I almost wanted to yell at her. What was the argument we'd had, then? What was *that* all about? Her jab at my wealth and leisurely lifestyle felt even more of an insult now that she was contradicting herself. Internalising it, I decided that I was still mad at her, and I turned even further away without letting on.

Fifteen minutes later, the parentals arrived home. As the door opened, a gust of wind joined them and they almost toppled into the foyer. Unravelling in much the same way I'd done from their gargantuan coats and scarves, neither of them looked too pleased. Mom rubbed her cold hands and blew on them for a moment, then saw us peaking in from the other room.

"This wind better die down before tomorrow night, or that Zeppelin ride won't happen!" she said.

"It'll be fine," muttered Hayley. "I'm pretty sure Eleanore can control the weather."

"I don't know…" Mom replied unsurely.

"We were just down at the hardware store," said Dad, petting Pigsworth as he came over. "We went to get a new wreath for the front door. When we woke up this morning, the old one was gone."

"With the wind," said Rachael sadly.

"If they cancel the ride, Annie will be beside herself."

"Great, then we'll have two of her," said Brendan quick-wittedly. "Where *is* she, anyway?"

"Out with Eleanore getting ready for tomorrow," I said, not letting my blank gaze move from a spot on the beige carpet.

*"Somebody has stolen my money!"*

The call came from upstairs, and a moment later the old hag herself came down. She was fully dressed in her usual dull-coloured attire — beige sweater and brown skirt, with stockings and black boots. Her metallic walking cane hovered on the stair below her, and she stood with her free hand clutching the top of the banister furiously. I could spot the veins from here.

"Ma, not now, we're busy."

"Lesley, I had thirteen hundred dollars in my bedside drawer last night vhen I vent to sleep. Now it is missing. I *demand* you find out who took it!"

I looked up at Dad.

"Will they reschedule the Zeppelin?"

"I'm not sure, sweetie."

"Listen to me, for crying out loud!" yelled Grandma. "We have a pick-pocket in our house! I demand to interrogate everybody."

Mom finally gave in with a tired moan, and turned to face her.

"Nobody that lives in this house would dare go into your bedroom. Especially since you keep the door open all the time. Maybe you left it somewhere else and forgot about it. Although I must say, that is a *lot* of money to have lying around. Why wasn't it in the bank?"

"I don't trust bank tellers. My money was there vhen I fell asleep last night and when I voke up, it was gone."

"I'm sure you just haven't looked properly," said Mom, giving me and Brendan a cheeky grin.

Grandma Helen suddenly raised that veiny hand of hers.

Pointing her scary finger, she muttered: "When did my only living daughter lose all respect for me? I vill not leave my room until you find out who took it! Do you hear me? I am not senile. It has been stolen!"

With that, she turned around and stormed back upstairs. To our great surprise, she slammed her door shut.

# 24

# GENTRY & URIAH

The daylight was fading very slowly, much slower than usual at this time of year. Chloe timed it on her watch until she couldn't see anything outside, with the exception of the glow from the snowmobile's headlights.

In the front sat two identical twin brothers by the names of Gentry and Uriah. They were large, burly men with coarse brown beards. Identical maroon beanies covered their bald heads, and they were dressed in the same red plaid flannel shirts, with brown corduroys and weathered black boots. Their cheeks were their most distinguishable features, for they were puffy and rosy from joy. These were the happiest twins to be in the land of the living. Naturally, Candice got along with them swimmingly.

"*On the eighth day of Christmas, my true love gave to me…*" the three of them sang together.

Uriah started: "*Eight maids a milking!*"

Then Gentry: "*Seven swans a swimming!*"

Candice: *"Six geese a laying!"*

They turned to Chloe, who shook her head.

*"Fiiiive gooolden riiiings!"*

The three of them continued on like this. They took such glee in knowing it off by heart, the cabin hot with their sticky breaths. Chloe wished she could wind down the window and stick her head out into the freezing winter air to scream. She wasn't even sure how long it had been since they'd left the confines of the hotel. A day? A week? Twenty minutes? There was no end in sight, and the two giant men in front wouldn't give them any details, no matter how often they asked. All they would say is: "Horn-Horn is only a little way off!"

Perplexed by it all, Chloe sat as far across the backseat from her sister as she could, and resented her for being so happy throughout the journey. As the threesome wound down their singing, Chloe took a jab at her sister in hopes of spoiling her mood.

"Whatever happened to that dog?" she reminded her. "What was his name again? Sudentry?"

"He's back at the hotel with…"

"No, not that one. The *first* one."

"Chloe, you made that up."

"I did not! Gentry, Uriah, before we made it to the hotel we were driving a car. When I opened the trunk, a dog jumped out and his collar said his name was Sudentry. He was as real as the four of us sitting right here."

"Sudentry? I've never heard that name before," said Uriah.

"Neither had I. I'm not even confident it's a real word."

"Perhaps, then," said Gentry slowly, "you imagined it after all. The mind is known to brew up some strange things. Maybe in the moment your brain couldn't come up with a real name fast enough, so it threw together some arbitrary letters."

Chloe sank back and thought about this for a moment.

"Maybe," she admitted calmly. "But then, why was Vonda's dog named Sudentry?"

"It doesn't mean to say it's not true. When Uriah and I became medics — and this was a *very* long time ago — we treated a man with an equally strange name. I can't actually remember it, can you?"

"No," said Uriah, and he continued on for his brother. "But this man's name was so unusual that every time one of the staff at the hospital tried to repeat it off by heart, they couldn't. As I recall, it wasn't even that long of a name. There was just something about it.

It was like trying to remember a random set of digits."

"Was he foreign?" asked Candice.

"No, he wasn't," said Gentry. "But come to think of it, this was also during the winter when we nearly died. Sometimes I think a period in time can be cursed."

"Oh, I believe that, too," said Candice. "Do you, Chloe?"

"No."

"Tell us about how you nearly died, Gentry!"

The bigger of the twins let out a sigh as he cast his mind back.

"Well, it's all a bit of a blur now. The two of us were much, much younger, and were ambulance drivers at the time. We got a call that two lovers had taken their lives by jumping off a cliff. Being the middle of January, we couldn't take the ambulance as the roads were blocked with snow. So we had to borrow a snowmobile to make it to the scene. It took us a very long time, as there was a big blizzard, just like this one.

"Sure enough, we found the couple's car on the edge of a cliff. We tried to find our way down to the bottom through a safer route, but ended up getting lost. Then Uriah, who was driving, miscalculated the road and we ended up rolling down a snowy embankment. We were very badly injured, although thankfully somebody had seen the accident and called for some more backup. But we were trapped in the cabin without heating for about... three hours, I'd say. I got some frostbite on my toes, while Uriah didn't get any. We were lucky to make it out."

"How awful," said Candice, shifting closer to her sister. "And those poor people who committed suicide. We're lucky that we've never been through an experience like that."

"No big, life-altering injuries?" asked Uriah.

Chloe shook her head.

"None that we know of. Although we're still waiting on Candice's test results."

"Lucky," remarked Gentry, staring out ahead at the endless snow flying past in the cold night.

Chloe tilted her head.

"Careful," she corrected him.

For some reason, they spent the next ten minutes in silence, the sounds of the engine and the shudders as they went over snow humps distracting from the conversation. Without saying a word, each sister knew that the other felt uncomfortable, spooked even, by the story told. To add to their disturbances, the brothers seemed to have changed personalities. They stared ahead out of the windshield, lost in their dark thoughts. They'd been nothing but cheerful since the pickup outside the hotel. And after so many hours, it made no sense.

Suddenly, Chloe spotted a glowing sign outside her window. She could barely believe her eyes as the snow seemed to disappear in an instant, and the snowmobile rolled casually into a lit-up filling station.

"*Candice!*" she yelled, for her sister's eyes were closed.

Startled by the sudden declaration, Candice checked outside and let out a gasp. "I told you we weren't far away from civilisation!"

Chloe was quick to open the door on her side.

"Thank God. I've been needing to pee for hours. Candice, get us some food while we wait!"

The sisters burst into the convenience store. Chloe rushed for the bathroom, while Candice made her way to the candy in front of the counter. A short Chinese man stood behind it, watching as she swallowed about ten chocolate bars without chewing. By the time she'd finished, she reached into her pocket and threw him some cash. Then, Chloe arrived, looking zen after her bathroom break. She grabbed two extra bars and gave the man some cash as well.

"Where are we?" she asked, stuffing her face.

The look on the clerk's face was that of confusion.

"Hartford," he said.

Candice giggled happily, and the two sisters hugged.

"That's not far! Thank you, Su…"

Squinting to read his name tag, she stopped.

"Your name is Sudentry?"

"Yeah."

"You know that thing where you hear a name for the first time, then all of a sudden it's everywhere?"

Sudentry shrugged and his eyes turned to the sudden movement of headlights passing through the convenience store. Someone was moving their car around outside. As he watched, his eyes grew wider and wider, and his face lost all colour.

Chloe and Candice turned, and saw as the snowmobile they'd arrived in casually left the filling station and headed off into the night.

"Hey! *Hey!*" yelled Chloe, getting to the automatic doors and watching Gentry and Uriah disappear.

The two identical men inside the cabin turned their heads, their eyes locking for a moment on Chloe.

*Where are they going?* she thought angrily.

Then the snowmobile was lost to the darkness.

"That was our bloody ride!" Candice joined her sister at the doors, and quickly yelled out at them: *"Thanks for nothing!* I've said it a million times, Chloe. You cannot trust twins."

Chloe backed inside again. Her face was a blank canvas, drained of colour just like the clerk's.

"That was them…" said Sudentry.

"Who?" asked Candice, stopping between the two of them. "What's going on? Why do you look like you've seen a ghost?"

"Because I have."

Candice felt Chloe squeeze tightly to her left arm.

"People around here call them 'The Hanging Brothers'. They were wanted for a slew of murders. They would make people hang themselves in their own attics. During a police chase in the fifties they drove their snowmobile off a cliff, and were never seen alive again. But the spooky thing is they've been spotted countless times over the years around these parts. Never aged, always coming in and out of snowstorms, just like the one they disappeared into…"

A sense of fear and dread clung to the recycled air. Candice put her arm around Chloe, silent and shaking.

# 25

# BEGLEY'S NICKY

As the sun rose across a cloudless sky, the two sisters took a moment on the side of the road to admire the view. After walking almost catatonic along the road for over six hours, chilled to the bone, they were finally starting to come to terms with the night before.

"We should have just stayed in the filling station."

"Until what, another ghost-mobile arrived? I think not! Look, that sign back there said Alexandria is only fifty kilometres away! That's not far!"

An approaching vehicle slowly came into view, and once again Candice stuck her thumb out. For the tenth time in one night, the car ignored them.

"Stop doing that," Chloe insisted.

"One of them will stop!"

"Great. I can't wait to get hacked to pieces."

"The odds of being abducted while hitchhiking is much less likely than a baseball player choking to death on an ant-hill when he dives for a home run!"

Chloe nodded. "I'm pretty sure you just made that up."

"I'll take my chances hitchhiking…" said Candice, tired of her sister's behaviour. "You know something, Chloe? You and I are very different people! And I don't mean that as an insult, I really don't!"

"I'd never take it as anything other than a compliment."

"You are a glass half-empty sort of person, and I could never be like that. I choose to see the good in every situation! Like when the police found those girls in Uncle Norman's basement. He'd fed them so well! They acclimated easily."

"I'm not spiteful, if that's what you're getting at. I just don't like people questioning the likelihood of a situation. I judge things at face value."

"And how do you judge what happened to us, then? The two men in the snowmobile, and the hotel in the middle of a blizzard?"

Chloe shrugged. "I don't know, alright? Stop pestering me about it. I just want to get home as quickly as possible."

Another engine was roaring towards them quickly from behind, and as the sole headlight lit up their surroundings just that little bit more, Candice grabbed hold of Chloe merrily. "Then join me, sister, in jutting your thumb! Do it for my sake, if not for your own! Tell the universe you believe in it! Trust it! Do it, sister!"

Chloe shrugged her off in annoyance. *"Alright, alright."*

She threw her thumb out as the motorcycle drove towards them. Delighted, Candice stared down the driver and stuck her thumb out, too. She even kicked her hips out flirtatiously in case that helped.

To their utmost surprise, the motorcycle slowed down and finally came to a stop right in front of them. Chloe couldn't believe her eyes, and she pushed Candice forward with all her might. Hopefully she would be in bed with a hot water bottle and a nice cup of hot chocolate within the next hour.

———— • • • ————

I was thrilled to wake up that morning, but was surprised to open my eyes ten seconds before my alarm went off. It'd happened quite a few times in my life, and I wondered if it was my body's alarm clock setting itself naturally. Either way, it was still weird when it happened.

Hayley was fast asleep in her bed, but I knew this time that she'd slept the whole night through. I also knew that she'd swallowed a sleeping pill from a pack she stole from her mother's bathroom. Now it looked like her sleeping schedule was back on track. Given her grievances with JT's mother, I was glad she wouldn't be cranky and snappy that night at the party.

I noticed right away that Grandma's bedroom door was closed. She was still in a furious mood, and to be honest I sort of knew where she was coming from. If somebody in my family stole money from my bedside table I would be furious. Besides, I'd also noticed an odd attitude change towards her in the past few days. Brendan would sit in the same room as her, but he wouldn't interact with her at all. When I questioned him about it, he told me that Grandma had been racist towards his friend Aron, and that sealed the deal for me as well. Mom and Dad were stressed because of her highly-strung nature, and Annie hadn't really been very warm to her since she ruined her birthday party all those years ago. Rachael, closer to her Jewish heritage than the rest of us, naturally couldn't stand her. The longer Grandma Helen stayed, the more cantankerous she was becoming. It was making Christmas quite miserable, an idea all Gellars despised with fervour.

"Will we be seeing her at all today?" asked Annie, as we gathered around the kitchen to eat breakfast.

"Who cares?" said Brendan.

Mom tsked at him, not bothering to tell him off. Dad was behind her filling the dishwasher, and as he turned it on to its cycle, he faced me. "Have you heard from the hardware store yet?"

"Dad, please, we've got too much going on today to worry about work!"

I noticed Mom giving me the side-eye and it disheartened me a little. Our fight was still there, in the back of my mind, and I knew she was biting her tongue.

"Everybody out of the kitchen after breakfast," said Annie suddenly, heaving herself up. "Mom and I are spending the day cooking for the party tonight, and I thought we'd add a few extra things for me to take on the Zeppelin. I'm getting picked up at two-thirty."

"What are you baking?" asked Aunt Rachael, who stumbled into the room half asleep.

"Brownies! If I see Thomas Noel, I'm going to offer him one, so they have to be extra special. Then for the rest of my life I can tell people that Thomas Noel ate something I made."

"Special brownies, huh?" she said, walking blindly to the fridge to start making her breakfast. "I can help you out a bit if you want. As your dear father knows, I'm the only good cook in our family. Except for that one time I burned his eyebrows off making French toast."

———  · · ·  ———

Begley was the motorcycle driver's name.

He was a tall man, ripped to kingdom come, in his late forties with short greying hair and a tattoo on his neck of the number five. Despite his rough exterior, he was the chattiest person either Chloe or Candice had ever met. He told them about his brother, Nicky, who he was going back to Horn-Horn to meet. Their mother was sick and needed money, so he was heading there to win the Motorcycle Competition that night. Wouldn't she be surprised when he collected his brother, the winner's money, and be by her hospital bedside by Christmas Eve?

The three of them travelled in the chilly winter morning until finally, at ten o'clock, they turned off the highway near Dalrymple and made their way towards the nearest mall. The motorcycle, scratched and groaning under the excess weight, eventually signalled to turn into the parking lot. With so many shoppers desperate for last-minute Christmas presents, all of the spots were taken. Begley took the advice of the two sisters (one pressed up behind him, the other in the sidecar), and decided to simply park it on the sidewalk near the entrance.

"Desperate times call for desperate measures," said Chloe.

As they walked through the mall, Begley kept his sunglasses on. He walked behind the two sisters, and checked over his shoulder continuously. "I've got a lot of enemies around here," he said. "Mainly loan sharks. My brother Nicky is mentally handicapped. It takes a lot of money to care for him. People don't understand his way of thinking, either. He's got savant syndrome, knows the most ridiculous trivia, but gets himself into a lot of trouble. Most of the time I swoop down in the eleventh hour and save him."

"How very admirable to take care of your sibling like that!" said Candice in earnest.

"Some say admirable, others say... foolish," muttered Chloe. "There's the powder room up ahead. Excuse us, Begley. We'll be right back."

The sisters rushed for the bathrooms. Urine hissing into the toilet bowl like angry cobras, Chloe forced herself to finish before Candice and was out to greet Begley in record time.

"So," she said, unsure of how to flirt these days, and knowing she didn't look great. "What does the tattoo stand for?"

"That's how many times I've been arrested."

"Oh..."

"It's okay. I got the tattoo done as a way to stop myself from getting into any more trouble. If I do get arrested again, I'll have to write over it."

"Well, five can turn into six real easy."

Begley tried to check it. "Damn. Needs an update."

"I have a self-made tattoo of a seismograph measure on my ankle. Truth be told, it was the beginning of the word 'Mother' but I vomited five seconds in, and couldn't go through with the rest."

"That's funny. Nicky tattoo'd himself once, when we were younger. Tried to put his name on his elbow but it ended up looking like 'Foghorn'. So I took him to a real tattoo parlour and made them fix it into an image of a lie-detector test. What are the odds?"

Chloe smiled and batted her eyelids.

Begley finally caught on. "Do you like tattoos?"

Chloe didn't answer, but made sure her lips were properly moistened. As she ran her tongue along her top lip, she gazed down. "Wow, Begley, is that a gun in your pocket, or are you just happy to see me?"

Candice finally came out, shaking her hands dry. Oblivious to the flirting, she wiped her nose with a heavy snotty sound and cracked her fingers. "Well! Sorry about that! Apparently every meal I've had this month decided to vacate the premises all at once. Been constipated for *weeks*. Can't tell you how relieved I am! I feel like I've had an enema... How much further is it to Horn-Horn?"

"Only fifteen more miles..." said Begley, grimacing.

Chloe and Candice high-fived each other. "First thing I'm going to do when I get home is throw out that Christmas tree!" said Candice happily. "If it hasn't run off already!"

With that they started to walk towards the exits. As they continued, Candice chatted to Begley about motorcycles, and what time the race started that night. Chloe, on the other hand, couldn't help but notice how the security guards were watching them. Moving slowly but steadily with them. When at the last minute a smaller guard grabbed his walkie-talkie, Chloe decided to interrupt her two compadres to ask them what was going on. But before she could, Begley grabbed the two of them by the back of their heads and shouted: *"Move!"*

The two sisters immediately did as they were told, bolting out of the mall and towards the parked motorcycle. As they reached it, two cop cars swung around the corner and skidded to a halt in front of them.

*"Get on the bike!"* shouted Begley, pulling out a gun.

"Begley!" cried Chloe. "I thought you were happy to —"

One, two, three cops hopped out of their vehicles and hid behind their doors. Pointing guns at them, they yelled to freeze. Chloe and Candice were on the back of the bike now, hands up in the air, happy to surrender. But to their surprise, Begley then hopped on the bike as well. He started it up and swung it around, then shot at the tyres of one of the police cars. With a hideous screeching of rubber, the motorcycle flipped around and bolted out of the parking lot and towards the highway, the sound of the angry engine almost drowning out the screams of the two captive sisters.

Two miles away, as they pulled off the highway and into the manky shadows of an underpass, Begley finally decided that it was safe. The police giving chase had disappeared, and there wasn't another car in sight. A few homeless people sitting on the kerb nearby watched as their motorcycle came to a stop behind a blue dumpster. Chloe and Candice immediately jumped off and sprinted five feet before turning around to face the tattoo'd man. He too climbed off the bike, and turned to face them. "That was close," he said.

Chloe stared, her mouth hung open in surprise. "What is the matter with you? Why did you do that?"

"They were after me," he said.

"Why did you involve us?"

Begley laughed. "You got back on the bike."

"You *told* us to!"

"It was more a suggestion."

Momentarily speechless, Chloe put a hand to her forehead and looked about. There were small warehouses nearby, mostly automobile shops and rundown factories, all of which were closed. "I've got to phone someone," she said to herself. "All we wanted was to get a lift to Horn-Horn."

"Yeah, and I told you, no worries. I'll get you there."

"Legally!"

"Look, it'll take all of fifty minutes to get there. I'll drop you off downtown and that'll be that."

Candice, hugging herself to keep warm, shook her head. "No, thank you. We'd rather walk."

"But this area is no place for ladies. You'll get in trouble."

"We *are* in trouble!" said Candice. "First, we got lost in a blizzard. Then we got a lift from two ghosts. Now, we're fugitives! You should be ashamed of yourself, Begley! What would your brother think?"

"I think Nicky would tell you to stop complaining."

"No!" snapped Candice. "Nicky would not! We're going now, and then we're going to the police and telling them everything. Come on, Chloe."

The two girls turned on their heels and trotted off down the gravel road. Frozen, they clutched at one another and tried to think of where to go. How long would it take them to get away from this underpass? Would anybody even help them? What was next, a goblin taxi driver?

The motorcycle started up and Begley drove past them, very quickly blocking their path to freedom. To their horror, he had his gun cocked and pointed at them.

"Actually, Nicky would tell you to get on the bike."

He pulled a pair of handcuffs out from his jacket pocket.

"You don't have to do this," said Chloe. "I have a cat."

Begley hopped off the bike and pushed the two girls forward. He shoved Candice, who fell face first into the sidecar. Head down where her feet should be, she noticed two things down there: a paper bag, and a *Tiro the Barber-Librarian* doll. Turning to look up, she saw Chloe get shoved violently, colliding with her. Begley reached over, grabbed the paper bag, pulled out a big wad of rope from inside, and quickly bound the two sisters together, back-to-back.

"This is ridiculous!" snapped Candice, as she heard the click of the handcuffs attaching them to the side-rail. "If only I'd stood up to my Christmas Tree!"

Begley climbed back onto the bike, and the three of them shot off down the road again.

"Cherish this Christmas, Candice," said Chloe, leaning her head back. "I have a funny feeling it'll be our last."

# 26

# THE NEW AND IMPAIRED
# ANNIE GELLAR

We busied ourselves around the house. Every once in a while Brendan and I would walk past the kitchen area to sticky-beak as Mom and Aunt Rachael helped Annie bake her special brownies. Most of the time Annie would look up and yell at us to go away, but we insisted we were simply 'passing through'.

She was nervous. I could tell. I would be too, if I were going on the ride. *But*, I thought contently, *I'm not.* I was instead going to focus my attention on the party that night. I was over the moon to be going, as was everybody else. JT called at about one-thirty to speak to Hayley, and had a quick conversation with Dad. I don't know what they talked about, but Dad mentioned something about candles. I wondered if they needed us to go down to the hardware store to get some. I didn't want to go, because I was still waiting on a call for a job there. Plus, you know, Morgan.

Finally, at one-thirty, Annie suddenly bolted from the kitchen and raced for the stairs.

"I'm going to have a shower and get ready!" she declared loudly. "Nobody bother me until I come down!"

The lights flickered just as the sound of the pipes shuddered in the walls. Aunt Rachael looked worriedly to Dad, who was sitting in his Barcalounger. He was flipping through today's newspaper and didn't look bothered.

"The wind," muttered Rachael.

"Please," said Dad. "They wouldn't cancel that thing if the air itself caught fire."

Half an hour later, Annie came down the stairs. It was honestly like that scene from *She's All That*. Dad was the first to glance up, leaning around in his chair to get a proper look. Brendan's jaw dropped at the sight of her. Annie's hair was curled and put up in a giant beehive-style not dissimilar to many of the ones I'd witnessed first-hand in the fifties. She wasn't wearing her glasses any more, either. She had just the right amount of make-up on to cover her bulging acne, and she was dressed in the most gorgeous canary-yellow gown I'd ever seen (obviously borrowed from the likes of Eleanore). The only thing that ruined her grand descent was how she tripped on the last step; she quickly nursed her twisted ankle and hobbled towards us.

"You look like a completely different person," said Mom.

Annie couldn't hold it in any longer, and a tremendous smile burst forth. Her braces reflected from every light source possible.

"Whoa!" said Brendan, squinting. "There she is!"

Annie fumbled for the kitchen bench to rest against.

"Eleanore's optometrist couldn't make me contacts in such a short amount of time, so I'll have to be blind for most of the night. I feel bad; she said she's going to sue him."

"Oh, but Annie!" said Rachael. "You won't be able to enjoy the fireworks, and all the views from the ride!"

Annie reached into her cleavage and pulled out her glasses.

"I'll sneak them on when nobody's looking."

As the next half hour came and went, we busied ourselves around the house in preparation for the party that night. Brendan's tuxedo arrived — the nearby dry-cleaners did deliveries — and he decided to put it on now rather than later. Mom took the opportunity to take a snapshot of the three of us, which I didn't particularly appreciate very much given it made me look like a wandering vagrant who happened to walk by as they were taking the photo. Just as she finished winding the disposable camera, somebody knocked on the door again. Annie jumped a mile in the air and ran to open it, almost smacking against it in her effort. Eleanore was at the door, as was her entire family. They were all rugged up in giant puffer jackets and fur coats, but Eleanore's make-up and hair was just as brilliant as Annie's. When we let them in, they scoped around the house and rubbed their hands to warm up.

"You look amazing!" said Eleanore, making my sister spin around for her. "Oh, hello, everybody. You've all met my family? Eric, Ella-May, Elliot & Eliza."

We waved at them and they waved back, but they had very fake put-on smiles. Sneers, almost. It didn't sit well with me. They obviously thought very little of us.

"I see your neck has healed quickly," I remarked, noticing she wasn't sporting that gigantic neck-brace anymore.

Eleanore ignored me, choosing to immediately pay attention to a painting on the wall by the front door.

"This is stunning! Your family has very good taste in art."

Dad snickered. "Thank you. I painted that myself."

"Oh, you paint?" said Ella-May, clutching onto Elliot for dear life. "We know a lot of people in the art world. In fact, so does Margie." She laughed to herself for a moment, and then explained: "That's our pet-name for Marguerite Walker."

Dad hopped up and came over, gliding a hand across his beloved painting. "I call it 'Leonard's Wake'. See the heavy brush-strokes? The gritty blacks amongst the colours? I was inspired by Akira Kurosawa."

Eleanore breathed in through her teeth. "Sorry, I don't really follow *Pokémon*."

"He was an artist, honey," said Eric. "Ichabod, this is superb. Perhaps one day we can commission a few paintings for the school. What do you say?"

"Happy to oblige."

"Wonderful new! We'll set a date, then. Goodness, the Gellar children are looking very presentable tonight. W... Oh, hello, Cassie, I didn't see you there. Anyway, we can't sit and chat. Have to rush. Are you ready?"

He turned to the gorgeous Annie, who blinded us yet again

with an impromptu smile.

Mom and Aunt Rachael carried three plates of brownies with them to the door, and I lazily got up from the couch to see where they were taking them. As I got to the open door, I saw a giant limousine pulled up outside. The driver hopped out and opened the trunk so they could put the brownies in.

"*A limousine?*" I called, and pouted a little.

"Oh, be happy for her," said Dad. "Annie's never had friends before. You've got plenty."

"I wouldn't exactly call Eleanore her friend, Dad. This is a business deal."

"All friendships are business deals."

"That's a grim outlook," I muttered, waving to my sister as she excitedly hopped into the back of the limousine with the Parkers.

I *was* happy for her, I realised. It was a once in a lifetime experience. Even though the winds were strong and the air was cold, these weren't the things she'd remember about tonight.

———  . . .  ———

As the chill of the afternoon somehow seeped in through the cracks, I busied myself upstairs getting ready. Hayley was up and avoiding me now, choosing to hang out in Annie's empty bedroom while I tested some make-up on my slowly fading black-eyes. I wondered what Annie was doing. Getting a briefing from that Cora Corali woman, most likely. Would she be at the school already? Were the cast already there? I tried not to feel jealous, but we were talking about the cast of *The Prefect Family*...

It was hard not to be.

Grandma Helen finally came downstairs at around five. By that time, we were all fully dressed up and waiting patiently for six o'clock to come along so we could leave for the party.

The matriarch of sorts came and joined us, watching the television. We didn't speak to her, and she didn't look at any of us either. She sat on one of the armchairs, placed her hands between her knees, and didn't complain about what we were watching. Which wasn't really particularly troublesome, anyway.

It was *A Very Brady Christmas*.

Brendan was enthralled. Mike Brady was trapped inside a building, which had fallen down on top of him. As the family gathered outside, they suddenly decided to start singing: '*O Come, All Ye Faithful*'.

Aunt Rachael, leaning forward, put a hand to her mouth.

"They're not. Tell me they're not going to do it."

Sure enough, singing a Christmas carol helped Mike climb out of the debris and towards a happy ending. Touched, Brendan wiped some tears from his eyes, while Rachael scoffed in her seat.

"Hopefully there are better options to watch on TV tonight."

"Are you sure you don't want to come with us?" asked Mom. "They said you could."

"No, thanks. I'll hang out here with my new best friend!"

Rachael nudged her head towards Grandma Helen.

"I won't be keeping you company," the old woman finally spoke, and she checked her wristwatch. "I have made plans."

"What?" said Mom. "With who?"

"None of your business."

Suddenly, a car horn beeped from the driveway.

"Speaking of which! I'll be back later."

We watched as Grandma Helen grabbed her handbag from the staircase, wrapped herself up in her big purple jacket and scarf, and hobbled out the front door.

"Ichabod!" cried Mom. "Stop her!"

"How? I'd hit her with my motorcycle, but it was stolen."

Mom scowled as something clicked.

"Of course! She's going to protest at that stupid motorcycle race downtown. I guarantee it. Well, you know what, Ichabod? Fine. Just fine. I don't care. She can protest and get pneumonia all she likes. We're busy tonight. Come on everyone. Let's go.

She stood up, clearly furious, and went to get her own jacket.

"But the party doesn't start for another forty minutes," I said.

"Sometimes it's good to be abnormally early."

Dad, Brendan and I exchanged concerned glances. Then, just as Mom got her first arm through its sleeve, a very loud scuttling noise sounded from upstairs.

"Oh, shut up, you stupid rats!" she yelled.

# 27

# SHOWTIME

The crowd was immense. People, rugged up in their winter best, stood cheering as motorcycle after motorcycle piled into the old Horn-Horn Raceway. The circuit had been abandoned for decades, only used for irregular events such as these. Now after its annual clean-up, Grandma Helen gazed around her as she made her way towards her allocated seat in the disabled spots below. When the man who helped her to her seat asked her something, she had to get him to repeat himself twice. Not because she was old and deaf, but because she'd put earplugs in before hopping out of the cab. Damned if she was going to hear the ignorant yells of the damn, oafish illiterate boobs surrounding her.

Ahead of her across the circuit she could see the dastardly vermin on their bikes, dozens of them, lining up in rows as they were verified to compete. Many of them were dressed up in ridiculous outfits: one rider wore a wicked witch's outfit, another had a Papier-mâché of several reindeers surrounding him. Then there was a woman in a bikini, someone wearing a Grim Reaper's outfit, and even a man in a Santa costume with two women tied and restrained in his sidecar.

"Attention seekers," muttered Grandma Helen, and she promptly pulled out a packet of tobacco to get her juices going.

———— · · · ————

Not very far away, Principal Parker stared at the television as it aired the motorcycle race. He glanced across the Teacher's Lounge at the fifty people rushing around, and his eyes landed on his daughter. Her ruby sequinned dress was a little low-cut for his liking, but it did indeed make her look beautiful. Next to her was Annie, who he could see was fumbling her way towards the bathrooms.

"It's time! Everybody, it's time!" called Cora Corali, the head producer, a deeply tanned woman with a bob of wavy brown hair. As beautiful as anybody who had actually been on *The Prefect Family*,

Cora was dolled up, wearing a stunning white dress that flowed about like magic.

"Stop what you're doing and line up as we talked about before. We'll lead you out to the football field. Remember the rehearsals a few hours ago? This will be the exact same thing, except with a real crowd this time. Annie, please Annie, no. This way."

She went to guide the very blind Annie back into the room.

"Am I meant to link arms with her the *entire* time?" asked Eleanore, as Annie grabbed onto her for dear life. "People will think we're a couple."

Principal Parker laughed and stood behind her, and brushed a few stray strands of hair off his daughter's very tanned neck.

"Eleanore, manners."

Ms. Weiss, wearing a beautiful pink dress her mother had once owned, joined his side and linked arms with him.

"I hope people think that about us!" she said jokingly.

Unfortunately, Parker was born without a sense of humour.

"Oh, Eric, lighten up," she muttered.

Behind them, a man stood in a complete tuxedo, with a top-hat, a large, bushy moustache, and an eye-patch. Red-faced, he began tugging at his tight collar.

"Is it me or is it hot in here?"

"Who are you again?" asked Ms. Weiss.

"I'm the... I told you before, I'm Pepper O. Salt. I'm the entertainment. My girlfriend got me the job."

"Eh?" said Ms. Weiss, and she turned to her partner, who whispered: "Magician."

"Has anybody seen her? Yay high, unwashed hair, cranky face. Responds in grunts?"

"Nobody's seen your imaginary girlfriend, Houdini," said Cora Corali. "Okay. On three, the doors will open. Prepare for blindness."

If Pepper had turned around at that exact moment, he would have spotted his girlfriend. In fact, as the press cameras flashed and blinded them on cue, the Croxley sisters' gagged and blindfolded faces appeared on the television in the corner.

———— . . . ————

Normally we would have driven up to the Walker mansion. However, Mom was in a prickly mood, and whenever that happened she would take it out on the car. Her obsession with cutting down on gas usage was paramount, so we found ourselves hiking up Gentleman's Court. This didn't bode well for our limbs, especially since we were all dressed up and bound tightly for the night. I was wearing a candy-cane coloured skirt and a maroon blouse with a big bow covering my cleavage. It was all I could do to manage carrying a bowl of punch, while Dad held a tray of pulled pork, and Mom a gigantic wrapped box which sported the family's gift to the Walkers. None of us knew what was inside, but Mom insisted it was expensive and in good taste.

"Probably our dignity..." I muttered.

The Walker mansion was lit-up from every angle possible. The gates were wide-open, and car after car was parked on the unloved muddy embankments surrounding it. As we made our way up the steep ascent, I noticed a little hill nearby that was being set up by caterers in white suits. Small tables with wine and poppers lined the insides of a temporary tent-like structure. What it was for, I had no idea. Surely we wouldn't be spending any time outside in this breezy, wintery weather.

"Somebody carry me," said Brendan, sweating in his tux.

When we finally got to the front door, Mom put the gift down for a moment and turned to us. She looked at me, then at Brendan, and finally her husband.

"Ichabod," she scolded, wiping his cheek of a kiss-stain.

"Hey, you're the one who put it there!"

"Brendan, no pranks or speaking out of line. Cassie, don't mention your Grandmother. I'm a very big fan of Marguerite Troubridge; it means a lot to me that you all behave."

"Don't you mean *Margie?*" said Brendan.

Dad and I laughed, but the deadly stare that followed from our mother was enough to snap some sense into my little brother.

"Last one for the night, I swear," he insisted.

The door swung open.

We jumped in surprise, for we had yet to knock on it. Standing there in a beautiful navy mermaid gown, Marguerite looked over our faces, saw me, and opened her mouth in a big toothy smile. It was kind of scary. I was half expecting her entire face to peel inside out.

"The Gellar family!" she said, as if announcing the lottery.

To my surprise, Mom didn't respond. Usually she was the head of the family when it came to social interactions, but for once she was speechless. She stared at the hostess, a grim look on her face.

Sensing something wrong, Dad pushed forward and waved. "Ichabod Gellar. It's lovely to finally meet you, Mrs. Walker."

"Please, call me Margie!" she said, and she guided us in.

"*Margie...*" muttered Brendan.

I suppressed a grin.

Three very awkward things happened in that moment. They were so fast and surreal that it took a while for everything to sink in. One, Dad went to kiss Marguerite's hand just as she removed it to welcome two staff members who were rushing over. His hand accidentally touched her breast instead. To my surprise, one of the staff members was none other than Morgan from the hardware store. The other staff member promptly began taking off our coats, starting with Mom's. Suddenly, it became clear why she'd gone so silent at the front door. She appeared to be wearing the exact same navy mermaid gown as Marguerite.

"Oh," said Dad, tucking his hands under his arms.

"Oh," said Mom, looking down at her dress in shame.

"Oh," said Morgan, recognising me.

"Oy vey..." muttered Brendan, embarrassed for us all.

Ever the class act, Marguerite turned on her heels and said: "Welcome, welcome! Morgan and Benjamin will take your coats. This lovely young girl behind me is Suzannah; she is my *'Complimentary Colleen'* for the evening. It's a very popular practice which is trending in Marseille, hiring a maid to praise you at functions."

A woman in black peeped from behind her and waved to us, then quickly complimented Mom on her stunning dress (which was quite clever since it also served as a compliment to Marguerite).

"Follow me, follow me," the hostess started to walk away, and raised her hands in the air. "I'll take this opportunity to introduce you to the other guests! Come along, come along, don't dilly-dally!"

"Excellent crowd control, Madam Troubridge!" said Suzannah.

I was certain we were all red-faced. As we went down the long hallway, a rush of conversation sounded from ahead. Entering the familiar parlour room I'd recently decorated, we were suddenly at the mercy of a dozen eyes. Standing about the room, nibbling and drinking, were the other guests. Some I knew, some I didn't.

"Last ones to arrive!" declared Marguerite.

*So much for being 'abnormally early'*, I thought.

"Attention, attention," she continued in a French accent, catching the crowd's notice. "It appears we all took advantage of the half-price sale down at '*Kak! Spinaldi*' this week…"

Marguerite waved her hands outwards, revealing her fellow women across the room. All of them were dressed in identical navy mermaid gowns. This caused the room to erupt in a genteel laughter, the women half-embarrassed.

Mom and Marguerite linked arms like long-lost soulmates.

"May I introduce to you the Gellar family," our host told her captivated audience. "They live in Philips Drive. You youngens already know Cassie from school; well this is her mother Lesley, father Ichabod, and younger brother Brendan. There's another daughter, Annie, but she is unable to make it tonight as she is Eleanore Parker's guest on the Zeppelin ride. Well, Gellars, welcome! Mi casa es tu casa. Soltarse el pelo!"

Taking this opportunity to move away from my family, letting them fend for themselves, I decided to join the conversation going on between JT, Hayley and Tommy Walker. They were standing next to the base of the bent Christmas tree, using the nearby table of hors d'oeuvres to place their drinks on.

"Hey," said Hayley, cutting in.

"Lee," I replied.

"Huh?"

"That's your name, don't wear it out."

"Whatever…" she said, confused.

Her eyes immediately scanned what I was wearing. I couldn't tell if it was a good or bad look. In turn, I drank up the anomaly that was her smart-wear: a black linen top and dress. I'd never seen her in such girly clothes. It looked… unnatural. She also sported white socks up to her knees, and Mary Jane shoes. To top it off, she sported a black Alice headband. This was not the Hayley Gauche I knew.

Not to say JT wasn't surprising in his dark green suit, either. His beanie was nowhere in sight. Instead, a future afro was growing, slow but steady.

"You kids scrub up very nicely," said Mr. Walker, wearing almost the exact same suit as his son, only in maroon. "Now, if you'll excuse me, I think I hear a cork popping."

Left alone, the three of us hummed over our outfits, quickly finding ourselves unable to resist laughing stupidly.

Hayley nudged my arm. "Did you hear about Greg?"

"No, what's wrong?"

JT looked unimpressed.

"He's not coming tonight. His mother's in hospital again."

"Oh," I said, looking down. I knew something was up with his mother, but he never talked about it. "Is she alright?"

"Who knows with her?" said Hayley. "I…"

She was about to elaborate when JT nudged her in the side. Wednesday and Friday were slinking over.

"Hello, boys," said Friday meanly, dressed in a lovely pink dress.

Each Saviour had a glass of champagne in their hands.

"Have you tried the wine?" asked Wednesday. "It's divine. And it's not even nine! Just needs a squirt of lime. JT, is it true you are having fireworks later?"

JT undid his green bow-tie a little bit.

"First off, don't kid yourselves if you think we're handing out real champagne to minors. Secondly, no, there'll be fireworks at the school when the Zeppelin returns later tonight. We're only setting up a viewing station down the hill. Best spot in town to see them, in my opinion."

"I wonder how they're going?" said Wednesday, dressed in a gorgeous blue ballgown. Her voice wobbled at the last second. I think she'd wanted to go with Eleanore the most.

"I'm sure they're all french-kissing each other," said Hayley, turning sour all of a sudden. When nobody responded, she added: "That sounded like a better insult in my head. They're probably being snobby aristocratic pig-swine up there. I've heard all celebrities are like that."

"No, we met Uma Harlow's twin, and she's lovely," I insisted.

*"Uma Harlow has a twin?"* said the Saviours together.

Suddenly full of intense aggression, they practically pinned me against the hoer d'oeuvres table to interrogate me further.

*"What's her name?"*

# 28

## A
## FACE IN THE
## CROWD

*Netti Zawistowski!* For billionth time, I'm on list. Didn't even have this much trouble getting into Simi Fest. I'm… Right there. See? Beneath your thumb. No, you've smudged it. It says Netti. Netti Zawistowski."

The security guard gave the dowdy woman with scruffy brown hair and big blue eyes a doubtful stare. As they stood outside Horn-Horn High-High's incredibly packed football field, Netti scoped the crowd for somebody on her team.

Suddenly, she caught sight of…

"Hey!" she called out, then turned back to the guard. "Okay, look, big pregnant lady over there. Huge, uh, looks to be faking. See her? She is with me. I left my lan… landmark… with my assistant inside, so I… I have forgotten her name, but I… *Audrey!*"

The one and only Audrey Mercy turned at the sound of her

name, and waddled over.

"Hi, Netti! Is everything alright?"

"Hello. Please tell security officer that I am part of..." she sighed, getting tired of speaking English, "... crew of program."

Audrey smirked, and pulled her lanyard out from between her breasts. She flashed it at the security guard.

"She's with us! That's Uma Harlow's twin, you know!"

The security guard didn't care.

Netti rushed through the barrier, and hugged Audrey in appreciation. The two of them began walking back towards the side of the football field, where their crew was preparing.

"I don't like people knowing me as famous association!" shouted Netti, her tiny voice barely piercing through the surrounding crowd of hundreds. She was hunched into her warm winter jacket. "Thank you for rescuing me! Is Uma nearly ready?"

"Just waiting for you!" shouted Audrey, pushing her way ahead. "Don't slow down for me! I'll catch up! It's my ankles! They're like rhino feet right now!"

Netti turned to look at the people surrounding the cast and crew's private tent on the side of the field, then turned back.

"I am happy to take... time with you. Yes?"

Audrey smiled. "Oh. Alright! Thank you!"

Netti helped Audrey to hobble the rest of the way.

Around them, the crowds were piling into their seats. Vendors and funfair employees lined the edges of the field, while a man they knew only as Pepper the Magician was on a stage pulling a rabbit out of his top hat. Across from him was a local rock band, who performed Christmas renditions quite terribly, although the dozen or so people rocking out in front of the stage seemed to be into it.

Beyond the school, very little traffic crowded the streets, and a gaggle of owls relished in the newfound kingdom. Eight of them landed gently in the middle of Stirrup Avenue, until suddenly a giant Harley Davidson disturbed the peace and sped twice as fast as the speed limit allowed. It shot down one street, up another, through alleyways until at last the growing roar of the crowd became almost overwhelming. This crowd, however, was not from the school, and as the rider with the slender woman straddling him from behind drove through the main entrance, they were relieved to see that the Annual Motorcycle Race in front of them was yet to commence.

"Don't take so long next time," cursed the rider, Sam.

"We made it, didn't we?" snarled his girlfriend from behind.

As they revved their way through admissions, they signed their names and drove into the crowd of fellow participants. Among them were cruisers, scooters, a Ural, and even an old-fashioned velomobile.

"These costumes are wild!" said Sam's girlfriend, Melinda.

She marvelled at the odd riders and their attire. One man had a bunch of papier-mâché reindeer attached to his torso. There was the Grim Reaper, Mrs. Claus, a dwarf dressed as an elf...

One particularly muscular rider, wearing a sleeveless Santa top, had two women in his sidecar. They appeared to be part of his costume, sitting back-to-back, despondent, their eyes and mouths covered with gaffer tape and their hands tied up.

Pulling up beside them, Melinda gave them a dirty look, while her partner admired the motorcycle.

"Bit sexist, don't you think, Sam?" she said under her breath.

"It's kind of hot."

Melinda smacked his shoulder gently.

As she turned to check out the crowds in their seats, someone in particular caught her eye. In fact, the old woman's bright blue eyes jumped out at her. Sitting in one of the front rows, eating popcorn.

"That..." said Melinda furiously.

Without bothering to explain anything to her boyfriend, she hopped off the back of his motorbike. Making sure to keep her eye on the target ahead, she strutted determinedly across the circuit, past men with headpieces who told her to stop while they set up. The camera crews ignored her as a group of Christmas Carollers sung on a stage in the middle of the grounds. The closer she got, the more certain Melinda was that it was the same woman.

"Hey!" she called as she reached the railing. "You!"

Grandma Helen sat back in her seat, her eyes boggling.

"You remember me?" asked Melinda, incensed, stopping at the metal railing between the two of them. "The other day at the mall when we drove past, you spit on me. I bet you remember me now."

Grandma turned in her seat and looked around at the crowd. None of the protestors were here yet, and the race would be starting soon. When she turned back, Melinda smacked her hands against the railing in front of her.

"I'm talking to you!" she yelled.

The man sitting next to Grandma, who'd been watching the entire time, stood up. "Hey, hey, easy."

"Mind your business, beefcake."

He fished inside his winter jacket and pulled out a police badge. "How about now?"

"What, I'm supposed to be intimidated by that? Look, Officer..." she squinted to read. "I don't even know how to pronounce that. This woman, *she's* the one who spat on *me* the other day. I want her charged!"

"She nearly ran me over outside the shops on her ugly motorcycle," said Grandma Helen, standing up. "I demand you arrest her for attempted murder."

"This is outrageous! *I'm* pressing charges, do you hear me? You are not going to get away with this."

"Go and tell your cheating boyfriend over there —"

Melinda jumped the railing, and came close to striking the old woman, but luckily the police officer got in her way. Soon Sam had abandoned his motorcycle and joined in the hustle, wrestling with the officer. Members of the crowd around them helped out, and soon an all-out-brawl was going on.

Grandma Helen somehow crawled beneath a pair of feet and watched from a distance as the nearby cameras turned away from the singers, zooming in on what was happening.

Leaving her cane behind in the mess, she hobbled for the exit.

# 29
## ALL ABOARD!

We were ushered into the large dining room at ten to seven. It was a very long room, decorated in beige and mahogany, with sprinkles of Christmas strewn across the two rectangular dining tables. Golden candle frames, tinsel hanging from the chandeliers, and baubles in glass bowls. I couldn't help but notice a candle-holder with nine unlit candles on it.

I nudged Dad's cummerbund.

"Menorah at nine o'clock."

He swirled around to check behind him. When I recalled that clocks startled his senses, I pointed instead.

"Ichabod and Lesley, you two are sitting right next to me," said Marguerite, and she linked arms with Mom again.

Not surprisingly, she led them to the head of the table, right next to the candle-holder. A lighter was placed upright next to it, and I knew at once that Marguerite was simply covering all of her bases.

I was guided to my designated seat by Morgan, who'd yet to speak to me about anything other than the relief of clothing and the direction of the nearest bathroom. As he pushed my seat in for me, he grabbed my red and green napkin and placed it on my lap. I knew I was going bright red, but at least this time I didn't look like an allergic pufferfish.

"Watch your hands there, buster," said Brendan, as my hardware friend repeated the same courtesy with his own napkin. "Buy me a drink first!"

JT sat opposite me, and when our eyes met I couldn't help but notice he looked a little panicky. His eyes quickly darted down to the end of the table and back again. I followed his short gaze and noticed that Hayley was being seated very far away, and did not look pleased about it. But then again, she did not look at all surprised. Rather than jumping to his girlfriend's defence, JT instead poured himself a glass of chilled non-alcoholic wine from the ice bucket before us.

"Maybe she's in trouble," said Brendan, cottoning on, and he called out to her: "Have you been a *bad litt*—"

"Stop," I said, clutching firmly at his thigh. I turned back to my friend. "JT, she can't sit all the way over there on her own. Look, Friday is next to her. They'll murder each other."

JT sipped his wine.

"This is why I hate Christmas," he muttered.

I eyed the vacant seat next to him.

"She can take Greg's spot. He's not coming. Hayley!"

I put my arm up to call her. To my surprise, JT grabbed it and pulled it down for me.

"No. Allocated seats."

I really didn't understand, but decided not to push it. We were guests after all, and maybe Hayley preferred it down there. I got comfortable in my chair, secretly poured myself some of the *real* red wine, and took to idly chatting to those around me.

I couldn't help but notice, though, that Marguerite was now giving me a rather unimpressed gaze from where she sat.

———— • • • ————

Annie was overwhelmed. Despite her best efforts in doing her own make-up, a team were now reapplying it while she sat in a leather swivel chair. It wasn't to her taste — they'd applied it too thick and bronzed, so that now she looked like a wax figurine. Still, this was how it was done in the business, apparently. Surrounded by people rushing about, she pulled her glasses from between her breasts, tired of not being able to see.

"My eyes hurt," she kept insisting, but the make-up artists told her to do without.

"Do you see *any* of the stars?" asked Eleanore, getting her make-up done in the seat next to her.

"I can't see anyone."

"I swear it's like they're keeping them from us."

"They'll be on the Zeppelin," said Annie, closing her eyes to rest. "Besides, we were promised handshakes. It's meant to be for the broadcast."

"Yeah, but now I'm wondering if they're being sneaky. Maybe they meant the radio broadcast."

Annie sighed, irritated by her negativity. "Eleanore, don't you ever get tired of being on edge all the time?"

Eleanore was about to snap back with something about her being ugly, but refrained.

"Yes," she answered honestly.

She leaned back in her chair and sighed.

"I'm sure you're right. Anyway, I can't relax. It's not in my genes. I'll relax when we've safely landed back on the football field at nine-thirty."

Annie turned curiously, tilting her head.

"Why's that?"

"I'm *terrified* of heights."

"Then… why did you sign up for this?" laughed Annie.

"Because everybody was telling me to, and I didn't think we'd actually win! But then we get to meet the cast and Thomas Noel, and I'm so excited for that, but all I'll be thinking about is the fact that we're a hundred feet up in the air and I won't even be able to look out the window without freaking out!"

"Wow," said Annie. "So you *are* human."

Eleanore shook her head.

"I'm really not, I swear. I've taken, like, twelve Xanax and they've done nothing. I even went down to Spliffany's last weekend to see if she had anything, but she swears she's clean now. Nothing is working, and I can't even…"

She was almost hyperventilating now; she knocked the make-up artist's brush away from her face and grabbed Annie's wrist.

"I don't think I can do this."

Pressed for time, noticing that people were getting more and more rushed around them, Annie smiled at her.

"It's okay. Look, take these…"

Thinking quickly, she fished in between her boobs and brought out her pair of glasses again.

"Put these on. You won't be able to see a thing."

Eleanore took the glasses off her and inspected their dimensions suspiciously.

"As long as they don't make me look ugly…" she said.

She put them on and leaned in close to the mirror to get a good look. She turned back, flabbergasted.

"I look amazing!" she said, baring her teeth in a wide grin.

Cora Corali reared her frenetic head through the tent's main entrance and grabbed the girls by the arms, yanking them out into the open. Both were blind, and stumbled forward. Music was screeching all around them, mingling into the sounds of the crowd cheering, the vendor music, and some sort of engine roaring above.

"It's here!" cried Netti from nearby.

"Good luck, Annie and Eleanore!" came Audrey's voice.

"No, I'm not ready," muttered Eleanore, turning her head this way and that. "I need to see my… *Wait!*"

Both girls looked up into the sky as a giant gust of warm wind greeted them from above, and they spotted a great big blurry grey mass growing larger and larger. It looked as if the moon was falling down. The crowds cheered louder yet, the wind howling, and the ground rumbled as the Zeppelin landed in front of them on the football field.

"We can do this, trust me!" said Annie, clutching at Eleanore's shaking hands.

Through the crowd they could hear whistling, and occasionally people calling out their names. A mega-phone was roaring information about *The Prefect Family*, naming those onboard, the flight-plan, the pilot, and then…

Before they knew it, they'd walked up the steps and were safely inside the airship. Cora guided them from behind until they reached the end of a short grey hallway. Beyond that was a ballroom, grand in size and very expensive looking, with a bar on each end. Cora let them go as the select few made their way in behind them…

— . . . —

I wasn't aware until it started that this was a full course dinner we'd involved ourselves in. Just as I was about to judge the tiny portion size of the sweet potatoes, the caviar it was accompanied with did set off my suspicions. Finally, when the fifth set of food was placed in front of me, I cottoned on at long last.

"They'll be lifting off soon," said JT, checking his watch.

Out of curiosity, I began counting heads. With over thirty guests packed into one room, spread across two long tables, I guess I knew maybe half of them. I caught Tanya's eye on the other table as she sat with her mother, father, sister and cousin. She didn't look like she was having much fun. Wednesday was the only other teen on her table, and besides from not liking one another, they were basically at opposite ends.

Shortly after, the music playing from the speakers softened and the lights dimmed. A clinking against glass could be heard behind us, so I turned to see Marguerite as she stood up. With her smile as broad as ever, she suddenly started singing in a very high operatic pitch. Brendan's hands flew to cover his ears, while the rest of us paid attention. I wasn't a huge fan of opera, but it was hard to deny what a lovely voice she had. It was smooth but firm, delicate but ferocious. When she finished, we applauded her and one by one we gave her a standing ovation.

"Brava, Ms. Troubridge! Excellent as always!" cried her Complimentary Colleen, Suzannah.

"Your mother is so talented," I said to JT, when our next courses were being served. "She sounds just as good in real life as she does on her records. Hey, who are all the people in this room? I don't recognise a lot of them."

JT leaned in to whisper.

"That's Friday's mother and father down the end, and her little sister Dima sitting next to Hayley. Then over there, we've got Wednesday and her parents, Tanya and her family, Mr. & Mrs. Wanke and their daughter Cherilyn, who's in Annie's year... And your parents. If the Zeppelin ride wasn't on, we'd also have the wonderful company of the Parkers and Ms. Weiss."

"So exclusive," said Brendan in a mock hush. He fidgeted around in his seat. "Pray tell. Is anyone else's butt itchy?"

"Brendan!"

"No, not like... inside the crack. I mean the meaty part. The *glutes*. I'm not talking about my squinting anus, you pervert."

Mr. Walker piped up from nearby.

"That's from a lack of proper circulation to your piriformis muscle. As you mentioned, it has nothing to do with your rectum."

"I'm sorry about him. He gets restless," I muttered.

"No need to apologise, Cassie. He was speaking technical jargon, which, as an expert in the Amblyopia field, I greatly appreciate. Feel free to stand up or go for a walk at any time, young man."

"Thanks chief, I'm just curious. Would *love* some wine, though."

Brendan made a reach for the real stuff, but I blocked him off.

Finally, after drinking three wines myself, I felt my ears begin to burn. I knew when enough was enough. I excused myself to go to the bathroom, and insisted my brother tag along with me.

"Are we poo pals now?" he asked as we left the room.

"No, I thought you could do with a walk. Mom asked you to be polite, and that was really embarrassing back there."

"Says you," he muttered.

We made our way down a long hallway until we were in a little holding room that led to the sole guest bathroom.

"Jeez, Brendan, I thought you were more mature than that."

"Give me a break. I'm not in there swinging naked from the chandelier, you know. I asked a question. Mr. Walker even said he appreciated it."

"He was being polite!"

"That man's drunk as a sailor; he was not being polite. I think the problem here is that everybody is acting uptight around the Walkers because they want to impress them. But why? They're ordinary people, just like the rest of us. I hate it when people fawn over others because they think they're special. I don't care who the Walkers are, and you didn't care either before you knew —"

"Brendan, stop, you're making this into something it's not. Why don't we..."

"No, everyone in this family keeps acting like they're so much older and smarter, and that I'm a little child —"

"You *are* a little child!" I snapped.

If looks could kill, my brother would've murdered me on the spot. His cheeks turned pink and then he backed away. A moment later I heard his footsteps running back towards the dining room.

I stood there in the hallway for a while, keeping my eyes closed, letting the quiet wash over me. I felt so tired from all of these fights I was having lately. Christmas was supposed to be a time of peace.

"Are you alright?" a voice called out eventually.

I slowly opened my eyes. Morgan stood there in his white tuxedo, an empty tray under his right arm. My brain immediately rewired and kicked into high gear, and I became a hot stinking mess in no time at all.

"Yes! Hi!"

There was a beat.

"Everything okay?" he rephrased.

"Just need a break from the people," I said.

"You look well."

I didn't know how to respond. "Um... Thank you."

"I mean..." he rolled his eyes and smiled, "you looked under the weather last time I saw you."

I thought back.

"At the store..."

It felt like a lifetime ago. The fifteenth century, in fact.

"You were with your Aunt?"

"I'm feeling much better," I said. "*And* I'm going to bring in a new résumé. One that isn't... ripped in half. I haven't done it yet because... This has been a very busy week."

I thought guiltily about the ridiculous amount of down-time I'd had. He didn't need to know that.

"Well, hurry up. It'll be nice to have somebody relatively normal to talk to on my shifts."

"Speaking of shifts... How many jobs do you have?"

"I work at the bakery and the hardware store. I also know the Coopers, so that's how I got this job... but that's it."

"Oh, you know the Coopers? As in, Greg Cooper?"

"Yeah, my mother is a receptionist at your school, and knew Mrs. Cooper when she worked there. Small world, huh? Or small town, anyway."

So much information. Who was Morgan's mother? And when did Greg's mother work at the school? Suddenly I put a hand to my mouth as I remembered something.

"Oh. You know... she went into hospital today. Greg's mother, Mrs. Cooper. I don't know why. Did you know that?"

He frowned. "No, I didn't. I'll call my mother during my break. She might not have heard because she's down at the school watching the Zeppelin take off."

"And you know Greg, too?"

"Sort of. Not a lot. I graduated high school in May so I haven't seen him in a while. Are you... Is he... Do you guys hang out a lot?"

I shrugged. "Yeah. He's really nice."

"Bit quiet though."

"Right?" I snickered. "And he always stares at you, even when it makes you uncomfortable."

"I was going to ask..." said Morgan, beaming from ear-to-ear.

We stood there grinning at each other for a moment longer, until finally I just said what he wanted to hear.

"We're only friends, though."

He nodded, looked down, and immediately went an intense shade of red. I'd never seen that colour on a healthy person before. Feeling terrible for him, and panicking slightly myself, I tried to change the subject as smoothly as possible.

"Need help doughing?"

He lost some of the colour purely out of confusion.

"Huh?"

I shook my head. "Never mind. I'd better get back some time. I mean, now. I'll see you around, Morgan..."

I held out my hand for some reason, and he shook it.

"Tucker."

"Morgan Tucker... Tucker... Oh, you're Ms. Chin-Tucker's son! The Asian lady at reception."

*Why did you have to add that last part?* I asked myself angrily.

"Yeah," he said with a smirk. "I'll tell her you said hi."

Morgan's sweaty hand let go and he trotted off down the hallway. I got up and went back into the dining room, apologising for taking so long, and making sure to keep myself turned away from Brendan.

———— • • • ————

Beyond the ballroom, decked in gold with rows of tall tables lining the sides, there was a hallway that led to a grand dining hall. The producers, cast and guests ate their dinners together at the two very long mahogany tables.

Across from her, Annie stared in awe at Thomas Noel, squinting in her short-sightedness. Even sitting down, he seemed to be a great deal shorter than she'd been prepared for. On *The Prefect Family* they'd always made him out to be over six feet tall. In fact, there was a running gag about it. In real life, however, he practically needed a booster seat to see over the table-top.

Uma Harlow was sitting next to him, dolled up in an extravagant gown with giant frilly pieces jutting out at the shoulders — a clear grab for attention. She looked different, as well. Less glamorous and more unimpressed with her surrounding company. Something about her nose was off, too. It was sharper than usual.

Annie had been needing to pee for quite a while, especially given all she was allowed to drink was soft drink, and her body-tight yellow dress was pressing in on her stomach. However, a very tense Eleanore was practically cutting off the circulation to her right wrist, begging her not to leave her sight, so she'd remained in her seat. Bladder in great distress, she tried to distract herself by looking around the lavish dining hall they sat in.

The Zeppelin was like an optical illusion — although impressive in its size on the football field, it was nothing compared to the grandeur flaunted inside. Annie wondered how it even managed to get off the ground with the amount of people, furniture and machinery it was forced to carry into the air with it. The further up they went, the more people ventured out of the dining hall after dinner, back into the ballroom in order to see Horn-Horn's lights from the bay windows on either side of the airship. It was quite a sight to see, and all but one person was enamoured by it.

"You should see the views," said Annie, as she dragged the Saviour to one of the windows. She snatched her glasses back. "There's Doowhacky Road, Gangrene Avenue, Belly Button Place. The curve to the beach... Oh! There's Paolo's ice-cream stand! Jeez, I tell you... the amount of owls I can see right now would *shock* you. They must be forming a coup."

Eleanore sat on a seat nearby, making sure to keep her eyes away from the sides of the ship's gondola. She was on her fourth drink since it started, and could only focus on one thing: not passing out. When at last it was time to serve desert, both Annie and Cora Corali had to help her across the ballroom and into the dining hall again.

"I just don't understand how an airship can have such gigantic rooms!" Eleanore whimpered, tears streaming down her worried face. "Why haven't we crashed yet!?"

"Holy Moses, I did not come here for this," said Cora, letting go of her and heading towards her own seat near one of the lesser-known stars.

Annie almost crumpled under the Saviour's surprising weight. She helped Eleanore back to her seat at their dining table, then grabbed at her face and squished her cheeks tight.

"You need to snap out of this. It's ruining your whole night. In a few minutes we are going to be able to talk to our favourite people in the world, right there in front of us, see? And I *need* you to be yourself, Eleanore. Please! We are not going to crash. You need to stop thinking about that. Also, the notion of it is making my throat constrict a little. But mainly, I need you to do this for *you!*"

Eleanore's eyes exploded with a new river of tears.

"I can't be this high!" she sobbed. "I can't. I can't be here. I feel like something awful is going to happen! Please, let me off! You have to let me off! Let me off!"

The Saviour stood up, immediately losing balance and collapsing against the table.

*"LET ME OFF RIGHT NOW! I NEED TO BE ON THE GROUND!"*

As people rushed over to help, Annie stepped back from her seat and watched helplessly. Eleanore let out a troubled scream, struggling against those who grabbed at her wrists and tried to pin her down.

# 30
## NAZI THAT COMING

Freezing cold on the sidewalk, the old woman didn't even look up as *'The Uma'* flew overhead. People in the circuit nearby were cheering, the music was playing loud, and the race was nearly over. She huddled like a homeless person into her large jacket and rested her painful hip against the nearest trash-can.

"Hey, Bird Lady!"

Grandma Helen looked up to see a hearse in front of her. Despite its headlights obscuring the driver from view, she knew exactly who it was.

"Vhy did you come here?"

"See, I love getting frostbite," said Rachael. "I thought I'd try it out. Maybe Santa will give me a stump for Christmas."

"Stop," said Helen moodily.

Rachael wheezed out a laugh: "Alright, alright. Get in the car."

Helen did as she was told. Buckling herself into the passenger seat, she put her frozen hands right up to the heater under the dashboard. As they drove away, she was surprised to hear some familiar music playing on the speakers.

"You like Jo Stafford?" asked Rachael, turning it up.

"*You* like Jo Stafford?"

"Sure! Who can resist the original creeper girl?"

"Eh?"

"*I Remember You? You Belong To Me? I'll Be Seeing You?* All cleverly disguised as love songs, but only a *true* fan can see through the lyrics. Jo was a *stalker*."

"I don't follow. Do you like her music or not?"

"No. That's why I play her music, you see. 'Cause I hate it."

"You are driving me mad! Answer a question for once in your life. Vhy did you come here? How did you know I'd be outside?"

"Because there I was, making myself a cup of hot chocolate and nestling into the couch, when lo-and-behold breaking news interrupts my program. A fight has broken out at the motorcycle race. What should I see in the background? Why, a metal walking cane being smashed into the head of a dead-beat with face tattoos, and a little old woman hobbling away in the background. I thought to myself: 'Should I call Lesley? Interrupt her exciting dinner with the Walkers?' Or do I drive down there and see if she needs my help? I waited twenty minutes in case you got a cab home, then when you didn't arrive I thought: 'Hey! I'll pop downtown. Why not?' Either way, I figured I'd grab some McDonald's so it wouldn't be a total waste of my time. I guess now that I know you're alright, the most pressing matter is…"

She reached behind her seat for something.

"Are you in the mood for McNuggets or a McPhilly?"

Grandma took the packet of nuggets. As she began to eat them, she eyed her son-in-law's sister, who was carefully driving through the downtown streets of Horn-Horn.

"Jews always have ulterior motives. You only wanted to have one over on me."

Rachael's eyes almost exploded from their sockets. Furious, she pulled the hearse over to the side of the road.

"What is your problem, Helen!?"

"You are. You've always been my problem."

"I'm not your problem. I drove down here out of *concern*, and you've insulted me in my very own car! No, there's something else. Whatever it is, you've got to figure it out because I am not the only one in this family who is getting absolutely sick and tired of your horse crap."

Helen huffed and laughed. "We are not family."

"Uh, news flash. We most definitely are. I'm not especially fond of this fact, either, y'know. My brother and your daughter have bound us together forever. And you know what? As disturbing as it is, we're a lot more alike than you think."

"Ha! You're a childless, unwed woman who is well past her expiry date. I don't see any prospects in your future. You should hear the things they say about *you* when you're not around. How on earth are *we* alike?"

"Because when this holiday is over, that's it. Good riddance to bad rubbish. We go home."

"And?"

"They'll be glad to see the back of us."

"That's not true…"

"Oh, really? No? Look me in the eye and tell me I'm wrong. See, this is what irks me about you, Helen. You think you know everything, and then you… you… This may surprise you to learn, but I've accepted my place in this family. I may be childless and alone and old, but that's my choice."

"Good grief, don't be so melodramatic," said Helen slowly, embarrassed for her little outburst. "You're not that old, and technically you're attractive enough. Women like you can always find someone. I'm sure a Jew boy will want to settle down and start a family with you eventually."

"I don't think so," said Rachael, her nerves on edge. "Nobody wants someone who…"

It seemed she'd said too much. She pulled back immediately.

Helen stopped eating, cottoning on.

"Who can't… what?"

Rachael let out a trembling sigh as she succumbed to the inevitable. She crossed her arms and stared daggers at the old woman across from her.

"Don't act so surprised. You are a witch, after all. This is the part where you rub it in my face and go: 'One less kike in the world to worry about'."

"No, that's… I would never…"

"Well, the truth is it makes me unwanted. And you're unwanted. So, that's how we're alike. Do you think I don't see the way Ichabod looks at me? I know what they say when I'm not there, because I think it myself. And you know what they say about you when you're not there. because you see it in their eyes."

Helen felt a strange sense of alienation from her own body. She gazed at the woman next to her, whose face exhibited no more signs of depravity or flightiness. A seriousness had swept over her, changing her appearance forever.

"Now I know why you were so angry with me at Annie's birthday. I didn't know that about you."

Rachael wiped her eyes and looked out the window.

"There are some things people shouldn't be expected to share."

They sat in silence, letting the conversation marinate in their thoughts for a while. Eventually, Helen cleared her throat.

"I lost a child once."

Rachael turned to her, taken aback in the moment. She noticed that the old lady's bright blue eyes were just as watery as hers, lost in another time.

"What you people choose to ignore is that ve *had* to be... We did not have a choice back then. I am not a monster, as much as you'd like to think I am. No, many of us were just normal people. We never wanted any of that to happen. It was like there was a giant cloud of evil over the world back then. When I realised I was... The man, he... We were not married, so... I had no choice... Well, Victor knows about it. Lesley and Deanna as well, although she has taken it to heaven with her. And now you know. Are you happy?"

"Oh yeah, ecstatic."

A deafening rush of motorcycles zoomed past at such a rate that the two women almost hit their heads on the roof in fright. Howls of excitement and firecrackers popping carried away with them, and Grandma Helen put her hands to her ears.

"That's it, I've had it vith these motorcycles!"

Rachael collected herself and flipped the indicator on to merge back into the traffic.

"What happened to that group of protestors you were meeting?"

"They didn't show up."

"Sounds about right. Let's go home."

They drove on in silence, climbing the steep road leading to Philips Street. Helen stared out at the ocean on the horizon across from her. Up in the sky, she began to count the stars, for the clouds were slowly drifting apart.

Amongst the millions, an oddly green star stood out suddenly. As she stared at it, more clouds parted and revealed a distinctly pink star next to that, and then a blue one next to that. Struck by their beauty, she closed her eyes and wondered about what she would do next.

Rachael thought the same thing.

# 31

## ONE OF
## THESE THINGS...

Cora Corali was a good, hard-working girl. That's what
she kept telling the people onboard, anyway. She'd made
up a tremendous success story of her life, oozing confidence and professionalism with every step she made.

However, this hiccup with the high school student in the dining room had caused a chain reaction, and soon things were deviat-
ing greatly from her tightly-structured plan.

During a quick bathroom break, she delicately touched up her
lipstick and adjusted her bob-cut. Encouragement by way of persis-
tent gaze in the mirror, she embodied the epitome of a successful,
top-tier television producer. Even if it was all a lie.

This crazy girl losing her mind was nothing to worry about,
Cora kept telling herself; she just had severe vertigo and was not
having a mental breakdown because of the pressures she was facing
from the producers of the show. No, that *definitely wasn't it, she defi-*

*nitely wasn't manic and in fact neither was Cora what are you talking about if I was manic the tell-tale signs would be uh-oh I think this might be what they're*

"Oh boy," she held her breath, and then left the bathroom. "One thing at a time, Cora… *Oh!*"

Straight out the door, she ran directly into a man wearing a black dinner suit and top-hat. His fake moustache almost fell off in the collision, and he collected the deck of cards which had toppled out of his cufflinks.

"Apologies, my dearest lady!" declared Pepper O. Salt.

He clumsily grabbed her hand to kiss it. Cora wriggled out of his grip, popped a mysterious pill into her mouth, and chewed on it as she tried to get past him.

"Men's bathrooms are on the other side of the ship," she said.

Pepper adjusted his black eye-patch.

"I was checking the engines. These hands don't just do magic tricks, you know. I'm also a skilled electrician by trade! Electrician by day, magician by…"

The lights went out, frightening them both.

"… night."

They flickered back on.

"Tada!" he said jokingly.

"Very impressive," said Cora, but his bragging was starting to aggravate her. "Did you ever find your imaginary girlfriend?"

Realising what little respect she had for him, Pepper decided not to answer, giving up on her and disappearing through another door that said: 'CREW ONLY'. By the time Cora reached the ballroom, she'd put the strange interaction to the back of her mind.

Annie turned in her seat by the window.

"Is Eleanore alright?" she asked Cora.

"No, I don't think she is, actually. Nothing is working on her. I got her on the bandwagon, and zilch. I'm tempted to slip something into her drink. If she doesn't calm down, we'll have to descend sooner than planned."

Annie covered her mouth. "Oh, no!"

"Relax, it's an emergency…"

"No, I mean about finishing early. That's awful! Although since you brought it up, Eleanore already popped a load of Xanax before we came on board. She told me."

"Great, another thing I'll have to monitor. Well, everything happens for a reason, I guess. The cast are really freaked out, too. They refuse to step foot in the same room as her."

"How many rooms does this Zeppelin have, anyway?"

"I think I read twelve on this one. Three of them are crew areas, two are above us where the hydrogen and helium are, and then there's the control car where the pilot is. You should have seen these things during the Second World War. They were something else. Of course, we've come a long way since then with technology, safety, electrical structure and all that, but the..."

Her voice trailed off.

"I'll be right back," she said.

Cora ventured down the narrow corridor, her steps echoing against the metal walls. She found the door marked 'CREW ONLY', beyond which lay the heart of the Zeppelin. As she opened the door and peered in, she immediately noticed the faint scent of engine oil tinging the air. Above her, the vast expanse of the Zeppelin's envelope loomed, filled with helium and interspersed with smaller air-filled ballonets. Narrow metal walkways wound around the envelope, providing access for maintenance and inspections.

The area was completely deserted.

Deciding to respect the 'CREW ONLY' sign, Cora quietly closed the door and decided to explore the passenger areas instead.

— • • • —

The five motorcycles that grouped together after the race hooned onto the beach-front. Riding down the pier, they parked side-by-side in the darkness. There was Sam, his girlfriend Melinda, then there was Terry and his wife Rhonda, a man simply known as Legs, a woman named Cathy, and last but not least the mysterious Begley, sporting two hot pieces of ass tied up in his sidecar.

Begley scooped his trophy up from beneath Chloe's legs, and raised it above his head. The others roared in applause, shouting and punching the air.

"This is going straight to the pawn shop tomorrow," said Begley. "Then I'm going to shout my mother to a beautiful hot meal at the fanciest restaurant this side of her hospital."

"I don't think they'll let her out for that, Begley..."

"They'll do what I tell them to," he replied, and he grabbed the gun from his pants pocket.

The others responded in delight, and cheered him again. Melinda, on the other hand, wasn't too pleased with his behaviour. Her eyes fell upon the two women, now lying down in the sidecar.

"Since the race is over, maybe you should untie your girlfriends. Or is that, like, some kind of weird sex thing you're into?"

Begley could barely see her in the dim, red light of Terry and Rhonda's brake lights. He turned back to Chloe and Candice, whose duct-taped heads tilted from side-to-side.

"They're fine," he said.

Suddenly Sam, with his giant arms, picked Melinda's tiny frame clear off the wooden pier.

"Let's tie you up too and see how you like it!" he joked.

She kicked and yelled until he let her go.

"That's not funny," she insisted, her feet planted firmly again.

Her attitude ruined the mood for Sam, who in turn became moody, and they departed shortly after. One by one, the others followed suit, deciding to head towards a favourite bar a few towns away, by the old highway. Begley insisted he would join them one day in the new year, but not tonight.

When Legs and his Harley disappeared onto the main road and zipped through the far-off trees, Begley put the trophy back into the sidecar, and pulled the gaffer tape off the sisters' eyes. Bewildered, Chloe forced Candice to sit up with her, and they both let out terrified, muffled moans through her gags.

Begley lit a cigarette from his pack. The light from below cast evil shadows across his face. He inhaled, looked out at the calm ocean, and then turned to check out the hilly town behind him. His eyes landed on a low-flying aircraft, probably that Zeppelin he'd heard about. Clouds parting, it blended well with the startling amount of stars on display.

"Why are you two so afraid of me?" he asked the sisters. "It's not like I'm going to kill you or anything. I'm not a murderer, you know. I'll drop you off somewhere soon, I promise. Just... not yet. I need your help finding my brother, Nicky.

"Last time I saw him was a few days ago, when we were casing a few of the houses around here. We do it every year at Christmastime, mainly for him, really. I don't think he understands what we're doing, though. He *is* retarded. In small towns like this, people are usually too enamoured by the tinsel to worry about burglars, so they make it easy for us. But here's the kicker, ladies. We don't steal things for ourselves. We give it to the poor!"

Begley cackled, a heavy smoker's laugh.

"Well, usually. Thing is, we were right in the middle of looting a place recently when I let it slip that I might have pocketed a few hundred thousand over the years. You know, to pay the bills and what-not. Well, Honest Nicky didn't like that. An honest retard, can you believe it? He nearly got us caught. He kept telling me: 'It's Christmas, it's Christmas, you don't steal from the poor!', but he doesn't know. He doesn't realise! What *I* have to do in order to keep us going."

Begley was suddenly in a rage, and he kicked the front tyre of the motorcycle. It barely moved.

"Anyway, it just became too much for me. So I... I left him. There. I admit it. I'm not proud of it. I had a moment. But of course, he can't take care of himself, and I'm the only one he's got, so... That's the real reason I've come back to Horn-Horn. I guess guilt got the better of me. Plus, my mother would disown me if I rocked up at the hospital to visit without him.

"He'll be sleeping under a pier like this one, or camping out on the beach somewhere. I don't know where. But I do know *him*. He'll be nearby. The only thing I can think to do is to drive around the streets calling out his name. Maybe he'll... Who knows? I just wish I could remember the last place we broke into. It might help somehow..."

Begley stared down at the sisters for a moment, as if they were responding with helpful suggestions instead of lying absolutely still.

"Then as promised, I'll let you go."

He flicked his finished cigarette at Candice. It caught in her hair. She quickly flinched and rolled over on her side, taking Chloe with her. Now facing towards the sky, Chloe immediately noticed one green, one pink and one blue star, all twinkling above.

"So ladies, which area shall we start with?" asked Begley. "Deadbeat central, or what about the Hills? I hear the affluent neighbourhoods have the best parties this time of year."

The engine started. Chloe and Candice found themselves shuddering along the wooden pier, across the cement walkway and back onto the smooth, main road.

———— • • • ————

Dinner finally ended after *twelve* courses. I counted them be-cause I wanted to see how far it would go. Well, it went far. Yet it never got to a point where I needed to undo any buttons.

"Five stars to the caterers!" I declared as we all made our way for the entertainment lounge.

"I've never been so well-fed," I heard my mother comment.

"Neither have I," said Brendan purposefully.

His comment stuck out like a sore thumb. Silence ensued, until Marguerite asked the house to play 'holiday carols'. A raging heavy metal track with extremely explicit language roared around us, and Mr. Walker promptly ran to a remote control on the wall to tune it back to a more appropriate song.

"What's up with your brother tonight?" asked Hayley, grabbing JT's butt while no one was looking. "I asked him to pass the butter during the tenth course, and then the little twerp told me to ask again in… 'igpay atinlay'? Whatever that means."

"Pig Latin," said JT.

Hayley immediately turned on him. "What'd you call me?"

"He's been iffy for a while now. I don't get it," I remarked, watching Brendan as he took off his jacket and untucked his shirt. He reached for the punch-bowl several times before Dad finally picked him up and carried him into another room.

I decided it was time to change the subject.

"Have you heard from Greg?"

"Nope," said JT. "Hasn't texted me. He's been through this before. He'll contact us when he's ready."

"What do you mean before? Has his mother been…?"

"Cassie," said Hayley, grabbing my shoulders and leaning in. "When Greg wants to tell you what's going on, he will."

"Jeez, Hayley."

"Jeez yourself, Jonathan," she muttered, and she returned her gaze to me. "Our friend JT here thinks I'm rude when I speak to people, but in my mind I'm only being honest."

As punishment for telling her off, Hayley kicked one of her legs back and it struck JT in the groin. He doubled over. I told her to be careful, and quickly checked to see if he was okay. He recovered just as fast, grinning with delight.

They were such a weird couple.

"Excuse me, everybody," said Marguerite, holding her lit-up phone in her right hand. "I've just received a message from the mayor, Ellana Fork-Flame. Apparently due to unseen circumstances, the Zeppelin will be returning to the football field very shortly. No additional information has been given, although everything seems to be fine. However, she suggests in about twenty minutes or so we head on over to the outside party, where we'll be serving delectable finger-foods and champagne. We'll have a perfect vantage point of the Zeppelin as it flies directly overhead, and then we'll see the fire-works! Isn't that exciting?"

"It is!" declared her Complimentary Colleen. "It *is* exciting!"

Marguerite turned to her husband, whispered something in his ear, and returned her attention to those nearest.

"Hmmm. Wonder what happened..?" muttered JT.

"Probably Eleanore. Afraid of heights..." said Hayley.

"It's got to be the wind," I told them, although I hadn't noticed any gusts when I looked out the window.

In fact, the sky was clearing up rather fantastically.

———— • • • ————

The cast of *The Prefect Family*, at least the ones who were at-tending, were now slowly leaving the green room. One by one, they made their way back towards the ballroom, after producers con-vinced most of them to at least try and socialise during the final half-hour of being in the air.

Travis McGuire, who'd been hired by the show to stand in for Thomas Noel (on account of his uncanny resemblance) snuck out last but not least, just as Annie walked past. Upon seeing him, she immediately slipped on nothing and tumbled face-first into the car-peted ground. McGuire reacted immediately, forgetting to put on his deeper voice, and helped her up.

"Oh, my gosh all-mighty!" he said in his squeaky, southern drawl. "Ma'am, I am beyond sorry for that altercation and I sincerely hope I can make it up to you."

Annie towered over him, for he didn't have his platform shoes on. Looking down, she noticed a giant bald-spot on the back of his head. Something a twenty-one year old most likely wouldn't have.

"You're not Thomas Noel..." she said in confusion.

She righted herself and took off down the corridor.

Cora Corali was in the near-empty dining room, talking amongst a group of executives and a few crew members at one of the large tables. When she saw Annie's pale and shocked face, with a strange red circle on her forehead, she begged to ask the question:

"What now?"

Annie explained her experience, sitting down at their table.

"Does Thomas Noel even exist?" she asked.

"Of course he does, but he's not on this Zeppelin," Cora told her. "He's snowboarding in Aspen with his parents. In fact, none of the big stars are here. The only one that actually accompanied us to Horn-Horn was Uma Harlow, with her sister."

"Oh..."

"And even *they've* swapped identities until all of this is over," Cora added nonchalantly.

Annie stared wild-eyed, her mouth agape.

"We can't risk the cast being killed in a Zeppelin ride!" said Cora defensively. "Hello? That's management 101. *Don't put all your eggs in one basket'*. We hire lookalikes and then shoot them from far away. Didn't you notice the closest cameras on that football field were in the bleachers? And the crates and crates of Vaseline for the lenses?"

Annie's mind was a whirl of confusion.

"So... Uma Harlow's *twin* is in the ballroom right now? Then who did I see hanging out with Audrey Mercy on the football field?"

"The *real* Uma Harlow. She has been pretending to be her sister since arriving in town. Neither of them are foreign, either; they're from California originally. Uma is working on her Polish accent for a new film role."

Annie sat stock still, her brain close to imploding. She cast her mind back to the interaction she'd had with Netti Zawistowski at the school luncheon. Who she'd assumed was Netti Zawistowski, anyway.

*I met Uma Harlow!"* she exclaimed, beaming.

At that moment, one of the security guards burst through the door, causing Cora and Annie to jump in fright.

"No sign of him," he said to the executives. "We'll check the kitchen again. It's like he just... disappeared into thin air."

"The sign of a true magician..." muttered Cora bitterly. "Alright, that settles it. Everybody out of here. This is now a security breach. Back to the ballroom, thank you."

"What's going on?" asked Annie, as the people around her began to shuffle towards the exit.

Hastily, Cora Corali guided her out.

"You wouldn't believe it. That magician on board, remember him? The... electrician, or whatever he claimed to be. He told us his name was Pepper O. Salt. Should've been the first give-away. Well, there's no such person. Pepper O. Salt doesn't exist! Whoever we met, he is *not* authorised to be onboard this Zeppelin."

# 32

## INAY INOVAY
## ERITASVAY

A s the party made their way across the ugly outside of the Walker residence, we were greeted by the entire staff in their jolly white tuxedos. They led us over to four giant tents, all with heaters inside, and an array of assortments on the tables spread across them. From where we stood, we could see in almost every direction, since we were so high up. The Zeppelin, I was told, would no longer rise from the west and descend into Horn-Horn from behind us. It would instead be coming in from the north. The fireworks would go off on the school football field five minutes before the Zeppelin would descend and, hopefully, safely land back where it started.

"I wonder if I should call Ella-May," said Marguerite, as we peered down into the darkness of Horn-Horn. "She may want to bring the family up to join us since it's finishing early."

"And, of course, your little bundle of joy is welcome, too," said

Tommy Walker, nodding to my parents. He either thought Annie was an infant, or couldn't remember her name. Given how much he'd had to drink, it was probably both.

Marguerite started to randomly sing again. This time it didn't seem that many people wanted to hear it. They were enjoying the hors d'oeuvres too much. Even Suzannah the Complimentary Colleen looked to be feigning her enamour this time, a generic smile plastered like a stock photo below droopy, glazed eyes.

I could tell it was giving Mom a headache, too, by the way she tilted her head (traits you pick up on after living with someone for sixteen years). It didn't help that we had no news about what was going on with the Zeppelin, either. On top of that, Brendan was acting like a little brat. He'd been banished by Dad to sit in JT's art studio for half-an-hour, which was basically just the den with a few couches, easels and computers to keep him company.

"My hands are freezing," said Hayley, hugging JT.

Her beanie-less boyfriend looked around slyly, then muttered under his breath: "Put them…"

"Huh?" said Hayley, not hearing.

*"Put them…"*

Cottoning on to what they were attempting, I turned away.

"Hey, Dad. How long before we can see the Zeppelin?"

Dad checked his watch. "Twelve minutes."

"Look at those stars," someone pointed off towards the ocean.

Three gigantic and colourful stars were shining bright. They were so startling that their reflections shimmied across the calm sea below them.

"That's beautiful," my mother said, coming and standing next to me. "I've never seen them before. What are they?"

"I might go in and check my astrology books from the library," said Mr. Walker, clearly eager to find the answer.

"Astronomy," I corrected him as he headed off.

Tommy stopped dead in his tracks, then walked back.

"That's what I said," he informed me with a smile.

"Oh, no, you said *astrology*. That's like divination and stuff. It's from *Harry Potter*," I said with an innocent smile.

"But I didn't say astrology. I said astronomy. I'll go get my *astronomy* books from the library."

It dawned on me that we both knew what he'd said. I held my tongue, feeling uncomfortable, and watched him walk back inside the house. Breathing out in relief, I turned to Mom and she shrugged, not sure what to make of our rather strange interaction.

"Excuse me!" yelled Tommy Walker.

Turning in surprise at his immediate return, I noticed he was now looking directly at my parents, a hint of displeasure on his face.

"Mr. and Mrs. Gellar," he said, much more quietly. "Your son is in the dining room, and he appears to be drunk."

Although stunned, not another word was needed. I chased after Mom and Dad, barrelling into the foyer and down the hallway until we entered the used dining room. Dancing to some sort of seventies disco music, Brendan wasn't wearing any pants. Simply his shirt, underwear and socks. In his hands was a bottle of Merlot. Mom instantly ran to him and snatched the half-empty bottle away from him.

"Fine, you cankeep it. Taste like *crab anyway*."

The voice that came out of my little brother's mouth was not his. It was as if he were possessed. He stumbled, stuttered and tripped over his words.

"Ichabod!" cried Mom. "I said give him *one glass*."

"I did," my father responded in disbelief. He stood by my side at the entrance, just as shocked as I was.

"*I'm sneaky!*" said Brendan. "Took more when you weren't lookin'. This and another've been my buddies downstairs. Personally I don't veal like it's done *nowt*... to *NOWT*."

Mom stuttered, panicking inside, and then turned back to us.

"Why are you both standing there? *Help me!* I don't know... What should we do?"

"I'm not dying, I'm just drunk, you Nazi trollop."

Taken aback by his choice of words, Mom reached out and smacked him across the face. The sound of it echoed around us in the near-empty room. It seemed to have some kind of affect on him, but it was strange. Brendan gazed up at her through bloodshot eyes, his cheeks flushed and his lips pouted. I couldn't tell if he was angry or about to cry.

"I hate you!" Brendan yelled.

Suddenly, he rammed her over. She tripped backwards, and I caught her. Dad immediately moved forward. He bent down on one knee to get to his level, and grabbed his only son's tiny shoulders in his arms.

"Don't you *ever* hit your mother," he said in a deep, serious voice. "No matter what is going on, no matter how bad you're feeling. *DON'T EVER HIT YOUR MOTHER!*"

He shook him enough to set off the waterworks. But this fight wasn't over for Brendan. He forced himself out of his father's grip and backed away until he reached one of the tables.

"I hate it here," he said, tears streaming down his face. He wiped his nose with his white sleeve. "I hate all of you. If Annie was here I'd tell her, too. You're self-centred and mean and...forgetful... and I want a new family."

His words were like daggers. Mom moved forward timidly.

"They say the truth comes out when you're drunk," she said gently. "Well, Brendan, I'm really sorry you feel that way. How can we help you feel better?"

"I want to go back to Salem," he said quietly. "I want my old bedroom and my old school. I want to go back to normal."

"We've only been here for three months," said Dad. "You've got to give it a little more time."

Brendan turned to me, his eyes reflecting in the dim light. "Don't you miss it? Before Zag. Life was better."

I felt something inside of me ache, as if my lungs had collapsed. I wasn't sure how to explain it to him.

"Brendan, no. I was really lonely."

Abandoned, he knocked my hand away as I went to reach for him. He was tired of listening, but at least he'd calmed down.

This was when Mom decided to step in again. She came forward and grabbed him under his arm gently.

"We can talk about this w hen you're sober. We're going home."

"*Stop touching me!*" he snapped, roaring back into force. He ripped out of her grip and pointed at her. "*You're* the worst."

"Me?" said Mom, shocked. "What did *I* do?"

Brendan stared her down for a moment, crossed his arms, and said quite clearly: "You forgot my birthday."

As my mind thought over the previous month, it very quickly dawned on me that he was absolutely right. His birthday had been on the tenth, and we'd skipped over it entirely.

Mom hovered in her place. She was locked in a stare-off with Brendan, as if frozen in time. A second later something shifted in her expression. She said: "Excuse me," under her breath, and barrelled past us to rush away.

# 33

# POLLUX AND THE CASTORY

D oes anybody know where Eleanore Parker is?" called Cora Corali, resisting the urge to rip some hair from her head as she re-counted the list of passengers. "We cannot land this thing until we have every single passenger accounted for, and since one of them is an imposter and the other is a guest, I'll ask again: Does anybody know where Eleanore Parker is?"

"I'm right here!" called an old woman, sat with the other cast.

"No, Baroness, not you…"

Cora went to speak in a low voice to another in command.

"I didn't know we had a magician…" someone commented.

"He's probably just a crazy fan," said the Thomas Noel impersonator. "They're not paying me enough for them tonight."

Every guest aboard was gathered in the ballroom, and had been for twenty minutes. As the producers scoped over their legal documents and the security guards went off in pairs to search for the imposter, Annie and the others were bound to this one room until everything was sorted. But everything was not sorted. Eleanore Parker was nowhere to be found.

Worried, stressed and tired of her high-heels, Annie hiked up her canary yellow dress and gazed out the nearest window, spotting the lights from the football field on the horizon. They were getting closer and closer.

Then a thought popped into her head. Technically, this was an emergency. She could make a wish. It trumped the Christmas rule of banning wishes during December.

"I wish I could see what's really going on..." she whispered.

"What did you say?" asked Uma Harlow by her side, who as it turns out was the real Netti Zawistowski.

"Nothing!" choked Annie, spitting out a wad of glitter.

"You should probably get that seen to," said the real Netti.

Just like that, a dozen psychic images flashed in front of Annie's vision. Ms. Weiss was standing in the middle of the football field, chatting to Principal Parker about the hold-up. Ella-May, Elliot and Eliza were watching from the stands, while Miss. Terr, Ms. Chin-Tucker and Ms. Winch sat with the rest of the faculty in their special front-seats, huddled together in the freezing night air.

*No, that's not what I need to see.*

Annie forced the image into the back of her mind. Instead, she saw a man riding a motorcycle around the streets of Horn-Horn, checking out houses, hoping to recognise any of them. Beside him in the sidecar were two women bound and tied up.

*Uh... no, not that, either.*

Another image, this one of Grandma Helen sitting on the couch watching television with Aunt Rachael.

Annie swiped in her mind one more time, until finally she saw Eleanore's face. She was in the green room all by herself, eating a packet of chips from the vending machine. Her make-up was smeared from crying, her hair disheveled, although she looked calm and relaxed and, most importantly, safe.

"I wish I could sneak into the green room without anybody noticing I'm gone," muttered Annie.

Soon she'd snuck down the hallway and past an alarming amount of security guards, none of which saw her as she walked by. Finally, she found the door to the green room, checked that the coast was clear, and snuck in. Shutting the door behind her, she faced

Eleanore front on, who stood up from the sofa.

"There you are," the Saviour said to Annie. "I've been asking to see you forever. Are we really heading back early?"

Annie was sweating from stress. "Yes. Haven't you heard?"

"This is great; my little meltdown has caused the entire production to shut down," sobbed Eleanore, and she put her hands over her eyes to cry again. "This is beyond humiliating. I can't believe this is happening to me. I'll never live this down. Like, legitimately, ever. I'll be that eighty-four-year-old who embarrassed herself as a teenager. This is even worse than the time I sponsored that whale who killed all those orphans."

"Never mind. We've got to get out of here, right now!"

Annie rushed over and grabbed her, but as she did she spotted a pair of black shoes hiding behind the nearest table. Quickly, she pulled Eleanore into the corner of the room as Pepper O. Salt, the magician… electrician… imposter… popped up from his hiding place.

"What is going on?" yelled Eleanore, furious at Annie's reaction, but also furious at the man. "Sir, you should have made your presence known!"

"Pardonnez moi, mon cherie…" said Pepper.

He lifted his top hat, revealing a rabbit underneath.

"I am simply hiding here for my next *tour de magie…* "

"He's lying," said Annie. "He's not meant to be onboard. I think he's trying to…"

"Yes? Trying to what?" asked Pepper, twirling his ridiculous fake moustache with a spare hand. Something in his only visible eye sparkled, as if he were waiting for her to say something very specific.

Annie stopped and stared for a moment, and realised that she had another way of finding out the truth.

"I wish to know exactly what you're up to!"

The look on Pepper's face changed instantly. His good pupil dilated, it was clear even from across the room. A sinister grin spread across his face.

"Thank you," he said serenely.

Everything Annie needed to know quickly rushed into her head. Who he was. Where he was from. What he was after. A chill ran down her spine, and she became greatly distressed as she realised he was between them and the only exit.

"Who is this man?" asked Eleanore in annoyance.

Pepper O. Salt's grin changed before their very eyes, and fear gripped the girls tightly as one thing above all else became suddenly very clear: this was not a human in front of them. The colour of his face shifted into a deep purple, his shoulders swelled in size, and giant claws emerged from the ends of his knuckles. A new set of teeth, sharp and yellow, appeared in front of his old ones. He raised his mutated arms up into the air, and giant purple streams of very bright electricity seeped out of the ceiling above and draped across his body.

"I knew it, you see…" he said, his voice now a deep, rolling vibrato. It sounded like he was made of static electricity. "I knew it had to be one of you."

"Wait," said Eleanore, whose face was pale and stretched in disbelief. "H-H-Hang on…"

Pepper pointed a long, black index finger at Eleanore, who held out her arms in defence. The conducted electricity immediately streamed across the room. It catapulted into the Saviour, picking her up and violently throwing her out of the nearest window. Glass shattering, body flailing, Eleanore Parker soared through the silent night sky, falling to her doom miles below.

More electricity filled the green room, shocking Annie violently as she made a run for the door. Despite the currents surging through her body, she clutched the doorknob and pulled. Her hand suddenly burned from the contact, and she let go just as she managed to squeeze through. A moment later there was a gigantic, sonic explosion. The door flew outwards, narrowly missing her, and a sharp wind barrelled across her bare shoulders. Still, she stared ahead, determined, and ran into the ballroom to get help.

To her horror, all of the guests were on fire. Cora screamed as her clothes erupted into flames, and her hair fizzled away. Uma Harlow's twin, the Thomas Noel impersonator, the security guards, they were all caught in the static uproar. Annie tripped in shock as the fire reached her too. Lying on the ground, she tried to call out for a wish, but instead belched a giant fireball which turned blue around the edges. Covering her mouth and pressing against the ground, she wished in her head for it to stop and for everybody to be healed.

Just like that, silence enveloped the entire room. The static had ceased immediately, the half-burnt people in the ballroom no longer writhed in agony but instead lay perfectly still, unconscious and unharmed. Annie hopped up on her knees, weak, and checked her bare arms and hair for any signs of burning. Nothing. She was healed. Everybody was healed.

Fury overtaking her sense of fear, she stormed back towards the green room, the power of wishes her only plan of combat. The inside of the room was burnt black, and Pepper O. Salt stood by the shattered window, his fake moustache and top hat vanishing with the wind. His entire body was twice its normal size, dark purple muscles having ripped through his clothes, his features distorted and bulbous like a werewolf. Whatever he was, he was not from around here, nor had he ever been. He was a mutant.

"You killed Eleanore. *You killed her!*" yelled Annie, shaking.

Pepper lurched forward, a deep growl rattling from his throat.

"If you wished to know what I was up to," he said in his static voice, "then you know where I am from."

"Danube."

"And you know what I'm going to do next."

"I won't let you, Pepper!" she declared, trying not to cry.

"*Pepper?*" he said in disbelief.

His teeth spread even wider as he allowed himself to grin.

"You know my real name. *Use it.*"

It was true. After making the last wish, Annie now knew everything about him:

He was born on the planet of Danube. His real name was Pollux. His parents, mutated hybrids, who'd abandoned him when he was nine, never bothered to tell him what his surname was. He grew up with the birth gift of conducting electricity, although not much more. He spent the rest of his childhood practicing to be a magician, as he assumed disappearing was what his parents did professionally. However, it crossed into his adulthood, and he became quite adept at spinning magic tricks to those desperate enough to pay him any attention. He eventually found himself hired by the Palace of Danube, only to charm the little ones. Still, the fact remained that he wasn't a particularly *good* magician, and so he took up the role of jester as a means of extra finance. Finally, after being kicked off stage for not being funny, he threw in his jiggly hat and stormed out of the Palace forever. He ventured into the banished woods behind the Palace of Danube, furious with everyone and everything. But the woods were banned from use by order of Duke Wilson of Elmer. Inhabitants who ventured in could never return to the Palace, ever again. These woods, called '*The Castory*' were suspected to contain mysterious dark spots where time and space would bend in curious ways. The lowest forms of life, exiled or fed up with the laws of Danube, would flock there to seek refuge. There were no laws in 'The Castory'. Nothing there was good or bad. Amongst the hundreds of miles of dense, dead trees, who knew what secrets lurked? Nobody had ever gone in for long enough to discover. But Pepper, or Pollux, found a group of exiled kindred spirits amongst the snow. And as their friendships grew, they learnt how to build and work off each other until finally they made a great, big house. Three storeys tall, made of magical wood from magical trees, hidden in the middle of the 'Great Planes', an empty region of 'The Castory' that was devoid of life. Caught in a one-hundred-year-old blizzard, it suited the group perfectly. Nothing ever came or went, except for the same two lost souls venturing in and out, who didn't realise they were travelling in circles throughout space and time.

Then, one day while he was outside barrelling snow, Pollux saw something in the distance. Up in the sky, amongst the heavy, falling snowflakes. A golden dime of light pierced the white, and stayed in its place. As Pollux got closer to it, he realised that it wasn't very high up in the sky at all. He quickly built a snowman with three balled layers, stood on its hips, and reached the glowing dime. As soon as he touched it, he knew what it was. It was a rip. He'd been warned about these, as they were something the Palace was looking for. They were dangerous. They allowed access to other places in the universe.

Still furious with the people of Danube for everything they'd done to him, he pulled at the dime and held onto its edges while the sky around him fell away, as if a giant mile-long curtain had been yanked from its fittings. All around him, a giant vista of blue sky appeared and then, suddenly, it mingled into his world and the snow began to fall as if nothing had happened.

When he returned to his wooden home, he told the others what had happened. Gianna, Karloff, Vonda, McGideon and his lover Nora were all deeply intrigued by the notion of an escape route. The eldest of them all, a withered woman named Atsina (who had once been a Child of Crux) lay in her bed upstairs and told Pollux what it was. The rip in time and space was so large that it was now finely smoothed out on each side, and impossible to tell where one world began and the other ended. It was a short-cut to the Planet of Earth. One that nobody on Danube knew about.

So the group started to venture in. Sometimes all together, then one by one. Pollux became obsessed with the other world, going through and witnessing amazing sights, while the others grew concerned of the bright and ever-changing places they would visit each time.

Then one day, the old decrepit woman upstairs told him something about herself. When she was younger, before she had matured, Atsina was owned by a mighty sorcerer who used her wishing abilities to destroy many powerful enemies in the universe. When she stood up to him, instead of killing her, he simply smashed her body under his foot. Her body died, she told him. But she learned quickly that when you kill the body of a Child of Crux, you do not kill the soul living inside of it. So she lived from then on in her broken body, crushed under the foot of a sorcerer who had since been destroyed. Her body, kept together by centuries of magic, was a shell of a thing and once it separated entirely, her soul would find one part of that and remain in it forever, until she eventually found another source of life to cling onto and take over.

"Why do you continue living?" asked Pollux.

"Because I cannot stop living," answered Atsina.

Furious at the idea that other Crux children were being abused in this same way, Pollux continued venturing into other worlds. Causing accidents. Inadvertently killing owners of a Child of Crux, then swooping in and claiming them for himself. Pollux had over one hundred Children of Crux, hidden in the basement of his three-storey home, locked away in their clay heads. *Safe from harm.*

Because Pollux was still bound by the laws of nature, so say the Heads of the Universe, he pressed into every crevice of every law and every rule, every forbidden wish and every grey area, until he found a place that was soft enough to crush under his persistence. He couldn't wish to find out how many Crux children were in each town, for they were protected by not only wood, but by the deep magic indebted to their privacy. No, he couldn't find out in the traditional way, but he could sneak around the edges of these rules, looking for weaknesses, and find out when a new one would appear through a privacy loophole. Coming from 'The Castory' which was out of Danube's jurisdiction, nobody would ever know that he'd managed to work his way around the rules.

Then in September, a new Child of Crux found itself without an owner in the woods of Horn-Horn. It was quickly claimed, and that's when Pollux set up his plan. Knowing that the new owner was a girl and had a sister, he took on his more placid human-like form and sussed out the girls in town, eventually landing on half a dozen suspects. First, the Mayor, who had a sister, but her involvement was quickly dispelled. Then, a woman named Bernadette, who also had a sister but was also only eight weeks old. This whittling down of suspects was an arduous task, naturally, that by the time November rolled around Pollux was setting his sights on Chloe and Candice Croxley. He donned his disguise — Pepper O. Salt, a pretentious electrician who thought very highly of himself and wore ridiculous outfits that quite literally looked like a costume. "What better way to disguise myself than by making it *look* like a disguise?" was his way of thinking, and his lover Nora, who had stayed behind in *'The Castory'* to look after the Crux children in the basement, agreed with him.

Candice, he quickly surmised, wasn't interested in men. So he moved on to Chloe. He stalked her, figured out where she lived, and soon found out that she liked to eat dinner alone at a nearby restaurant. He made sure to meet her there one night, charm her only slightly so as not to accidentally fall in love, and then while he dug his claws into her daily habits he scoped for any signs of a Child of Crux in her life. He thought he'd nabbed her when he discovered Candice kept a bunch of toys in her apartment, but she soon told him that she was storing them for a friend's son.

Now realising that they were not hiding a Child of Crux, he realised he had to ditch them, for he had a few other very interesting candidates to investigate. He quickly infected their drinks with wild hallucinogens, and while they imagined some sort of terrifying nightmare he drove them into Horn-Horn's Haunted Woods by the old abandoned train station, where they walked through the secret abyss that led into *'The Castory'*. They hiked for miles through the empty space, with nothing but a blizzard to keep them company. Finally, they found the house with Pollux's companions. As he'd done with countless other dead ends over the years, instead of simply killing them he would essentially lead them down hallucinogenic rabbit holes, until the rabbits in those holes would guide them back into their own world. Gentry and Uriah were two spirits he'd met out in his wanderings. They were escaping the law in a snowmobile, having accidentally driven through the abyss. It was a funny thing: every twelve or thirteen days they would reappear through the blizzard and greet the outcasts in their wooden home, which they labelled as a hotel for wanderers to find them easier. Soon, Gentry and Uriah would pack up and head off through the snow again. The next time they'd return after twelve or thirteen days, they wouldn't remember a thing about their last visit.

So, Pollux figured, *if they keep coming back-and-forth from this world and the other, why not use them to send back the people I've poisoned? Then these poor infected souls can go back to their normal lives, oblivious to what really happened.*

Why, Pollux was sure that the Croxley sisters would be home by now, if Gentry and Uriah had dropped them off the day before. Since Chloe and Candice were definitely not the owners of a Child of Crux, he knew that it could only be one of two others. His first suspects, the Gellar family, who had been the talk of the town since a fierce moose attack a few months earlier.

Of course, there was the Parker residence next door as well. The daughter Eleanore also had a sister. So Pollux knew that it had to be one of them. Seeing the Zeppelin ride as a fantastic opportunity, he set things into motion, slithering his way behind the scenes, setting up his details so that he could easily sneak onboard, pretending to be the entertainment, and the electrician. Once inside he would test the both of them, Eleanore and Annie, to see if one of them would break under pressure. When suddenly Annie came out with exactly what he was looking for.

*A wish.*

"I told you," said Annie as she stood in the doorway. "I know everything. I know you were the one who threw a ball at Cassie's head in the auditorium. You knew it wouldn't kill her, otherwise you wouldn't be able to claim the Child of Crux for yourself. But the ball gave her a concussion, which could later kill her on its own."

"It didn't work," said Pollux. His hideous new set of fangs were glistening in the shattered light-fittings from above, and his gigantic torso seemed to be heaving and swelling with every passing moment. "All guess work. I wasn't sure if it was Eleanore, either, so I pushed your sister over while they were trying to hang that star on top of your friend's Christmas Tree. I was hiding behind the bookshelf, cloaked by magic. Eleanore Parker's death would have been by Cassie's hand, not mine. Inadvertently, you see, so I could claim her Child of Crux. Unfortunately, her friends below broke her fall, but it doesn't matter in the end because she was not the owner. You are."

More knowledge was seeping into Annie's mind about him, revelation after revelation. "You even glued my brother's eyes shut with magic. Why? You knew he wasn't the owner."

"He's smart, that's why," said Pollux with an angry grunt. "I told you, I observe everything from a distance before I engage. I could see that he was going to piece everything together, so I passed on a virus from another world. It was harmless, wasn't it? Went away after a few days. I told you, I don't seek to harm."

"If you were so determined not to harm any innocent people, *why did you throw Eleanore Parker out the window?*" said Annie, breathing in heavily as she tried not to cry.

Pollux shrugged, not giving it another thought. "Collateral. Now that you know everything about why I'm here, why don't you wish to find out what I'm going to do next? Dinner up the road is over. Everyone will be going home soon."

Annie hesitated. Things couldn't possibly get any worse. Like ripping off a bandaid, she made the wish in her head to find out, and immediately she saw what he was planning on doing. They were going to drive the Zeppelin away from the school. Up the hill, towards the homes. Directly into the Gellar house, killing its inhabitants. However, Pollux wouldn't be driving the airship. Annie would be doing it, so that Pollux could claim Zag for himself. Poor Zag, hibernating in the attic, snatched away from his Earth home in the night, his previous owner dead in the carnage downstairs.

"Like hell!" screamed Annie, a fearlessness taking over her mind and body as never before. Thinking about Aunt Rachael, Grandma Helen, Pigsworth, Tigger, and the rest of her family, she let out a scream of rage and raced towards Pollux. More electricity quickly pummelled her senses, and she was lifted off the ground. Searing pain rippled through every nerve as the currents carried her out of the burnt green room and down the hallway, past the group of unconscious guests in the ballroom. A door ahead burst open, showing two unconscious men slumped in their seats, facing a giant window. Annie realised immediately that she was being forced into the cockpit. Behind her the giant, hulking purple body of Pollux followed. When Annie had hovered over the top of one of the unconscious pilots, his body was whisked to the side by magic. Suddenly the feeling came back to her body, the electricity leaving at once, and she flopped down in the vacated seat. Exhausted, she had just enough energy to turn around and face Pollux.

"You're going to make me crash into my own house?"

"You could always give up your Child of Crux, and save your family. Leave this mess behind."

"I can't," said Annie automatically.

Pollux's eyes glistened.

"That's right. Because *you* are not the owner. Your sister is. The best you can do is make wishes. You're second fiddle."

Annie didn't know how to respond, and she found the electricity surging again through her neck and wrists this time. She was forced to face ahead, gripping the rudder with one hand and pulling down a lever with the other. Ahead of them out the window, darkness seemed to be lit up by rows and rows of warm street lights, houses, and stars reflecting across the ocean.

The distinct sensation of being in an elevator took over; they were now descending very rapidly.

# 34

## PARKER KNOWS BEST

I s it just me, or does it look like it's…"
Eric Parker took the binoculars away from his face and
squinted at the sight on the horizon. He stood in the
very back row of bleachers on the football field. The music, cheering and entertainment was reaching fever pitch around them,
piercing to the ears. He could've sworn that he heard the town's
tornado siren booming from the lighthouse on the cliff. As his
wife huddled into him for warmth, a spot of glimmering ruby
caught Eric's eye in the crowd. To his utmost disbelief, his eldest
daughter came limping onto the field.

Ella-May saw her, too. She rushed down the stairs and chased
after her, pulling off her own giant puffer jacket and wrapping it
over Eleanore's bruised and cut shoulders. Blood was pouring from
her head, hair wildly unkempt, neck at an unusual angle. By the time
Eric and the twins had reached her, she'd leaned forward and silently
puked onto her bare feet.

"Oh, honey," said Eric, noticing the cameras clicking away from all angles. "Let's get you inside. Amelia, keys. Pocket."

Ms. Terr, who had rushed over with Ms. Winch to assist, promptly put her hand into Eric's right pants pocket to search for the school's keys.

"Teacher's Lounge," muttered Eric to his wife.

Ella-May reached down to the twins.

"Go to Ms. Weiss over there. Tell her to keep her eye on you."

The empty hallways appeared sterile in the incandescent lights as the three Parkers hurried around each corner. Pushing the doors inward, Eric helped Eleanore sit down on one of the giant, red sofas near the blackened windows of the Teacher's Lounge. Ella-May made it a point to put a stack of chairs in front of the doors to stop anyone else from coming in.

"Did the Zeppelin land?" she asked by the water-cooler.

Eric looked over at her, and shook his head grimly.

"Then how..?"

Ella-May handed a plastic cup of water to her daughter, who sat dazed, unlike herself, staring off into space. Now that they were in better lighting, Eleanore appeared much worse than before. Her skin was a cross between sickly white and a deep magenta. Two black eyes, a gaping hole in her left shoulder, and a slash across her right thigh. Strangest of all, the light had gone from her eyes.

After a few measly sips, Eleanore smacked her dry lips and gazed up at her parents expectantly.

"Should I..?" started Ella-May.

"No, she's fine," said Eric, and he smiled down at his daughter. "Sugar plum, can you tell me what happened? How did you get down from the Zeppelin before it landed?"

Eleanore's eyes were wider than they'd ever been.

"I fell."

"That's impossible! They were miles up. She'd be dead if it were true..." said Ella-May, putting a hand to her forehead.

"Maybe she fell into some trees," said Eric, shrugging her off sharply. "Sweetheart, what made you fall?"

With this question, Eleanore's eyes began to water. Dropping the plastic cup onto the linoleum floor, she put her hands to her mouth as she began to hyperventilate.

"That awful man pushed me!"

"What awful man, honey?"

"Th... The one who... The magician. He used... *magic.*"

Ella-May stuttered incoherently for a moment.

"C-Clearly she's not-t thinking straight. We need to call an ambulance for her right away. Dr. Aunders, he..."

*"No, wait!"*

Eleanore stood up, catching her father's attention further.

"They're in trouble, Daddy..."

"Who is?" he asked gently.

Eleanore grabbed Eric's sleeve and squeezed tight.

"The people on the Zeppelin. I think it's going to crash."

# 35

# BLACK & WHITE & BLUE

L ook! There they are!"
Somebody in the freezing crowd called out. Just as Hayley and JT were about to go inside to get warm, they turned at the voice and saw what everybody else saw.

*'The Uma'* roared over the hill, so low that they could make out the light fixtures of the chandelier in the ballroom. It flew on by, narrowly missing the nearest telephone pole, and continued on its way down into the heart of Horn-Horn, towards the school.

"That was a bit close, wasn't it?" said JT.

"Dramatics, I'd say," muttered Hayley, noticing for the twentieth time that night as Marguerite eyed her up and down. "Hey, Jonathan… I might go home."

"What? It's early."

"Yeah, but the Gellars, and Brendan and…"

Not believing her excuse, JT turned to see what she was frowning at. He quickly turned back. "Ignore her," he said.

"I really am tired. I just want to go to bed. All these crazy hours at the bakery are making me..."

"Jonathan, darling!" called Marguerite loudly. "Will you come here a second?"

Hayley was watching her now not in contempt, but in disbelief. "You're kidding me..." she muttered.

JT turned around again. Marguerite was presently standing next to Cherilyn Wanke, an exceptionally pretty black girl he knew from school with a rather unfortunate surname, whose family was a part of their rich social circles. Marguerite had been trying to hook them up for over a year. Now she was shamelessly making another attempt, right in front of Hayley.

JT grabbed her shoulders.

"I'll get rid of her in two seconds," he promised. "Then let's go inside and watch a movie in my room on the computer. You can choose which one."

"No," said Hayley, frowning heavier than she'd ever done in her life. "I'm not in the mood. Especially now. I'm going ho... back to the Gellars."

"Well, at least..." said JT, and he grabbed her hand in his and guided her with him as they ventured towards the two women waiting for him. "Hi, Cher. Mom, Hayley's not feeling well, so she's going home." He made it a point to wrap his spare arm around her. "Cher, you've met my girlfriend Hayley, right?"

"Yes," said Cherilyn, her neck stretched in competition.

"What a shame you have to leave," said Marguerite, giving Hayley the distinct impression that she in fact felt the opposite of regret. "Don't forget your little basket of treats at the front door before you go. Jonathan, you can show Cherilyn the projector in the basement..." She nudged Hayley away from him and turned her back on her. "The men of the house can't quite figure out what's wrong with it, but I know *you* are good with this sort of stuff, my dear!"

Furious, Hayley stormed away with her head down.

"Hey," said JT angrily, grabbing his mother's hand.

He excused the both of them. When they had walked far enough away from Cherilyn and other curious listeners, he let go.

"Hayley is my girlfriend..."

"What? I said goodbye, and told her about the..."

"You know what I'm talking about. I can't believe after all of those trips to Scarborough, and all your work with the homeless that you'd base your opinions on someone over…"

"Oh, Jonathan, don't kid yourself," muttered Marguerite angrily, keeping a content smile on her face in case others were looking. "It has nothing to do with her wealth. Cherilyn is a lovely girl, she's on her way to Princeton and she is, quite frankly, above your batting average, if I can be honest. You're wasting your time on that other girl as if you'll actually have a future with her!"

"I might," said JT. "That's for me to decide."

"No, it is *not!*"

Marguerite didn't say anything else, but JT could see it in her now: a burden festering beyond her dark brown eyes.

"She's my girlfriend," he repeated.

Marguerite shook her head in pity, turning to walk away before their argument became more heated.

"It doesn't matter…" she started.

A scream came from the crowd higher up on the hill. JT looked to see his father rushing towards a group of people pointing off into the distance. Marguerite let out a gasp — she'd already seen it, and ran up the hill to get a better look. JT gave chase, and as he did he felt a sudden warm wind hit him from behind. All at once the breeze became a strong gale, and the party found themselves struggling to stay upright. The plastic trestles and chairs from the outside area were being blown about. Morgan and a few of the other waiters in their white uniforms tried to catch them, but the winds were so strong that some of them disappeared over the fence and into the beyond.

"What is *that!?*" a woman cried.

JT reached the top of the hill with the rest of the onlookers and turned to see what they were looking at. Down in the heart of Horn-Horn, past the school and towards the beach, was a bulbous, billowing circle of white cloud. Churning at a terrifying speed, it looked like a giant avalanche was about to hit the town. Then, with a sick feeling in his stomach, JT spotted a tiny little silhouette against the oncoming white.

"The Zeppelin!" he called to his parents, who covered their mouths in horror.

———— · · · ————

On the football field at Horn-Horn High-High, the crowd of hundreds began to run. Gale force winds stripped the tents, many of them blowing up into the air and crashing down on people. The winds were so strong that Eliza Parker toppled backwards in the bleachers and landed on the concrete below, where she grabbed at her left wrist and began to cry. Ms. Weiss rushed over and held onto her, but was quickly knocked flat as Elliot's light form tumbled into her from behind.

Rushing out of one of the last standing tents, Audrey Mercy and the woman known as Netti Zawistowski held onto each other as people running past collided, bins toppled over and rubbish soared through the sky. Netti was suddenly rammed into Audrey's pregnant stomach with force.

"Oh my God!" she cried, grabbing at her automatically. Accent vanishing with the wind, her Valley Girl came through. "Audrey, I'm sooo sorry! Are you, like, okay?"

Audrey didn't notice the change in dialect, for a huge spotlight seemed to be shining upon them. She turned to see as the Zeppelin careened through the sky above and descended quickly, right on top of them. People began to scream, louder than the winds or the engines, and the two women could do nothing but watch in disbelief.

Just before it reached them, a tremendous white billowing cloud took over the sky, blanketing everything in mist. The Zeppelin, as if a toy, shot off in the direction it had come, but not before striking one of the stadium lights. A fierce explosion of shattered glass and sparks was swept up in the gale.

Audrey squinted through the heavy winds, and pointed at the Zeppelin as its back-end momentarily burst into flames.

"Oh, 'The Uma', Netti!"

Parts of nearby roofs and loose tiles were soaring through the air, debris and people and animals and mayhem soaring about everywhere, and then... The mysterious cloud vanished.

The warm mist slowly faded away, and in the sudden stillness of the night, Audrey thought for a moment that she was looking out upon devastation. With tremendous relief, she realised that most of the people lying flat on the ground were doing so not from injuries, but in order to remain safe. Finally, with the chill of winter seeping back into the air, the people began to sit up, move, and just like that the world was back to normal. Quickly, panic took over as everybody made a mad dash for the exits. But Netti, or Uma rather, remained standing still, looking up into the night sky curiously.

"Okay, but, like... *where* the *hell* did the *Zeppelin* go?"

# 36

## THE
## ABYSS

Annie was relieved, as she went to wipe the sweat from her brow, that she was finally able to move her hands away from the controls. Pollux, who'd shifted back into his old human form, seemed to be staring out the front window, an equal amount of confusion on his face.

"Did you do that?" she asked him.

Pollux didn't answer. They had just gone for the ride of their lives. A billowing plume of angry white cloud had come out of nowhere, just as they were descending back towards the school grounds. They seemed to still be stuck inside it, only now it wasn't turbulently knocking them back-and-forth.

Pollux pushed Annie out of her chair.

"I'm going to drive this thing now," he said.

He sat down and grabbed the controls, but when he turned left and right, it didn't seem to make much of a difference. Outside the window was nothing but pure, blinding white.

"It's night time. Where is this glow coming from?" he muttered to himself angrily.

Annie stood by the side of him, not sure what she should do. If she struck him over the head, it probably wouldn't hurt him very much. If she wished him dead, that strange denial sound would come from nowhere, he would hear it, and then possibly kill her for the attempt on his life. All of these thoughts flashed through her mind, when suddenly she noticed somebody else standing at the open door: Cora Corali.

It was as if nothing had happened to her, brown bob high and tanned skin fresh. Not a hint of burning flesh; her white, flowing dress looked untouched. The most noticeable difference was that, unlike the unconscious guests in the ballroom, Cora was very much awake and aware of everything going on. She leaned against the door, a deeply unimpressed look on her face.

"Hey, Pepper," she said confidently. When he turned around, she remarked: *"Remember me?"*

Cora's face melted away in front of them. Annie let out a scream as her skeleton reflected the bright white outside the window. A moment later a new face had grown back, almost as pale as the skeleton had been, and of a woman she'd never met before.

"Nora!" whispered Pepper, confusion written on his face.

"No, that's just a name I made up. Cora is my real name."

"What?"

The face of Nora melted away, and Cora's original grew back just as quickly. She winked at Annie, and then smirked at the man behind the controls.

"Since you're a magician, Pollux, I'd like to see a magic trick. How about you disappear?"

Cora Corali clicked her fingers, and Annie covered her eyes as the man sitting next to her exploded in a huge, bloody mess. Covered in his entrails, Annie stared in disbelief at Cora, who only had a few red spots on her white dress. She'd barely moved from her lean against the door, and as she came into the cockpit she brushed the spare seat of chunks and sat down in it.

"He was a terrible magician," she muttered. "You can sit now."

Cora clicked her fingers again. Any trace of Pollux, or his body parts, vanished from sight, and Annie felt herself dragged back into the clean pilot's seat.

"Relax," said Cora, noticing her shaking. "The worst is over. You must be wondering what's going on. Well, so was I for a while. I guess now is as good a time as any to tell you. Unless you'd like me to send you home with no memories?"

*That wouldn't be half bad,* thought Annie truthfully.

"I don't imagine we've got very long, so I'll make it quick. I suppose I should introduce myself first. My name is Cora Corali, and I am from Summers City. How much do you know about the planet of Danube?"

Annie shrugged, barely finding her voice to answer. "Small parts," she managed.

"In case you don't know, Danube is a tidally locked planet. One side is facing the sun, the other is always in darkness. The Palace of Danube is on the dark side, which is why it's always winter there. That's where Queen Ursula lives, in the Palace protected by the giant dome of ice. Do you know that much?"

Annie nodded.

"Summers City is, you guessed it, on the side facing the sun. It's also considered the slums of the planet. Every child needs to be born in Summers City and then lose their parents in order to be considered a Child of Crux. If they're born on the dark side, and can grant wishes, they're not a Child of Crux. Why? I don't know. Unfortunately, I don't make those rules, the Heads of the Universe do.

"The problem with a Child of Crux is that, even though they're orphaned, it doesn't always mean that they don't have other family members to look after them. That's why I'm here. I'm looking for a Child of Crux. Not just any one, but a particular one."

"My one?" asked Annie gently.

"Yes. My brother died, a long time ago, and he made me promise that his child would not become a slave. Unfortunately, the Palace of Danube intervened. There's a black market under the Fa-Fa Belt, you know, and they sell them to unseemly characters.

"And this is where Pollux came into it. I met him once when I was undercover at the Palace of Danube, in my disguise of 'Nora'. I caught an act of his when he was entertaining a crowd. Something about his stupidity intrigued me — I felt like I could use him to my advantage. And I was right, but I never expected him to become quite as useful as he turned out to be. You see, he left the Palace in a rage. They didn't respect his act, he was a laughing stock, they didn't think he could become a truly great magician. So when he left, I followed him. Into the deep, dark banished woods on the outskirts of the Palace. He led me to a group of others, all of them Danubian outcasts, and they lived in peace at a house, deep in the snow, named after the woods we were in: 'The Castory'.

"I know about that place," said Annie. "When I…"

"Made a wish earlier, I know. I heard you. I was pretending to be unconscious with the others when you first discovered who Pepper really was. Well, Pollux took me in, trusted me, and never even wondered where I was from. I think this was because of my disguise. As you saw a second ago, 'Nora' is very pale, just like everybody in the Palace of Danube. My normal complexion as Cora is very dark, so I could never let him see that side, as it would tip him off. Everybody from Summers City lives a hard life, and we are always in the sun. Anyway, I think my beauty as Nora blinded him from asking questions about where I came from, and I played with his emotions to get him to tell me everything. And he told me all about the basement full of clay heads. Each one with a Child of Crux inside, over one hundred of them, better off stowed away down there than out in the universe, their powers being abused by so many.

"The truth is, I did consider setting them all free. Who knows how long they'd been there for? Even once they are of age and the Crux curse is lifted, if they're kept in their clay heads they might not even know that they're free. But their lives aren't important to me. That's not why I'm here.

"Through a great secret network of Danubians from Summers City, I found out that a Child of Crux was in Horn-Horn, and sure enough it was *my* brother's child."

"How did you know that?" asked Annie.

"My connections are very thorough. They work with the Palace of Danube *and* your governments in order to keep humans in the dark. When these connections tell me they've found the Child of Crux I'm looking for, I believe them. So, with that, I told Pollux about the Child of Crux in Horn-Horn. He immediately left 'The Castory' and made his way through that secret abyss in the air he found, the one that connects that world with this world. He thought he left me behind, but I quickly got a lift from two gentlemen who were travelling through in their snowmobile, and set my own plan. The secret network supplied me with forged papers and security in order to pass as a producer of that television program you like, and I took over the control of the Zeppelin, which I knew Pollux was going to use to crash into the owners."

"How did you change how you looked, so he wouldn't recognise you? Queen Ursula could do that, but said it was painful and hard to keep up for so long."

"Because of this," she said, and she pulled a small pill-box from her jacket pocket. Inside was a set of glowing, amber pills... tablets... something. She popped one in her mouth and swallowed. A second later, Annie was looking at the face of Nora again. Somebody heavier, rounder in the face, with long red hair and skin as pale as snow. "It's something one of my connections has been cooking up in an experimental chamber... My features don't *actually* change, they only appear to, and only to whoever I want. Case in point..." She shook her head, and the old Cora came back again, short brown hair now resting in its normal state, while her freckled and tanned complexion smiled back at Annie. "Can you understand where all of this is coming from now? I *used* Pollux to do the dirty work. He figured out who the new owner is. I don't have to guess anymore. I know. That's why I sent us through the abyss, in order to give us time, and that is when I decided to end his useless life. His ideas of protecting a Child of Crux were dangerous. He had to go."

Annie turned to look out the window at the white void all around them. "Is this through the abyss?"

"Yes," said Cora, and she grabbed the steering device in front of her. "With a little bit of luck, we'll have appeared near '*The Castory*'. I need to stop inside our house and let them know what's going on. None of them could stand Pollux; they were all in on the plan to get rid of him."

Annie watched as Cora Corali continued to steer, but as ten minutes came and went, the white failed to waver. "There's one thing I don't understand, though," she said. "Does this mean you're planning on taking away *my* Child of Crux?"

Cora half turned to her. "Well, Annie. I'm only going to ask. But we're family. It's important to me, and my brother."

Annie thought about it, and watched out the window at the white, unsure of what she thought about this. Would Zag really be better off with Cora Corali, who was, now that she thought about it, his aunt? She thought of Aunt Rachael, and what she would do if she were orphaned. *Of course Rachael would be the first choice to look after us*, she realised.

"I'll have to talk it over with my sister, Cassie. But... if you think it's for the best… alright."

A darkness appeared through the white, and before Annie could even raise her hand to point, the distinct image of dead trees came into view below. Hundreds of them, stretching out for miles, and directly ahead of them sat a large, empty space of white. Amongst this white sat a triple storey house, and on the roof Annie spotted, even from this height, the word: '*ASTOR*' in block writing.

"We've found it!" said Cora, sounding relieved. "I've never cast a spell that doesn't work. Now that Pollux is gone, I'll set the Children of Crux free from the basement, and we'll go back through the abyss and land this thing on the school football field. We'll wake the passengers in the ballroom and wipe their memories, and it'll be like it never happened."

The Zeppelin touched down with a hefty thud on the snow below. Ahead of them, the giant hotel looked picturesque, like a scene in a movie, far too perfect for the situation they were in. Its towering presence was jarring against the white surroundings.

"Alright, let's go," said Cora.

Annie followed her, and they made their way through the dimly lit ballroom. Strewn across the carpeted floor were the people from *The Prefect Family*. Producers, fake cast, security guards, and a dozen more. Each and every one of them was out like a light, and wouldn't be waking up until Cora wanted them to. Which wouldn't be any time soon. She pried open the door leading outside, and kicked at the steps that led down to the snowy ground. Annie stood behind her, gazing out at the blizzard of snow which seemed to go on forever and ever beyond the dead trees surrounding them. Cold in her dress, her skin erupted in goosebumps, and noticing, Cora clicked her fingers again and a large insulated green jacket covered her, then pants and snow-boots swept over her bottom half to keep her warm.

"Is this Danube?" she asked, following outside.

"Yes," said Cora. "The cold side. Dismal, isn't it?"

Annie landed heavily in the snow, her new boots sinking almost two feet, and as she looked up at the hotel she got a sense of where she was. This was another planet. She was standing on another planet, yet it was so similar to the cold regions on Earth. This was the planet Ursula came from, and in actual fact, the Palace was not that far away.

"Astor…" said Annie, reading the sign on the roof.

Cora bent down and picked up some snow, rolled it into a giant ball, and threw it at the sign. Snow that had been sitting on the roof started to fall like a mini-avalanche, and the sign became clearer. It wasn't *'Astor'* at all. It was *'Castory'*.

The two of them burst through the front door, into the abandoned foyer where Chloe & Candice had arrived mere days earlier. Now, with all of the lights off, it looked scary and uninviting, and Annie immediately felt a sense of unease. Turning to Cora, she noticed she too was looking about in concern.

"Nobody's here… They're always here…"

"Should we call out to them?" asked Annie, wondering why she was speaking in such a quiet voice.

Cora suddenly rushed down the hallway and out of sight. Annie chased her, down a narrow hallway until they reached a wooden door. Cora muttered to herself for a moment, and then flung the door open. Inside was nothing but darkness, but she reached out for a light-switch and turned it on. Down the stairs Annie could see into the basement, just like a regular basement at home, only this one was completely empty.

"Oh no," said Cora, her breath shallow. "They're gone. They… The basement, all of the clay heads, the… There were one hundred of them down here. The ones that Pollux had been collecting. I don't understand why they've been taken."

"Who took them?"

Cora's face dropped even further, and she ran off again. By the time Annie caught up to her, she was racing two steps at a time up the flight of stairs.

The first door on the left, Room One, was wide open.

"No!" she cried.

Annie quickly followed and went into the room, turning on the light-switch at once. This was no room. This was a disaster. Curtains had been torn from the window, every item of clothing, every quilt and pillow and content on the upturned chest of drawers was now shredded on the ground, ripped to pieces, as if a giant tornado had swept through.

"They took Atsina with them. I *hope* they took Atsina!"

"Is Atsina a Child of Crux?" asked Annie, watching as Cora ventured into the empty wardrobe and came out in a panic. She knew the answer, of course, for she'd wished to earlier.

"The most damaged Child of Crux I've ever met. She was determined to stay in her old body. Pollux hid her from ownership until she was seventeen. That's the age a Child of Crux is when the curse is broken. They can't be owned after that, because they're no longer considered a child..."

Cora picked something up from the floor — a purple shawl.

"I can't believe they'd take her away, not with her body in such a fragile state. They must have felt... Oh, Vonda, why? I refuse to believe Karloff would help move her. Or Gianna, or McGideon for that matter... Unless... They mustn't have felt safe here."

"But you told me... You told me '*The Castory*' was in the middle of nowhere, and that this *was* safe. And I thought you said you hated them!"

"No, I hated Pollux. We all did. We let him think he ruled this place. They were all in on my plan to get rid of him. They're my family, just like your Child of Crux. I need them. I can't imagine where they would have gone. We didn't have another plan..."

The woman Annie was looking at now was no longer the strong and powerful one from the Zeppelin. This was a fragile woman, much like how she'd appeared before the ride, when she was pretending to be a producer on *The Prefect Family*. They made their way back downstairs, and as she checked behind the front counter, Annie could tell that Cora was close to devastation.

"Maybe they didn't leave on purpose," suggested Annie. "Could the people from the Palace have found this place? Do they go searching in the banished woods?"

Cora wiped her tears away. "You're right. You must be right. That's the only reason they would've left. They've either been captured by the Palace, or were tipped off that they were on their way."

"You don't have anything to worry about, then!" said Annie reassuringly. "I happen to be on very good terms with Queen Ursula. All we have to do is go to the Palace and tell them exactly what has happened, and she will let them go, I swear! Then she can help us get back through the abyss and everything will return to normal. You'll see. Come on, let's go back to the Zeppelin."

Cora immediately put her hands up.

"You're on good terms with Queen Ursula?"

"Yes. That's how we got our Child of Crux."

Cora let out a short laugh of disbelief, and then covered her mouth. "Oh, no... No, no, no. You're not... No..."

She tipped forward and back, side-to-side and then grabbed onto the front desk behind her to steady herself.

"I don't believe this. What bad luck."

"What is it?" asked Annie.

"You're the ones they're talking about. I should've realised. The new Earth owners who took the Child of Crux from Queen Ursula and Duke Wilson of Elmer. Of course you are!" Cora put her face into her hands and began to breathe in and out loudly. "You have no idea what kind of trouble you're in."

Annie didn't know what to say. She tilted her head in curiosity, while a sudden sensation of panic sent a chill down her spine.

"I know something they don't want you to know," said Cora. "It was only a few months ago I heard about it for the first time, through my connections in Summers City. They didn't name any names. Just that somebody on Earth had taken over the rights of Queen Ursula's Child of Crux. They weren't going out of their way to get the child back, because it's… Oh, no… That means my brother's… and… was Ursula's, and… Oh, *no.*"

"What's going on? What don't I know?"

Cora Corali looked on, as if suddenly afraid of her.

"They're going to kill you," she said bluntly.

Annie's head was already filled with so much information that for a moment, she couldn't take it in. She let the words settle in her mind before she said calmly: "Who?"

"Queen Ursula, of course. And Duke Wilson. The whole damn Palace of Danube have got it planned out. You're dead."

"That's ridiculous! Why would they want to kill me?"

"They want the Child of Crux back. *Our* Child of Crux."

"But if they kill us, they can't. It's one of the rules!"

"*They* aren't going to kill you. The *comet* will. When it hits, they'll swoop in and claim the Child of Crux."

"*What comet!?*" screamed Annie, her face red with panic.

"This is ridiculous. Come here…"

Pushing away from the front desk, Cora Corali guided Annie, now sobbing uncontrollably, into another room. Smelling of smoke and mould, it was dark and colder than the others. Cora invited Annie to sit down next to her at the linoleum table, which had an array of clutter spread across it. Half-empty glasses of whiskey, two ashtrays, and an abandoned card game never to be finished.

"Listen carefully. It's very important," insisted Cora, her voice low. "You and your family are in danger. Do you understand me? Actual danger. It may sound absurd, but there's a comet hurtling through space right now. It's going to hit Earth next year. Trust me, Danube knows all about it. They'd prefer you and your sister stayed in the dark, though. And don't worry, it's not a very big comet. It won't destroy the Earth or anything…"

Cora paused, figuring out how to continue.

"Just you…"

Annie had never been more captivated in her life. Her legs had gone numb, her breath tight in her throat as she listened on.

"By sheer bad luck, it just so happens the comet is going to strike Horn-Horn. It'll destroy everything and everyone, including you and your sister, the town of Alexandria next door, the island of Tallulah a mile away…

"Do you understand why they're not stopping it, Annie? Danube *wants* it to hit. By keeping you and your sister oblivious, they're orchestrating your demise without directly causing it. Remember how Pollux was going to make you drive the Zeppelin into your own house, in order to kill your sister, so that he could claim your Child of Crux for himself? Danube is scheming to exploit the same loophole. Since the comet's movements are governed by the laws of physics and not influenced by conscious life, they will not be held accountable for your deaths. And I know for a fact that they're taking extreme measures to ensure no information about this leaks into, or out of, Horn-Horn."

Cora Corali leaned back, allowing Annie to absorb everything she'd said. When the human didn't speak, she added:

"I can't believe I stumbled across that town. *The* town they've been talking about. Of course, they've kept Horn-Horn's name out of the Danubian news. They don't want sight-seeing exploits before the big impact…"

"None of this is true…" said Annie at last. "It can't be… Why should I believe you? Queen Ursula saved our lives; she doesn't want to kill us. This doesn't make any sense!"

"I'd say it's Duke Wilson pulling the strings. He's an artful dodger of sorts. Wouldn't put it past Ursula to sit back and allow it, though. If you think she's a saint, Annie, then you don't know the Queen of Danube very well."

Annie focused on a creased King of Hearts on the table. This world was so similar to her own. Why did Danube have a deck of cards just like those on Earth? In fact, why were they at a linoleum table… in a hotel… if they were on Danube?

"Not everyone on this planet wants to see you dead," said Cora, sympathetically holding out her hands to offer support. "Summers City is different. It's full of good, loving people. Sunlight goes a long way. Even though we're very far away from the sun compared to Earth, the atmosphere is thicker and it's tropical all year long. The Palace of Danube on the dark side breeds dark minds and souls. You must never trust a person who was born into the Palace. Not even one. They are all evil."

"What... what do you suggest I do about this... this comet? Should we leave town?"

"No," said Cora immediately. "That is the most dangerous thing you could possibly do. When we return, you should... Come on, let's go back inside the Zeppelin. We can't worry about my friends right now. I'll take you home, and we can discuss your Child of Crux ownership with your sister."

The two of them left the dark and abandoned hotel, ventured through the snow and back into the giant Zeppelin, which was a great deal colder now that the engines had been turned off. Annie walked ahead of Cora, into the ballroom, and looked across at the dozens of sleeping bodies. They all looked so peaceful. For a moment, she envied them.

"You can't go straight home and pack," said Cora. "Do you remember, about a month ago, how they brought in *Forgettenablers*? They were Danubians with birth gifts that allowed them to shape and mould other people's memories. The moment you let on that you know about the comet, they'll send one of those *Forgettenablers* down and wipe your memory clean. Annie, it's a miracle what happened tonight. All of it. If we hadn't come here, and gone into *'The Castory'*, we'd never have realised that my brother's child is your Child of Crux, and most importantly — I'd never have told you about *Guiltursaar*."

"What's Guiltursaar?"

"The comet. That's its name. Actually, it's not really a comet. It's an ancient sleeping monster that has been hibernating for thousands of millenniums. It's made up of materials so mysterious that even Danube doesn't know what they are. Nothing we've ever made can penetrate its shell."

"Horn-Horn is going to be crushed by a huge sleeping monster that falls from the sky?"

Cora pointed at her seriously. "Let that be the last time you ever utter those words, or else it will be on your head."

"If I can't let on that I know, how am I going to save my family? I can't let my family die. We *have* to leave town."

Cora frowned as she thought.

"I'll... We'll... I don't know. When I find Atsina and the others, we'll figure out a way to save you. Now, don't speak about this to anyone. Not even your your sister."

"I have to tell Cassie..."

"*No.*"

They stood there in silence for a while, looking at each other in exhaustion. The only sound they could hear was the whistling of the wind through the opened door across from them.

"Right, let's get our heads sorted," said Cora at last. "First things first. We'll set off and go back through the abyss to Horn-Horn and try to explain everything. I'd better organise some drinks for all of these unconscious passengers, so that they..."

Cora Corali stopped talking immediately. She could hear the crunching of footsteps in the snow outside.

Somebody was coming.

# 37

# SURPRISE, DISGUISE

Quickly, take this," said Cora, grabbing the packet from her pocket and handing one of the amber pills to Annie. "It'll make you appear differently to whoever you want it to. Make sure we stay together, because it wears off after half-an-hour."

Annie quickly put it in her mouth and swallowed.

Cora waved her arms about the ballroom and a giant black tarp-like sheet appeared out of thin air. It was so big, it covered the entire ballroom, and Annie realised that it was in fact covering up all of the sleeping human beings around them. When the tarp settled itself at last, it vanished from sight, as did the guests. To Annie's eyes, the ballroom looked completely empty.

The sound of heavy boots landed on the steps leading outside. Cora calmly guided Annie forward and the two of them locked eyes with the three men standing in the doorway. They looked similar, all of them clad in thick furs. They wore giant furred head caps, too, with black horns on each side. Heavily bearded, with the palest blue eyes Annie had ever seen, they stood at over six feet tall and carried strange, metallic looking instruments in their hands, shaped like harps. Or bows.

"Who are you?" said one of the men, his voice deep.

Annie, shaking terribly from fright, turned to Cora for help. To her amazement, Cora now looked like a man equally heavy-set and bearded, wearing a flannel top and dirty, faded pants.

"My name is Gentry, and this in my brother Uriah," said the man who had been Cora, and he tilted his head towards Annie. "We were just passing through when we found this machine next to our usual stop. No idea where it came from. Seems to be empty."

Two of the intruders moved into the Zeppelin and began to look around. They skirted the edges of the ballroom, one walking towards the bar on the left, the other checking down the hallway towards the cockpit. The last man, the one who had spoken, stayed in his place by the open door.

"Is this not from Earth?" said the one near the bar.

Annie turned to Cora, who shrugged. "I am not sure."

The three men clearly didn't believe them. As the two wandering around met at the other end of the ballroom, Annie noticed out of the corner of her eye that the magical tarp had failed to entirely cover the sleeping guests. A pair of high-heeled feet, seemingly without a body, were sticking out a few feet away from them. She let out a deep husky cough, and moved forward and kicked the feet under the tarp, just as the man at the door locked eyes with her again.

"What part of Danube are you from?" he asked Annie.

Annie quivered in her boots, almost too afraid to answer. Finally, she said: "The Queen's. Personal friends."

Cora froze in her place by her side. Her borrowed shoulders tensed, and Annie knew she'd messed up.

"Gentry and Uriah," said the lone man, and he turned around and walked down the steps into the snow.

Annie let out a long breath of relief. She'd said the right thing. They were going to leave them alone. Maybe they'd have enough time to get the Zeppelin up into the air and back through the abyss before the three of them realised.

"Come with us," said one of the other men. The two who had skirted the ballroom grabbed onto Cora and Annie, and soon they were all back out in the snow.

Annie's shaking was uncontrollable now, and she shared a dark look with Cora as they stood side-by-side, wondering what was going to happen. The two men let go of them and went over to the other man, who appeared to be speaking to his metallic bow. A voice seemed to be muttering back from it, although it was too quiet for Annie to hear, and was like a distant hum.

"Come with us," the same one repeated his order.

Two shards of long, sharp ice appeared in his hands, and he passed them to Annie and Cora. The moment they landed in their hands, they immediately tried to drop them. It was a sudden, intolerable pain that seared through their palms. No sooner, the pain went away and the cold, familiar temperature of ice greeted them like a great chill of relief. Annie checked her wrists — they were now shackled in ice.

"These will melt away eventually," said one of the men. "Come. We'll guide the Zeppelin."

The two others flung both arms up into the air, and what looked like giant, glowing yellow ropes lashed out of their sleeves and wrapped around the entire airship, tying together near the bottom in a Zeppelin bend. Suddenly, the great machine they'd arrived in began to rise again into the air, without the aid of an engine this time. Annie's anxiety skyrocketed — there was no way they'd get home now.

"Where are we going?" asked Cora in Gentry's voice.

The one leading the group answered slyly, almost as if he knew what they were up to. "We are taking you home, to the Palace of Danube. To see the Queen."

The group made their way through the snow, heading for the nearest stretch of dead trees. Annie checked behind her. The Zeppelin was following them half a mile above, their only means of escape.

# 38

## THE COLD, HARD TRUTH

It was not a pleasant evening, at least not in the Gellar household. We'd left without saying goodbye to the Walkers, Mom leading the way down the icy hill. Dad followed, carrying a half-drunken Brendan over his shoulder like a rag-doll. I lingered behind them, allowing myself to cry as we crossed the road into Philips Street. Aside from how humiliating the whole thing was, judgemental eyes peering at us as we made our way for the front door, I was mostly upset that we'd forgotten Brendan's birthday.

Dad took him up to bed right away. Aunt Rachael and Grandma Helen, who'd been watching from the lounge-room, knew something was definitely wrong, but nobody spoke a word. Mom locked herself in her room, and I went to the kitchen to make myself a cup of hot chocolate, hoping it would calm me down.

"What's wrong?"

Rachael had snuck up on me, and I started. This set the waterworks off again, and through a mumbled string of incoherent sentences, she finally got the gist of it and told me it was okay.

"It happens, oh, it happens," she said soothingly, letting me wipe my nose on her sleeve. "You didn't mean it, and he'll realise that eventually. There is nothing you can do about it, except apologise, and there are... Hey, look at me. There are much worse things that could happen than forgetting a birthday. You know what? It happened to me. Your father, bless him, was knee-deep in placenta I imagine, on my twenty-second birthday, because Annie was born three days before. He forgot. He forgot my birthday. Granted, he was the only one, but it stung."

"Aunt R-Rachael," I said through sobs, although I was calming down. "I'm s-sorry Dad forgot your birthday."

"Thank you," she said, and kissed me on my forehead.

Grandma Helen had snuck up on us in the same manner, and was leering menacingly by the counter without her cane. She pointed her danger finger at me.

"Shame on you for forgetting that boy's birthday!"

Aunt Rachael immediately stood between us.

"He is the best thing going for this family, and there is no good excuse for what you did. I am *deeply* ashamed of all of you. Vhen I realised the day after I arrived, that you'd somehow, *inconceivably* forgotten..."

"You *knew?*" I said through burning eyes.

"Don't try and blame this on me. *You* are the ones who forgot. There is no reasoning behind it, either, other than you are all so incredibly self-centred. I don't recognise any of you any more. What this town has done to you."

"Helen, you're making things worse," said Rachael, and she hugged me back into her bosom.

"Good. She needs to hear it. All this arguing with your friend about getting a job, and not being able to afford presents, then forgetting your own brother's birthday... You are *selfish*. You've become a rich, horrible girl. I'm ashamed of you."

I stopped Rachael's protests, and made my way out of the kitchen. "You're right, Grandma. I'm sorry. I'm sorry for everything."

I ran up the staircase, bursting into tears. But instead of going into my bedroom, I looked up at the attic door and thought about Zag. Poor little boy, locked away from everybody. I lowered the stairs as quietly as possible, and climbed into the rafters. On top of one of the empty packing boxes, his clay head sat exactly where I'd left it, collecting dust.

"Zag," I called quietly.

He didn't arrive in a puff of smoke. For a moment I looked around the darkened attic space. Maybe he was already out, preparing to jump from the shadows and scare me as a joke. I noticed the rat traps we'd set, two of them having snapped without a catch. I spotted Dad's red Santa outfit, thrown in a big, lumpy heap amongst a pile of old curtains and fabrics. Across from me, I noticed a large garland of mistletoe hanging from one of the rafters. Zag must have hung it in the past few days.

"Zag?" I said again.

I leaned over the clay head to see into the darkness better. To my horror, the Santa outfit amongst the curtains moved on its own. Somebody was in it, and they...

A giant rat darted out, and I let out a shrill scream and jumped onto the nearest pillar like a primate.

"*I wish the rats in this house would go away, and this is an emergency, so make it come true!*"

To my surprise, a giant mound of glitter rose in the back of my throat. I heaved and hacked for a good minute before it went away. Glad that the wish had worked, I lowered myself back onto the wooden posts and angrily grabbed the clay head. Despite Zag's initial warnings about turning it on, I rubbed vigorously.

"Come. Out. Zag."

Finally, he emerged in a puff of smoke. He was dressed not in his usual blue pyjamas, but in a festive green and red T-shirt and shorts, with giant maroon boots. The ends were curled inwards, and had bells on the ends.

"Why are you dressed like one of Santa's elves?"

"Me and Father Christmas have been trying to get into the festive spirit," said Zag. He grabbed the mistletoe. "Now you have to kiss me! It's the law."

"I wouldn't kiss you if my life depended on it," I said. "Why did you take so long to come when I called you?"

"I was busy studying," he said.

"Studying? What do you mean, studying?"

"About Christmas. I think I've learned everything about it. Origins, myths, right up to today's consumer-driven market. What's wrong?" He noticed my red eyes at last, and sat down by the clay head.

"Nothing…"

"How was the party?"

"A train-wreck," I muttered. I gazed into his blue eyes, which were wide and curious. "Well, I guess I'll go back downstairs… Goodnight."

"Goodnight," he called quietly, and he eagerly zipped through the air, disappearing in a puff of smoke again.

As I jumped back down onto the landing, I went into my room and lay down on my bed. I couldn't figure out what this new feeling was that I was battling with. I'd gone up there because I needed to feel better, and that gracing Zag with my presence would be a good deed, but he didn't seem to want me there. He was preoccupied with his studies. A sinking sensation overcame me, and it wasn't just because I'd landed on my LOL. Grandma was right. I was self-centred.

More than I'd realised.

The house began to rattle. Strong winds, which seemed to increase exponentially with every minute. Then I heard Rachael cry from downstairs: "It's a twister!"

Paranoid, I wandered back down the staircase and ventured to the open front door, where my aunt was standing on her own.

"What's wrong?" I asked.

Rachael pointed up into the near-bare oak trees above. High in the sky I could see things flying past, fast. Leaves, tiles, sheets of metal, and other debris. There were no clouds any more, and I noticed the three colourful stars glimmering in and out of view through some swaying branches.

"You think it's a tornado?" I said worriedly.

The winds suddenly died down, and only then did we realise how warm it had been. The natural chill of winter struck us again, and we went in and shut the door.

"That was weird," said Rachael, and she returned to the living room to keep warm.

To say I thought nothing else of it would be a lie — I did think about it, and kept thinking about it as I watched a Christmas movie in my room. But I knew how paranoid I was in general, ever since Zag had come into my life. Not every little thing was to do with magic, and as I cosied into my quilt I forced myself to accept that strong winds did not equal danger.

Annie would be fine.

# 39

## SCOOPED UP

They'd been trundling through the snow for a little over half-an-hour (during which Cora slipped Annie another pill to swallow), through the dead trees, struggling over giant rocky slopes. Just as Annie was about to ask for a chance to rest, they came to a small wooden door in the side of a snowy hill.

"Through there," ordered one of the three men, pointing.

Cora led the way, pulling at the black iron doorknob, then pushing the door to the side. Through it was nothing but darkness — a tiny black tunnel for them to climb through. If Annie hadn't been anxious before, she was near anaemia now. She followed Gentry's large form through, and turned to see if the three men were following. To her surprise, they shut the door behind her. Annie forced herself to breathe in and out slowly as the darkness enveloped them, and she whispered to Cora: "Where does this lead?"

"I don't know, but we can't go back," she replied, Gentry's

husky, deep voice reverberating around them. "Let's see where it takes us."

It was getting humid. The further in they went, the more dense the air, until finally Annie's ears popped. With nowhere to go, the tiny sounds they made with their palms and knees grazing the soil beneath them were dull and sudden. Finally, after what seemed an eternity, Cora pointed out how strange everything felt, and just like that the ground disappeared from beneath them.

Annie let out a panicked shriek, coming out in a male cry, and felt Cora glide past her. Falling endlessly into the darkness, they barely had time to collect their senses before they were swept up in a pool of water that slapped them from the side. Annie swam to the surface, which felt like it was on her left, and gasped for air. A bright, blue light shone down from above like a spotlight, and Annie caught sight of Cora, or Gentry, swimming by her side in the turbulent waters.

"It's alright," she said to her, sculling as best she could. "It's the Tumble-Dryer technique. We'll be out of it in a —"

A giant wave crashed into her, knocking the both of them deep under the surface. The light faded away, and Annie tried her best to hold her breath, but she could feel herself sinking deeper and deeper. Eventually, as the pressure greatened on her chest, she saw deep down something glowing. Her eyes were blurred from the water, but she knew what it was straight away. It was a giant water-plug at the very bottom of the pool. Just like the spotlight from above, it was glowing a vibrant blue, waiting for her to pull it. With what little strength she had left, she swam as fast as she could for it, and was about to grab the glowing chain when Cora, in her own body now, swooped in at the last minute and did it for her. Immediately, the two were sucked through the hole in the ground. The water seemed to evaporate, leaving the two to tumble down what looked like a slide in a giant warehouse — it was twisted and long, and Annie caught her breath as they slid down it into a giant pit of glowing, pink foam. Upon impact, the foam covered them from head to toe and Annie quickly found her footing and stood up. The foam only went up to her knees, and she grabbed onto Cora's flailing hands and pulled her up onto her feet.

"You're you again," she said to Cora.

"So are you," said Cora, looking her up and down.

"What was that?" asked Annie. She'd been stripped of her warm clothes and was now standing soaked in the canary yellow gown she'd started the night out in.

"Hang on," said Cora, and she scrunched up her features.

Hurricane force winds battered them from the right, knocking them both over into the foam again. But the foam was carried away with the winds, and Annie managed to climb to her feet again. Finally, the winds died down completely and the two were left standing there, disheveled but completely dry.

Cora opened her eyes. She'd been expecting that last part. She wiped some of her hair from her eyes and untangled her white dress. "That was a magical security measure. They call it the Tumble-Dryer. Before entering the Palace, you are sent through. It shows your loyalty, your true colours. That's why we're back to how we looked before. If your intentions are pure, and you don't wish to kill anybody in Danube, you swim to safety like we just did."

"And if you don't?"

"You drown. Look, over there. See? We're free to go."

A door had appeared in the side of the room, tiny, barely enough for the two girls to get through. Annie thanked her lucky stars that they were no longer big, burly men — however, she suspected the door would've been just that little bit bigger even if they had been.

Through the door, they were greeted with the place they'd started from — right in the middle of the cramped tunnel. Cora suggested they continue, as it would probably come to an end now that they'd passed the test. They followed on hands and knees through the darkness for another ten minutes, until far ahead a gentle red circle cast its light upon them. The two hurried along, eager to get out of the tunnel, no matter what was ahead. Finally, it became clear what it was — the red was from a giant curtain covering an exit hole, illuminated by a strong light behind it. Cora grabbed the curtain, ready to pull it back, but turned her head to listen for any noises on the other side.

"I can't hear anything, can you?" she asked Annie, who shook her head. Cora sighed. "I think we'd better change appearances again. If we're where I think we are, they won't know who Gentry and Uriah are, so we'll be no better off than if we just kept our original faces."

"Who should we look like, then?"

"Actually... I have an idea!"

Cora held her breath. Annie watched on as her body changed. Horrified and perplexed, a familiar face appeared in front of her.

"Cassie!" she cried.

"I'm not your sister," said Cora, shushing her with a finger to her mouth. "I only look like her. You should stay in your real form."

Annie checked her hands, and breathed out in relief, as they appeared to still be hers.

Beyond the curtain was a dungeon, cold and grey, only eight feet wide, with nothing else in it. Across from them was a flight of marble steps. Cora grabbed Annie's hand and the two of them rushed upstairs, through a medieval-looking entryway. There wasn't a soul to be seen, and as Annie admired the intricate details of the ceiling far above (much like a church), she noticed out of the nearest stain-glassed window that it was just as bright as it had been outside *'The Castory'*.

Suddenly, a thought occurred to her.

"I thought you said the Palace was on the dark side of Danube?" she said, stopping where she was. Her legs were still shaking from the swim.

Cora looked out the nearest arch window.

"It is," she said, "only they put a spell on the dome to make it look like the sun is shining during the day. Look ahead, something is going on over there!"

The two of them made their way towards a giant, closed wooden door. Beyond it they could hear a tremendous, rowdy commotion. Cora swung the door open; they were greeted to a giant circular room, with about one hundred Danubians inside.

The room was like a House of Parliament — at least that's what it looked like to Annie. Everybody was seated in curved pews, which all focused on a sort of stage in the middle of the room. The men and women of the court were yelling angrily at the sole figure standing in the middle of the stage, at a pulpit: it was Duke Wilson of Elmer.

This man, as far as Annie knew, was Second in Command after Queen Ursula. He was a man she'd trusted up until that day.

"Utmost rubbish!" he yelled over the protesting voices.

After a good while the crowd simmered down and he continued reading the parchment on the stand in front of him.

"It was an unfortunate incident, most definitely, but not as far-reaching as they'd like you to believe. Lady Angle can vouch for that. We have people on the site who have fed information for decades on the other side, and they will not be revealing any more to the people for quite a few decades. As I previously stated... *as I previously stated!...*" he yelled over the more bristled among him, "nothing has changed in the plan since day one. The Crux has managed to spread its bad luck throughout the town and we know exactly wh…"

His eyes landed on Cora, with her borrowed brown hair, red sweater and ripped jeans, and then to Annie.

"Meeting adjourned," he said to his listeners, and as they began to chatter amongst themselves, Duke Wilson collected his papers and rushed through a side door.

Before Annie had a chance to ask if he'd seen them, hands magically appeared out of the nearest wall and pulled the two of them into it. Cora and Annie suddenly found themselves in a giant room, circular again, lavish with wooden bookshelves, an iron fireplace, obscure art on the walls, a purple and leather-looking couch, a bed, a port window… and a giant, black shiny desk with a tall chair behind it. The two girls tripped as they came through the wall, and noticed Duke Wilson's grip on their necks. He let go of them and walked around his desk to his chair, with the slightest sound of rocks grinding together as he lowered himself into it.

"What, exactly, are you two doing here?" he asked.

Annie stared down at his clothes. He was wearing all black, and sported a giant cape that he'd flung over one side. He was old, strangely purple in colour today… and he looked agitated.

"We were abducted," said Cora.

Annie watched her sister speak for them, finding it in her shocked senses to nod in agreement.

"By whom?" he asked.

"I don't remember his name. He was tall, had black hair… wore a ridiculous fake moustache and eye-patch, top hat, dressed in a suit with a black dickie-bow. Went by the name… Pollux? Or…"

"… Pepper O. Salt," said Annie, followed by a gulp.

"There was a Zeppelin ride at our high school. We were just minding our own business, and he said he was going to drive the Zeppelin into our house to kill our Child of Crux!"

Annie was impressed by Cora's quick thinking. She was also surprised to see a box of tissues on Duke Wilson's desk, behind a strange yellow globe. He pushed the box to them, and Cora began to wipe her nose with it, putting on the show of her life.

"Pollux?" said Duke Wilson, turning to look out the port window at the fake setting sun, squinting as he cast his mind back. "I haven't thought about him for a very long time. His parents were magicians, you know. Didn't teach him very well, although he pursued a 'career' nonetheless. To this day, I don't see a lick of sense in having a magician when the world is filled with very real magic. Something of a human trait, I'd say..." He looked back at them, and sighed. "Tell me how you got here. The Heads of the Universe have informed me that your family have put a wishing ban upon your Child of Crux until your Christmas season is through, is that correct?"

"Yes," said Annie quickly, "although I've had to use it tonight to save our lives..."

Suddenly, an idea came to her. She wanted to see if Cora was telling the truth about the comet hitting in May. Could she elicit a response from him, to confirm it?

A burst of bravery overtook her senses, and she said carefully: "We promise we won't do that again until July, when it's Cassie's birthday. Would you mind, Duke Wilson? If we put up another wishing ban, at the beginning of July next year?"

For a moment, Duke Wilson didn't say anything. He sat back in his chair and took turns looking from one sister to the other. For a terrifying moment, Annie thought she'd said too much and revealed her cards.

Then, at long last, Wilson smiled and said to them: "We'll cross that bridge when we get to it."

Annie could see it. A look in his eyes, a danger she'd not seen until now. They would never cross that bridge. All this time, he'd played innocent. A man who came to the rescue when Rudnick van Pan and Just tried to kill them.

Wilson pressed a button on his desk, a sly smirk spreading across his painted face.

"I was wondering who that Zeppelin belonged to. Some of our rogue Sherpas brought it into the Palace during my meeting. Unfortunately, they demanded payment and things got ugly, so they were removed from the Palace before telling us who it belonged to. I'm sorry, they must have given you an awful fright. Did you try to run away from them?"

"Yes," said Cora, grabbing another tissue. "We found a door in the middle of some snowy woods, and it led us here."

"Ah, one of the entrances to the Tumble-Dryer. How fun. That must have been in the banished woods. You're lucky those Sherpas were the only ones you came across," said Duke Wilson, and he stood up and went over to his fireplace to warm up. "During our last pandemic, which was over five hundred years ago, many of the inhabitants of our Palace did not do as were required of them. Many seemed to think our restrictions were beneath them, a ploy to control and spy on them, and that we fabricated the whole thing for financial gain. Well, we made it very simple for them. They could either go by Danube's rules, or cast themselves out of our society and survive on their own in the outer-regions. Or worse, Summers City. The cretins that swarm there, my goodness…" He laughed, and grabbed a fire-poker to rustle up more flames in the fireplace. "I'm sure you've been versed aplenty on Summers City, on the sunny side of this planet. Your Child of Crux was born there, after all. Has always struck me as strange, how pale yours turned out, when usually they are fairly dark… Must've been an anomaly in… Anyway, I need to backtrack. The banished woods, ah yes, that's right… Where the most deplorable, dangerous criminals from Danube end up. There's no law there; as such you won't find a single redeemable soul. Nothing but trouble-makers, murderers, thieves, and worse. We'd blow it up if we could…"

Annie felt a chill run down her spine as Duke Wilson's face furrowed. A dark and deadly menace glistened in his eyes.

"How many people live in the woods?" asked Cora.

Wilson turned back to them and forced a smile. "Afraid we don't know, Cassie. It's not within our territory. You could form a coup and we wouldn't know until it happened. Now don't be getting any ideas," he chuckled and waved an index finger at them. "Stars above, it must be getting on for Christmas Day on your planet! Let's see what we can do to get you home as fast as possible."

He came over, waited for them to stand, and guided them out of a side door into yet another gigantic, marble entryway. Only this time they were greeted by hundreds and hundreds of people bustling about. Annie and Cora marvelled at them — some were human-like, many others were not. Some were blue, with legs sprouting out of their ears. Others were circular and squat with no legs at all, rolling about. Two of them looked exactly like Annie and Cora, only they quickly switched to that of Duke Wilson and Ursula, then back to Annie and Cora, and they ran off in their duties.

Only as the three of them hopped into a glass elevator did Annie realise they were in a mammoth, extravagant transport station. Beyond the marble walls she could see giant, translucent bubbles. Through their transparent, pink hues she spotted dozens upon dozens of creatures sitting down on equally translucent seats inside. Bubble-trains.

"It will take a while, unfortunately, but it's very comfortable travel. You'll feel like you're floating on a cloud. A bubble, in fact!" said Duke Wilson, guiding them cheerfully towards an iron gate.

Cora eyed Annie nervously. "Duke Wilson, as wonderful as that sounds... Don't you think it would be wiser to go back the way we came? The thing is, the Zeppelin was brought here by magic, a sort of wind tunnel I think, or a storm-front... and there were a lot of people watching it in the skies of Horn-Horn. If we returned any other way, even *without* the Zeppelin, it would raise eyebrows. It's probably best if we return the same way we left... On the Zeppelin?"

Duke Wilson paused with his hands on the iron gate, thinking. He looked across the vast station, at the many commuters rushing to catch their bubbles. "Cassie, you are far wiser than I. That is the best idea you've ever had."

Annie tried not to scoff at this back-handed compliment, but was overcome with relief as Wilson ordered the two of them to catch a 'bullet-bubble' with him. She soon found herself pushed inside a bubble no bigger than the average car, with Cora and Wilson by her side. Inside they sat on seats that appeared to be completely invisible, but comfortable and squishy.

"Knight's Bridge," said Wilson.

The bubble shot off into the sky.

Annie wet herself a little as the grand roof of the station seemed to melt away behind them, and the chilled, white sky momentarily blinded her. They were a mile above Danube now, with the walls of the iced dome visible all around. Before them, spread out, was a giant world of blue and white. Giant mountains in the distance, dark crevices and cracks in the ice. It was the most beautiful thing Annie had ever seen with her own eyes. And glowing like the nerves inside a human brain, directly below them, she spotted the great Palace of Danube, lit up with a million tiny lights reflecting the manufactured setting sun. *This really is another world,* she thought to herself in dazzlement, although soon the enchantment wore off as she realised what this meant: *We are screwed.* The bubble began to descend just as quickly as it had shot off, but now they were falling into a different area of the Palace. Between some funny looking trees, Annie spotted strange, long yellow lights coming from a big, grey ball sitting in the middle of a tremendous bridge. The bubble quickly shot down towards it, and soon it became clear what it was — the Zeppelin, stationary, with the giant glowing ropes still tied around it from the dismissed Sherpas.

The bubble landed gently on the concrete road of the bridge, and popped in a comical fashion. The three of them fell an inch to the ground, and when they wiped themselves off they rushed to the stairs of the Zeppelin. The door leading inside opened above, and Duke Wilson waited for Annie and Cora to walk in before shutting the door behind him.

Annie was hugely relieved to see that the ballroom was still empty, and as she moved forward she kicked around at an area where she thought the magical tarp might be, the one that covered all of the unconscious guests. She stretched her leg out, trying to act subtle about it, but couldn't find anything. A moment later she noticed Cora attempting the same thing.

"They're gone," said Duke Wilson behind them.

Annie turned and noticed that he was talking to her. Her heart started to beat quickly, and she made an innocent 'hmm?' sound in her throat, but she could see it in his eyes now. He knew.

"You're not fooling anybody," he said in a tone so different from his previous one that it made even Cora stop in her tracks by the bar area.

"Sorry?" said Annie in a hush.

"Let me be frank," said Duke Wilson. He walked past Annie and through the empty space of the ballroom. "We found the bodies the moment we opened her up. It was *not* a good disguise. Only took our magical interpreter two minutes and forty-three seconds to uncover them, and he's our very best. I wish I'd kept him handy before sending him off again."

He turned back and skirted around Annie, who was now visibly shaking in fear. As he looked her up and down, he snickered and licked his lips.

"Who are you?" he asked finally.

Annie could do nothing but stare back in bewilderment. What did he mean, who was she? Couldn't he *see* who she was? She was Annie Gellar, seventeen, from Horn-Horn. Across from him was Cassie Gellar, sixteen, also from Horn-Horn, although not really. Because of the hidden group of humans in the ballroom, did he now doubt what he could see?

"I'm Annie... G-Gellar," she stuttered in a high voice.

He leered closer, and closer, until he was inches away from her. She noticed a rank smell of sulphur, and a strange redness to his otherwise brown eyes, just like Pothosia's.

"I'm not Duke of this world without reason," he said, in a threateningly low voice. "My birth gift is to communicate with others via electrical currents, something of a talent shared with that oafish magician, but it also gives me an insight to people's inner vibrations. It's like a spattering of colour to each individual, and I can see it in both of you. Now, it's not something I forget, and since I've met Cassandra Gellar the First, and her sister Annie on multiple occasions, believe me when I say you two are not who you say you are."

It was the pills they'd taken. Annie knew it. Although she was most definitely Annie Gellar, the pill's magic was still working on her, just as it was on Cora. It must have given off a different energy, a different current, that fooled him into thinking she was somebody else. How could she explain this, though, without giving away Cora's real identity? A woman off the grid, living in the banished woods with Pollux, a dead giveaway for 'The Castory'. She'd never be able to return, never be able to find out what happened to her friends.

In an instant, the Duke was pushed over and Cora grabbed Annie's arm. "Run!" she said, and the two of them tore down the nearest hallway to escape.

Duke Wilson did something very strange to the air then: it rippled with power and the two girls were nearly destroyed as it skimmed over them. Electricity, Annie realised, and she noticed Cora's borrowed hair begin to rise with the static.

"You go in here, and I'll go in there," said Cora, and she pushed Annie through an entryway that said: 'STAFF ONLY'.

Annie pressed against the other side of the door and caught her breath. The smell of fuel and metal was overwhelming. She was in a giant room that seemed to stretch on forever, above and beyond. A maze of metal-works lay before her: ladders, walkways and frameworks. She was in a control room. The outer shell of the Zeppelin was within reach. All she needed to do was light a match, or tear at the fabric. She knew how dangerous it was to be in here, but she didn't have much time to think about this as the door-handle behind her began to jiggle.

Annie snuck away as quickly as possible, running up a flight of metal stairs and hiding behind the first bulbous tank she could find. The door she'd come from opened loudly, and for a moment there wasn't a breath of sound, for the Zeppelin was not... But wait. The gradual roaring of engines began to churn away, and the gas tank in front of Annie started to hiss, and slowly but surely she felt the sense of being in an elevator again… The Zeppelin was rising into the air! Cora must have gone into the control car and started it up.

Was Duke Wilson going to go and find her? Annie peeked around the corner to see if he'd left, but he was only five feet away from her. Her heart nearly left her body, and she stayed still as he glided past, looking all around at the machinery, then checking the corners of his eyes for any movements.

She took her chance and wiggled between the gas cylinder and a now warm iron stove-looking object with a temperature gauge on it. Her yellow dress catching slightly on one of its knobs, she had to stop herself from running down the steps in order to unhook it without making any noise. As she did, she saw that Duke Wilson was checking two storeys above her, between some very noisy machines.

Annie finally got to her feet and ran as quickly as she could for the door. The noise around her was deafening now, and she didn't dare look back in case he was watching. Finally, as she reached the door she heard him yell out from far away. She turned, spotting him three storeys up, quite near the curved top, and he raised his hands, full of electricity, towards her.

"Stop!" he yelled.

Annie covered her mouth in horror.

*"Stop!"* she yelled back at him, but it was too late. The magical fireball he'd conjured in his hands to throw at her caught in the air and spread above. Before she knew what was happening, a giant explosion blossomed in front of her. She flew backwards, heat almost burning her to a crisp, and she smacked heavily into the corner in the hallway outside. Giant flames burst through the doorway at her, and she stretched out of its influence just in time. Stunned, she automatically found her footing and bounded into the ballroom. To her utmost surprise, the entire place was packed with the familiar guests from the television show, all of them clearly in mid-conversation, at the bars, some of them dancing. Dazed, perturbed, sensing she may be looking at ghosts, Annie backtracked. She ran lopsided down the hallway, past the now singed-doorway leading to the burned inner workings of the Zeppelin, and found Cora at last in the pilot's seat, navigating the machine with all her might over Danube.

"He's set fire to the place and killed himself!" shrieked Annie, grabbing the back of Cora's seat as she made a sharp turn to the left.

"You can't kill Duke Wilson," said Cora, sticking her tongue out as she aimed the Zeppelin towards a dark mass in the distance.

"He's like a Child of Crux. Indestructible in his own way. He probably just set fire to the Zeppelin, that's all."

"That's all? We'll crash before we get away!"

"Or die trying. Look at that, it's the banished woods up ahead. I'll do the best I can to aim for the abyss, and hopefully we'll reappear in Horn-Horn exactly where we left off."

"If Duke Wilson's still alive, it won't matter. He'll stop us."

"I've set a dozen magic traps around the Zeppelin to keep him preoccupied until we get through. Did you see the guests in the ballroom? That's one of them. I've shown his daughter to him in the control room, which will have definitely spooked him. Any other hallucinations will come to him and slow him down before he can get to us here."

"But if we get through, once we land…"

"It'll be too late for him to do anything! We'll be back in Horn-Horn by then. He thinks you're pretending to be Annie Gellar. He was right about me pretending to be Cassie, but he has no idea that it really *is* you here! Once we get through, all you have to do is insist you're the real Annie, and pretend like you weren't here at all. I'll go back to how I normally look, and be just another face in the crowd, which means if he confronts you and your sister, she'll corroborate your story and insist it wasn't you two. He thinks we're imposters, so let's make sure he keeps thinking it!"

There was another explosion from above them.

"We're nearly there. Look!" said Cora, pointing out the windshield to the dark mass of dead trees that stretched on and on into the distance — the banished woods.

"What about the others?" asked Annie in panic. "The humans, the guests from Horn-Horn? We can't leave them here on Danube."

"They're already taken care of, don't worry."

"How?"

"They're in the ballroom!"

Annie looked over her shoulder, managing to see a tiny portion of the ballroom down the hallway, and a few people walking past and chatting.

"They're unconscious under that tarp, remember?"

"But Duke Wilson said he found them straight away! His… decipherer, his magic man, the one who…"

"Solved it in two minutes; I heard that too. He's not as powerful as I am. I put a tarp *over* the tarp. He thinks he found them, but he didn't. I'm a master of illusion! Much better than Pollux."

Annie tried to wrap her mind around the situation. "So the real guests are unconscious underneath those fake moving guests in the ballroom?"

"You're smart, Annie!" exclaimed Cora, grinning like she was having the time of her life. "Now, come on. Let's go back to Horn-Horn!"

The Zeppelin catapulted downwards, heading directly for the banished woods, turning at almost a ninety-degree angle. Annie let out a terrible moan as she struggled to stay upright.

Suddenly outside, colourful spears of light began to glimmer past them, and for a moment Annie thought they were fireworks. That was until Cora cried: "They're shooting at us! Danube is shooting at us, from all angles! Get down, quick."

The glass windows surrounding them burst inwards, and giant balls of glowing red magma shot into the room, piercing the walls, door, narrowly missing Annie and Cora. The two of them abandoned their stations and ducked to the ground. Flames were erupting all throughout the Zeppelin, every inch of it. A shrieking, snapping sound was the loudest of all — the giant, glowing ropes that had been wrapped around the Zeppelin by the Sherpas were fraying, breaking away as the energetic beams shot through them.

Deafened by the noises, Cora and Annie crawled down the hallway and into the ballroom. Through the shower of angry missiles, bullets and explosions, they could see that the entire ballroom was set on fire yet again, and a hideous blue and green burst forth like a flower. The imaginary guests were still going about their business, getting drinks, chatting, dancing, not even a little bit affected by the pandemonium around them. They really were like ghosts, Annie realised, a great magical hallucination. Underneath them was a tarp, invisible to the eye, and the real guests were fast asleep underneath, completely protected.

Annie and Cora lay on the edges of the ballroom, curled into balls on the ground, covering their ears and keeping their eyes shut, and for a while they assumed this was the end. They were going to crash in a fiery mess, perishing from the lack of oxygen, or the flames that would cascade across their fragile flesh... but then, all at once, the heavy bombardments stopped.

Harsh silence followed.

Annie was the first to look up. The ghostly guests had vanished; lying down now were the real guests, fast asleep, appearing like a massacre of dead bodies all around her. The flames were no more. All of the windows were broken, and half of the promenade deck sticking out from the rest of the capsule was blow apart. Annie felt a warm breeze enter the Zeppelin, and as she walked over to the broken windows, she let out a gasp at what she saw outside.

Nothing but a great, swirling void of grey clouds, in every direction, churning quickly and energetically, appearing to be growing closer and closer, but also further and further. Annie ran to the other side of the Zeppelin and looked out, and found the same sight beyond.

"The abyss," said a calm voice from behind her. Cora was getting up off her knees, wiping herself down and looking past Annie at the clouds beyond. "This is what it looks like to be caught between worlds. The worst punishment Danube can ever think of. We're lucky because we're in a machine, and we'll cross through into Horn-Horn soon. But sometimes, if you're really bad, the people of Danube will curse you to an eternity in these clouds. There's no way out. You'll float forever."

Annie stared out at the abyss, which she now thought was aptly titled. A sense of exhaustion overtook her. "At least it's warm…"

All at once, the clouds parted, and complete and utter darkness took over. Annie steadied herself, panicking as she'd been right near an open window. A few moments later, she spotted lights below, many of them, which were coming closer and closer. Then she spotted a lighthouse on the edge of a cliff, by the ocean, and growing nearer and nearer was…

"Horn-Horn!" she cried, pointing. "We're back. Oh, thank goodness. What do we do now?"

"Land," said Cora, her breath showing as she spoke.

Annie turned to see her running as fast as she could down the hallway for the cockpit again. She took one last look at the lighthouse as it disappeared below, and chased after her. Tearing around the corner and sitting in the seat next to her, Annie noticed that she was Cora Corali again, no longer in disguise. The pills they'd taken must have worn off.

"It might be a bumpy ride," said Cora.

Annie took a deep breath of the now wintery air. "After tonight, I'm game for anything."

The town looked completely different at night, and from up above it was impossible to make out where they were. Fortunately, the Zeppelin's lights had all been destroyed in the complexities of war, so as the two of them squinted into the darkness they had little in the way of distraction. And that is the way they sat for quite a while. Cora guided the rudder easily with one hand, and Annie sat with her hands tucked between her legs to keep them warm.

"We'll land where we took off," said Cora.

How strange it would look, Annie realised as she agreed. The crowd would be waiting for their return, only to find everybody passed out in the ballroom, with a mere two of its guests awake to greet the cameras.

*What a scoop!*

# 40

# A BAD FEELING

I'd decided to paint my toenails Christmas colours, every second one red and green. Although I was mentally exhausted, I was waiting up until Annie came home. I needed her to tell me everything, to brighten my mood and distract me from the disaster that was the Walker Dinner. When I heard the front door open downstairs, I hobbled bare-foot to the landing and looked down. To my surprise, it was JT, who had burst through the door with not so much as a knock.

"Have you heard?"

I noticed Grandma Helen opening her closed bedroom door. One look at our visitor, and she urged me to call the police.

"That's my friend, Grandma," I said, hobbling down the stairs quickly to greet him. "I haven't heard anything. JT, what's going on?"

Hayley emerged from around the corner, with a mug of her Pandora coffee in both hands. One look at JT, and she let out an angry moan.

"Go home, Jonathan! I told you I'm not in the mood to talk to you right now."

"This isn't about you…"

"You're right, it's not me, it's her."

"No, I…"

Hayley nearly spilled her coffee as she ran down the stairs, and she kicked at him with her own bare feet.

"Get out, get out, get out," she demanded, and he started to backtrack out the door.

I protested for them to stop, and chased after them, but finally Hayley had abused him enough that he took one giant leap out of the front door.

"STOP!" he yelled at her in a way I'd never heard him speak before. It was like another person's voice booming out. It echoed through the bare oak trees and down the street, and a moment later I heard my father as he opened the sliding door to his bedroom balcony above us.

"Excuse me, it is very late. Some of us are trying to sleep."

"Dad, you've been watching the skies since we got home."

"Have not," he lied.

I thought this may have quashed the clamour, but JT tipped his head back and addressed my father immediately, in that same determined voice: "Mr. Gellar, the Zeppelin had an accident, and they can't find it."

Mom's head popped out on the balcony behind Dad, silhouetted against the light from their room. "What do you mean, they can't find it?" she asked nervously.

"That's what I was trying to say. My mother said something about a freak wind that came…"

"I *knew* that weather was going to be trouble!" snapped Aunt Rachael, appearing by the doorway in her black pyjamas. "Where were they last seen?"

"Over the school. Lots of people were hurt, about a dozen ambulances were called. We saw it all from my house. It was really scary…" JT looked to Hayley for support, but she was staring off into the trees above us in curiosity. "What?" he said, turning.

"Have you ever noticed those three stars before?" she asked, pointing between the bare branches. The three colourful stars were twinkling more brightly than ever. Pink, green and blue.

"We saw them earlier," said Mom, at the same time as Grandma Helen, who poked her head out of the door behind Rachael.

After a moment of standing out in the cold, Mom said: "I'm coming down." Half a minute later, she barged past Grandma, having grabbed her jacket by the door. "JT, do you think we might be able to see better from your house?"

"I guess," said JT, shrugging.

"Lesley, you should stay here, it's not safe," said Grandma suddenly, trying to grab her hand. "Something isn't right. I have a bad feeling. The same one I get when…"

"Ma, I have the same bad feeling. That's why I'm not staying here. Ichabod, keep the phone close in case it rings. The rest of you… Stay here."

"No, Mom —"

"Cassie, for the love of God, I said *stay here!*"

I wasn't one to argue when she got this serious. Her wrath was straight from Grandma Helen. With that, she took off through the oak trees towards the road with JT. The rest of us started to pile back inside to keep warm, our minds aflutter. Nerves had taken hold of my stomach. Forgotten were the troubles we'd had with Brendan, who was sleeping it off upstairs, while any animosity with Grandma was put to rest. As I shut the door, I wondered what else could possibly go wrong tonight.

And then I saw it.

Through the trees, over the fence, was the Parker family coming home early. And, huddled between them as they rushed for the front door, with a pink blanket over her shoulders, was none other than Eleanore Parker herself.

"Cassie," my father called in the foyer, and when I turned to look at him he raised his eyebrows, not willing to let me out of his sight for even a second.

*I have a bad feeling, too,* I thought as I shut the door.

# 41

## THE
## FINAL
## MAGIC TRICK

While they were slowly gliding towards the football stadium, Cora gave Annie a task to keep her occupied. Going around to each and every unconscious guest, she slipped them a pill. These weren't like the ones they'd taken to appear different to those on Danube. Instead, these blue pills from the same packet would hydrate them, and would gradually wake them up. Just in time, Cora informed her, for the Zeppelin to land and come to terms with what had happened.

*And what did happen?* Annie wondered.

By the time they landed, Duke Wilson would've finally escaped from the maze of magic tricks Cora had laid out for him. The camera crews at the school, as well as the hundreds of people on the football field, not to mention those at home watching on television… How would Duke Wilson manage this unfortunate situation?

Perhaps he would pretend to be one of the disturbed guests, emerging dazed and befuddled and losing himself in the crowd before magically heading back to Danube. That was a very smart idea. After all, it was what Cora and Annie were planning on doing. Once they'd landed, they would sneak back into the ballroom and lay down between the guests, and be the first to 'wake up in confusion'.

"You're lucky you've been asleep this whole time..." said Annie, closing one of the sleeping guest's lips shut and making sure they swallowed the blue pill.

Thinking of how glad she would be to hop into bed that night, she automatically pushed a pill into the mouth of a guest lying near the bar, whose head was half tilted up against the corner of a bar stool. Pinching the man's lips closed to make sure he swallowed, Annie waited, and waited, busying herself by looking at the Waxing Crescent across from her... Still, the man refused to swallow. Usually they did it straight away, but this time...

Annie turned back to check on him, and was surprised to discover his eyes were wide open, locked on hers. A second later he was upright, clasping at the sides of his head in dismay. He grabbed onto the nearest chair to steady himself, focussing on Annie again.

"Don't touch me," he said in a deep voice, and he wiped his dark blazer clean. "What happened?"

"The Z..." started Annie, but she didn't know what to say. For the first time that night, she was speechless.

The man had been in the make-up tent, as part of the crew. He waited for Annie to say more, then his eyes slowly drifted across the crowd of unconscious guests surrounding them.

"*What's happening!?*" he screamed loudly.

Annie put her hands out to quieten the panicking man, but he swung his fists out and nearly struck her. A moment later he ran over to the door, figured out its mechanics, and kicked it open.

"No, stop!" cried Annie, and she ran forward.

Like a predator, Duke Wilson appeared out of the darkness, pushing past a bizarre optical barrier behind him. His face strained in a physical and mental struggle as he managed to pierce through the last of Cora's magic tricks.

"Got you!" he yelled, grabbing the man in a blind rage.

With one determined push, he sent the guest flying with all his might out of the open door. Only this time, the man didn't fall down. He fell up. Annie watched in confusion. His cries of fear disappeared into the night sky, and Duke Wilson leaned against the edge of the opened door and peered above.

"Enjoy the abyss!" he said with a cold laugh.

Annie ducked the moment he turned back around. She lay flat on her back in the dimly lit ballroom, her gaze fixed on the singed ceiling and the rows of broken light fixtures. Amidst the sprawl of unconscious bodies, she blended seamlessly.

A face lost in the chaos.

They'd taken too long, she realised. Cora remained in the control room, with her back to the entrance. The intruder had penetrated her magic tricks earlier than expected. But then again, he was Duke Wilson of Elmer — a man whose intellect surpassed most mortal bounds.

"I know you're in here," his voice sliced through the silence, echoing off the elegant marble walls. He stood by the open door, a shadow against the moonlit darkness. "Your friend, the one masquerading as Cassandra Gellar the First, is gone. I dispatched him to the abyss. A fate worse than death. Surrender now, and I promise a swift end."

Annie's breaths came shallow and rapid as she lay among the inert forms of five others. His footsteps drew closer, each a frigid reminder of her vulnerability.

And then, there it was—the outline of his silhouette in her peripherals. He stepped into view, his eyes glinting in the moonlight. They swept across the room, lingering on the person beside her, until finally... they locked onto her.

"Why, hello there," he said with a sly smirk.

# 42

## CRASH
## MANIA

From her vantage point at the gate, Marguerite Walker could see through her binoculars as the Zeppelin appeared to head towards Horn-Horn High-High. Where had it come from? The same burst of clouds seemed to have come out of nowhere and disappeared just as quickly, but instead of engulfing the airship, it spat it out this time by the bay area.

The guests had abandoned the party, all rather abruptly after the gale force winds left nothing else but the very house behind them standing. Others were called to the school — where the brunt of the damage took place. Then there was her son, chasing after that girlfriend of his. Marguerite was glad to see him returning from down the hill; for a moment she thought he was coming back with Hayley. On second glance, it appeared to be...

"Lesley!" Marguerite cried, unlocking the gates again.

"Where is the Zeppelin?" asked Mom in a panic, her cheeks

flushed from the cold.

Marguerite handed over the binoculars. "See for yourself, dear."

Mom let out a sigh of relief as she spotted the airship. She skimmed across its side, and then at the words *'The Uma'*, which were half covered by what looked like burn marks. She looked without the binoculars — they were so close that she didn't need them now, and giant black lacerations were streaked across the Zeppelin's body. Half of the control car was dangling perilously from its hinges, while flames seemed to be coming from deep inside the airship, for it had a sense of gentle glowing between its frames.

"What happened to it?" asked JT in a concerned hush.

"I haven't the faintest. I think it's trying to land," said Marguerite. "Lesley, how is Brendan?"

Mom ignored her and, not taking her eyes off the Zeppelin, began to run up the hill towards the house for an even higher vantage point.

———— · · · ————

I sat with the rest of my family in the living room while the end of *It's A Wonderful Life* played on the television.

I was lost in my thoughts. The Zeppelin must have landed. There was no other way Eleanore Parker could've gotten off. Unless she was dead, and I saw a ghost outside, which was doubtful. I couldn't even talk to anyone about it. The only people in my family that knew anything out of the ordinary was Annie, currently MIA, and Brendan, currently DUI.

I looked from Rachael, to Grandma Helen, Hayley, and then Dad... and realised none of them were watching the movie, either. Rachael's gaze remained fixed on the ground, and Dad was watching the window. Grandma Helen fidgeted terribly in her seat.

Finally, she said: "Curse it! I'm going after her."

Dad was the first to follow her lead. He rushed to the door, grabbed his jacket, and reasoned with himself: "We'll go to the corner of Philips Street and Gentleman's Court, see if we can spot Lesley, and then we'll come home again. We're not that far away if Brendan needs us."

"I agree," I said, kicking into my fluffy slippers and helping Grandma into her giant coat.

Minutes later, we were walking down Philips Street.

Rachael and Grandma Helen were far behind the rest of us, as Grandma had misplaced her cane somewhere and was walking slower. Ahead of us, high up in the sky, sat those three glowing, colourful stars. A spare cloud appeared, and was quickly ushered on by strong winds that were too high up to affect us.

Then, as we got to the corner, where the teenage oaks on the opposite side of the road ended, we stopped to stare at the sight before us. The Zeppelin was pitted against the calm ocean — only it was much, much closer. It moved at such a rate that it couldn't have been more than a few streets away.

"Isn't it meant to be landing at the school?" asked Hayley.

"That was the plan…" muttered Rachael, squinting. "It could be making a quick detour for some reason… but…"

Her voice trailed off as something else became clear.

"Guys, it's… it's coming right…"

Dad grabbed hold of me first, then Hayley.

"Get back to the house. Now. *Now!*"

With those words, we turned and ran back up the hill.

— • • • —

Duke Wilson stepped over the slumbering forms, his intense gaze fixed upon Annie.

"Still in disguise, I see," he remarked, seizing the sides of her yellow top to lift her. "Why not reveal your true self? Unless you'd prefer an eternity spent in the void."

Annie's scream echoed as he dragged her toward the open door. The frigid night air stung her eyes, and she clung to the doorframe, resisting. Her glasses slipped from her face. They vanished below, only to quickly reappear, defying gravity, soaring into the sky above and toward the abyss.

Unexpectedly, a colossal wooden telephone pole appeared, crashing against the Zeppelin's side. Metal screeched, sparks danced, and flames licked the airship's exterior. Wilson's weight heaved against Annie in the violence, bringing her to her knees; he tumbled out of the Zeppelin altogether, managing to cling to the bottom of the doorway with his bare fingers, which had been chipped of their layers of paint.

Annie left him, her heart pounding. For a split second, she could've sworn she glimpsed the sprawling Emmett property below

— a stark contrast to the downtown area near the school where they were meant to be heading. Panic surged as she entered the cockpit. Ahead lay a street flanked by adolescent oaks, and half a dozen figures sprinting for their lives

"What are you doing?" asked Annie. "That's my street!"

Cora's eyes remained fixed on a single house.

"I'm taking your Child of Crux. Nothing personal, Annie. I'm sorry I couldn't tell you before. I knew you'd try and stop me."

"But you'll kill everyone inside!"

Cora's smile was chilling.

"Not quite. Everybody knows you can't kill a Child of Crux!"

Annie should have known. She should've known that Cora wouldn't play fair. They'd warned her — people played dirty when it came to Crux ownership. And now, as Cora Corali hurtled the Zeppelin toward their house on Philips Street, Annie's heart raced at the thought of her family inside. Vulnerable, human.

Except for Zag, who couldn't die because he was a Child of Crux. By crashing the Zeppelin into their home, Cora would inadvertently kill Zag's owners. Then she could claim him for herself and escape, leaving the Gellars to perish in the fiery blaze.

"*No!*" Annie screamed, wrestling for control.

Instincts took over. She lunged at Cora and bared her teeth, sinking them into Cora's right ear. Blood filled her mouth; Cora released the controls in disbelief. The two of them tumbled to the carpeted floor, locked in a desperate struggle.

———— · · · ————

We dashed forward, Rachael, Hayley, and Dad leading the way as we sprinted up the street toward our house. The Zeppelin's engine roared behind us, and I struggled to push Grandma Helen, who couldn't run very fast due to her hip.

"Faster, Grandma!"

The shrieking of metal, followed by a thunderous explosion. Lights illuminated the sky from behind, casting our shadows on the sidewalk as we reached the front of our property. In that critical moment, I turned around, leaving Grandma to forge ahead. The Zeppelin descended upon us, soaring over the teenage oaks. It had collided with a telephone pole, and a man dangled from the open door. I opened my mouth to scream, but another engine sound to my right diverted my attention. A motorcycle came out of nowhere, zigzagging up the street as its rider desperately tried to evade the oncoming airship. I leapt aside in fear, witnessing the motorcycle collide with Grandma Helen, knocking her clean off her feet.

*"Oh my God!"* I gasped, hand covering mouth.

The motorcycle flipped and tumbled, sparks flying in all directions. The two handcuffed ladies in the sidecar were flung onto the grass, while the driver bore the brunt of its weight.

"My motorbike!" Dad shouted, pointing at its yellow finish and the dented bumper sticker that read: *'Too Fat To Carpool.'*

For a moment, we had forgotten about the most pressing issue of all. As Rachael reached Helen's body in the middle of the road, we gaped in horror as the Zeppelin plummeted earthward. The top branches of the oak trees in the front of our property snapped away. Five or six trees collapsed against their siblings. The world seemed to hold its breath as chaos unfolded around us.

— · · · —

Annie grappled with Cora on the ground, her once-white dress now marred by bloodstains. She sank her teeth into Cora's neck, then her shoulders, wrists, and even her nose.

*"I'll kill you before you kill my family!"* Annie's voice trembled.

Cora's response was equally primal — an angry moan followed by a surge of magical electricity that shot from her forehead. The bolt struck Annie's shoulder, leaving her stunned but unharmed. She glanced out the window in a panic. What she saw defied belief: hurtling toward them was her very own house, its windows aglow. Someone stood in the circular attic window, eyes wide with disbelief.

"I wish for a big gust of wind!" yelled Annie.

In that moment, she unwittingly made the best wish of her life. A wad of glitter caught in her throat, and the Zeppelin slowly began to rise again. But Annie wasn't done.

"I wish we were free of this goddamn Zeppelin!"

Suddenly, the ground vanished beneath them. Annie found herself suspended in mid-air. Cora twisted like a cat, attempting to right herself gracefully. In her desperation, Annie glimpsed a series of strange sights: three vivid and colourful stars shining above, the fifty or so sleeping guests now plummeting alongside her... and there amongst them, most astonishingly, was Duke Wilson.

With a tremendous boom that shook birds from their perches, the human mass crashed through the roof of the house below.

Annie landed on something particularly large and lumpy, which quickly let out a cry of pain...

———— · · · ————

Gripped with fear, we witnessed something that defied logic. I tore my gaze away from Grandma Helen — sprawled on the road, her moans echoing in the night, illuminated by the motorcycle's crimson taillights — and turned toward the the figures who had fallen from the Zeppelin. Against all reason, the airship had managed to soar back up into the sky.

"They... they hit the roof!" yelled Hayley uncertainly.

The Zeppelin slowly continued on its journey, until it disappeared over the pine trees behind our property.

"All those people... they must have jumped," I called to Dad. "You stay with Grandma, I'll check on Brendan!"

———— · · · ————

Up on the hill, Marguerite accepted a cocktail from Morgan, without bothering to thank him. He was tired, she could tell, but she didn't want to clean up the mess the wind had made. Besides, she was in no mood to be forgiving — the storm had brought a premature end to her highly organised Christmas party.

"It vanished into those trees..." she informed Mom.

"That's impossible. Philips Street is down there."

"Lesley, I assure you, it's not. I have excellent eyesight, in fact, the best in my family."

"I can vouch for that!"

Marguerite frowned. "Go *home*, Suzannah."

Tommy Walker strutted down the hill. Fresh drink in hand, he appeared utterly unfazed by the chaos around him.

"Marguerite, my dear, most of the staff are waiting to be paid before they leave. Your cheque book, or mine?"

"Mine, of course. It's in the bureau. *Wait...* "

Marguerite grasped his hand, as if sensing something. For a suspended moment, time seemed to freeze, until finally...

"Bedside drawer."

Tommy turned to leave, and just as he did, a tremendous sight unfolded before them. Rising like a celestial dawn, *'The Uma'* — or what remained of it — reared its flame-covered, driverless body over the hill, soaring past them in a noisy whir. Mom, JT, and Marguerite instinctively ducked, their breaths catching as it grazed past, allowing them to witness its final descent. The air vibrated with a gigantic, crippling sound as wood and glass shattered, followed by a fireball that heated up the entire hill. The Zeppelin crashed with furious force into the Walker Mansion, where it finally — *finally* — came to rest amidst a towering inferno.

"My cheque book, then," said Tommy, letting out a tired sigh and reaching for his back pocket.

# 43

# CROWDED HOUSE

I ran up the stairs and burst into Brendan's room. His pyjamas had twisted around in his sleep, and he sat upright
in bed, looking moody.

"Zag's being loud," he muttered, pointing upwards.

I went into the hallway and grabbed the stringer. The attic ladder collapsed down on me, bringing with it the body of a woman in
a green cocktail dress. She groaned and looked about as she lay on
the landing carpet below. Concerned but not deterred, I climbed up
the wooden steps and peered into the attic.

Once, the clay head atop a packing box was a familiar sight,
adorned with mistletoe and surrounded by scattered rat-traps and an
old Santa costume heaped in a corner. But tonight, everything was
changed. Fifty souls lay sprawled across wooden beams, their moans
echoing, hands clutching at aching backs, necks, and legs. Above
them, a colossal hole in the roof revealed a star-studded sky — three
colourful ones in particular blazing with unwavering intensity."

Annie crawled off a portly man in crimson robes, who emitted a strangely familiar groan of pain. Across from her lay Duke Wilson, pinned beneath a tangle of fallen guests, unmoving. In her dazed state, it took Annie a moment to notice Cora, seated perfectly upright in her blood-stained white dress. Bare legs crossed, calmly surveying the attic, it was apparent she was looking for something. Annie came to this conclusion just in time, as their eyes landed on the clay head directly in front of them.

"Wait!" cried Annie, her head spinning.

Cora reached it first, cradling the artefact in her bruised hands.

"Dear one," she whispered to it, voice soft. "Come forth, and…"

From the hollow eyes, nose, and mouth of the clay head, a whisper-thin fog emerged; a spectral white veil that clung to the air, carrying with it the scent of magic. Ethereal and elusive, it wove itself around the clay head before condensing into a familiar, physical form. And there stood Zag. His features, etched in wonder, mirrored the astonishment that now danced across Cora's face.

"Who are you?" he asked.

Cora Corali turned to Annie, gripping the nearest pillar.

"Your Child of Crux is a boy?" she inquired.

Annie nodded gently, her eyes wide.

Cora released the clay head abruptly, letting it drop.

"Wrong one…" she muttered.

A flourish of magic erupted in a spectacular shower of green and yellow sparkles, enveloping her completely. When they dissipated, Cora was gone.

"Zag!" I whispered across from him. "Get back in your clay head, quick! Before somebody sees you."

Obeying without hesitation, he returned to his misty form and slipped back into the lifeless sculpture.

Duke Wilson emerged from the tangle of unconscious bodies, his demeanour changed. His eyes held a manic intensity. Annie clung to me, fear etched on her face as Wilson approached.

"You," he sneered, directing his gaze at my sister.

"Duke Wilson, what are you doing here?" I demanded, my voice steady despite the tension.

Wilson shifted his attention to me, then to the clay head lying on the ground.

"Did you and your sister come to Danube today?"

I glanced at Annie. Her wide-eyed expression mirrored my

own. "No," I replied truthfully.

Wilson scanned the room, as if assessing the energy in the air.

"Is something the matter?" Annie's voice trembled.

"Not at all," he answered swiftly. "As you can tell by this horrible debacle, we've had a bit of an upsetting night. I think it's best if I make myself scarce before these people wake up. Cassandra Gellar the First, I'll contact you soon."

"Yeah, no rush this time, alright?"

Duke Wilson's dark and moody eyes were the last to vanish into thin air. Just in the nick of time, for Dad pushed past me and squeezed into the attic. His breath was ragged from the frantic climb up the stairs.

"An ambulance is on its way, Rachael thinks your grandmother's hip is broken, and..." His voice trailed off as he finally noticed Annie's presence, and the injured guests strewn about. "What the...?"

Annie, ever the quick thinker, stepped forward.

"The bottom of the Zeppelin collapsed just as we were going overhead!" she told him. Her eyes were wide, and the hug she gave him desperate. "Dad, I was so scared!"

He hugged her back, but his gaze shifted over his shoulder.

"Can you believe that guy had my motorcycle?" he said to me. "And those women on the back... Chloe and Candice Croxley!"

I muttered in frustration, trying to cast my mind back to the last time I'd seen the Croxley sisters. I simply couldn't.

"Man, what is going *on* tonight?" I declared angrily.

———— . . . ————

Half-an-hour later, as every ambulance available came to cart the dazed and confused guests off to hospital, the final set of nurses tended to Grandma Helen. I stayed by my grandmother's side as they lifted her into the back of their truck.

"Grandma, we'll get to the hospital as soon as we can, I swear."

"Thank you, Cassie," she said, smiling. "I do not mind all that much! I found this little doll on the ground. It must have been in the sidecar of that motorcycle... We shall keep each other company."

Grandma revealed a *Tiro the Barber-Librarian* doll from under her blanket, and tugged at its pull-string.

A voice called out: *"All hail ze Germans!"*

"I think I vould like to keep this," she said with a quiet thrill.

"Besides, now I can die a happy woman."

"Why?"

Grandma's doped-up eyes filled with joyous tears. "Thirteen!"

The ambulance drove away down the street, and I walked back over to Aunt Rachael, who was sitting with Chloe and Candice on the sidewalk. The two sisters were covered in bruises, their eyebrows missing, but they appeared generally unscathed. Except, it seemed, for their minds.

"Sudentry," muttered Chloe. "Two of them. In the snow."

"Yes, and the cliff. We fell," said Candice.

"Onto a haunted hotel. Then the twins."

"Ghost twins. Hitchhiked, and… Begley."

"Looking for Nicky. Won the race. Scoped the streets…"

Rachael didn't know what to say, so she patted the both of them on their backs. "It's been a hard night for everyone."

When another ambulance arrived ten minutes later, they tended to the Croxleys' abductor — the tall man with tattoos who had been driving the motorcycle. *Dad's* motorcycle. His name was Begley, and unfortunately his right leg was fractured. Rachael offered to splint it for him, but he refused.

"He must've snuck into our house the night the window was broken!" Dad's voice cracked, rage barely contained.

"You made it too easy," Begley rasped, lips curling into a grin.

Despite the pain radiating from his fractured leg, he seemed to find amusement in our predicament.

"No love lost, though," he added nonchalantly, as if discussing the weather. "It had a crappy mill, anyway."

Hayley, the firebrand, couldn't resist. "Wow, what an evil turd!"

It was at this moment my mild-mannered father, who'd never thrown a punch in his life, leaned forward. His hand shot out, connecting with Begley's nose — a resounding smack that caused the abductor to recoil, shock etching new lines on his face.

"SMIDSY," said Dad, and he walked back toward the house.

I trailed him up the driveway, just as one of the many cops on the scene emerged from our front door. Behind him followed two more officers and a portly man in a Santa outfit.

"We found this guy up in the attic," the lead officer informed my father, who looked like he was barely listening to begin with. "Definitely wasn't on the Zeppelin ride. Claims he's been up there for over a week."

Dad shook his head, clearly done with surprises for the night. The squatter — overweight, balding, and emitting a month's worth of stench through his mangy Santa suit — waved at me from his handcuffs. "Hello, Cassie!"

"Do you know him?" asked a cop, eyeing me.

"No..." I said honestly, shaking my head.

I cast my mind back. A terrible, awful, disturbing thought occurred to me in that moment. Of the many times I'd gone into the attic to visit Zag, there was always a sneaking suspicion that somebody else was up there with me, watching. In fact, how many times had Zag mentioned the fact that he'd been talking to the jolly fat man himself? Poor, clueless Zag, starved for company, desperate to learn about Christmas... As I inspected the intruder's chubby torso, I realised in horror that my father's discarded Santa costume in the attic had concealed a living, breathing person this entire time.

"Looks like he stepped on a rat-trap a few days ago," said another police officer, pointing to the man's bruised, bare feet. "I think that big toe is broken. Better put him in the back of that ambulance before it goes. Oh, and we found thirteen hundred dollars on him. I'm assuming it's yours?"

"That's Grandma's!" I exclaimed, snatching it off the cop in disbelief. "She was... he must have... Dad!"

"It's fine... all fine..." my father replied distantly.

Rachael, Hayley, and Annie joined us by the letterbox, their tired expressions mirroring mine as we watched them lift the stowaway into the back of the last ambulance for the night.

In the dim glow of the interior, the man in the Santa costume drew a sharp breath. His eyes locked onto the other occupant — a fellow criminal. Recognition dawned.

"*Begley!*" he cried.

Begley turned, incredulous. "*Nicky!*"

# SATURDAY ⭐
### THE 22<sup>nd</sup>

# 44

## BERTHA

Mom returned home with a fantastical story from Gentleman's Court, and in turn was relayed an equally mind-blowing tale from Philips Street. She was quick to hop in the car, heading to the hospital before midnight. She insisted we all stay home and sleep it off, at which point Dad imposed a new house law to keep us in line. If we betrayed him, we wouldn't get presents for Christmas, he said. I knew he was bluffing, but we all needed a good night's sleep. More than anyone else was Annie, who locked herself in her room and refused to talk about what'd happened.

Unfortunately, Hayley and I sat up chatting about everything until one in the morning. She'd yet to hear from JT after the argument where she'd kicked him, and after Mom had told us about the Zeppelin crashing into his house she wasn't sure whether to be glad he hadn't responded, or be the better person and text him in support.

"I'd say, you text him first," I suggested.

"No way! I think I might break up with him."

"Hayley," I muttered, tucking my right hand under my pillow to get comfortable. "Don't be overdramatic."

"I'm not…"

I turned back around and looked at her through the darkness of my bedroom. "Are you serious?"

"His parents hate me," she said quietly.

As my eyes grew accustomed to the darkness, I bit my lip hard, trying to come up with a helpful response.

"Whatever you think is best, Hayles."

"It'll screw up the group, though, right?"

"Oh! Greg!" I sat up and flicked on the light. "His mother."

Hayley moaned from the light-source, and the topic.

"Don't worry about it, Cassie. Don't worry. If you're going to the hospital tomorrow, you'll probably run into him anyway. Then you can french kiss all you like." She mimicked kissing disgustingly, and laughed at her own joke. "Turn off the light. I'm tired."

We sat in the dark for a little while longer, completely silent, although neither of us was in the mood for sleep yet.

"We were pretty lucky tonight," said Hayley suddenly.

"Yeah…" I muttered, thinking about it all.

— . . . —

Alexandria General Hospital had a vaguely familiar look to it as we drove into the parking lot, but I was sure I'd never been there before. Rugged up in our winter best, only myself, Dad and Rachael were visiting — Brendan was sleeping off his hangover, and Annie had flat-out refused to leave the house.

To my surprise, there seemed to be a great deal of patients I recognised from school. Wednesday and Friday turned their backs on me the moment we walked into the waiting room, William from our class was there too, and so was Tanya, sitting nearest to the re-ception desk. I waved to her as we checked in.

"What happened?" I asked her.

She cricked her neck and crossed her legs, sighing as she did. "Well," she muttered, "my mother got hit in the head last night dur-ing those strong winds. Everybody else is here because apparently there was a huge storm that hit the school."

"I heard," I said, sitting down in the spare seat next to her as Dad and Rachael talked to one of the nurses. "Did you know that JT's house was hit by the Zeppelin?"

"No," she said, eyes growing wide. "Is..?"

"Everybody's fine," I insisted with a smile. "The whole place was gutted, though. They can't live there anymore, so they're moving into Hayley's house for a while."

"Quite the demotion," said Tanya, and she gazed at the crowds of people around us. "We're lucky nothing else happened. I heard Eleanore got the worst of it. She's in bed now and her parents told my parents that she'll be there for a while."

I thought about how I'd seen the Saviour the night before.

Suddenly I spotted Ms. Weiss, walking out of a room with a doctor, who then called Audrey Mercy's name. A hunched figure who'd been sitting two seats away from me moved, revealing herself. She waddled eagerly down the hallway to meet the doctor, and just as she did I spotted Greg coming out of another room. Our eyes locked; he immediately turned away and disappeared out of sight.

"Cassie, come on."

The voice of my aunt brought me back to reality, and I noticed her and Dad were walking through the swinging doors that led into the ICU unit. I stood up.

"Okay, I'd better go. I hope your mother is okay."

"Thanks," said Tanya. "Same with your grandmother. I heard what happened. Sorry."

"Thanks," I said, and we shared a smile.

I was glad that she was being nice to me again, but as I thought about it more, I became impatient and decided I'd had enough of this on-and-off-again angst between us.

"Hey, Tanya. Do you want to be my friend?"

Tanya bit her bottom lip as trouble brewed in her big, brown eyes. Eventually, in a high voice, she said: "No, thanks."

"Oh..."

I turned immediately, embarrassed. I'd thought the outcome to my question would be the polar opposite, and now I didn't know what to do. As I got closer to the swinging doors, I felt a sense of frustration, so I turned back to her.

"Can I ask why?"

It seemed Tanya had been expecting this, for she shrugged one shoulder, saying with a wince: "You're kind of a dick."

I went red. Not willing to torture myself any further, I turned around and chased after my father and aunt, eventually catching up to them as they walked into Room B6. We were immediately greeted by Mom, sitting in a chair next to Grandma Helen, who was sitting upright in her bed.

"You look flustered," she said to me. "Did you run here?"

I was glad that she was so on the ball. Considering she was in ICU, it was impressive. "I'm fine," I muttered, trying not to think about what Tanya had just said to me. I raised by eyebrows at my mother. "How's everything?"

"Broken hip, of course," said Mom, and I noticed she was holding Grandma's hand in hers. This was the most affection I'd ever seen between the two of them. "She finally needs a hip replacement. It only took thirteen motorcycles to do the trick. But she'll be here for a while. On top of that, she's got five broken toes, one broken finger, and lacerations on her back from when the motorcycle dragged her along the road." Her voice caught in her throat, and she took a moment to swallow.

"Lesley," said Grandma Helen quietly. "I'm okay."

"It's just a lot," said Mom, using her spare hand to wipe a tear from one of her eyes. "I'm tired. And you aren't helping anything by cussing at that lovely lady who was in here earlier delivering meals. She doesn't get paid, you know."

"Not surprised, her food was awful."

"You didn't seem to think so when you ate that egg sandwich she gave you," sighed Mom. "Anyway, I've offered to hire her company to deliver to our house when you get out. I expect you to be a little bit nicer to her next time you see her."

"Her name was Jasmina. You know what that means."

Mom didn't respond to this, perhaps having gone through similar conversations with her in the past. She rubbed her hand and said: "Alright, Ma. But at least be polite to your nurse when she comes in." She turned to me, and said: "An hour ago your grandmother barked in response to all of her questions." She turned back to her mother. "She's not here to steal your kidneys, she's here to help. I know it's an inconvenience being here, but you need to be polite. And stop pressing the white switch next to your bed. That's for emergencies only."

"They told me to."

"No, use the black one on your other side."

*"I thought the switch was white!"*

For a moment it looked like she was trying to sit up, but her rage disappeared with a pain that showed in her face, and she finally settled down enough to sheepishly apologise.

"How's Brendan?" Mom asked us, scoping the room.

"Out like a light," said Dad.

"Good. He's grounded until he's fifty, so he might as well sleep some of it off. Cassie, I've seen a lot of people from school around here. Have you found out what happened last night?"

"Yeah, I've picked up bits and pieces. Hayley told me before that the Zeppelin was about to land on the football field at the school, and then this huge storm front came out of nowhere and blasted it off-course. They lost control, and that's when it crashed into JT's house."

"Boy, that was a scary thing to see," said Mom, blowing upwards to wipe the hairs from her forehead. "Nobody was terribly injured though, right?"

"Only Eleanore..."

"I'm not sure I like this town," said Helen suddenly.

"I'm starting to feel the same way," said Rachael, squatting down on the ground and crossing her feet to get comfortable. "Bad vibes, you know?"

"If Eric Parker wasn't so preoccupied with Eleanore, I'm sure he'd be completely humiliated by what happened. I can't imagine the field day they'll be having with this on the news. Any word on how the crew of the TV show are doing?" asked Mom.

We all shrugged, for nobody had a clue. I don't think anybody cared, either. The rose-coloured glasses we'd watched *The Prefect Family* through were well and truly worn out.

———  · · ·  ———

We'd agreed to stay for at least three hours before going home. Grandma Helen would be there for a while, so her feelings weren't hurt at the notion of our absence. Since all we were doing was sitting in her room, I waited until she dozed off for a while, and snuck out to snoop around.

To be honest, I was mostly using it as an excuse to look for Greg. After twice stalking the same area, I finally spotted him grabbing some snacks from a vending machine. I snuck up behind him and poked with both hands into his sides. He jolted in surprise, and spun around. He looked stressed like I'd never seen him before. In fact, he looked at least ten years older, a vertical crease between his eyebrows showing. When he saw it was me, he relaxed into himself and handed me a packet of my favourite chocolate snacks.

"I was going to bring these to you," he said.

"Oh, thank you, I love these."

"I know."

We stood there for a little while, as I ripped the packet open and feasted on the chocolate bullets. I hadn't eaten anything all day, so I must have looked like a ravenous pig. I even snorted, briefly.

"How's your grandmother?" he asked at last.

"Broken hip, broken toes, broken everything," I said, covering my full mouth. "But she'll be fine. How's... how's your mother?"

Greg smiled. "As good as she'll ever be."

I waited for him to share more, but he didn't, and after a moment of silence I couldn't bear it any longer, so I changed the subject.

"I feel like I've hardly seen you since school ended."

"Just goes to show how important education is, hey. Have you done much else this week?"

I shrugged.

"No," I said honestly, trying not to think of how depressed I'd been all week. "You?"

"No," he said, going red. He pointed down the hallway. "I'd better get back to my mother."

"Okay, cool. Well, I'll... see you?"

Waiting for him to agree, I noticed that he wasn't moving, his focus completely on the ground. He looked troubled.

"This is stupid," he said.

"What is?"

He opened his mouth, but stuttered before saying: "W-We hardly know each other."

I knew I was going just as red as he was. What did he mean? It was said in such a way that its meaning could easily be misconstrued. Was he criticising me?

Confused, I said in a very quiet voice: "Huh?"

To my great surprise, his eyes locked on mine. A mischievous look appeared, or maybe a confident look. I wasn't sure. It seemed determined.

"Let's go out some time," he said coolly. "Just you and me."

*Don't panic. Don't panic. Don't panic!*

"Alright then," I replied, with not a hint of emotion showing.

I began to walk backwards, heading for Grandma Helen's room again. As soon as I turned the nearest corner, I allowed a grin to spread widely across my face.

*Did that really just happen?* I asked myself in disbelief.

———— . . . ————

I tried not to appear too excited as we packed our stuff to go home a few hours later. Rachael led the way, followed by Dad; I lingered and said goodbye to my mother and grandmother before joining the others.

Alone, Mom and Grandma Helen closed their eyes. They breathed in, both grateful for the quiet room at last. The only sounds to be heard were the machines beeping, and nurses shuffling back-and-forth outside.

"I called Pa this morning," said Mom.

Helen's eyes opened wide in disbelief. "What?"

"I had to let him know what was going on."

"Lesley, you shouldn't have… How d…"

"He told me who Bertha is."

Helen's lips thinned. "Oh, he did, did he?"

"Bertha's not a woman. She's a motorcycle."

"That's right."

"Why did you let me think it was another woman? Ma, I thought he was having an affair."

"I'd rather you think that. Don't you know how much I hate motorcycles? Surely I've drilled that into your head by now! How do you think I felt, coming home one day and seeing it in my driveway? Learning that Victor had spent half of his pension on it, probably in some vain attempt to recapture his youth!"

"It's just a motorcycle. You didn't have to leave him for it."

"Lesley, your husband owns a motorcycle, too. This family seems to think I am joking when I express my dislike for them. Almost dying each time I've been hit is a very traumatic thing to go through. Not to mention painful. Skin grafts, splints. Pins. Scars. I can't even walk by a repair lot because of the smell of burning rubber. Yet you all make light of these experiences. I don't understand why. I've now been struck by thirteen motorcycles. They make me uncomfortable, and that should be enough. Imagine how I felt, Lesley.

Your father knows how much I despise them, yet he went out and bought one anyway. So how dare you sit there and tell me I am the one in the wrong here!"

"Alright, I understand. I'm sorry. And I'm sorry that Ichabod's motorcycle offended you so much. I didn't know. But Pa told me he got rid of it as soon as you left. He said to apologise, that he didn't know what he was thinking. Most of all, he wanted me to tell you that he loves you and is sorry about what happened last night."

"He got rid of Bertha? I suppose that's a step in the right…"

"He wants you to come home, Ma."

Grandma Helen didn't say anything, she simply turned away and scoffed. Although she kept her eyes closed, she said: "Tell him I'll think about it."

Mom smiled. In Helen's world, that meant yes.

# 45

## G'S THESE D'S

It could have been that they were used to better standards of living, or perhaps the previous night's disaster was taking its toll, for Marguerite Walker appeared to have gained a permanent sneer when I saw her next. I'd been invited over to Hayley's house that afternoon to help rearrange things for the Walker family to move in. Steve wouldn't be home until January now, and Mrs. Gauche (who I'd crossed paths with in the hospital) was confident her ass would be properly healed by mid-January at the latest. This came as a relief to Hayley, who admitted that even though she liked living in our house, there was nothing quite like home. I understood where she was coming from.

"Hayley, dear," called Marguerite from upstairs, "would you mind all that much if I cleaned up a bit in the master bedroom? A layer of dust seems to have fallen in the weeks since abandonment."

I was downstairs with Hayley and JT, moving the couch to the side of the tiny lounge-room in order to fit in Tommy Walker's entire saxophone collection. Hayley frowned at her words, and called: "Fine!" before muttering to me: "...even though it has always been like that..."

"You're taking this exceptionally well," I said to her. JT handed me something called a 'bass saxophone', which looked exactly like the rest of them, only on steroids.

"Ah, what can I do?" she replied. When I giggled, her gaze lingered. "No, I'm asking you. What can I do?"

Tommy came downstairs then, and saw how we'd placed his most prized possessions. "Do you think maybe we could put a cloth over that thing in the corner?" he asked casually, waving. "It doesn't seem to match my..."

Hayley's look silenced him, for he'd been referring to the very dated television, her own most prized possession.

A hustle of movers in blue overalls came in from the back door, having had a 'much earned' break from carting all of the furniture in. When they saw what we were doing, the head of the company asked Hayley, JT and I to stop bringing stuff in, as we weren't covered by their insurance.

"Insurance for bringing things into my own house?" said Hayley loudly, and JT intentionally repeated what she'd said with only a millisecond between them. When Hayley turned on him, he shrugged. "What? It's my house too now. We're domesticated."

He rested his head on her shoulder until she shrugged it off. I caught her glance and remembered our conversation the night before. *She's puckered at both ends,* I thought.

Marguerite and Tommy graciously offered to take us all out for pizzas as a thank you for helping them move. But none of us were in the mood to have a busy night after last night, and it was agreed that we'd take a rain-check on the matter. They decided to treat themselves to a romantic candle-lit dinner at one of the restaurants downtown, which left the three of us alone to talk candidly about things.

"I'll never watch that show again," said Hayley, referring to *The Prefect Family.* She was disgusted that not one of the stars had been on the Zeppelin ride, a piece of news that had sent shockwaves throughout the country, among other things. "I don't even like Thomas Noel anymore. I'm so disappointed in him."

We'd been watching the news reports on TV, and his face appeared above the scrolling banner. Just like that, he'd lost his charming nature. I didn't like him anymore at all, my respect for the actor gone down the toilet since the scandal. The executives on TV were grasping at straws now, making up excuses like how they'd found the head of the network tied up in her home and that somebody had pretended to be her on the ride. None of us believed this. It sounded melodramatic, as if made up by one of the writers on the show.

"It was always kind of trashy," muttered JT, his left arm wrapped around Hayley on the couch.

"It'll be off the air within a year," she responded.

"Fine by me," I said scathingly.

"Greg will be hard to convert, though. He always likes to be the one with an opinion, you wait and see. Sly bastard."

With the mention of Greg, my mind cast back to our conversation. Nothing on the screen in front of me got through to my brain, and as the next ad-break came on I turned in my seat to face my friends. "Speaking of Greg, I saw him at the hospital. Guess what?"

JT and Hayley did not look curious, in fact they looked fed up with me. "What did you say?" they asked together.

I shrunk into my seat, afraid.

"I didn't say anything. He... I think he asked me out."

The two of them pouted in surprise, and shrugged to each other. Finally, JT said: "You *think* he asked you out?"

"I'm sure of it," I said, only realising it as I said it out loud. "He bought me a snack from the vending machine, and we had one of those awkward conversations, you know the ones..."

*"Good God, do we know!* We see you two every day at school," muttered JT in exhaustion, clawing at his eyes.

"Well," I continued, "I was just about to end the... awkward conversation... when he said that these... awkward conversations... were getting ridiculous, and that we never saw each other."

"It's true," said Hayley, leaning back into JT and balancing her bowl of popcorn between her knees as she got comfortable. "You never spend any time alone with him, because of me and this big bag of useless getting in the way."

"I guess it didn't help that he couldn't come to the party last night," said JT, and he looked at me. "I hope you didn't pester him about his mother..."

"No, not at all," I insisted, and I leant closer to them, as if paranoid other people could hear. "He was in a pretty okay mood, in fact he said she was fine. But then he did it. He asked me out. I think."

"He either did or he didn't," insisted Hayley.

I stared her dead in the eyes. "He said: 'Why don't we go out some time? Just you and me.'"

Both of my friends immediately ooh'ed, which relieved me so much in the moment that I let out a breath as I smiled. This was a good sign. But then I thought of the one thing that got in the way of my happiness.

"The only thing is," I admitted sheepishly, "I sort of have a crush on someone else, too. And it's kind of going really well."

"No way!" Hayley exclaimed, nearly knocking her bowl over as she sat upright. "Shut up! Get out! Be quiet! Silence the baby! Who and when, why and woof?"

"Just some guy in town. We've been flirting a lot lately, and he was sussing about Greg last night. When I let him know that Greg was just a friend, he seemed really relieved."

"Does he go to our school? What's his name?"

"He graduated last year," I explained.

Hayley made an excited sound, urging me to continue.

"He's Morgan. You know, from the bakery. And he works at that hardware store in town."

"Wait..." grumbled Hayley slowly. "*Morgan* Morgan? *He's* the guy who made you feel like a walrus?"

"No, I said I felt I *looked* like a walrus. I kept... you know... putting my foot in it..."

They waited.

"Because I like him!"

"That is not a piece of information you shared," observed Hayley, glancing at her boyfriend.

"Have I met him?" asked JT.

"I don't think so... Oh, well, actually. Yes, you have. He was a waiter at your party last night."

JT squinted in thought for a moment.

"Morgan..." he said slowly, eventually cottoning on. "Morgan. Wait... *that* Morgan? You have a crush on *Morgan?*"

"Yeah?" I nervously confirmed.

JT erupted into laughter, tilting his head back so far that I glimpsed the pink roof of his mouth. He sounded like an animal being slaughtered.

"You've got a crush on Morgan Tucker," he giggled, tears streaming down his face. "Lordy, Lordy, Lordy..."

"Jonathan."

JT composed himself swiftly "You're right. This is serious.

Morgan will never go on a date with you."

I felt ugly in that moment, and yearned to bite my nails.

"Why not?" I asked, my tone bitter.

"Because Morgan Tucker is as queer as an eighteen dollar bill."

I anticipated a punchline.

"Nah," I replied, grinning.

"It's not confirmed..." Hayley began hesitantly. "But... I mean, everyone at school thought so. Morgan never had a girlfriend, and he was always trying to hang out with Greg. To the point where Greg kind of got weirded out. Don't get me wrong, Morgan's lovely, but I'd be surprised if he was... *into you?*"

She said this with an uncomfortable cringe, as if she were pulling my teeth instead of my leg. The way I felt, maybe she was pulling my teeth. I thought back to the conversations I'd had with Morgan. No, he was definitely flirting with me. Although he was always impeccably dressed... but that was because I only ever saw him in a work uniform... But he was so lovely and friendly... Plus, he blushed last night when I said I wasn't dating Greg... because I was cutting to the chase, and he was embarrassed that I knew he liked......

I sat forward in my seat.

*"He's into Greg!?"*

Feeling uncomfortable, JT went to busy himself in the kitchen. Hayley seized the moment and moved to the armchair next to mine to talk privately.

"We swear we won't tell anyone that you fancied him. For your own dignity. But keep it hush, because we think maybe..."

She looked up, then around, paranoid.

"What?"

"I probably shouldn't say this to you right now, given what's going on, but... Well, JT thinks... and he would be furious if he knew I told you this... But he thinks... that maybe... *just maybe...* Greg fancies Morgan too."

I took this information in and tried to reason with it. "But you told me Greg was weirded out by him."

"Yeah, so there's being weirded out, and then there's overcompensating, you know? I didn't think much of this theory at first either, but as someone who spends the most amount of time with Greg, JT would know. And since I'm the person who spends the *second* most amount of time with Greg..." She paused for breath. "It's not the worst theory."

Rather than feeling the crippling sensation of rejection, I sat back and let these possibilities wash over me. Was Greg gay? Is that why nothing had happened, and why he would gape at me like a neanderthal? Maybe I was right, he wasn't aware he was doing it, and that perhaps there really was nothing to these long staring spells. It was possible that he may be a bit simple. I couldn't remember every interaction we'd had, although now I was deeply suspicious of each one.

"I'd better not be his test subject," I said to Hayley angrily.

"I don't know what you are. Maybe we're wrong. Maybe he's just flattered that Morgan likes him. I mean, if I found out a girl had a crush on me, I wouldn't totally hate it. But it doesn't mean I'd want to pop on matching wedding gowns and trot down the aisle with her."

"Hayley, he kissed me!"

*He's young,* called an ominous voice in my head, like a ghoul.

In a sudden moment of clarity, it dawned on me that my feelings for Morgan weren't as deep as I'd initially believed. The realisation that he was gay swiftly extinguished any romantic spark I had for him. However, when it came to Greg, the situation was different. My crush on him remained as strong as ever. I found myself unwilling to accept the truth, clinging to the hope that it wasn't real.

*Not Greg. Please, not Greg!* I thought desperately.

For the rest of the night, Hayley and JT talked quietly about the news, the hospital, the school, the gutted mansion, Christmas… I responded when spoken to, but vaguely. I felt like I was in a sort of strange, lucid dream.

At least I didn't have to worry about Morgan anymore.

# 46

## EAT SOME WORMS

Life felt like it was a bit more on track the following day. After a very restful night's sleep, I woke up around nine a.m. feeling like I could run a marathon. I didn't even care about gay rumours or the fact that my favourite show had betrayed me. Life was mine for the taking.

Brendan was still unwell, but at least today he was responsive as I went down for breakfast. He was sitting on the couch reading a book, and he startled easily when I spritely jumped the last step.

"I thought you were Mom or Dad," he said in a croak, and he sipped from a giant glass of water on the coffee table next to him.

"How are you…?" I began, but stopped to watch as he took his time swilling the entire glass, nearly a full litre, until there was nothing left. "Brendan… are you pregnant?"

"I think I'm dying," he told me, and he doggy-eared his book page. "Something's not right."

"I wouldn't know, because I've never had one, but I think this is your very first hangover. I can't believe you beat me to it."

He sat back in his armchair and let out a gigantic, monstrous belch that caused a sleeping Tigger to leap from his spot in front of the crackling fireplace.

"None of this is fair! *None of this is fair!*" he said, curling into a ball and rocking back-and-forth.

"You got drunk at a party," I said. "You're eleven years old, Brendan, what did you expect? A pat on the back?"

He glanced up, his eyes tiny slits on his pale face. "I am *twelve!*" he said, almost loud enough to wake the family. But something in his voice calmed down in the end, and he let it go.

Kicking myself internally, I said: "I only meant that…"

"I know what you meant," he muttered. He turned away. "And I know why you forgot."

For a moment, I was a little bit scared. "You do?"

"Yup. You forgot… you all forgot… because they made you forget. All of them. Up there."

I waited for a better explanation, praying that this wasn't the beginning of his unraveling. "Who?"

"Danube."

"Ohhh. Brendan, they didn't mess with our… Oh *wait*, they *did!*" I said, knowing how dumb I sounded. Quite poetically, I'd forgotten that Danube had sent down *Forgettenablers* in disguise as students and teachers, residents of Horn-Horn, in order to make everybody forget about our trip to the other world. They'd even wiped Mom and Dad's memories in order for them to live a normal life. The idea of this relieved me greatly, as the guilt I'd felt about forgetting his birthday was almost crippling. There had been no excuse, up until this moment.

"Well, I'm still… I'm still sorry," I said earnestly, sitting down next to him. "The only constellation is that this Christmas, you'll be getting a *lot* of presents. I overheard Mom and Dad talking about it at the hospital. Expect the world, buddy."

"Consolation."

I shrugged. "Alright, expect that, too. But Brendan, you need to know how sorry we all are. We're so, so sorry."

"I know," he said with a tired smile.

"Especially Mom."

He didn't answer, but instead he burst into tears. My heart

ached, and it took every ounce of me not to cry along with him. I rubbed his back for a while, watching as Tigger slowly came back into the room, twirling around until he was comfortable returning to his place in front of the fire.

"Nobody likes me," my brother said.

"Oh Brendan, we *love* you! What are you talking about?"

"You can love someone and not like who they are as a person. You love Grandma Helen, but you don't like her. Same with Annie."

"That's true, I guess…" I said slowly, thinking back to how Tanya had called it like it was back at the hospital. "You really don't think anyone likes you? What about your friend, Aron? Your teachers like you, Candice Croxley adores you, and Elliot Parker next door seems to *really* like you…"

I could tell he didn't believe a word of it. Instead of pushing the matter, I grabbed his tiny shoulders and pulled him into a hug.

"So what if nobody likes you?" I told him. "That's the story of my life, Brendan. Nobody has ever liked me, and I used to think to myself all the time how *awful* I must really be. You have to realise, it's not you, it's them. Look at how many people hated me back in Salem. I had one friend! One! Nicole. And even she didn't really like me. You've got Aron, but you've also got me and Annie as friends. You know, being twelve… with sisters who are older… in a few years time it won't seem as big an age gap, and we'll be able to talk about anything and everything to each other… I *do* love Annie, and I *do* like her as a person, but it's because I know her so well that I've learned what she's like. Just let people in, Brendan. Once you do that, they'll see what you're really like… and if they don't like you then, well… in my opinion, there's something wrong with them."

He looked up at me, his poor eyes crusting heavily after his infection, and he nodded. After that, we didn't say anything else. I sat with him until Annie and Rachael came downstairs, by which point my brother's tears had dried and they were none the wiser.

# 47

# OVER (AND UNDER) OLD GROUND

Mom and Dad were on the school committee, which meant that they had to go and clean the school at lunchtime with the aid of other parents in the community. The freak storm hadn't damaged much, as it wasn't even close to twister weather, but it was enough that trash cans had sprayed about like confetti, tree branches had fallen, and the odd windows were smashed in from debris.

"You know, you girls could come and help us!" said Mom, and she leaned in to me. "I could even give you a hundred dollars to go towards Christmas presents if you do a good job. Brendan, get dressed, you're working."

I agreed because I needed the money, and immediately I felt like I was weak with anaemia (how I always felt when the threat of physical labour loomed overhead). Annie decided to come, and so did Aunt Rachael, who was bored of the hospital and wanted to tag along just so she could sticky-beak at the damage done.

"You're shameless," said Dad, but for the first time since she'd arrived, he ended his sentence with a short smirk.

"If I'm shameless, you're shameless," she replied, and suddenly she twirled on the spot in the foyer. "I'll meet you guys there. My car needs to stretch her legs."

The school was packed with parents and the occasional student. It didn't look too bad. The only issue I could see from the parking lot was the mass amounts of litter strewn across the yard. I remarked to a very grumpy Brendan as we hopped out of the car that I felt robbed of Christmas, being back at school so early. He didn't giggle at my discomfort the way he usually did, and as I watched Mom sternly order him about, a sad thought occurred to me. Maybe this was how he was going to be from now on.

Up near the front gate, which looked perfect if not for the fallen sign, Dad and Rachael busied themselves lifting it back up.

"Icky, you're glowing," Aunt Rachael said as they struggled under its weight. "Are you on Isotretinoin?"

Dad grunted, and they fit the sign back into place. "No, but Annie's just starting on it. Maybe it's rubbing off on me."

Rachael shrugged, not sure about his mood. He was staring off at the teepee-shaped reception building now, which was a little further down the slope. She followed his gaze, watching as a flock of white birds took off nearby and soon became a part of the picturesque horizon.

"I'm glad you came, Rach," he said.

Aunt Rachael hugged herself as the last strands of sunlight were finally blocked by the midday clouds.

"Me too, Ichabod," she replied. "It's been nice."

This seemed to confirm something to Dad, who shifted his weight on the sign he was resting against.

"Saw your bags when I went past your car," he muttered. "Were you going to tell the others?"

Rachael shook her head.

"They'll be devastated you're not staying, you know."

"I know."

"Even Helen will be…"

"I don't give a damn what anyone else thinks. I'm going to stay with Mom and Dad in Philadelphia for a while."

"See you at Annie's twenty-first, then."

"Hey, don't give me that," she retorted sharply. "You can't treat me like a piece of gum on your shoe this whole time and then expect me to feel guilty when I finally…"

Rachael didn't bother to finish. They'd been through this a million times before. Instead, she changed the subject.

"Your attitude towards Helen sure has changed," she said.

Dad looked on, astonished at what she was implying. "That's because she was nearly killed!"

"Exactly. Is that all it would take for me?"

Rachael barely finished the sentence before her emotions got the better of her, and she turned away as she tried to control herself. Dad was glad of this, for the sadness he felt inside threatened to explode from him in what seemed like waves.

Mom was walking up the slope now, unaware of the conversation between them. Just before she got within ear-shot, he muttered quietly to his sister: "You never change. Why do you always have to make things so difficult?"

Rachael's wide, watering eyes locked on his own.

"Funny… that's the same thing you said to me last time."

She put on a false smile for Mom as she arrived. Then, with not even a glance behind her, she walked away.

———  · · ·  ———

The giant football field looked like a bomb had gone off.

Annie, Brendan and I walked through the metal gates on the sides, and looked around in awe. There were remnants of stages, ripped billboard signs, upturned ice-cream machines, and trash. Trash everywhere.

"At least nobody was hurt," said Brendan.

Annie and I turned to him in confusion. Was he not aware that the nearby hospital was full of people who would beg to differ?

"I mean, at least nobody *died*," he clarified. He was still a nasty shade of white, emphasised by the black jumper he was wearing to shield himself from the cold.

"Most of them have a pretty good excuse not to come and clean up," sighed Annie, and she poked at a piece of rubbish with the stoke she'd been given at the front, then put it in the black trash bag she was carrying. "I fell through the roof and I don't even have a single cut on me!"

"Poor you," I muttered, sensing her angst.

"Oh, leave me alone, I'm not in the mood," she said angrily, and she stormed off in a huff.

Brendan and I walked around the field for a while, smiling as we passed people we sort of knew from around town. Eventually, I said to him in a quiet voice: "You know... I think it's really unusual that Principal Parker isn't here."

"Didn't Eleanore get hurt, though?" asked Brendan.

"Yeah, but..." I scrunched up my nose as I thought about it all. Something smelled fishy, both figuratively and literally. "I would've thought he'd at least send... you know... *others*. Like Elliot and Eliza. Ella-May. The Shaloms. God, even Ms. Weiss isn't here. I don't see any of them. It's really weird."

"First world problems," said Brendan quietly, and he staked a dead fish. "Tell me the wind didn't carry this from the ocean."

To my great horror, Ms. Chin-Tucker came walking towards us, with two boys in tow. One of them was Morgan, and the other boy was about Brendan's age. Strangely, he looked identical to Morgan, only about two feet shorter.

"Hello, Cassie!" said Ms. Chin-Tucker, her trademark warm smile causing every crease in her face to resurface. "Oh, how is your sister doing?"

"Great! She's over there helping out," I said, pointing. "This is my brother, Brendan. Brendan, this is Ms. Chin —"

"— *Please*... don't call me that. I hate it. I'm sure you can guess why. I try to get the students to call me Jean. And these are my sons, Morgan and Howard."

*Man,* I thought, *they sure do like their old-person names.*

"We've met before," said Morgan, his smile almost as wide as his mother's. "Cassie handed in her résumé to the hut."

"Oh, is *this* the girl you were talking about?" said Jean.

If I hadn't been briefed on the cold hard truth the previous night, I would have taken this as a very promising sign.

"What a small town. You know, he wouldn't shut up about you. This and that, about how intuitive you seemed, and that you're friends with Greg Cooper, too."

As the school receptionist went on and on, I paid attention to Morgan in my peripherals, curious to his reaction. If he'd been embarrassed about the fact that he apparently never stopped talking about me, it certainly didn't show. The truth of the matter was solidified in my mind, though, the moment she brought up Greg's name. Morgan immediately flushed in the ears, the same way he'd done the other night, and he tried to change the subject without making it too obvious. But I was perceptive. And kind. I allowed the distraction to flow.

Eventually they told us they'd better continue cleaning, and that they were heading in the opposite direction to us. Morgan said goodbye to me and mentioned how he hoped I'd get a call from the manager of *Hogan's Hardware Hut* soon, and we wished them a Merry Christmas with as much energy as either of us could muster, and then we parted ways.

I was surprised that I was not the only one who let out a gargantuan sigh the moment they were out of sight.

"Great," muttered Brendan. "More names to remember."

———— · · · ————

Annie walked past the Walkers, trying not to smirk as a disgusted-looking Marguerite coyly dropped a soda can into a trash-bag Tommy was holding open. JT, who was behind them and rolling his eyes, waved at her. Annie waved back, and was considering going over to talk to him (for she thought he was quite smart), when a voice called her name from nearby.

At first Annie couldn't see anyone, and wondered if she'd imagined it, but then it came again, and her eyes locked on the face underneath the nearest bleachers. Taken aback by who she was seeing, she waited until the Walkers, and then a couple of other parents, passed by. Then she ran down the tiny steps and underneath the giant seating. It was dark and nasty down there, but devoid of any trash. Unfortunately, this was the last thing she cared about, for the person who had called her name was Cora Corali.

Blind fury raced through Annie's body, and she pointed at the tanned woman, dressed in a grey jacket and beanie to fit in.

"Stay away from me and my family," she said intensely.

Before she could walk away, Cora pleaded: "Wait, we need to talk. It's serious."

"You tried to kill me and my family to get Zag. You're lucky I don't dob you in to Danube, you horrible…"

"Listen to me, Annie, listen… They can't hear us here."

"Who?"

"Danube. We're under the bleachers."

"What's your point?"

"They can't hear conversations when we're... Don't you know anything? You own a Child of Crux and you don't know about the wood rule?"

"No, I guess I don't. Enlighten me, *please*."

"Danube can't track you or hear you through wood. I'm assuming your sister has... Zag... locked away in something wooden? Like in the basement? Or a wardrobe?"

Annie's eyes flickered.

"In the wardrobe. That's smart. Well, the same rules apply here. They can't hear a word we're saying because the bleachers are made of wooden stands. There may be gaps in them, but it all does the same. So we can speak now and they won't hear a thing. Is there anything you'd like to say to me... In confidence?"

Annie's face was still stretched in rage.

"The only thing I want to say to you is... is..." The rage quickly petered out, and she covered her mouth as fear finally took control. "Can you save us from the comet?" she asked shakily.

Cora didn't show any sympathy for the crying girl in front of her, nor did she look away in disrespect. "I can't, but you can. Find an excuse to get away from here. As soon as possible. Don't try and save the townspeople, they'll bog you down. Get the whole family to go away on vacation, and while you're there make sure you never ever come back. Does anyone else know what I told you about Duke Wilson and the comet?"

Annie sniffled, and wiped her nose with her jacket sleeve.

"No, I'm too scared to mention it. I can't even tell my sister. She'll... I'm *afraid*."

"Good, don't tell her. There's more to this town than you can see, Annie. *Believe me*. Things even Duke Wilson doesn't know about. You don't want to stay here. You can't trust anybody."

"Why should I trust you?"

"I got you home safe and sound, didn't I? Even if I... Well... If it weren't for me, you'd still be in the dark about Duke Wilson, and he showed his true colours to you just as I'd said he would, didn't he? Obviously you believe me about the comet, otherwise you wouldn't be asking me for help."

"When we leave, should we.... should we take Zag?"

Cora stared, then looked across the football field through the wooden slats. "It's up to you. But I wouldn't leave him. He's your only leverage."

"How?"

"Think about it. They're wiping out the town so his owner will be killed naturally. That means, they want him back. As long as you have him nearby, they can't hurt you. They'll kidnap the clay head the day before the comet strikes, wait it out until you and your family die, and then since his owner is dead, Duke Wilson will agree to be the new owner. First come, first serve. That means no matter what, keep your eyes on the clay head."

"Cassie told me people start to rot when they steal a clay head from its rightful owner."

"Look, I've read the plans, do you believe me or not?"

"Yes. Yes, I do…"

"They've hired someone who will steal it the day before, just like Pothosia did. It takes time to rot, and once you return the clay head to its rightful owner, you stop rotting and go back to normal. Does it make sense now?"

Annie could not stop shivering. She wasn't sure if it was from the cold or the fear. Her mind was growing weak, and a migraine started in her temples. She knew what she had to do.

"Can you help me more?" she asked the informant.

Cora Corali stepped back into the shadows, unsure. Her eyes, gleaming in the darkness, never looked away. "Only if you can help me find the Child of Crux I'm looking for."

Annie suddenly remembered the brother Cora had mentioned, the one who had died in Summers City. She'd thought Zag was the one, but he wasn't… because he was a…

"There's another Child of Crux in Horn-Horn?"

Cora's eyes remained chillingly steady as they observed Annie's human form. "Yes," she said eventually. "A girl. I want her. I'll do anything for her, because she's my family. You know how hard and for how long I've been looking. It's going to be hard without Pollux. I've nearly figured it out. Maybe you can help me with this. In return, I'll help you and your family escape."

"An escape for an escape," Annie muttered gently, thinking it over some. Eventually, having calmed down a lot, she said: "I can always wish to know where she is."

"No!" said Cora immediately. "All wishes made through a Child of Crux are taken into consideration by the Heads of the Universe before being granted. This takes all of half a millisecond most of the time, but Duke Wilson works hand-in-hand with them. You have to do this the hard way. Without wishes."

"How can I possibly find a Child of Crux in this town without magic? You expect me to get lost in the woods again?" Suddenly, she cast her mind back to the fallen trees in the forest, long ago after our first day of school. "He was *hiding*..." she gasped in realisation, putting a hand to her mouth.

"We're in agreement then? No trickery this time. You help me and I'll help you. I give you my word."

"Alright," said Annie.

To her great surprise, it started to pour with rain. It only lasted for five seconds, and in that time Annie noted that the rain was coming from underneath the bleachers with them. Outside, where people were walking around picking up garbage, nothing had happened at all, and they were none the wiser.

"What the hell was that?" asked Annie, after it stopped.

"Promise rain," Cora said, smiling. Her once curled and perfect hair was now wet and flat under her beanie, and she wiped some strands away from her eyes. "It's an ancient magic that binds our words together. So now you know that I am serious, Annie, and that legally we must both stay true to our promises. But since you are a human, I suppose you'll want a handshake."

Annie backed away, not forgetting that this woman had tried to kill her a few days earlier. "How do we keep in contact?"

Cora thought for a moment. "Good question," she muttered quietly. "Since you can't wish to see me, perhaps we'll have to improvise. Allow me to create a portal into your house."

Annie didn't like the sound of this, and she voiced as such.

"Perhaps another rain promise is needed so you know I'm not up to anything else. I'm only here for the Child of Crux. I give you my word, alright?"

"A... Alright," said Annie.

She'd barely finished speaking before another downpour drenched them from head-to-toe, all in the space of five seconds.

"Please don't do that again. It's winter!" she insisted angrily. "The portal goes into the basement, and that is the only place in the house you're allowed."

"Fine. I'll leave notes around if I have any information."

"Ingenious," said Annie, and she checked to see if anybody was nearby. "What's your Child of Crux's name, anyway?"

"We called her Adreanna Knight."

Annie thought this over.

"Adreanna Knight... Alright, fine. I'll try and find her. But if I can't, does that mean you..?"

"If you can't, then I won't help you leave when you need to. But if you *do* find her, I will try and save you and your family until the very last second. I've given you my word."

"*HEY!*" somebody yelled from behind them.

Annie had barely spun around before catching sight of Miss. Terr standing there, bundled up in a tight leather jacket, almost unrecognisable in her casual clothes. Annie gaped in horror, then turned back to Cora, only to find that she'd vanished.

"Yeah?" snapped Annie, turning back to Miss. Terr.

"The rubbish is out there, Pippi," said the gym teacher, and she pointed to the football field beyond the bleachers.

"Sorry," said Annie, and she wiped her soaked hair out of her eyes. She was in such a state that she stopped herself from leaving right away, and built up enough courage to say to Miss. Terr: "You know, I'm here voluntarily, and anyway, you really shouldn't talk to people like that. It's very rude."

Miss. Terr looked quite taken aback.

"My apologies," she exclaimed.

Annie didn't stick around to find out if she was being sincere.

# MONDAY
## THE 24th

# 48

## 'TIS THE **REASON**
## TO BE **JOLLY**

Here it was, at long last.

After all the trials and tribulations of the most eventful year of my life, we'd finally arrived on what was normally my favourite day of the year. However, Aunt Rachael had split unexpectedly the day before, leaving everybody (even Mom) in very low spirits. Annie tried her best to look on the bright side, admitting that it was nice now that Helen and Hayley had moved out as well, and that it felt like the house was ours again. I wasn't even sure if my sister believed her own words, because she was pulling strands of hair out all night. To the point that, as I was the last to bed, I noticed a big blonde hairball caught up in Pigsworth's collar while taking him outside to pee.

At least Zag was back downstairs and in the safety of my wardrobe, where he would be staying from now on. That Christmas Eve morning, as I stretched in bed, he greeted me at the open wardrobe doors, his bottom half still wedged inside the magical clay head between my shoes. Even he admitted *he* felt happier to be back where he belonged. In fact, he now had an appreciation for it after being hidden up in the attic with a man he no longer believed to be the real Santa Claus.

"That guy gave me something before he was arrested. Said he found them while lurking around. It takes on a whole new meaning now that I know about..."

His voice trailed off.

Curious, I opened my crusty eyes. Zag was holding Hayley's bright-pink underwear in his tiny hands.

"Oh!" I screamed, almost as if I'd seen a rat.

Eventually, things calmed down and I placed the missing underwear into my sock drawer for safe keeping. I wondered what else that squatter had taken whenever he'd snuck downstairs.

"I don't think I quite understand Christmas," said Zag, a slight grimace still on his face. "All this time learning about it, trying to feel what you feel. You said that something just... clicks. Well, I gotta say, I don't get it. Maybe it's a human thing."

I rolled over, tapping my covers so he'd join me on the bed.

"It's probably because *we're* not feeling it," I admitted sadly. "Aunt Rachael and Grandma Helen are gone. We missed Brendan's birthday, too, and... gosh, that night in the attic. It's a miracle nobody saw you up there! We've had a stressful month. I don't know about the others, but..."

I turned my head to look out the window at the naked oak trees, some with fractured crowns from the Zeppelin's near miss.

"Part of me wishes we could skip Christmas this year..."

"Your wish is my command," said Zag, sitting up.

My use of the magic word had been accidental, and I clamped a hand to my mouth in horror. "No, Zag! I didn't mean it, really... *Please, I need it! Zag!*"

By the time I'd blurted out my most inner-thoughts, I realised Zagreus was only joking. A big grin spread across his face.

"Relax, it doesn't work like that. Besides, the wishing ban you made doesn't end until tomorrow."

I sat back in relief.

Well, at least I knew how I really felt about the matter. Maybe, no matter what, I would always love Christmas. And, I suppose, it was foolish to think that every single year would be good. Downright naïve, some might say. I waited until Zag disappeared back into his clay head, then continued to gaze out the window for a good half-an-hour before forcing myself to get up.

After cleaning my teeth, I left the bathroom to head downstairs. I could hear the rest of my family pottering around noisily in the kitchroom, my brother in particular letting out a gargantuan laugh. This rare occurrence excited me; I raced down the flight of stairs in such a hurry that I sprained one of my ankles.

"Ow! Oh…" I muttered, crawling on all fours.

Mom, Dad, Annie and Brendan stopped what they were doing.

"Are you alright?" asked Mom, by the toaster.

"No, I… I need… coffee!"

Brendan laughed again from the lounge area; I turned to see him sitting on the couch, surrounded by an immense crowd of presents: A life-sized version of *Tiro the Barber-Librarian* was sitting by his side, a new red bike, a springy purple pogo stick, and a wealth of little knick-knacks. Books, a plush *Babar,* a mound of new CD's, *Power Rangers* figurines… Brendan's cheeks were so puffed with joy that they looked like they were ready to burst.

"Since we forgot about Brendan's birthday this year, he gets to celebrate it today," explained Dad, sitting on a stool by the counter and savouring a mug of Hayley's left-over Pandora.

*"And then there's tomorrow! Then there's tomorrow!"*

"Yes," said Dad, turning to me without smiling. "Christmas is tomorrow. Didn't you hear?"

Mom and Annie, both of whom were unresponsive while baking in the kitchen, avoided meeting my gaze. It felt like a business deal was going on or something.

"Mom…?" I called out slowly, checking in on her.

Busy mixing a bowl of white icing for her traditional gingerbread hut, my mother finally met my eye-line.

"Who says you can't buy your child's happiness?" she said.

Things were okay between them, I realised gladly.

"At least you surprised him this year!" my sister added.

———— • • • ————

For the rest of the day, we spent time together doing typical family things. We went for a walk, played with the pets, helped Brendan set up his new backyard basketball court (yes), and argued throughout each activity. Then, during a heated game of Yahtzee that afternoon, we received a visit from the Croxley sisters. Recently discharged from Alexandria General, they appeared at the front door with permanently surprised looks on their faces (eyebrows having been ripped off the night of the Zeppelin crash).

With them they brought a rainbow cake for Brendan's birthday, which Candice told us she'd made twelve hours earlier from scratch. It was meant to feature a frosted drawing of my brother's face on top, but it looked to me more like Noddy than anyone I'd ever met. Still, Brendan couldn't believe it, and with the arrival of his friend Aron an hour later I wondered if he was over the idea that nobody liked him.

"Candice, thank you, but… this is too much," said Mom graciously, preparing the cake by the kitchen counter.

"Nonsense, it's my pleasure!" said Candice, helping to poke twelve candles into Brendan-Noddy's features. Her North London accent tripped over her words as she rushed to finish each sentence. "Besides, I haven't slept in days, although I was temporarily forced into unconsciousness by the doctors at the hospital. I needed something to do last night, and this kept me occupied until dawn, so here we are! *Not to mention this riveting individual couldn't distract me if her life depended on it…*"

Candice whispered this last part, and tilted her head towards her rather despondent sister on the couch. Chloe's unusually lethargic movements hinted at her deeply doped state. She was most definitely on something strong enough to put a horse into a coma, which became evident when Annie offered her some pretzels from a bowl. Chloe aimed, and missed. Aimed, and missed. The bowl *and* her mouth, that is.

"As you can tell," said Candice, twitching, "we're polar opposites when it comes to treatment."

———— • • • ————

Brendan's mood, already ecstatic, somehow improved as the afternoon slipped into an early winter's night. Our small party lounged about the kitchroom merrily until, eventually, Mrs. Hasmutt came to pick Aron up. Shortly after that, the Croxleys informed us that it was time for them to leave, too.

"Nighttime medication waits for nobody!" said Chloe in a slur.

Alone again, the five of us quickly ate dinner, then made ourselves comfortable in the lounge to watch *Home Alone*. However, barely ten minutes had passed when we were interrupted by yet another unforeseen knock on the front door, this time accompanied by the muffled strains of festive singing.

"Mom, if it's carollers, can I spit on them?" asked Brendan. "In honour of Grandma."

"For the last time, she's not dead!" I yelled at him.

When Annie, who'd been acting very unusual all day, answered and let out a cry of delight, we bolted from out seats and sprang into the foyer to see what all the fuss was about. Marguerite was singing a carol at the top of her lungs. Bundled up behind her was her husband, JT, Hayley, and Greg.

"Surprise!" said Marguerite in her usually dynamic way. "We thought we would invite you to join us. We're heading downtown to sing carols at Our Lady Church. Half of the town will be there. It shall be wonderful and magical and exciting, and won't smell of dog urine at all!"

Hayley groaned ferociously in the back.

"That wasn't the dog," she muttered. "That was Steve, and you can't smell it because it happened five years ago, and I'm sorry I told you about it in the first place!"

"I know what I sme-e-ell!" Marguerite sang operatically.

— • • • —

Twenty minutes later we'd all driven down to Our Lady of Horn-Horn, a lavish Catholic Church half-covered in the lazy mush-snow from the day, but lit beautifully in and out with romantic fairy lights, tinsel, mistletoe, and the nativity scene greeting us near the door. Inside, deeply brown since its inception in the seventies, I spotted many, many people from school. Not a single person looked sad or stressed after what'd happened.

To my surprise, I even saw the entire Parker family (minus Eleanore, of course), along with Wednesday's family (all twelve of them!) and Friday's (man, her parents were old). Eric Parker was in a corner talking to a tall, slender woman with short blonde hair wearing a power-suit, clutching the shoulders of a little girl in a fairy outfit. Mom pointed out in awe that this was the Mayor of Horn-Horn, Ellana Fork-Flame, and her daughter Astrid.

Parting ways, Parker initially turned to walk towards us, but for some reason stopped and struck up a conversation with somebody else instead. It was very rude, and very obvious.

"That was unusual," said Tommy, without delay.

"I don't know *what's* gotten into the people of this town. Nobody has taken my calls these past few days. They've turned their backs on us overnight, as if the Zeppelin crashing into our house was *our* fault! Honestly. I thought they were our friends!" whispered Marguerite, so only we could hear.

"This might be a great time to tell you, then. I'm not friends with Eleanore," admitted JT. "She's *nasty*."

"We already knew that; your father and I simply enjoy watching you squirm each year," muttered Marguerite quickly. She waved at Ella-May Parker, who promptly grabbed Mrs. Shalom and turned the other way.

"I'm sure it's just a misunderstanding," said Dad.

"The same," declared Marguerite, spinning her protective shawl around dramatically, "cannot be said for the lack of menorahs in this establishment! What an atrocity!"

Dad seemed to be dumbfounded. "It's... a... church?"

"Jesus was Jewish, you know," said JT.

"If Jesus was Jewish, then what is Christianity exactly?"

Dad turned eagerly to answer Hayley's question: "It's complicated, but it all starts with the fact that the term *Jew* is used in two senses when it comes to this. There's those who are *ethnically* Jewish, and then there are those who are only *religiously* Jewish. Jesus was a Jew in both senses, but boy does it get even more complicated from there..."

I shared an amused look with my siblings. For all his schvitzing while Aunt Rachael was in town, it seemed Ichabod Michael Gellar was still a proud Jewish boy at heart.

———— • • • ————

We made our way into the chapel not long after, which was temporarily cleared of its pews for the masses (of people). JT suggested the four of us distance ourselves from the others, so we snuck away to the front. Greg had been hot on my tail all night; I could tell he was making sure we stood shoulder-to-shoulder — but I think even he was finding our newfound proximity to be too intense, especially as the growing crowd quickly encroached on our already limited personal space. Within minutes, we were essentially trapped. Wedged. Slowly grinding and sweating against each other.

Once the chapel was suffocatingly full, a side-door opened and the crowd hushed. An elderly man, known as Reverend Ronald Cool, walked through and made his way to the front. He was dressed in a long, black cassock, with a white surplice draped over it, and a colourful stole around his neck. With his ever-present smile at the ready, he began the service by giving a profound yet extremely succinct sermon crafted specifically for the occasion. Knowing most of us were only there for the carols, he quickly thanked his congregation for their year of hard work, for decking the church in Christmas decorations, and by welcoming those visiting Our Lady of Horn-Horn that night from other faiths. His closing remarks made us laugh the most — he suggested the tremendous tree in the corner had surely been decorated by the spirit of Liberace himself.

Encouraged by his parting humour, we opened our songbooks, guided by the organist in the gallery above. As if by magic, our voices created a tremendous euphony of Christmas hymns, echoing beautifully throughout the giant chapel.

———  . . .  ———

"Merry Christmas!" said JT, as we left the Church.

"Merry Christmas!" I called back.

"Happy Hanukkah!" declared Hayley.

"Hayles, Hanukkah is over."

"Shut up, Jonathan…"

"Good-ah bye! I will never forget-ah you!" I yelled, waving until my friends had disappeared into the darkness of the adjacent parking lot. I'd not said goodbye to Greg, but only because we'd practically made love in the packed chapel for an hour.

"Who would've thought?" said Annie. "Cassie Gellar, *popular*."

On the drive home, tired from all the singing, I found myself dwelling on her words. If only my newfound popularity had been the biggest surprise of the year. I thought about Danube, Ursula, van Pan, Pothosia… not to mention everything that had happened *this month alone*… the Zeppelin ride, Duke Wilson appearing with a multitude of others in our attic, Brendan's birthday, Dad's motorcycle, Morgan, Aunt Rachael, Grandma Helen…

Then my mind wandered to Zag. I immediately regretted not

bringing him tonight, whether invisible or magically posing as a brooch on my jacket. I realised, far too late, that our trip to church would have explained the feeling of Christmas to him perfectly.

**TUESDAY**

**25th**

# 49

# ONCE IN A GREEN FLASH

Yes, that's right, I fell asleep sitting up in bed licking a giant lollipop. Mom had let us all open a wrapped present before midnight, and I'd picked one that'd seemed enticing. I was disappointed as I'd been hoping it would be a straightening-iron, but instead of wallowing in my failed attempt, I instead decided to sit up watching repeats of *Designing Women* on the television until my head quite literally dropped to one side.

When I woke up, I knew immediately what day it was. The sun was only just rising outside. Lips sticky, gums itching a little, I hopped out of bed and went to the window, grabbing my dressing-gown which had been thrown on my desk chair. Over the top of the bare oaks, half of which were splintered and torn apart from the damage done on Friday night, I caught sight of a little green sliver on the edge of the oceanic horizon. I'd learned about this phenomenon from Ms. Weiss in class not even two weeks ago. Only now, as I glimpsed the brief green flash with my own eyes, did I re-call her explanation. Joyful at the unexpected sighting, I gazed across my room at the wardrobe, and had an epiphany. Tucking the idea into the back of my mind for later, I slowly crept down the hallway.

I knocked quietly on Brendan's door, not surprised in the least when he energetically swung it open a moment later. I crossed the hall to knock on Annie's, and she too emerged in record time.

We knew the rules. Downstairs, we would find all of our presents laid out on the couch waiting for us. It was a tradition. Some of them would surprise us, some of them we knew about when we saw them wrapped shoddily under the tree, but most of all they would thrill us to our very toes. And this year was no exception.

The entire living room was engulfed in unnatural blackness, by what we thought at first to be a new opening, an extension put on the house. Creeping closer, Brendan was the first to let out a hushed, deep moan of surprise at the gigantic television, the biggest screen we'd ever seen outside of a cinema complex. Annie and I squealed, because goddamn it, we were girls. Brendan did the same, because goddamn it, he was gay, and it was Christmas!

Once we'd gotten over the surprise, and Brendan blinded us by turning it on for the first time, Annie and I scoped the couches for something else of interest. Amongst the crowded seating were two basketballs, obviously for Brendan's new outdoor court, but they had cards attached to them which had our names on them. Annie grabbed hers first and opened it, and read the letter out loud:

"Dear Annie," she said, shaking in delight, pushing Brendan away as he clamoured on top of her, "your father and mother love you very much. Please accept this invitation to get your..." She looked up at me, almost losing herself in shock, "... Please accept this invitation to get your *eyes lasered* so you can finally have the per-fect vision to see what a perfect daughter you are to us..." She couldn't finish, for she began to sob. Eventually, she waved her hands over her face, and took off her glasses to wipe her tears. "Boy, we really should have waited for them to wake up before opening these!"

"It's a bit weepy," I said, not feeling the emotion as much as her. I opened my letter and began to read it:

"Dear Cassie, your father and mother... yeah-yeah... Since we are sick of driving you everywhere, please... *FIND A PURPLE VOLKSWAGEN BEETLE PARKED IN THE GARAGE!*"

In one sentence, I'd managed to shoot back up onto my feet

and yell at the top of my lungs. I immediately dropped the letter, took a deep breath, and let out the most blood-curdling scream I could ever make.

"Where's mine! Where the hell is mine!" cried Brendan, searching for his own card.

"Your birthday was yesterday," Annie said, wiping her eyes.

Brendan didn't look any older than eleven as he pouted, but he eventually found his own card wedged inside the lower branches of our now lit-up Christmas tree. He gave himself a paper-cut as he tore the envelope open with an index finger.

"Ouch!… Okay, Dear Bren — blah-blah, and… our gift to you is up in our bedroom. You cannot receive it until we are all woken up and… *Pfft!* No way. What's this garbage?"

He stormed off up the stairs. Annie and I quickly followed. By the time we'd reached the landing, our little brother was hovering directly opposite Mom and Dad's closed bedroom door. To our surprise, he violently kicked it open with one of his bare feet. I heard Mom let out a guttural scream, then use the F word.

Brendan entered without hesitation. Annie pushed me out of the way, but I was hot on her heels; the three of us jumped on top of our parents' waterbed in excitement. Crying, laughing, thanking them with kisses planted upon their grumpy cheeks.

"You still need to get a job…" said Mom in a sleepy voice.

"*Of course!* Of course," I declared.

I was about to make more future promises to her, when there came a strange *'yip!'* sound next to me. We stopped fussing.

"What was that?" asked Annie.

"I think it was the smoke alarm battery."

"Sounded like a dog to me," said Brendan.

We turned to our parents again in a deadly serious manner. It was very unlikely to be the case, as Mom had rolled over to go back to sleep, and Dad's eyes were closed. But then suddenly, despite this, we watched as his eyebrows raised.

"What'd you expect? We love ya more than our luggage."

Through the sheets waddled a tiny puppy, barely the size of Brendan's foot. Instead of screaming, the three of us remained completely silent, turning into gentle beasts. It was beige, with tiny floppy ears and a round head that looked comically large against its body. We coo'ed, letting its wet, black nose sniff around us.

"Hi," I said in a high pitched whisper.

I looked over at Mom, who was smiling at us.

"Technically he's Brendan's," she said, "and technically he's not our gift. He's a joint gift from your aunt and grandmother."

"Did they check with you guys first?" inquired Annie, handing the ball fur over to Brendan.

"Of course. Actually, it was more serendipitous than that. Shelby Tanner was telling us that a dog in the pound had given birth a month ago, and all of the puppies but one had been adopted. We mentioned it to Rachael, who mentioned it to Helen, and they thought it would be a perfect present to give to Brendan, to… and I quote them both… 'match Annie's and Cassie's gifts'."

"Thank them for me…" said Brendan.

"You can thank them yourself. We bought you a calligraphy set for Christmas, too. It's downstairs. You can start this afternoon and write one out for Grandma."

"Is it a boy or a girl?" asked Annie.

"We prefer to call her Helen, otherwise she gets mad."

"Ichabod," muttered Mom. "It's a boy. No name yet. That's for Brendan to decide."

My little brother, eyes puffy from shock and sleep, stared down at the puppy in his hands, who had taken to chewing on his fingers.

"What's your name?" he asked it, sweetly. "Let's see. You guys kept him a secret, the best kept secret you've ever managed to keep from me… Keepey! I think we should call him Keepey."

"No!" we all cried, and I added: "That sounds dumb."

"Alright, sorry…" said Brendan, blushing. He thought some more. "You've been keeping him under lock and key all month, so… What about Lachlan?"

Nobody made to protest.

"Lachlan…" each one of us took turns saying it.

The five of us sat on the bed, mulling over it, watching in silence as the puppy made a slobbery mess of Brendan's fingers.

"Welcome to the family, Lachlan."

My brother's words were spoken softly; I sensed immediately that he was in love.

———— • • • ————

We spent the next hour downstairs, introducing Pigsworth and Tigger to Lachlan, making breakfast, and handing out the rest of our gifts to one another.

Eventually, I snuck away from the others and into the cold garage, where I ran my hands gently along the finish of my new Beetle. Its colour was a deeply vivid purple; it seemed to match brilliantly with Dad's yellow motorcycle, lying broken in the corner. To honour its fallen compadre, I peeled off the *'Too Fat To Carpool'* bumper sticker and gave it a brand new home, directly above my right brake-light.

———— · · · ————

Another hour passed. Annie began to clean up the lounge, diligently picking up the remnants of their early morning celebrations — the scattered wrapping paper and discarded packaging. Lodged in the crevices of the sofa, her fingers brushed against the envelope bearing her name on it. When she'd torn the edges open in haste earlier, she'd assumed it only contained a letter from her parents and therefore discarded it carelessly. Now, however, she finally noticed an unaccounted thickness inside. Concealed within its folds, Annie extracted five items that looked rectangular, laminated, official...

"What are these?" Annie asked, pulling them out.

Mom, brewing a coffee, glanced casually across the room.

"Plane tickets," she informed her. "Your new eye doctor isn't in Horn-Horn. He's in Salem."

Brendan stopped jumping around on his new pogo stick.

"You three keep talking about how homesick you are, so... Thought it was time to organise a visit. At the end of January. Only for a week. You know, if everybody still wants to."

Brendan didn't say anything, but he pranced away on his pogo stick merrily enough. Annie didn't seem as excited as we were, but was the first to agree on going. I was happy, of course, because Salem still felt like home... sort of... I think it was the normalcy I missed more than anything, and a return trip wouldn't change that.

But I'd think about that later on, I assured myself, because it was now nearly eight in the morning. I was cutting it rather slim with my plan. I ran upstairs to get dressed, nudged the wardrobe doors open again, and grabbed hold of the clay head.

"Merry Christmas..." I whispered into its hollow mouth.

A silent stream of white vapour poured out. Zag appeared by my side, wearing a red and green elf costume.

"Merry Christmas!" he said, his buck teeth protruding wider than ever as he smiled up at me. Outstretched in one of his hands was a single candy cane. "Here you go, I made it myself!"

"Thank you," I said gladly, unwrapping it.

The moment I put it in my mouth, I gagged so involuntarily that I couldn't fake in the least.

"Oh, Zag, what... What flavour is this?"

"Undiluted pine sap. I thought these grew on Christmas trees."

"No, they're... We put them on. They're made from candy."

"Oops. Sorry."

I recovered quickly. "It's okay. Look, I have an idea. You wanted me to prove to you what Christmas was all about, right?"

"Right."

"Well then, Zagreus Wendig... Let's go for a drive."

———— . . . ————

Flavour Street looked warm and inviting, with the sunrise casting golden rays down its reflective road; however it was deceiving, as the morning frost was still thick and dangerous for cars such as mine. My own, brand new, purple Volkswagen Beetle. As I turned into the street, going at the pace of a snail, Zag peeked his head out the side window to see where he was going, taking off his seatbelt for the twentieth time.

"Hey! Nope. Back on, please."

"There's no point. Everybody knows you can't kill a Child of Crux..." he grumbled, inconvenienced. Still, he obliged, and looked out the windshield instead. "Why are we here?"

"You'll see."

"See what? Nobody's even awake yet, and it's freezing out!"

"I thought of it this morning when the sun rose. I saw this tiny flash of green. It made me think of... and then I remembered what Pothosia told me in her letter, and... you came to mind. After that, it all sort of fit together in my mind like a really neat puzzle."

"I think the new car smell is getting to you."

"Look!" I said.

Right on cue, the front door of the wooden house opposite us opened wide. It was a lovely, white double-storey, with two brick chimneys, and black shutters on the windows. A large verandah spread around the entire house.

Zag squinted. "Is that the Uranus lady?"

I watched, hidden behind tinted windows. Ms. Weiss came out of her front door in her pink dressing-gown and slippers. Sure enough, she reached down to grab her newspaper from the front porch, taking a while in her old age to stand up again. As she stretched out her back, her eyes scanned past my unfamiliar car and down the street, pausing for a moment as she took in the picturesque world that surrounded us.

"Cassie, I don't get it," muttered Zag.

I shushed him, then said: "Watch."

To my disappointment, Ms. Weiss turned to go back inside.

"Oh no, she didn't see it!" I moaned miserably.

"What are you talking about? Didn't see what?" asked Zag.

"In her front garden. *Look!*"

Finally, he noticed what I was pointing at.

Hundreds of garden gnomes magically appeared across my teacher's garden. They posed amongst potted plants, peeked out from the frost-covered branches of bare trees, nestled in the icy flower beds, and lined her verandah like soldiers. It was as if they'd never left, simply reemerging from a respite in the garden's shadows.

"I remember you telling me about this…" whispered Zag.

He climbed over my lap to roll down my window. The cold morning air quickly seeped in; he leaned his elbows against the window-ledge to get a better view.

"Charles and his garden gnomes. They went missing after Just, but… Pothosia promised to give them back to her on Christmas morning, which is… right now…" He gulped nervously. "Oh no, she's going inside, Cassie! Do something…"

Without thinking, I yelled: *"Hey, Jocelyn!"*

Panic-stricken, Zag cranked my window back up in a frenzied hurry, and we ducked in our seats. Gripped by the tension, the two of us watched as my teacher snapped around and scoured the street.

"That was close," Zag muttered, sinking further down.

Suspicious, but unsure of her own hearing, Ms. Weiss slowly gave in and turned to walk back inside with her newspaper.

Finally, she caught sight of one by the door.

Then another.

*And another…*

Even from the car we could see her face drop. Grabbing the corners of her verandah for support, Ms. Weiss spun around as she noticed the hundreds of garden gnomes surrounding her, each one unique and old and precious to her in ways we'd never understand...

"It's perfect," Zag marvelled, his eyes shining as hers welled up.

Ms. Weiss let out a big laugh, revealing her garish mouth-plate. *"It'sh a Chrishmush meecle!"* she declared.

I shook my head, and murmured: "Well... almost perfect."

Zag sat back in his seat, captivated and silent.

"I get it now," he said softly.

Prying my eyes away from Ms. Weiss, I gazed down at the little boy sitting next to me. His red hair was bright against his pale skin, and his pointy ears peeked out from underneath.

"Merry Christmas, Cassie."

I felt a surge of happiness, and inhaled the crisp morning air.

"Merry Christmas, Zag."

# 50

## EVERYBODY KNOWS

Christmas Day in Horn-Horn was mild compared to other years, weather-wise. While the winds blew and the heaters kept everybody feeling safe and warm, stores were closed and most people stayed home. It was a day to spend with family, after all, for whether one was religious, atheist or agnostic, Christmas mattered to a variety of different people, and in different ways.

The Shaloms, all twelve of them, stayed up late playing board games. The Sheppards sat on their laptops, working hard but together for once. Greg Cooper sat with his mother in a hospital room, while his father slept soundlessly in the chair next to him. Hayley sat alone in her room with Scruffster, while JT and his parents watched the television downstairs together. Tanya was bickering with her cousin and sister, complaining that Derek overcrowded the house, while Cindy insisted that Venus the dog was the cause of all this bad energy. Meanwhile, Ellana Fork-Flame sent her daughter

Astrid to sleep at precisely nine o'clock. As she did, she caught sight of two owls flying by her second-floor window. They joined their parliament in the skies, then traveled across the town, over the darkened pier and towards the lighthouse on the cliff. The bright lamps inside the tower spun around, shooting beams of white into the distance and back again. For a split second, as he made his way to his immaculate upstairs kingdom on Philips Street, Eric Parker glimpsed its white radiance through a window, shimmering behind the dancing, bare branches in his front lawn.

Reaching the landing, he checked his watch. It was nearly midnight. He poked his head into the twins' bedroom, catching their sleeping faces in the moving night-light. Satisfied, he moved on, spotting the sleeping figure of Eleanore in her own darkened bedroom. He lingered for a moment, watching her breathing while she slept, until finally he went to check on his wife. As expected, Ella-May was fast asleep as well, sitting upright in bed with the television on. She'd taken another pill.

"Daddy?"

A voice came from behind him, gentle but unexpected.

He turned his head to one side. "Hmm?"

"Who were those people?"

"What people, sweetheart?"

"The ones you were talking to downstairs for so long."

"That was the television, darling. Go back to sleep."

"But I recognised some of the voices."

Eric walked back across the landing and met his daughter, who was hidden in the shadows of her bedroom. He rested his right arm against the door and smiled warmly at her.

"Eleanore," he said, gently urging her to forget about it. "Angel. You shouldn't be standing. Go back to bed."

"But... I'm thirsty..." she said drowsily, taking a step forward.

Eric saw her in the clear light of the hallway, the warm light doing nothing to soften the deep black bruises hollowing out her now anorexic face. All but skin and bones, a shell of the beauty she'd once prided herself upon, she teetered on her feet, dressed in nothing but her pink silk nighty. The jagged edges of her collar bones seemed to shriek out to Eric, the light showing just how much weight she'd lost. And he knew that by morning...

"There's water on your bedside, see?"

Helping her under the covers, Eric guided the full glass of water to her lips as she gulped it down, without so much as a breath in-between. Finished, he placed the glass down and stood up to leave.

"I'm going to bed now, honey. It's time you sleep too, alright?"

"Alright," said her bones, hidden in the darkness.

Eric walked to the door to leave, stopping by its threshold.

"Daddy," called Eleanore, "what's wrong with me?"

Eyes focused on the white shag carpeting beneath his loafers, he smiled and said: "Absolutely nothing, honey."

He waited until her breathing became steady and soft again, then slipped out of the room. He paused in the hallway, trying to calm his racing heart. He inhaled deeply, and fixed his eyes on the window opposite him.

A different source of light flickered outside suddenly, catching his attention. It was not from the lighthouse this time. Eric moved to the staircase to get a better view. It was a star, he realised, just as another one appeared next to it, and then another. Through the swaying branches, twinkling as the wind blew, he gazed thoughtfully up at the three coloured stars.

Things would be fine. He had to believe that, deep down. Yet fear of the unknown gnawed at him. It was fear that had ruined their last Christmas together. Fear that forced him to sedate his wife and twins so they wouldn't panic.

Shortly before succumbing, Eliza had managed to ask one final, slurred question to her father: "Is Eleanore going to die..?"

"No, don't be ridiculous!" he'd insisted angrily, unable to bear the idea. "Your sister is most certainly not going to die!"

Now, as the familiar sense of generational duty washed over him, Eric Parker turned away from the window and walked back downstairs, determined to pour himself a tougher drink.

*Besides,* he thought to himself, *everybody knows you can't kill a Child of Crux.*

# OTHER BOOKS IN THIS SERIES

*'Horn–Horn' (Book #1)*

*'Horn–Horn, Cracked' (Book #2)*

# <u>DID YOU LIKE THIS BOOK?</u>

## WHY NOT LEAVE A REVIEW AT
## GOODREADS AND AMAZON!

*Did you know that reviews are an essential part of a book's success? By writing a review, you're not only helping the author, you are helping other people find 'The Horn-Horn Series'!*

*All books in this series are available at these leading retailers:*

# ABOUT THE AUTHOR

Tommy Lellan was born in London and moved to Melbourne at the age of two. When not writing, he is found performing pop/rock and composing scores.

Follow him on Social Media: *@tommylellan* or visit his website at *www.tommylellan.com*